NIGHT TERRORS

New Stories of the Vampire Wars

Edited and Co-authored by
JONATHAN MABERRY

With Field Reporting by
LARRY CORREIA
JAMES A. MOORE
JEREMY ROBINSON
JOHN EVERSON
KEITH R.A. DECANDIDO
HANK SCHWAEBLE
SCOTT NICHOLSON
MARCUS PELEGRIMAS
TIM WAGGONER
SCOTT SIGLER
WESTON OCHSE
SAM ORION NOVA WEST-MENSCH

IDW

Become our fan on Facebook **facebook.com/idwpublishing**
Follow us on Twitter **@idwpublishing**
Subscribe to us on YouTube **youtube.com/idwpublishing**
See what's new on Tumblr **tumblr.idwpublishing.com**
Check us out on Instagram **instagram.com/idwpublishing**

978-1-63140-272-2   18 17 16 15   1 2 3 4

EDITED BY
JONATHAN MABERRY

COLLECTION EDITS BY
JUSTIN EISINGER
AND ALONZO SIMON

EDITORAL ASSISTANCE BY
LAUREN GENNAWEY
AND ZAC BOONE

COVER ART BY
TREVOR HUTCHISON

COLLECTION DESIGN BY
GILBERTO LAZCANO

V-WARS, VOL. 3: NIGHT TERRORS. DECEMBER 2015. FIRST PRINTING.
V-WARS © 2015 Idea and Design Works, LLC. All Rights Reserved. The IDW
logo is registered in the U.S. Patent and Trademark Office. IDW Publishing, a
division of Idea and Design Works, LLC. Editorial offices: 2765 Truxtun Road,
San Diego, CA 92106. Any similarities to persons living or dead are purely
coincidental. With the exception of artwork used for review purposes, none of
the contents of this publication may be reprinted without the permission of
Idea and Design Works, LLC. Printed in Canada.

IDW Publishing does not read or accept unsolicited submissions of ideas,
stories, or artwork.

Ted Adams, CEO & Publisher
Greg Goldstein, President & COO
Robbie Robbins, EVP/Sr. Graphic Artist
Chris Ryall, Chief Creative Officer/Editor-in-Chief
Matthew Ruzicka, CPA, Chief Financial Officer
Alan Payne, VP of Sales
Dirk Wood, VP of Marketing
Lorelei Bunjes, VP of Digital Services
Jeff Webber, VP of Digital Publishing & Business Development

IDW founded by Ted Adams, Alex Garner, Kris Oprisko, and Robbie Robbins

CONTENTS

"BREAKING NEWS" PT. 1

Jonathan Maberry

Upper East Side
New York City

You can't drink away the apocalypse.

You can't smoke it away or snort it away.

Can't laugh it away, cry it away, or fuck it away.

Yuki Nitobe knew that for sure. She'd tried it all. Repeatedly. Since the outbreak, since she broke the story about the existence of vampires, Yuki had gone to every height, dropped to every depth, explored every extreme.

To not know.

To have it not be.

To put things back the way they were.

But, like the song says, you can't unring a bell.

You can't unhear a scream.

You can't unsee the blood.

And no matter how hard, how long, how well, or how desperately you search, you can't find the reset button that puts it all back together again.

Yuki knew it.

She did.

She stood on the balcony of her apartment on the upper East Side, watching the city burn. Knowing that the world was burning, too.

"Are you coming back to bed?"

Yuki half turned at the sound of his voice—deep, soft, cultured. Strange in ways both good and bad, with a timbre beyond the range ⸝

human vocal patterns. There was a low, almost subsonic hum when he spoke, like the drone of a Tibetan monk. She knew he couldn't control it. It was part of who he was—what he was.

From the first time she'd heard it more than a year ago, it had frightened her. Terrified her. She'd awakened from a drugged sleep, tied to a chair with a hood over her face. She hadn't even remembered being abducted, though the bruises and torn clothes testified to the fight she put up. The drug, some kind of synthetic ketamine, wiped most of it out. What mattered was that she was there, in a darkened room in some unknown place, bound and helpless.

With vampires all around her.

And him.

Martyn.

Only a voice at first, and then a face, a body, a personality once he removed the hood.

It was so strange to be that completely terrified, that deeply repulsed, and yet that powerfully attracted all in the same moment. That was Martyn, though. A beautiful black man with eyes the color of blood and the voice of a god. Or a demon.

Martyn. Mannered, elegant, even respectful in his way. Marginally so during the first moments of that abduction, much more so when he dropped the pretense of being her executioner and revealed his truth.

Martyn was a vampire in the service of the Crimson Queen. He was the chief field operative of that secret empire. A fixer, an enabler, a solver of problems. Occasionally an executioner. Always an ambassador.

Not of good will.

Nor of bad.

He was the proxy for the will of the queen.

He was her Metatron, speaking for her so that she could remain apart, aloof, enshadowed, safe.

Yuki stood on the balcony, shivering in a hot wind. Cold from within, she pulled the folds of her silk robe around her slender body, discovering no warmth within it.

"Yuki—?" he called from inside.

When she didn't answer, she heard the soft rustle of his body as he slid across the bed, and then the nearly silent pad of his bare feet on the hardwood floor. She didn't turn as Martyn came out onto the balcony.

At first he sought to wrap his heavy arm around her shoulders, but when he found no reaction, Martyn withdrew his touch. That was his way. Never impolite. Never intrusive. Not since that first day.

He moved a few feet away and leaned his forearms on the rail, his brown skin painted gold by the firelight. He wore only black boxers and a single ruby teardrop earring. There were scars on his big arms and back and chest that he would never explain beyond saying, "Life is life."

Life is life.

Such a strange, vague way to explain a life clearly lived in the storm lands.

Yuki had her own scars now. Some branded into her flesh from splinters, as bullets had chewed apart a room in which she nearly died— a hospital room where patient zero of the vampire plague, Michael Fayne, had begun a rampage of slaughter. Yuki wore the reminders of her mortality on her skin. Every time she stood naked in front a mirror that lesson was reinforced. And there were other scars, too—each one marking a different day, a distinct event of the V-Wars. She told Martyn about some of them. Others she did not. Scars can be a deeply personal thing, like insights gained in meditation. It wasn't required to explain them or proselytize because of them. Martyn understood that about her, and she about him.

Just as she knew and respected the secrets he kept.

Now they stood apart but together on her balcony, watching how the smoke from dozens of fires lit the midnight sky over Manhattan. Towers of smoke rose toward the great pall that hung over the city, and it was like looking at the pillars supporting the smoky ceiling of Hell itself. The knobbed columns and rippling roof reflected the fires in hues of Halloween orange and chimney red. And the soundtrack was the constant whine of sirens as firefighters raced from place to place, all while knowing that the demons of flame owned the night.

"You want to be out there," murmured Martyn, "don't you?"

She shrugged. Said nothing.

"If you want to go, Yuki, I can get you a car, some people. Protection. Whatever you need."

Still nothing.

He straightened and turned to face her, leaning a hip against the rail. She glanced at him.

"Why are you making that face?" she asked.

"You're crying."

Yuki touched her cheek, then studied her fingertips, surprised to see them glisten. She rubbed them dry on her sleeve.

"How many people do you think died tonight?" she asked. "No, tell me how many you think will be dead by morning? By the time this is over?"

Martyn sighed. "What does the tally matter?"

She almost wheeled on him, almost snarled. Instead she fought to keep her words from launching at him like knives. "Because they're dying, damn it. It's wrong. It's fucking insane."

He smiled. A faint, small thing. "You miss my point, love. Don't mistake my question for indifference."

"Then what was it?"

Martyn ticked his head toward the burning city. "Ever since this war started, the whole world's gone nuts. Everyone on both sides. There hasn't been one battle that's ended in what any sane person could call a victory. People are dying on both sides, and people are dying when they're caught between those sides. Bloods and Beats, soldiers and guerrillas, the innocent and the guilty. This isn't a war. Not really. This is some kind of internal conflict within the body of the human race. This is the right and left hands bashing each other and tearing at the flesh of their own body because both want to be dominant and each thinks that dominance is possible. It isn't. Self-murder is the only outcome of this kind of conflict. You know it, the Queen knows it, Luther Swann knows it, and I know it. How many others? A few thousand? The Queen's empire and those random cool minds who are able to step back from their own fears and look at the world as a single living thing. That's all. And stacked against us are eight billion people who are ruled by hate and fear and greed."

"I don't need a fucking sermon, Martyn."

"That's not what it is. It's a reality check, Yuki."

She wiped at fresh tears that burned on her cheeks. "You think I'm standing here with my eyes closed? Fuck you."

He smiled again. Every bit as sad as before. "No. That's not what I'm saying, and I think you know it. We're both standing here observing this. Witnessing it. A year ago—sure, you'd have been down there in the streets. So would I. Six months ago you'd have been broadcasting live from the inferno. Six months ago I'd have been in the trenches doing what had to be done. That was who we were."

The tears wouldn't stop. She came and placed her palms on the flat hardness of his chest and leaned her forehead against him.

"What happened to us?" she whispered. "Why aren't we out there now?"

Martyn took her in his arms, trailing his fingers down the curve of her back, kissing her hair, sharing his warmth with her even though his flesh was cold. So much colder than hers.

"We fought this war, Yuki," he murmured, "each of us in our own way. You in front of the camera, me in the shadows. Both of us trying to tell the truth and finding only deaf ears. What happened to us? God… it's so obvious, and that's what makes it hurt so bad."

"Tell me," she begged.

"We lost our faith," he said. "In God, because why would any god allow this? In the system, because we now know, without doubt, that it doesn't work. In the value of truth, because no matter how much we shout everyone thinks we're telling lies. And in ourselves, Yuki, because I guess we both found out that the myths we believed in about ourselves are nothing but bullshit."

Her hands curled into small, hard fists, and she slowly pounded them against his chest.

"No," she said, though she meant "yes."

Siren calls floated like banshees around them. There were screams and gunshots from forty-nine stories below. A phalanx of Apache attack helicopters flew past the burning spike of the Chrysler building. A spiraling worm of smoke came whipping from another building, and suddenly the lead helicopter exploded as a rocket-propelled grenade slammed into its rotor. A split second later, the other five Apaches responded with Hellfire missiles that struck the building where the RPG had come from, turning its glass facade into a firestorm of burning splinters.

Yuki and Martyn recoiled from it even though her apartment was many blocks away.

What had begun as a series of coordinated attacks by a militant V-Cell had escalated into a full-blown battle.

Yuki's knees buckled and she sagged down, pulling Martyn with her as they huddled together. Not for fear of what was happening out there, but in terror at what was happening inside their own broken hearts.

"ABSENCE OF LIGHT" PT. 1

Larry Correia

Seattle, Washington

T he mob pushed and screamed and chanted their slogans, stinking of sweat, adrenalin, and excitement. The air was moist from recent rain evaporating off of sweatshirts and hoodies, and hot from hundreds of packed-in bodies. Marko and his vampires passed between the protestors, and the hardest thing in the world was not killing them all.

These humans are nominally on our side. These are the useful idiots. Killing them—now—would be a waste of resources. Marko had ordered his men to hurt as few of the protesters during the op as possible. He'd had to beat that lesson into his soldiers. Some of his men were more feral than others, so in a few cases the beating had been literal. Some of his recruits struggled with the concept of discipline.

The street was absolutely full of bodies. Most of them were young, impressionable, and passionate. The ones who were showing their faces thought they could make a difference, naively believing their slogans, hashtags, and painted cardboard signs were going to change the world. The protestors hiding their identities were just eager to break shit. From the smell he could tell that some of their backpacks contained all the fixings to make Molotov cocktails. So far the masked hooligans were behaving themselves. The broken glass and burning cars would come later. The day belonged to the activists. The looters believed the night belonged to them… In reality it belonged to the vampires, and as tempting as it was to show these idiots who was really in charge, a riot made one hell of a good distraction.

The other side of the street was a sea of flashing red and blue lights. Seattle PD had learned their lesson about protests a few times over the last decade, and that was before 11V1 kicked societal order in the balls. The cops were ready behind batons and shields, tear gas launcher and pepper balls. If it weren't for all of the news crews recording the peaceful protest, the street would already be filled with gas. The cops and the looters both knew what was coming next, but there were *rules* to the fall of an empire. If the forces of law and order jumped the gun, morons would rant on Twitter, politicians would feign outrage, and a bureaucrat somewhere might be inconvenienced. Pretenses had to be kept up. So the street-level decision makers would be forced to coddle the mob until the situation spiraled out of control, turning into a complete clusterfuck, and then overreact to contain it. That was the yin and yang of riot control.

All those years the government had spent training him how to overthrow governments, and Marko had never realized just how entertaining it would be to screw with his own. Before he had turned Marko had been Army Special Forces. His job had been to train and lead indigenous forces behind enemy lines. "Force multiplication," they called it. Now he was training vampires. He'd collected these individual predators and molded them into a real unit. Same tactics, new war.

One of his vampires appeared at his side. Even with the bandana covering his face, he could tell it was Basco just from how smoothly he moved between the humans. Basco had been a tough bastard when he was still human. Making him bloodthirsty and fast as lightning had only made him an even better soldier. "In my country, we'd run a belt-fed across a mob like this. A hundred rounds and problem solved."

"Where's the fun in that?"

His vampires were wired, tense, and ready. They were hungry. Not just for blood—he'd kept their feeding to a minimum so as to not tip off the local authorities—but for action. They'd been planning this op for weeks, ever since word of the vaccine experiments had leaked. The news conference this morning had simply bumped up their timeline. The protestors had already been here anyway. His men had already been working the locals and stirring up the radical elements, so it hadn't taken much of a push to get the riot kiddies fired up. His people had been bussing them in all day.

Marko was wearing a black hoodie and a plastic Guy Fawkes mask. The irony of a bunch of lefty atheists using a Catholic fanatic as their symbol caused him no end of amusement, but he was guessing there weren't a lot of War College grads in this bunch. He needed the mask because the NSA was certain to be running facial recognition programs against the footage. As a bonus the hood hid his radio headset. "Target is in sight."

The Iwashiro building didn't look that impressive. It was just another plain old office cube. The real prize was inside. There were a hundred medical research companies looking for the Holy Grail, but if the rumors were true, Iwashiro Biomedical had been making real progress on understanding the vampire virus—mostly because they had zero ethics—and according to this morning's press conference, they'd made a real breakthrough.

"Sniper is in position."

"Breaching team is in position."

Every mutation was different. Some of his best soldiers couldn't operate well in the sunlight, so they'd move once the sun was safely behind the buildings to the west. At the same time, his kill teams would start taking out vital employees who hadn't come to work today because of the protests. If everything went according to plan, by the end of the night the technology to produce a screener would be in vampire hands, and every human who understood how to make more would be dead. "Assault team blend in and wait for my signal. We've got sundown in thirty."

The angry mob was here because Iwashiro had been caught doing illegal experiments on vampire *volunteers*. Some girls wearing duct tape over their mouths—symbolic of who knew what—went marching past, waving signs that declared "Vampires Are People Too."

Marko smiled behind his mask. *No… We're so much better.*

"Look at all those hippies."

"Just try not to run any of them over, Solo," Matt Kovac told their driver.

"General May hates when I run over civilians. Look at all that flannel. I can't tell if they're homeless or college students." He honked the horn as twenty people jaywalked in front of them. Somebody threw a beer can at their car and it bounced off the hood. "You little son of a bitch!"

"Be cool, man. It's a rental. It's on the company card."

"It's the principle of the thing," Solo muttered as the kids flipped them the bird, but eventually they meandered out of the way so he could keep driving. "Big Dog's team gets to pop tangos while we have to grade rent-a-cops. Fantastic. Hang on, police checkpoint ahead."

Toolbox was in the back seat. He leaned forward to see better. "Cops are diverting traffic like it's a parade or something. Can you believe this nonsense, Show?"

Kovac didn't like his call sign, but Showdown had stuck. Get in one Mexican standoff with a crazy vampire, and pretty soon everybody in V-8 was telling exaggerated stories about it, but as a new team leader, it had helped establish cred with the vets. It usually got shortened to Show for brevity's sake.

V-8 was the military's elite special response unit for vampire problems. Their personnel were some of the finest operators available, recruited from every branch of the service. Kovac had been Army SF himself, following in his deceased father's footsteps. It wasn't until after he'd been with V-8 for a while that he'd learned his father wasn't *exactly* deceased.

"Pull over there."

The four of them were out of uniform—rocking the business casual as Solo put it—and driving a Honda. Normally when V-8 rolled up on a site, they were hard to miss—what with the armored vehicles and top-end military gear—but the General had told them to be discreet today. If Kovac had realized that the streets were going to be filled with cops in helmets, face shields, and vests, they'd have brought their fun stuff. It was a sad comment on the state of the world that they wouldn't have stuck out that much.

Kovac rolled his window down and showed his ID to the police officers on the corner. "How's it going, officer?"

"Mostly vandalism and graffiti so far, but they're just getting warmed up," the cop said as he read the card. Behind him, a stoned white guy dressed in tie-dye clothing and sporting dreadlocks was trying to put a peace sign bumper sticker on the cop car's windshield. "Aw, stop that! You guys go through. My boss said to expect you. Head that way."

The cops moved a wooden barricade and waved them through. Solo drove between a SWAT van and an MRAP, honking so that the riot squad would get out of his way. They got some surly glances from the other side of those Lexan face shields. They could see a lot more of the protestors now, and Kovac was surprised to see how damned many of them there were.

"Glad that's not our problem," Kovac muttered.

People were milling around in groups, and the atmosphere was charged. The rumble of crowd noise was overwhelming. Iwashiro Biomedical had been working on a vaccine for I1V1, which just about every sane person would agree was a good thing, but if people could throw a fit about animal testing, they got downright pissed when a company got caught illegally testing drugs on vampires.

"Today's lesson is, if you're going to do stupid shit, don't get caught!" Solo exclaimed.

"Like these assholes care about the civil rights of vampires. Okay, maybe the chicks do, but there are two kinds of guys who come to things like this," Toolbox explained. "The ones who are trying to impress the activist girls so they can get laid and the ones who want to break a window and get a free TV... Mute here was an observer in Libya with me. Those protests were sure different than this, huh?"

Mute spoke for the first time since they'd left the airport. "More AK-47s."

"Yeah, and not so many pussies sporting anarchy symbols."

Since it was the focal point of the protestors' outrage, the cops had formed around the front of the Iwashiro building. The police here didn't know who they were, but their car had been let through, so that was good enough to make a hole for them to pass.

"Weak-ass metal fence around the perimeter. Couple of decorative concrete planters would stop a car bomb from getting right under the facing," Solo said as he gave the place the once over. "Not exactly impressed on first glance. A little bit of creative landscaping would make this place a lot harder to crash… And make it look nicer too. My dad's a landscaper. I should give them his card."

Inside the visitor parking lot was a little guard shack manned by rent-a-cops. The glass wasn't even thick enough to be bullet resistant. The guards inside looked nervous and distracted, which was understandable since there were a few thousand people a couple hundred yards away who thought their employer was the capitalist antichrist. "What's your business here?"

He held up his ID. "Captain Matthew Kovac, Vampire Counterinsurgency and Counterterrorism Field Team. You should be expecting us."

"The Army guys?"

"I'm Navy, but I let them hang out with me," Toolbox said quietly enough so the guard wouldn't hear.

"That's us."

The guard pushed a button and the flimsy bar lifted. It was the kind of thing kids could push out of the way when they didn't want to pay for parking. Solo drove up to the front of the building and parked. "Can you believe that? A laminated ID card I could make at Kinko's gets us right in without question. The General was smart to send us to review their security, because this place sucks."

"Be diplomatic," Kovac warned as he stepped out of the car. The four of them started toward the entrance. "It's their invention. We just need to make sure they're smart about keeping it safe until it's ready for release. The military isn't officially here. This is a completely civil matter. We're only supposed to assess."

"If they've actually got a working V-Screener, somebody should declare the whole place a national security risk and take it over," Toolbox suggested. "Nobody else has gotten a test to work yet. Can't we just say it's a public health emergency or something?"

"That's over my pay grade. Once the government gets its shit together, I'm sure they'll buy the thing, and if not, it'll go to court and the lawyers can fight. General May told me these guys are big donors with lots of Congress friends, so play it cool. He offered to protect it, but the best he could talk them into without a court order was allowing some advisors."

Two men in suits were waiting to greet them at the entrance. Kovac took one last glance back at the protestors. Most of them looked like they were attending a concert, but there were a few knots of them that made his instincts tingle. He'd often felt like that back in Afghanistan, rolling through a village, getting the eyeball from some of the locals that said *you are not wanted here*, and as soon as you were out of the way, those were the ones who were planting IEDs. Some of those kids were giving him that exact same vibe now.

Three men in white masks and black hoods were standing toward the front of the mob, arms folded, watching, too still compared to the excitement swirling around them, and Kovac felt the hairs on his arms stand up. A group moved between them, waving red flags, and when they passed, the men in the white masks were gone.

———•———

"You can tell that's your son. He looks just like you," Gregor said.

"Yeah, regular chip off the old block." It wasn't a surprise. He'd figured V-8 would get involved, and he'd known Matthew was working in this area. Marko keyed his radio as he moved smoothly through the masses. "We've got pros in the building. At least four. Plain clothes."

May's elite V-8 troops were no joke. They were recruited from the best, and his old friend had done a good job staffing his special unit with the type of get-the-job-done hard-asses who wouldn't get unnerved by little things like fighting creatures straight out of nightmares. It hadn't exactly been a shock to find out that his son had gone to work as a vampire killer. He'd always been a pretty straightforward good-versus-evil, protect-the-innocent type idealist, even as a little boy.

Now, somebody with even a scrap of human empathy would have kicked Matthew from his anti-vampire unit once he discovered his father had turned vampire, but General May wasn't the type to let some little thing like personal bonds or family history stand in the way of using the right trigger puller for the job.

"You want to abort the mission?"

If they could steal the screener technology, it would be a powerful recruiting tool for their new army. He'd heard that the Red Court had already paid to get backdoor access to every DNA database in the world just in case. Far more importantly, the humans couldn't be allowed to have such a weapon. If they could know for certain who among them was destined to become a vampire, there would be no more recruits. The vampires who could still pass as humans would all get caught. They would lose their spies and insiders. Their race would be driven to extinction once again.

"Negative. Stick to the plan." He checked his watch. Sundown was in twenty five minutes.

Gregor was following him. The big vampire was eyeing some of the pretty girls hungrily. He'd not fed for a while, and his kind had an insatiable appetite. "With May's people here, you think it's a trap?"

"If it is, we'll make them regret it."

"What about your kid?"

That was a good question. Ever since his transformation, when Marko looked for that place where his feelings used to be, there was only a dark, empty hole. He had loved his boy. Hell, he'd doted on him. Matthew had emulated his father and tried to follow in his footsteps. Seeing his son wearing the same uniform had been the proudest moment of his life. At the end of his mortal existence, when he'd been chained and beaten, and the Syrians had begun to saw off his head, the last thing he'd thought of was his family. Only instead of dying, he'd turned, and never looked back.

When Marko thought of his family now, there was *nothing*.

"The mission comes first."

The review wasn't going well.

"You're a security expert? Have you ever fought vampires, Mr. Cook?"

The Head of Security for Iwashiro Biomedical hadn't been expecting to get grilled this hard this fast and was stumbling badly. "We had five volunteers here during the early testing phase and I was in charge of managing—"

"Not managed. I'm sure you're a fantastic zookeeper. I said *fought*."

"Well, no. I haven't, though one of our subjects did become unruly as a result of the drugs and caused some trouble, but as you can see outside we're working in close conjunction with local law enforcement. Between the police presence and our employees, we have a very secure facility."

Kovac had only been talking to this corporate goon for a few minutes and he was already running dangerously low on patience. He could have stormed this facility with a crack team of Girl Scouts. "I don't think you realize that, as of this morning's press conference, your company declared it has something that every vampire supremacist in the world wants. You've dealt with volunteers desperate enough for a cure that they'll let you do all sorts of things to them, but trust me, there are plenty of vampires out there who see your research as the effective end of their species, and they'll do whatever it takes to stop it."

"I've been doing this for years and think we're—"

Kovac cut him off. Tagging in Solo was dangerous, because he tended to be colorful in his descriptions, but it needed to be said. "Sergeant González, what do you do for a living?"

"I kill motherfucking vampires, sir."

"And what did you do before that?"

"I went to places that supposedly had good security, killed the people there, and took their stuff on behalf of the United States Army. I was extremely good at it, sir."

"In your professional opinion, are vampires much like regular security risks?"

"No, sir."

"How would you assess Iwashiro Biomedical's security against a potential organized vampire threat?"

"Woefully fucking inadequate."

"Well, there you go." Kovac leaned back in his chair. "That's pretty close to the assessment I'm going to give to General May, which he'll pass along to the president."

——•——

The conference room probably would have had a good view of the street, but they'd pulled the curtains. It was dark out there, light in here, and some chump in the crowd might have been tempted to pop off a few rounds at the enemy. Other than the security guards, the place was nearly deserted. Everyone who could stay home to avoid the protests had done so, except the CEO had proudly told them that the scientists vital to the screener and vaccine projects were still downstairs, bravely working away for the good of mankind, despite the danger outside. That might have sounded great on a press release, but Kovac didn't like having all of their vulnerable eggs in one basket.

Dr. Iwashiro was younger than expected for a CEO, probably only in his mid-thirties. Kovac had watched the morning's press conference on YouTube on the ride over. During that, Iwashiro had mentioned inheriting the company from his father. The CEO struck had him as somebody who was trying to overcompensate to get out of his father's shadow. Being the son of a legend and working in the same field was tough—Kovac got that better than anyone—but that didn't justify taking stupid risks. A few hours ago this man had rocked the world, yet now Iwashiro was listening intently as his security chief was being eviscerated. So far he was playing it close to the vest, and Kovac couldn't tell what he was thinking.

"If you won't accept our protection, at least let us provide a full security workup, Dr. Iwashiro. We understand the potential threats you face. We all come from special operations backgrounds."

"What did you do before becoming vampire experts?"

Vampires were so damned new and odd that he didn't think anyone actually qualified as an *expert*. Luther Swann maybe, as that dude was a walking encyclopedia of vampire trivia, but even then he was wrong half the time. "Gonzalez and I are both Army Special Forces and Morris is a SEAL."

"What's he?" the CEO nodded toward where Mute was sitting. The tall, thin man hadn't bothered to pull up a chair at the conference table, but instead was sitting on a couch by the windows, surfing the internet on a tablet.

"It's so classified you don't even want to know," Kovac said.

"James Bond level shit," Solo suggested.

"We can also bring in information security experts to prevent outside sabotage." Iwashiro Biomedical had a good IT department. He knew that because General May already had his guys at the NSA working on breaking into their files. But they'd be more interested in stopping corporate espionage. Kovac was worried about the research being destroyed rather than stolen. As a man who'd seen firsthand the horrors of vampirism, he'd love to see the screener technology leaked far and wide. Screw Iwashiro's bottom line; he wanted vampirism eradicated like small pox.

"I truly appreciate your offer, gentlemen, but this is *my* company. General May was rather demanding on the phone. I believe in cooperation, but you can see why I'd be hesitant to accept your help. Some of my advisors think that V-8 is overstating the danger of some sort of threat in order to gain access to my company's research."

"We've got ninety-nine bombings that disagree with your advisors," Toolbox said. "And that's just the stuff you've seen on TV."

"Yes, of course. Coordinated vampire terrorism. And stopping that justifies *everything*."

Kovac made an honest plea. "I can't share details about national security risks, but there are groups of vampires out there who are far more organized than anyone in the media suspects. Some extremely knowledgeable people have turned." As he said that, Solo and Toolbox gave him a curious look. Everybody on the Field Teams knew about *Showdown's dad*, but none of them liked to talk about him. "Some of these have been organizing and training cells. Their skillset makes them extremely dangerous."

Iwashiro gave him a patronizing smile. "Oh, I'm sure they are, but since we're on the topic of vampires, there's that old bit of folklore about how they can't come into your home unless invited. Today, we know that's a myth for vampires, but it has been my experience that it is true for the government. This is my house, gentlemen. Not General May's."

The CEO sure was a smug little bastard.

"Look, I'll level with you. I hope you make billions off your screener. I hope you spend the rest of your life sleeping on a giant pile of money in a house made out of gold bars. I just want to make sure the screener is kept safe. I can have the rest of my team here in a few hours and we can get this place locked down."

The Head of Security came back for more. "We've already got a secure facility. No one is going to try anything when there are hundreds of cops right outside."

"And in a few days when the protestors get bored and go home, the cops will go away, and then a vampire could walk right in here."

"You can't enter without scanning a badge!" Cook was getting upset. It was a good indicator of a man's lack of professionalism when every pointed out flaw was taken as a personal insult.

"They aren't exactly vault doors!" Solo exclaimed.

Toolbox grinned. "If it was me, I'd just follow an employee up to the door, let them swipe it with their badge, then shoot them."

Solo wasn't about to be outdone. "Or hell, take out an employee at home and steal their badge!"

"Our employees' personal information is kept private," Cook retorted.

Mute cleared his throat and held up his tablet. It was easy to forget he was even in the room. "Yeah, about that, I just got all of your employees' names and home addresses while we've been sitting here. Your HR director really needs to do something about his wi-fi settings."

"Holy shit, you people suck at this," Solo muttered.

———•———

Marko watched the sun disappear. It was remarkable how few vampires were actually light sensitive. *The movies got everything wrong.* "Execute phase one."

Bringing in agitators to rile up crowds and incite riots had been part of asymmetrical warfare since they'd invented the concept. Marko had agents placed through the crowd—some vampires, but most were easily duped or paid-off humans. It started simply enough, with windows shattering across several blocks and greedy morons rushing into stores to steal things. The smarter humans in the herd realized that the channel had just been flipped to a different station and tried to get the hell out of the way. The stupid got stuck in the middle, but even the panicked ones were useful meat shields and noise makers. By the time the rocks and bottles started raining on the cops, the riot had begun in earnest.

Killing the power had been a no brainer, and any big city grid had its exploitable vulnerabilities. Remote detonation took out a few choice lines, and five minutes after the first cop needed stitches from a brick to the face, half the lights in downtown Seattle were out. They could still see though, because by then some cars had been helpfully set on fire, and the flickering orange light and spreading smoke really added to the ambience.

All around them angry youths rushed forward, hurling things at the cops. No Molotovs yet, though. That was a downer. Marko had paid good money to have Molotovs here. The cops formed up in ranks, shoulder to shoulder, a wall of Kevlar and muscle, and they started forward, like a comparatively gentle, politically correct Roman legion.

Brave or drugged-up rioters rushed the line, kicking at the shields. Screaming and taunting, dancing around and hurling balloons filled with piss.

And they said vampires were savage…

"I love this stuff," Marko told Gregor and Basco. He could tell that both of his lieutenants were feeling the bloodlust too. They wanted to jump in there and start taking heads and drinking from necks like fountains. "Easy, boys. We'll feast tonight."

The cops turtled their way up, shields raised against the falling debris. He could hear the *thunk thunk* of projectiles bouncing off of plastic. They were wearing their gas masks, but they'd not started firing canisters yet. They were probably hoping for a quick clash and break to arrest the troublemakers, and then everybody could go home without any exciting news footage of downtown being gassed.

The main bodies clashed. The Seattle PD must have been drilling a lot, because they kept their formations and did a great job of rotating men in and out as their arms got tired. Groups of cops would part ranks, allowing another squad to rush through, surround some of the really unruly troublemakers, drag them down, cuff them, and drag them out of the fray. They must have had some good leaders in there keeping order. Marko picked out the guy calling the shots and keyed his radio. "These cops are too calm. Sniper team, up the fear. Your target is the tall black guy giving orders at the front of the MRAP. Don't kill him though. I want some screaming."

"Roger that."

Their shooters were hidden in the surrounding buildings, sitting back inside the rooms a bit so they wouldn't be spotted by the police snipers on the opposite rooftops, just like he'd taught them. The suppressed rifle was so quiet that there was no way anyone would hear it over the chaos in the street, but the cop fell over, blood spraying, as the .308 round tore through his knee. Marko had seen plenty of limb hits like that. The bone blew up like a grenade, fragments making all sorts of secondary wound channels. It would probably need to be amputated, but Marko had to hand it to the cop. Other than one quick bellow of shock he stayed calm, put pressure on it, and began calling for a medic, probably a fellow combat vet. Luckily some of the cops around him weren't as cool, and they started freaking out. By the time they'd dragged the wounded cop behind the armored vehicle, the SWAT cops were looking to blast the shooter, and somebody else had given the order to fire tear gas.

Then flaming bottles of gasoline were tossed toward the line, most shattering in the street, but a couple hit the cops. Those who'd come prepared had melted Styrofoam packing peanuts into the gasoline until it had gained the consistency of jelly. It was poor man's napalm, and that stuff stuck to riot shields and flesh, melting either rather easily.

"About damned time. Breaching team, you have one minute. Move. Assault team, kit up and execute on my signal." Marko and his men unslung their packs, knelt, and began getting their gear ready.

The 37mm tear-gas rounds hit the pavement, bouncing, sparking, and spitting. A noxious haze drifted through the street. The stupid humans who hadn't got out of the way in time really began to panic when they suddenly couldn't see or breathe right. A few fools were knocked down and trampled. By the time the gas washed over the hidden vampires, those who were still vulnerable to such things had already pulled on their own gas masks. The rest were taking out firearms, unfolding stocks, and racking charging handles.

Between the flickering fire, the spreading smoke, and the fog of gas, visibility was awful. A constant roar of shouting, screaming, and cursing filled the street. Nobody would see or hear them make their move, and if they did, by the time a response was organized they'd already be gone.

"Breaching team is in the truck."

He knew he couldn't bring up his own vehicle to ram the door with a protest in the way, so he'd had his stealthiest troops sneak into the Iwashiro parking lot last week to check the vehicles that were already there. They'd had plenty of time to make their own keys. The nice thing about being prepared was that, even when your timeline got moved up, a professional was ready to handle it.

The cops were pushing forward too fast now. Those that heard one of their own had just taken a bullet had started cracking skulls. The rioters reciprocated and now they had a good old fashioned slug fest on their hands. The law was pulling away from the target building and leaving gaps in their lines. *Wait for it...* Marko watched the whole beautiful thing unfold until all of the angles were right.

"Execute, execute, execute."

Ten vampires set out toward their target, and no one even saw them coming.

When the lights had gone out, Mute had pulled back the curtains to take a look outside. His voice was eerily calm as he warned them, "We've got incoming."

There was a crash below them that shook the whole building.

"What was that?" Iwashiro shouted as the four men from V-8 drew their guns. Cook fell out of his chair and hid under the desk. When normal people hear a big bang, their first reaction is surprise, and then puzzlement. In Kovac's line of work, it was assess and prepare to return fire.

Mute had his forehead to the glass and was peering down. "They rammed the front door with a truck."

Toolbox looked at Solo, as if embarrassed that he'd not mentioned that method of getting in. "I guess that works too!"

If it had been a car bomb, they'd already be dead. That meant they were about to raid the lab. "Box, call it in, then you and Mute take the north stairs. Me and Solo will take south." They had to counterattack, break the momentum. Time was of the essence. Any delay and the attackers would have to retreat because there were a whole lot of rein-forcements nearby. He turned to Iwashiro. "Have your security protect the lab and get the civilians out of here. Let's move."

"Told you so," Solo spat at Iwashiro as they left. The lights came back on within seconds. It made sense that a building that did sensitive medical research had a good backup power generator. They rushed past a handful of confused employees, to the stairs, and down, taking whole sets at a time. It was hell on the ankles, but riding an elevator into a potential gunfight was a great way to make yourself the proverbial fish in a barrel. They reached the main floor and headed toward the entrance.

Kovac took cover at a corner and risked a quick peek down the hall. A single headlight was visible through the dust swirling around the broken wall. The guards who'd been posted there had been hit and were lying on the ground, partially crushed by the debris. Solo moved up behind him. "If we're really lucky, that was just a stupid car accident, and we'll all laugh at it over beers later." Someone began screaming and it took a moment for Kovac to realize that there was a guard stuck beneath the truck. Solo started to move up, but Kovac signaled for him to hold.

There was a *chuff* noise of a suppressed gunshot, and the screaming stopped.

"So much for beers," Solo whispered.

There was a lot of movement around the wreck. A man moved in front of the headlight, crouched, with a stubby rifle at his shoulder. Before he could ID him as friend or foe, the man put a round into one of the unconscious bodies lying on the floor. *That would be foe.* Kovac leaned out, centered the front sight of the Sig M11 on the man's chest and pulled the trigger. Solo fired a split second later. The man went sideways, hit the wall, but stayed up. He saw them, opened a mouth full of jagged shark teeth, and screeched something incomprehensible. They opened up, striking him repeatedly, but he didn't go down.

"Vest!" Kovac warned, but by the time he could sight on his head, Solo had blown the vampire's brains out. That did the trick.

More vampires around the truck began flinging rounds their way. Solo hung his M9 around the corner and cranked off several more shots. The headlight went out. Then Kovac took a turn just as a vampire moved up behind the reception desk. He put a couple 9mm rounds into the wood and was rewarded with a surprised yelp from the other side. That slowed them for a second, but then the vampires came back shooting. Their heavier rounds zipped right through the walls. One of them was on full auto and Kovac had to pull back as several rounds pulverized his corner into dust and splinters.

He heard crashing, fearful cries, and more suppressed shooting. Some attackers must have entered before they'd gotten here. They'd been too slow to establish a bottleneck. There was a flash of movement, and Kovac fired at a vampire sprinting across the lobby. That one dove behind cover before he could put a round into him. Some vampires were just too damned fast. They were going to get flanked here. "Fall back."

"Cover me, Show."

He leaned out and started shooting, forcing the vampires to keep their heads down while Solo crossed the hallway. Then he followed. The two of them rushed back into the offices. Employees were running past them, and every bit of movement was making his nerves twitch. "Get out the back! Get out of here!" Kovac held up one hand as they approached a glass partition. He'd seen a dark reflection in it. Someone was moving up the other side, and this one wasn't dressed in a lab coat or a suit. They both took aim the split second a vampire with a hoody and a gun came around the side. They lit him up. The glass shattered. One eye socket turned into a gaping red hole and the vampire collapsed in a heap.

The slide was locked back on the Sig. "Reloading." He had two more mags on his belt, but they had not come here expecting a firefight. By the time Kovac had shoved a fresh mag into the gun, Solo had moved up on the dead vampire, taken his Tavor rifle, and lifted its bloody clothing to reveal that he was wearing a plate carrier and mag pouches beneath. "Bastards came loaded for a fight."

"Grab it and go. We've got to protect that lab."

There was more unsuppressed gunfire from that direction. Mute and Box had gotten in on the action. They'd dropped two but had no idea how many more there were. From the noise coming through the building, there were several, and from the dead bodies they passed, some of the vampires had gotten ahead of them. Most of the staff had been shot, but a few looked like they'd been ripped apart by wild animals and spread across the cubicles.

The men of V-8 had gotten really good at tuning out that sort of thing while in the zone. You dealt with the images later, once the job was done.

They reached the entrance to the lab just in time to see a grey, twisted, hunched-over *thing* rip a security guard's heart through his ribs. They both shot at it, and Kovac was positive he hit it, but it lurched across the carpet lightning fast and disappeared into the lab. A split second later it came back, cranking off a bunch of rounds on full auto their way. Bullets tore through the desks around them, but Kovac stayed up and shot it in the face that time. There was a splash of blood and teeth, but the thing just shrieked and pulled back, still annoyingly alive.

"I'm hit." Solo said, perfectly calm.

Kovac jerked his head over to see his partner sinking down as his leg slid out from under him. Blood was pumping out of Solo's thigh. "Damn it." He slunk over, trying to stay low behind the desks, until he reached Solo. "How bad."

"Bad." Solo was pulling his belt off. "Help me tourniquet this before I pass out."

Kovac did. Solo roared in pain when he cinched it up tight. His hands came away slick and red. "Take it easy." He kept risking quick peeks over the desk to make sure the grey vampire wasn't sneaking up while he pulled off his dress shirt to use it as a makeshift bandage. "Keep pressure on that."

"What the hell was that thing?" Solo asked through gritted teeth.

"One of the Indonesian types." He couldn't remember the name but he'd read about one in another team's report. "They're one of the fastest we've seen."

"What do you want to do, Show?"

"Carry you out the back."

"Hell no. That screener can ruin these suckers once and for all." Solo shoved the stolen rifle toward him. "Don't let them take it."

Solo was right, and judging by the continuous gunfire the rest of his team was occupied at the far end of the building. "Okay. Cover the hall and call Mute and Box. I'll hit the lab."

"BREAKING NEWS" PT. 2

Jonathan Maberry

44th Street near Ninth Avenue
New York City

Dr. Luther Swann leaned forward to peer past the driver's bulky shoulder. He gasped and stared. Everything beyond the hood of the car seemed to be burning, as if the limo had stopped with its front wheels on the doorstep to Hell.

"I thought you said this way was clear," bleated the man beside Swann.

"Don't worry, Barry," Swann assured him, "we're okay."

Barry Derkin, the tour manager for the OneWorld Initiative, was a thin, small man with the nervous tics of a little dog. Even at the best of times, he tended to yip and snap. For the last twenty minutes the driver, Hector, had been trying to get them to LaGuardia for a plane out, but every route was blocked. Traffic. Rioting crowds. And now the flaming debris of a building that was slowly collapsing beneath the weight of its own fiery immolation. One wall had already fallen, scattering flaming bricks and debris across Forty-fourth Street, and as they watched, a second wall crumbled, sending whirlwinds of fire into the air. Sparks swirled like clouds of fireflies. Even through the closed windows and air conditioning, the heat was like the breath of some great dragon.

"Back up," insisted Derkin. "Get us the hell out of here."

"Working on it, sir," said the driver. "Keep your doors locked."

Swann turned in his seat and looked out through the smoked rear window. All he could see were the headlights of a hundred other cars. The limo edged back, but then stopped because none of the cars behind it either would or could move.

"I said get us out of here," snapped Derkin, slapping the back of the driver's seat. Hector flinched, but Swann wondered if it was because he had to jump on himself to keep from snapping at Derkin.

"We can't get out," he said, laying a calming hand on Derkin's arm, but the manager shook the hand off.

"Don't fucking tell me what the fuck we can and fucking cannot do. I fucking well *ordered* you to get this fucking car the fuck out of here. What fucking part of that are you too fucking stupid to fucking understand?"

Hector's hands were tight on the steering wheel, the knuckles white with tension. However, when he spoke his voice was controlled. "I apologize for the inconvenience, gentlemen. Looks like we're in a gridlock because of the fires. May take a few minutes until the street is clear and then we'll be on our way."

The answer sounded scripted to Swann. He wondered if limo drivers had to take a course in how not to go ballistic on asshole clients. Probably. Almost certainly.

Derkin was a hard sell, though. He punched the back of the seat this time. "Don't give me that shit. How would you like to lose this fucking job you—"

Swann leaned so close to the manager that it made the man sit all the way back in his seat. Swann took a handful of Derkin's lapel—mindful that the nervous little man's suit cost more than Swann's entire wardrobe—and used the grip to pull them nearly nose to nose.

"Shut. The. Fuck. Up."

Derkin gaped at him, his mouth open but suddenly silent.

"Hector needs to pay attention to what's going on outside so he can do his best to keep us safe and get us out of here. He can't do that if we're yelling at him. And I don't think we're going to help matters by threatening him. Now, do us all a favor and zip your lips shut over your teeth while you still *have* teeth. Sound like a plan?"

Derkin stared at him with shock bordering on horror. His eyes clicked back and forth as if he kept trying and failing to find a trace of the Luther Swann he knew in either of the professor's eyes.

Swann could relate to his confusion. This was the first time he'd ever said or done anything like this, but he'd learned a lot of useful skills through observation during the months he was the civilian advisor to the Special Ops team V-8. He'd been in more than sixty firefights, ostensibly to provide real-time, on-the-ground intel on the many vampire species V-8 encountered, but more than once he'd walked away with blood on his hands. In Austin and Pepper Grove, in Trenton and San Francisco, and deep inside the earth in three separate underground facilities. Even once on an oil platform off the coast of Santa Barbara.

He'd learned about violence firsthand and he'd seen more of the vampire wars than any other civilian. Enough to break his heart, and maybe enough to harden it. Not to inure him to the pain and cultural tragedy of the V-Wars, but to help him grow up, to look for and embrace a different role in this part of history.

Threatening Derkin wasn't his finest moment, but it was a useful one. An act of necessary bullying.

He released the manager's lapel, smoothed it, patted it flat against the man's narrow chest, and turned away, both to allow the man to recompose and to assess the situation.

"Hector," he said quietly, "is there anything useful on the news?"

The driver had a Bluetooth in his ear. "Getting reports now from dispatch. This thing's spreading. More than thirty buildings engaged. News is calling it a coordinated terrorist attack."

"I don't understand these people," said Derkin weakly. "We've been working for months to change public opinion about vampires and now they go and do this?"

Hector turned in his seat. "Don't mean to contradict you, Mr. Derkin," he said, "but this isn't Bloods."

"What?" asked Derkin and Swann at the same time.

"CNN says that a group's already stepped forward to claim responsibility. Here, let me put it on so you can hear it. They're running a tape of it."

He punched some buttons on his console and the speakers cut in with the excited voice of Wolf Blitzer setting up a replay of an audio file.

"...credit for the series of devastating explosions that is ripping through the heart of Manhattan. What you're about to hear is a man—a very human man—who has chosen to withhold his identity, but has given what he calls a "war name." This is "God's Soldier" speaking on behalf of the Army of the Living."

There was a moment of silence and then a voice began speaking. Swann thought that it was definitely a male voice; however, it was distorted by one of those devices that make it sound like a machine speaking.

"I am God's Soldier and I am here to declare war—total and unrelenting war—on the bloodsucking fiends who have polluted our world. The Army of the Living has assembled and tonight brings the holy wrath of God against the devil's spawn who have come to steal our blood, our lives, our families, our faith. We will not abide it. The *Lord* will not abide it. Scripture is clear and there is no room for *in-ter-pre-ta-tion.*" He spaced out the word, over-pronouncing it in order to mock it. "Interpretation of scripture is the same as blasphemy. It is a crime against the Holy Word of our Lord God. The law is the law, and the punishment for all sin is Hell. Today, empowered by the Holy Word and in humble service to the laws of God, the Army of the Living has brought the fires of Hell to the vampires and to all of those who abide them, support them, protect them, fornicate with them, and allow them. Just as God has declared that man shall not lay with beasts and man shall not lay with other men, He has said that all evil shall not be suffered to live. The vampire is evil and must be burned out. He must be cut away like diseased flesh so that the whole of the body of God's children shall not share the infection. Tonight we have brought hellfire and holy wrath to the unholy. Be warned that God is merciful to His children, but He will not abide the creatures of Satan. The Army of the Living declares total war on the vampires and their supporters. Repent now and be saved. Defy the Lord God and burn. God bless America and God bless those who fear him."

Blitzer's voice returned, and he began reading the list of buildings that had been targeted in this wave of terrorism. Swann listened, but with each moment he felt himself falling, falling, falling. As if whatever tether of sanity and hope that bound him to the world had snapped.

"...New York Presbyterian Hospital... Mount Sinai Hospital... Bellevue Hospital... the offices of Amnesty International... the Center for

International Humanitarian Cooperation... the Non-Governmental Organization Committee on Disarmament, Peace and Security... the offices of PeaceWomen Project... the offices of Safe Horizon... the Tanenbaum Center for Interreligious Understanding... the offices of UNICEF... "

And on.

And on.

And on.

Beside him, Swann heard Derkin saying, "My god," over and over again. In the front seat, Hector crossed himself and then wiped tears from his eyes.

Far above, the sky was torn by the sound of rotors. Swann rolled down his window and looked up to see wave after wave of military helicopters fly into the glowing smoke.

Swann's phone rang and he dug it out of his pocket with numb fingers. He expected it to be Yuki, but it wasn't. Nor was it George Clooney, the celebrity CEO of OneWorld. Instead his phone displayed an icon of a red crown.

He closed his eyes, took a breath, and pressed the green button.

"Yes, your Majesty," he said softly.

"Are you still in New York?" asked the Crimson Queen.

"Yes."

"Are you safe?"

He didn't answer the question.

Quite frankly, there were too many possible meanings built into those three words; and far too many possible answers.

All of those answers were bad ones.

"ABSENCE OF LIGHT" PT. 2

Larry Correia

Marko checked his watch. It had been three minutes since they'd rammed the door. They were running out of time. He glanced around the laboratory. He'd memorized the blueprints, but it still felt like he was in the wrong place. It was far plainer than he'd expected. Laboratories were supposed to have all sorts of interesting devices, and Tesla coils, and bubbling vats, that sort of thing. This was mostly computers, and all of the fancy medical equipment looked like white or beige boxes. *Disappointing.*

He'd shot a few of the staff to make the point that he was in control. From the noise coming through the walls, the V-8 soldiers were being a pain in the ass and refusing to die. A couple of his assault team hadn't checked in, which meant they were probably dead. The breachers were holding the front door. Basco was watching one entrance to the lab and Gregor had the other. Meeker was off running an errand, and Doroshanko—who actually understood all this egghead stuff—was screwing around with their computers.

"Sniper team. Status outside?"

"I don't think the cops have made you yet. The riot is going crazy."

That had been money well spent. "Doroshanko, what've you got?"

He'd pulled his gloves off so he could type better. Marko could see the bones of his fingers through his weird, translucent skin. Some mutations were stranger than others. "I've taken most of their research, but there are a few files that have extra password protection."

Marko glanced at the scientists. He'd made them all kneel on the floor in a line. "Which one of you has the password?" They all looked at the floor. "Nobody?" He tore off his mask, went to the nearest idiot in a lab coat, and picked her up by the hair. There was a hot pressure in his face as the fangs grew, and then he sank them into her neck. His jaws clamped shut, slicing through the flesh. She kicked and thrashed and screamed as the wonderful blood filled his mouth and painted the walls. He unclenched his jaw, ripped his teeth out, and hurled her across the room. She slammed into a machine hard enough to smash a huge dent in the sheet metal and send sparks flying from it. Droplets of blood sprayed from his mouth as he shouted, "How about now? Anybody got the password now?"

"Market, the number forty two, underscore, the number twenty, blue!" shouted a young man. "All lowercase!"

"Thank you," Marko said as Doroshanko typed it in. The Moldovian vampire nodded when he was in. "Keep being helpful like that and you might just live through the next few minutes."

Gregor came in, dragging an Asian man by the tie. "Look what Meeker found hiding in a janitor's closet upstairs."

"That boy has a nose like a hound. Ah, Mr. Iwashiro. Just the man I've been looking for. I really enjoyed your press conference."

"Why are you doing this? We're trying to cure you!"

"Cure us?" Marko laughed. "You've got that backwards, Doc. Vampires *are* the cure. I'm preventing genocide here. I'm the good guy."

"Go to hell!"

The CEO had balls, Marko would give him that. He knew he was rather intimidating when he was covered in blood, with fangs sticking out and eyeballs filled red, and he'd get the truth out of the doctor eventually, but he didn't have time to screw around. "Gregor, bite off one of his fingers."

"What? No!" Iwashiro cried out as Gregor grabbed his hand. He strained and fought, but Gregor's mutation had turned him into an *asasabonsam*, and that bloodline was ridiculously strong. It was like watching a kid wrestle an adult. Gregor dragged the hand up, pried out a pinky, and smiled, revealing gray, flat teeth. "No! No!" And then Gregor chomped down and bit the finger clean off. Iwashiro screamed.

Gregor spit the severed pinky out. He saw that Marko was scowling at him. "What?"

"I thought you were hungry."

"I don't eat the *bones*, man."

Marko turned back to the weeping CEO. "We've got a problem. You said you had a prototype screener. I can't find it. Your people deny knowing where it is, and I'm pretty sure they're telling the truth." He glanced theatrically at the corpses. "So where is it?"

"I don't have it!"

"Another finger."

Gregor dragged the twitching, bleeding hand back up and shoved the ring finger between his iron teeth. *Chomp.* Iwashiro screamed again.

"Damn. Someone just experienced a drastic reduction in typing speed. Where is it?"

"I'm telling you! There is no screener! It isn't real!"

"Another."

Iwashiro screeched and babbled and fought. *Chomp.*

Gregor spit it at his feet. "I feel like I should be saving these. Make a necklace or something."

"Now you can't flip anyone off. Tell me what I want to know while you can still point."

"There's no screener. I lied! The press conference was a lie! I swear!" Iwashiro was desperate. Gregor clamped the last finger between his teeth, but didn't bite down yet.

"Explain."

"We're stuck, just like all our competitors. We can't get it to work right. We got so much bad publicity from the trials that our stock was in the toilet. I needed to do something or I was going to lose the company. Claiming to have a working screener was just to buy us time."

"You lied to boost your stock prices?" Marko had wasted his time and resources, and lost some vampires over a PR stunt? He didn't even need to tell Gregor anything that time.

Chomp.

With a stubby bullpup rifle on his shoulder, Kovac swept into the lab. There wasn't a vampire in sight. Moving quick and crouched, Kovac saw lots of blood, footprints tracking blood, and shell casings, but no vampires. There was a spatter trail from where he'd nailed the Indonesian in the face, and that blood had a purple tint to it, but after a few meters the trail disappeared; he'd either healed or got the bleeding to stop.

Room after room, nothing. His nerves were spiked. He was ready to react. A fraction of a second after he picked up a target, it would catch a 5.56 round. He'd been fighting vampires for a year, so Kovac knew to keep scanning, not just side to side, but also up and down, because some of these bastards liked to climb walls or stick to ceilings. Some could only be seen in your peripheral vision when they were holding still. Kovac listened, but it would be hard to pick up the stealthiest predator sneaking up on him with all that gunfire-related ringing in his ears. The worst part about operating by yourself was that no matter how good you were, you could only look in one direction at a time.

It had all happened too fast. In minutes the vampires had swept through and killed everyone, and they'd done it with an army of cops outside. It was too brazen, too slick. There was a gnawing feeling in his gut about who was behind this.

Kovac reached a closed door. There was a headless security guard sprawled in front of it. No sign of the head. He kicked the door in.

This room was a mess. It hardly seemed possible but there was even more blood everywhere. There was a pile of dead in white lab coats now dyed red. Judging by the splatter and the waist-high line of bullet holes in the wall, it looked like the scientists had been lined up, put on their knees, and then machine-gunned down.

There was so much blood that it was hard not to slip in it. He moved around a table and found Dr. Iwashiro flat on his back, staring at the ceiling, with his chest so torn open that his ribs were visible and his intestines were hanging out. Kovac swore under his breath. The vampires had fled.

Surprisingly, Iwashiro was still alive. On the other side of the red ribs, he could see purple lungs inflate. "I'm sorry."

It was such an odd thing to say when you were lying there disemboweled that Kovac didn't know what to say. He knelt next to the doctor and had to lower his head to hear the whispers.

"This is my fault. I lied. There was never a screener. My… fault… All a lie." He coughed up blood and went out.

"You son of a bitch." Kovac's phone buzzed. He pulled it out. The screen read *Toolbox*. "Are you guys okay?"

"Yeah, looks like the vamps are retreating."

"Listen. Solo's injured. He's in the hall by—"

"We're with him now. Where are you?"

"In the lab." There were footprints through the blood leading away. Three sets of them. "Iwashiro and all the scientists are dead. He just told me there was no screener. I think it was a scam. I've got three vamps on the move. I'm going after them." He stood up and followed the red path down the tile.

"Wait, Showdown. I'm coming to back you up."

"There's no time. They'll get away."

"You just said there was no screener. There's no reason not to wait. You go by yourself you're liable to get killed."

They all knew that was true. Only a fool ever went after a vampire by himself, let alone multiple vampires. Solo had gotten his call sign by being stupid enough to do that once. *"Wait just a damned a minute."*

"I can't do that, Box."

"You can't because you think it was your dad that did this. This feels like one of his ops. I know you want to put him down—"

"More than you can ever understand! He's gone evil, Box. I've got to stop him."

"Don't let your anger cloud your judgment, Captain."

"Catch up," Kovac ordered, then ended the call. He needed to concentrate.

———•———

They'd only been inside for a few minutes, but the riot had changed dramatically during that time. Maybe they'd been unconsciously spurred on by all the blood-spilling going on right under their noses, but the rioters were really charged up now. Maybe it was all the pent up aggression and worry since ancient horrors had started rearing their ugly heads again. Maybe the cattle were tired of getting bled and had begun to stampede—Marko didn't know, but shit had gotten real in the street. A bunch of kids had knocked one of the cops out of formation and were beating him like a piñata. A rioter was lying face down in a gutter, skull cracked open. There were wounded on both sides, and some of the cops looked ready to call it a night and open fire. It looked more like a battle than a riot, and the protestors had transformed into wannabe berserkers.

Into that mess, Marko Kovac melted. He pulled the plastic mask back on, put up the hood, and simply walked away. The rest of his vampires spread out; each of them would be taking a different route to the rally point and then they'd get out of town. The hungry among them would certainly feed along the way, and they'd earned it. Three of his new recruits hadn't checked in, which meant they were most likely dead or lost. But that's why he'd sent the inexperienced ones to roam the building, to cause trouble so his elite could focus on the mission. *What a waste.*

Basco had caught a bullet in the face. It would take weeks for the shattered bones around his mouth to heal, but luckily for him his kind fed through a spike in their tongue so he wouldn't go hungry. Gregor gave one last nod to his boss, and then his two lieutenants veered off. The last he saw of them was two shadows climbing up the side of a building to take to the rooftops. Gregor had picked up the scent of the college girls he'd fancied earlier, and the two of them were going to track those girls down and have a little party. They'd earned it.

As for Marko, he savored the chaos as he strolled through the riot. There was a lot of fear-stink over on the cop side. Their carefully drilled formations had fallen apart once they'd got word that one of their own had gotten shot, but there had been no more shots and no sign of the shooter. SWAT cops were spread out behind cover, rifles pointed at the surrounding buildings, scanning for threats. Now that they'd just found out that there'd been a massacre inside the building they were supposed to be protecting, they were really going to freak out.

He didn't know how it worked, but one of the abilities he'd picked up since he'd turned was being able to sense when he was being watched. It was more of an instinct really, a certain knowledge of where humans were looking, and how to avoid being there. In that one instant, he knew there

35

were eyes on him, but this time it was different. Normally he used the instinct to avoid the eyes of his prey, but this wasn't food, this was another predator stalking him. Marko kept his head down and kept walking until the feeling lessened just a bit, and the other predator kept scanning.

"Marko, you've got company," his sniper warned. *"One of the V-8 guys is moving your way."*

He froze—surrounded by fools and animals, in a fog of blinding gas and choking smoke, between the burning cars and the angry law—and took stock. The whole city was filled with anger tonight; it was unfocused and cruel, lashing out stupidly. But piercing through that haze was another anger, only this one was the righteous wrath of a warrior, focused like a laser beam, and sharper than any sword.

Marko slowly turned until he saw his son.

Across the mob, Matthew Kovac was searching for him. He was wearing a blood-stained white t-shirt and had an assault weapon hidden under one arm, concealed in one of the protestor's discarded red flags. The tattered bits were whipping in the hot wind behind him. The image made Marko think of a crusader for some reason. His boy was certainly dedicated enough. Brave too.

"I've got him in my sights. Want me to take the shot?"

Matthew hadn't made him yet. He didn't have the senses of a vampire. He was a strong man—a better man than Marko had been when he was still human, for sure—but he was still only a man, so he was out of his league, and he couldn't pick out his target through this chaos, but he sure as hell wasn't going to give up. The boy had never been a quitter.

Marko's instincts had evolved. He'd been blessed to become something more. Vampires had existed before, but they'd failed because they had not had officers like him to lead them. His people, his *true people* needed Marko to survive, to continue training the others, until the day the vampire army was strong enough to rise up and take what was rightfully theirs. Matthew was one of the humans who would end that dream.

"Marko, I've got the shot. Say the word."

Marko knew that if he let Matthew walk away tonight, his son would hunt him for the rest of his life. The smart thing to do was to end this here and now.

Except Marko had found an emotion in that pit he'd thought was empty. *Fatherly pride.*

He let Matthew follow him into the darkness. The best would win and the other would die.

"Hold your fire."

Marko Kovac faded back into the night.

"BREAKING NEWS" PT. 3

Jonathan Maberry

New York Harbor

T he boat bobbed in the water half a mile from the docks. Behind it the bulk of Lady Liberty rose up from her island, torch held high, her face sinister in the flickering light from the burning city. She no longer wore her mask of serene acceptance but instead seemed to sneer at the insults implied by the attacks.

That was how he saw it, and that amused the living fuck out of him.

He'd left his real name behind a long time ago, and he'd spent a lot of cash and gone to a hell of a lot of effort to make sure it had been sponged out of every database. No one who'd known his real name was still alive. That had taken some time, but it was a good kind of busy. Fun, in a nitpicky kind of way. And the looks on the faces of the people from the orphanage, the school, the foster homes... well, those looks were precious. He'd kept some of those shocked faces in a trunk. Just the faces. Steamed and pressed and lacquered so he could jerk off while looking at them spread out around whatever motel room he was in at the time. But after a while he wised up. That was evidence and it was stupid to ever drag evidence around. Trophy hunting was for chumps, and Rancid wasn't a chump.

Rancid.

That's what he called himself now. It's what anyone called him who wanted to do business with him. Sometimes people called him "Mr. Rancid," which he thought was hilarious as shit.

He sprawled naked in the pilot's chair, his thighs sticky with blood that hadn't yet dried, his cock growing gradually detumescent, his belly full of meat. He lifted his bottle and took a long swig. He loved bourbon, and this was a very good bottle of Pappy Van Winkle, but he longed for the days when whiskey could get him high. He ached to be drunk again, to be falling down sick, throw-up in your own bed shitfaced. The kind of drunk where he had to search the newspaper headlines to find out what kind of a night he'd had.

Or baked. Rancid used to love burning a few heavy blunts, especially the stuff he scored around college campuses, because nobody had seen weed like rich frat boys. Nobody. He remembered one batch he got at a Cornell house party. The weed had been spiked with some kind of new synthetic methylone called Krush that took him all the way to the rings of Saturn and goddamn near left him there. Dropping down off that high had been like falling off a bridge.

But that was then. Now not even smoking good crack could do more than tickle. Heroin might as well be a syringe full of baby piss for all the good it did. He'd even tried munching sixteen peyote buttons with an Apache dude he used to run with. The Apache tore his own eyes out, but all that happened to Rancid was a headache and the shits.

And that was when the change first started happening. Right after the Ice Virus thing hit the news. Since then? Nothing.

Well, he thought, rubbing at the blood on his inner thigh. Not *nothing*.

Blood did it.

Meat did it better.

Fresh, hot, and screaming.

Yeah, *that* was a fucking high.

Shame it didn't last more than a few hours.

The bourbon he kept knocking back was for sentimental reasons. And because there was nothing else left to drink on the boat. The fight with the owner and his family had been a lot of fun, but it was messy. Everything useful was smashed except the Pappy Van Winkle.

Controls weren't worth shit, either. The boat bobbed at the end of an anchor, but the engine was for shit. Rancid was pretty sure the hull was taking on water somewhere under the boards. Fuck it. He could swim if it came to it.

Wouldn't have to if those two nutsack brothers ever showed up with *his* boat.

They were getting close to being late, and he absolutely hated it when someone wasted his time. That was on the long list of things that pissed him off. And the longer he had to wait the more his being pissed off changed the shape of the conversation he'd have with whatever tardy offender was in question. Tonight it was Ballard and Billings. Or something. He always thought of them as the Balls Twins. Or some variation of that. The little one even looked like a scrotum. Wrinkly-faced motherfucker. The other one was taller, fatter and hairless. His head looked like a shaved testicle. Both of them were uglier than a pit bull's bunghole, but they were rich cocksuckers. Rich was good. It even bought them a little grace when it came to meeting timetables.

Like, maybe half an hour. Beyond that it was a direct insult and Rancid couldn't let that stand. He had a business to run and there were standards.

He sloshed the whiskey around in the bottle, enjoying the way the immense fires over in Manhattan seemed to be captured in cold miniature by the amber liquid. Really nice. He'd buy a snow globe of that if someone made it. That he'd keep, and it wouldn't be evidence. No one was ever going to connect him to those blazes and those bombs. No chance in hell.

That was for the nutsack twins. Ballard and Billings—if those really were their names—might go down for it, but no one could establish a chain of evidence that came anywhere near Rancid. He was very careful about that. Very, very careful.

That did not go the other way, though. Ballard and Billings thought that they were a film and opaque buffer between them and the people for whom they served as agents. That was incorrect. Rancid never got involved with anyone until he did the research that revealed all of the players in the game. And he'd been at this for a long, long time. Well before the V-Wars. Well before the first Gulf War. This was an old game, and he was a long-haul player.

He knew that the nutsack twins worked for a law firm that was on retainer to a family of ultra rich assholes who made their billions from military contracts and similar deals for urban pacification technologies. Those silver-spoon dickheads owned about a third of the House and Senate. And they had key people on their payroll who wore stars on their shoulders or had reserved parking status at 1600 Pennsylvania Avenue. They were clever bastards, though, and they used a lot of money to put dozens and dozens of layers between them and anything that even had a whiff of corruption. None of that protection or misdirection meant either jack or squat to Rancid. He had his own network and they, too, were everywhere. And they answered to Rancid.

They worshipped Rancid.

They carved his name in their skin. They'd kneel on broken glass to lick the sweat off his balls if he asked them to. And, at times, he had. Special cases.

Rancid seldom revealed how much he knew and never exposed his sources. He did not possess any personal codes of ethics or loyalty, but giving up a source weakened and shortened his reach. So he kept his secrets to himself until he needed a card to play, and then he'd only let someone peek at a single card in his hand. Just enough to let the other guy know the deck was stacked and Rancid was always the dealer.

It was fun.

And it was part of a long game Rancid was working. Something that followed no other agenda but his own, but the nutsack brothers and their bosses didn't know that.

The time wasn't right.

Nope, not yet.

In the sky the National Guard helicopters were flying around like they had something useful to do. Rancid laughed. There was no army to fight. Most of the bombs had been put in place days ago. Some had been there for weeks. One was even built into the wall of a new wing of a hospital, sealed up and totally out of sight until a little clock went "bing" and all that lovely C4 and ANFO and Semtex said a big, red hello to the Apple.

He started getting hard just thinking about it.

But the sound drew his attention away from the conflagration and he stood up and squinted through the gloom. The boat was a mile away, but he could see it and hear it. Even in human form he could smell the engine, because the wind was blowing this way. Rancid nodded to himself, downed the rest of the whiskey, and went below to find his pants. He hoped they weren't too bad off. After all, he wanted to look presentable when the scrotum brothers made him a very rich man.

"FAMILY TIES" PT. 1

James A. Moore

So running across rooftops seems to be my thing these days. Seriously. I grew up in San Francisco and never once went bouncing over rooftops, but damn near every time I leave town, it's back to jumping between buildings—or at least trying to. I got to Chicago, next thing I know it's the rooftops game. And here I am again and for the same reason. The cops kind of want to tear me a new asshole.

It's not what I intended, but with the cops after me again, it seemed like the best idea.

Different city this time, at least. I mean, what's the fun if the only people trying to kill you are all from the same town?

I got myself spotted in Seattle. I don't even know why the hell I went from San Francisco up that way except maybe I have always had a desire to see the Pike Place Starbucks. That's the very first location, according to the coffee shop legends. Turns out the place is busy.

I might have gotten out of town without any troubles, but Kang got hold of me. As the man who'd just fired me, I maybe could have told him to get bent, but I still owed him a lot, and he was offering money. He's also the head of the Triads in San Francisco's Chinatown. So pissing him off is never a good idea.

I was just supposed to shadow a guy for a few hours and watch while the dude took a package for Kang. If things went south, I was supposed to get to the guy, take the package, and get the hell away from there just as fast as I could. These days I'm pretty fast, so there's that.

Surprise! The guy I was supposed to tail was a vampire. I don't know what kind. How sad is that? I'm a vampire myself, but have no idea about the rest of the different types hanging around. He had pale skin, damn big teeth, and eyes that gave off a freaky light in the darkness. He was the sort that stays in the shadows, which complicated things for me, because that was where I was hiding.

You know what the problem with a lot of vampires is? They can see in the dark. Hell, I can. My sister, Anna, can. I'm not saying it's as great as those high tech night vision goggles, but it's good enough to let me read the newspaper at night on a park bench with no noticeable light.

Pale Face got on his cell phone and vanished not long after he made me. It wasn't hard to see me if you were another vampire, I guess. Some times hiding are harder than others.

I'm still learning a lot of stuff about myself. Here's a new one: When I get too stressed, it's hard to keep my human face in place. I start vamping out. In my case that means white fur on my skin to match my white hair. It also means big cat eyes and a small muzzle full of sharp teeth. You ever try to hide that sort of condition? It isn't easy. Mostly I do okay with a hoodie and some sunglasses. Sometimes not so much.

Maybe it was the fact I was wearing the shades on a rainy night. Whatever the case, I had cops trying to ask me questions four minutes after Mister Pasty got off his cell phone. First question out of the cop's mouth was, "May I see your ID?"

Rather than answer, I turned on my heel and hauled ass for the closest building. Part of me was wondering if Kang set me up. It was a small part, but there are rewards and then there are rewards. Humans United had put out a bounty on me. They called it "a reward for information leading to the capture and conviction of Jonathan Lei of San Francisco," but what they really meant was $100,000 for putting a cap in my ass and handing them my head. That's enough money to make people think twice.

I tried to push away thoughts of betrayal and booked it. Right into a dead-end alley. That's the problem with towns you don't know. You never can find a decent escape route. Might have helped if I'd actually looked around first, but I'll yell at myself for that another time.

Around the same time I started climbing, the rain went from drizzle to downpour. You ever try climbing a building in heavy rain? I don't recommend it as a method of calming the nerves. The good news for me was the claws. Seriously, those things come in damn handy. I sank them into the brick of the wall and pulled myself up. It's a lot like walking, one step at a time, only gravity is trying to yank you down and in my case the cops were taking it personally that I didn't want to wait around.

By the way, I could only use the claws on my hands. The ones on my feet weren't quite punching through the new shoes well enough to let me use them to climb.

Once I was on the rooftop I started running. I was beginning to think I'd made a clean getaway when I heard the 'copter.

I think the old days were better for vampires. I mean, okay, most of the vampire legends got a lot of things wrong. I didn't die, I didn't rise from my grave, and I'm not dead now, but there was a high fever and a coma when I got started, so I can see where that might be a problem for some people. I heard they used to put bells in people's graves because they used to bury a lot of folks alive. I think if I'd lived back a few decades they might have buried me, too.

As I was saying, the old vampires had it easier. People thought they were demons or worse, so they left them alone. On top of that, though, technologies have changed. Back in the day I might not have been spotted. These days? I got a quarter says some douchebag on the helicopter had night vision goggles or was tracking me on infrared.

They had no trouble keeping up with me or nailing me with the searchlights on that thing. Between the roaring chop of the blades, the guy on the bullhorn screaming for me to stop where I was, the wind from the helicopter trying to blow me off the building, the rain that was splashing into my face, and the searchlights, I was having a hell of a time staying on the roof.

To add to the fun, the cops fired a couple of warning rounds. That was about when I decided to avoid rooftops for a while.

I could have tried for a fire escape, I guess. I mean, if I'd spent the time looking, I might have found one, but I was still mostly blinded at the moment and I was definitely not thinking things through.

So I dropped over the side and did my best to climb down to an open window. The wind from the helicopter was even worse on the way down.

I dropped and skidded and slid until my feet found a window. I didn't bother knocking—I kicked the glass out of my way and dropped into the room.

No one was home. I call that lucky.

I landed on someone's desk. It was covered with stuffed animals and smelled like the sort of cheap perfume Anna used to wear when she was around ten.

I did my best to land on my feet and then I got out of the room. It was an apartment building, which explained the stuffed animals and kiddy cologne. I got out of the apartment, into the hallway, and down the stairs at a speed that would have shamed most pre-vampire athletes.

Five minutes later I was on the ground level and looking out through the front doors of the place. There were maybe a dozen cop cars in the area, judging by the lights I was seeing all over the place, but none were right in front of me.

That was going to change soon enough, and I knew there was no way in hell I was going to pass a close inspection, so I decided not to wait around.

I ran hard, with most of my worldly goods strapped to my back.

Not a single death. I call that a good day.

———•———

I don't have a lot of possessions these days. You really can't when you're a fugitive. One that I keep with me is a collection of thirty-seven oddly shaped lumps of lead. Each of them belongs to me, personally, and was taken from my body or forcibly expelled by my body as I healed.

Most of them came from a group of losers who wanted to kill me. The rest came from the cops that wanted to kill me for killing the first losers.

I left the first group dead. I keep reading stories about the cops. A few of them lived. A few of them died. Most are in comas.

That was my warning sign to leave San Francisco. Well, that and some asshole blowing up the apartment where I grew up.

I've been trying very hard not to think about my parents. If I don't think about them I don't have to consider that they're probably dead.

So what do you do when you've murdered several radical anti-vampire fanatics, ripped half the life force from a dozen or more cops, and been caught on film for the entire incident?

Leave town, duh.

My name is John Lei. Until recently I was as human as anyone else. Now I'm a Chinese vampire, near as I can tell. Legends call my type a "hopping ghost." I grew up on the stories. I know all about hopping ghosts and now I know more than anyone else alive.

Okay, that last part? Probably a bit of an exaggeration. I bet if the V-Virus hit China there's a whole lot of hopping ghosts, what with your genetic history being a part of what you become and all. Like I'm proud of saying I'm an Asian mutt and all American. But even in San Francisco's Chinatown, we just aren't that common. I've only ever seen one like me, and that's me. If there *are* more hopping ghosts, I have to wonder if they look like me or if they'd be radically different because they come from pure Chinese stock.

Kind of makes me wish I was better with speaking Mandarin or Cantonese. If I was, I bet I could blend in better over there than here in the U.S.

If you don't know about the V-Virus, you've been isolated from humanity for too long and are beyond my help.

Want to know the important part? What really matters? The world has gone bug-shit crazy. I turned on the news last night, after playing hide and go seek with the cops, and every damn story was about the Vampire Wars. I was sitting in my crappy little motel room just outside the city— ever notice that, no matter how big a dump, every hotel has TV and most of them have HBO? Weird, but true—and every channel that wasn't a movie or pay-per-view was going on about the latest insanities. It's gotten so bad that I'm basically a footnote. Not that I'm complaining.

Anyhow.

I'm watching the news, and in D.C. bombers have taken out national monuments. Apparently the Vampire Liberation Front is taking credit. So is the Anti-Vampire League of Decency. Seriously, though, who the hell comes up with these names? There are a lot of people who are willing to take the blame for the damage.

That's the big stuff. On the smaller side it actually gets worse as far as I'm concerned.

In Augusta, Georgia, a family of four was murdered two nights ago. The reason? The seven-year-old daughter was V-Virus positive. She hadn't actually attacked anyone, and there was a legal skirmish going on about whether or not she could attend public schools. I guess someone was afraid she'd actually win the case. The family fought back and they died for that. The little girl? Beheaded, with a stake driven through her heart.

Over in Mississippi the exact opposite happened. A non-vampire family was murdered on the same night. Dragged from their home and torn apart by a group of pale-skinned bikers. I guess they were hungry. I know how bad that can be. I try not to think about it.

On Craigslist I saw an ad that said for the right amount of money anyone could be a vampire. Like anyone would want to be, right? Only I can bet there were saps out there going for it, because there were other ads talking about where you could hook up with other "creatures of the night."

Were there vampires out there that could bite a person and make them into vampires? Was it a new scientific thing? Did they just shoot somebody up with infected blood and hope for the best? I was guessing, if it was anything, it was the latter. More likely it was just a scam. If not, we were all gonna be screwed over by a major Goth invasion.

In San Francisco, the police are still looking for me. They're beginning to think I might have left the area. Smart of them to notice. Maybe they're too busy worrying about that other thing that went down. I tell you, my hometown can't get out of the headlines these days.

Remember when the big headlines were about the war in Afghanistan or Pakistan—any Middle East country ending in "an"? Didn't matter. Every major article seemed to be about a new war.

I guess maybe that was really the first time I started thinking about my situation in an "Us or Them" way. I just thought we were all people. Not everyone sees it that way. Not on either side of the equation.

I don't carry my phone anymore. Not my old one. I have a new one. It's a burner. It has three numbers in it. The rest went away around the same time I got out of the Bay Area.

When I was done drying off and watching the latest news about the war on vampires, I looked at my burner. There were no new messages. There should have been. Things went bad and it wouldn't take Kang long to know that. Okay, maybe Pasty Face had gotten the package and done what he was supposed to. It was possible, I guess. But things had gone bad enough that there were cops and helicopters involved. That's the sort of bad Kang has always tried to avoid. That's why I didn't work for him anymore. There were too many incidents with cops and the deaths of a U.S. Senator and his family that I got framed for.

The more I thought about how deep in it I was, the more I thought I should pay my sister a visit.

Last time I saw my sister she told me I could join her in Chicago as her personal assistant or I could go the hell away. We used to be close. That was before the whole vampire thing changed us both. I got all the looks. She got all the strength and all the evil mastermind cunning. Anna was the main reason I was a fugitive. She framed me in the process of setting herself up as the head of the Chicago Triad.

We're really not that close anymore, but she was also all I had left.

When in doubt, see your family. I guess maybe it's always that way.

Once I'd made my mind up I gathered my possessions—bullets and all—and headed for the door.

And right outside the door was Pasty Face and he'd brought a couple of friends. Up close he was just as pale, but I got more details. Strong jaw line, looked like he was maybe Italian before he was turned. Black hair cut short and slicked back, but as it was raining again that could have just been the water works. The rest of the group looked like more of the same, only whereas Pasty was dressed in a nice suit and a trench coat, they were dressed like extras from *Grease*.

I dropped my worldly possessions and went into a combat stance.

Pasty held up a hand. "Wait. No one wants trouble."

I had my doubts and tried to confirm his motives. "That's why you had the cops coming after my ass yesterday, slick?"

"*You* were following *me*, not the other way around."

Okay, he had me there.

"I was supposed to keep an eye on you."

His brow wrinkled a lot. Enough that it distracted me from looking at his funky eyes. The others with him had the same sort of eyes. They were all glowing and letting off a red light. I'm telling you, that stuff gets hard to look away from. It's the little things that are out of place that mess with me the most.

"Who the hell wanted you watching me?"

"Kang? From San Francisco?" I figured he knew, of course.

"Who the fuck is Kang?"

I put my hands up as he took a step closer. Looked to me like the one who fucked up was, no surprise, me.

"Listen. I was just hired to make sure you picked up a package without getting hurt. You got hurt, I was supposed to grab the package."

All four of the dudes were making grumbling noises now.

Pasty waved a hand and the rest calmed down. "I don't fucking know or care who Kang is. You just cost me a deal and you need to make it right."

I stood back up and looked hard at Pasty. He was in charge, and I wasn't having a good time with this. The problem being that near as I could tell I had been set up by someone I trusted.

My mistake.

"I don't know or care what I cost you. I'm broke and I'm out of here." I shrugged. "You want compensation? Talk to Kang. I'll even give you his cell number."

It was the best I could do. I had seventy dollars on me and figured I'd need that to get to Chicago, so I wasn't paying him shit.

"I didn't say money. I want to talk to you about maybe joining us."

"Say what?" Gotta say I wasn't expecting a chance to join any new clubs.

"Join us. We've actually been looking for you. Well, she's been looking for you." The way he said "she" made me think I was supposed to have a clue who he was talking about. Nope, not a one. He shook his head. "You're John Lei, right?"

"Yeah, that's me. Who the hell are you with?"

"The Crimson Queen."

I had no idea what he was talking about. All I could think was there was a band by that name when my folks were kids. Or maybe I was getting the name wrong.

"Who?"

"Seriously, dude, where the hell have you been hiding?" That came from one of the would-be greasers.

"Kind of been laying low since they decided I was killing senators." I gave him the stink eye and he returned it with interest.

Pasty raised a hand again. "Just hear us out, okay? You want to meet with her. She's the real deal."

"I'm supposed to meet up with some people." I crouched and picked back up my pack, slinging it over my shoulder. I was done with this shit. "Why don't you give me a business card and I'll consider it."

Pasty shook his head. "Thing is, when the Crimson Queen makes an invitation, it's best to listen."

While Pasty was talking, one of his thugs was pulling a gun. I didn't see what type. I didn't have to see what type. All I needed to see was the holster, the business end of the gun aiming at me, and the look on the bastard's face. He intended to win brownie points by making me listen to him.

You know what I hate about guns? Everything.

"Put down the fucking gun!" I roared the words. I didn't mean to, but like I've said already, I have control issues when I'm stressed. I could feel my jaw changing, lengthening, and I could feel my teeth warping—that shit hurts, for the record—and when I spoke what was supposed to be a stern warning, it came out around the same volume as thunder. Most everyone looked surprised. Trigger-Happy pulled his gun the rest of the way and fired at me.

The bullet blew a hole right through my backpack when I was trying to get away. All of my souvenir lead went sailing. I would get over it. The good news was I'd have a chance to get over it.

I ran right for him.

I hadn't planned to. I'd meant to run the other way, but the part of me that didn't like getting shot at was also a lot more aggressive since my apartment got blown apart. Or maybe it was just getting louder.

Remember how I said I can run really fast? I can. I got to him in maybe one second. Unfortunately, he was fast too, and he nailed me in the stomach with a hard fist even as I reached him.

Vampires. Turns out a lot of them are faster than you'd think. To be fair, I didn't really have a lot of experience with other vampires aside from my sister, and the last time we fought she kicked my ass all over the place.

The greaser hit like a sledgehammer and I fell back. He hit me again, a good hook across my jaw. Before I could recover he was actually biting at me. I stopped him from reaching my neck by wedging my hand into his mouth. For a moment I was dazed by his punch but I woke right on up when his teeth broke skin and started gnawing bone.

After that every chance of negotiation went right on out of me.

I let myself go and felt the change finish itself. My claws carved trenches in the greaser's forehead and took out his eyes. He screamed and sprayed my blood across my face as he let go of my hand.

I elbowed his face because my hand hurt too much. His face broke. I stepped back and looked around just in time to get nailed by one of the other guys who'd only been watching a minute ago.

The first greaser was down and screaming, and the second one slammed me into the side of one of the cars in the parking lot of the motel. The car rocked on its tires and my head shattered the glass of the passenger's side door. It should have left me wrecked but all it really did was piss me off.

I don't know what language he was screaming in, I just know it wasn't English. Gotta be honest here and say I was a little busy trying not to get myself killed. My feet change shape when I get my monster on, and I kicked my shoes off because they were just getting in the way.

The bastard had a hand on my jaw and was bending me backward in an effort to cut my head off, near as I could tell. Judging by the pain, and the blood I felt flowing into my shirt collar, he was doing a damn fine job.

My left foot came around and swept his feet apart. While he was trying to keep his balance I did my very best to kick his balls to Texas. I didn't get the range I wanted, but he fell back shrieking.

I screamed too, and kicked him in the stomach. My claws cut his leather jacket to shreds, but I didn't have time to see if I got the body underneath. Instead I pushed him back and tried to find an easy way to get away from the scene.

Pasty took the opportunity to shoot me four times in the chest.

I have to say, he actually looked like he wasn't happy about the holes in my torso.

Instinct is a damned weird thing. It does what it has to in order to keep us alive, but that doesn't mean we always like it.

I had never fed on vampires before, but I did right then. There was no way to stop it, but I managed to at least curb the need to feed a little. I didn't rip everything there was to take from any of the four, but I dropped them all to the ground and left them hurting.

Most vampires seem to feed on blood or maybe even a little flesh. I don't. Near as I can tell I feed on life force, or if you're religious, maybe it's the soul. Whatever the case, I try not to do it. The first time I let myself go, I sucked the entire life out of the guy standing next to the guy who'd just whooped my ass. I missed. There wasn't a whole lot of aiming going on that time, anyway.

The next time is the footage almost everyone seems to know. I killed eighteen people without ever touching them. That's the sort of shit that gets you labeled as a terrorist, by the way—when they aren't just flat out calling you a monster.

I took Pasty Face's cell phone from its holster and looked down at him. He was alive, but he was also crawling around and dry-retching. "Call me. We can talk. But call me tomorrow, when you're feeling better."

It was all I could think to say.

I took off as fast as I could, my body still aching as the wounds healed themselves. I couldn't go back to my motel. They knew where I was staying, after all.

So instead I ran. I do that a lot. Some people would call me a coward with as much as I run. I prefer to think of myself as an opportunistic pacifist. I like not fighting and I'm deeply in love with the idea of staying alive.

So I opportunistically ran my ass away from the scene and then I just as opportunistically got the hell out of Seattle.

And where do you suppose I went?

Did you guess Chicago? Right you are. But between Chicago and Seattle I took another trip down to San Francisco. One more deal to handle. I had to have a talk with Kang.

"BREAKING NEWS" PT. 4

Jonathan Maberry

44th Street near Ninth Avenue
New York City

The screaming man came running out of the smoke.

His clothes flapped in rags, and his eyes were filled with such total horror and panic that Swann recoiled even though he was safe behind the bulletproof glass of the limo. The man ran into the thicket of stalled cars, weaving, slamming into some, staggering, falling, and getting back up. He was in full flight when he ran crotch-first into the Escalade's grill. The impact folded him in half and he bowed forward at high speed to smash his face on the hood. He rebounded, leaving a deep dent, and howled as fresh blood exploded from his nose and shattered mouth. He stood there, threw back his head and hurled a scream toward the sky.

"Christ!" cried Derkin.

Swann lunged for the door handle.

"Don't!" yelled Hector, but he was too late. Swann shouldered the door open and burst out into the smoke and noise. He ran to the bleeding man but stopped short, his hands almost touching. Almost, but he withheld with the atavistic dread people have about touching the blood of anyone, particularly strangers.

"What's wrong? Where are you hurt?" Swann fired the questions off despite being able to see the cause of the man's agony. The flaps of torn clothes were not clothes at all. The man *himself* had been shredded. Long strips of his flesh had been flayed backward and hung like streamers from his arms and chest and thighs. Blood welled and ran, but in other places there was the bright red and black of charred meat. Thousands of splinters of glass stood out from him like the needles of some perverse cactus.

The man screamed and screamed and screamed.

And then he stopped.

Just like that. As if something had reached inside of him and flipped a switch, throwing everything in the man's mind and soul into utter darkness. The mad light went out of his eyes and he puddled down to the ground, making no attempt to break his fall. He fell into a boneless sprawl at Swann's feet, and it happened with such dramatic finality that Swann knew—*knew*—that the man was dead. Not in a coma, not overcome with pain.

Dead. Gone.

Like that.

The driver's door opened and Hector put one foot out and hoisted his bulk halfway out. "Professor Swann, please... get back in the car."

"We... we... we have to do something," stammered Swann.

Hector suddenly reached inside his jacket and drew an automatic—a Glock 26. Swann had learned about guns while running with V-8. Strange how the mind assimilates details like that when bullets are spraying all around you and hostile vampires are running amuck.

Swann stared at the gun, and his eyes followed Hector's arm as it lifted and pointed. Not at him. Of course not.

He turned in line with Hector's aim and for a moment his mind was not able to process what he was seeing. It wasn't real. It was horror story stuff.

Then Luther Swann remembered that he lived inside a horror story. A monster story.

Vampires and vampire hunters.

Monsters of every possible description. That was all his world was. It was what defined the world.

Since the beginning of the first vampire war, Swann had waded through rivers of blood. His daughter had become a feral, ravenous thing that had murdered—no, *devoured*—her brother and mother. Swann had knelt in the rubble of destroyed homes and held civilians—women, children, the old, the bystanders—as their lives leaked from torn veins and their last breaths floated up to mingle with the gun smoke. As if the breath of the dying and the evidence of killing were no longer antithetical elements.

The world had gone mad. The V-Gene hadn't caused it, but the effect was there. Humans like himself and vampires of all kinds had found no common ground. Not even the ones, the many, who wanted that shared real estate.

The war was everything.

The climate of hatred had become the only atmosphere. It changed the color of the sun and the content of the dark.

And now this.

Now.

This.

The wall of smoke had been torn as figures staggered, ran, stumbled, crawled away from the bombs, looking for help and safety that did not exist in any way that would help.

Hundreds of people.

Thousands.

Flashes burned, rented by glass and debris, maimed and disfigured. Melted flesh and eyes boiled to whiteness in their sockets. Private flesh bared by clothes that had been stripped away by shockwaves of super-heated gas.

Thousands.

It was impossible to tell if they were the vampires the Army of the Living had launched this campaign to destroy. It was impossible in many cases to tell man from woman, not when flesh ran like tallow.

It was impossible to tell race or creed, ideology or affiliation. This was a mass of dying people in full flight of panic, ungoverned, uncontrolled, lost inside the one concept that still existed in their dying brains.

Escape.

Escape.

They ran forward, weeping bloody tears, hands reaching for anything to pull them out of hell. Mouths gasping for air that might somehow, impossibly, scrub clear seared lungs.

"Get in the car," barked Hector. "Doctor Swann, get in the car now."

"I… we… have to help… "

"We can't. God damn it, Doc, get in the fucking car."

And Luther Swann, to his shame, got into the fucking car.

"FAMİLY TİES" PT. 2

James A. Moore

So Kang and me, we worked things out. We both have our secrets. I never told him my sister was Hsi-Hsue-Kuei, the new leader of the Chicago Triad, and he never told me whether or not he sent me to follow Pasty Face because he wanted me to get caught up in something. We all have our little mysteries.

What I got out of it was a quick gig working as a bodyguard. The gig paid well.

I left San Francisco again and this time I left with cash and a few weapons. I'd left with cash before, but it hadn't gotten me very far. This time I left with enough to get me to Chicago along the roads and the highways, with stops for decent hotels and food.

Along the way I collected the bullets that worked their way out of my flesh. Time to start my collection again. I guess that makes me morbid, but really I like looking at those lumps and reminding myself how damn lucky I am to be alive.

I bought a junker on the way to Illinois. It cost me more than I wanted to spend, but I needed transport and the last damn thing I wanted to do was catch anyone's attention with a stolen car. I figured anyone driving an old enough piece of shit probably needed their car. Any of the good, newer stuff might have a Lo-Jack or something and I didn't need to have the cops on my ass for something like that when they were already looking to put a cap in said posterior.

So I got to Chicago, and it only took three days. I could have gotten there faster, but I was trying to lay low.

The only exciting thing that happened on the way was a call from

Pasty Face.

"Hello?"

"You stole my phone."

"Well, yeah. But let's be fair about this. You shot me." I thought about that and added, "A lot."

"So maybe I needed that phone, asshole."

"Give me an address. I'll send it back." I managed to avoid smiling. I figured he was about as likely to give me an address as I was to polish his shoes. I don't polish shoes, in case you were wondering.

"How long until you reach Chicago?"

"How the hell did you know… ?"

"There's an app for everything, John. I'm following the phone."

"So if I throw it out the window?"

"I'll lose you and be very pissed off. Don't piss me off. We're already in what could be called a strained relationship."

"Listen… What the hell is your name?"

"Marko."

"Listen, Marko, I don't know if you've noticed, but I'm kind of on the run from the feds and trying not to get myself killed by a bunch of trigger-happy vampires. So I'm gonna let you go. Text me an address and I send the phone. Don't text me an address and I leave the phone in the next convenience store I come to."

"I thought you wanted me to call you."

In fact I had told him to call me. I still wasn't really sure why. Except that the Crimson Queen was a name I was hearing more than I did most of the names out there. I mean, okay, the Coalition for Vampiric Freedoms was a thing, but from what I'd seen when I checked out their website, mostly they seemed to want donations so they could pay for the website. The Crimson Queen? When I was in San Francisco I heard about her. There was buzz going with the vampires I ran across—don't ask. It's a private thing—and on the Internet when I checked it.

Whatever part she was playing in the vampire wars, it was a big part and maybe growing bigger.

"We'll talk soon. Right now I have business to take care of. Text me an address."

I killed the call.

I was almost where I needed to be in order to see Anna. Last time I saw my sister, things went south fast. So, naturally, I was expecting a great family reunion.

I pulled out my burner and called the number Anna had given me. It rang twice before she picked up.

"I was wondering when you'd get around to calling me, John." Her voice was the same as always, soft and light. I felt that familiar pull at the old heartstrings. She was my little sister and I loved her.

Of course, she'd also started the whole damn mess that had me down as a threat to national security. She killed a senator, and I got the blame. That kind of put a downer on my affection levels.

"I'm in Chicago."

"Not smart. Not unless you're joining me."

I felt my jaw clench. I was trying to play it light, but she wasn't making it easy. My little sister managed to turn herself into the head of the Chicago Triad not long after she framed me for everything she could manage. I was a hopping ghost. Whatever she became when the virus hit her—she called herself a "blood-suck-demon," I called her a goddamn big, green ogre—she was bigger and badder than me, and I knew it and so did she. After she set me up she gave me an ultimatum: either I was with her or I was not welcome in town.

"Listen, Anna, we need to talk about mom and dad."

"They're dead. I know that. I looked into it." For a second she almost cracked. I almost heard genuine emotion in her voice, but then it went away, replaced by that detached business tone she'd learned to employ.

"Yeah? Well isn't that fucking special? Nice of you to give a damn!" I didn't mean to scream. I was trying for a nice, calm conversation but it wasn't working.

"I've been busy, John. I've been building something, okay?" That time her voice actually did break. I could see the look on her face, could imagine her blinking back tears, because I'd seen that look enough times over the years.

"Yeah. I know. I was there when you started remember?" I didn't scream the words. I kind of let them hiss out from between my teeth. I thought I'd dealt with all my anger issues when it came to Anna, but I was wrong.

"There are things going on that you don't know. Come meet me. Come alone."

"Tell me where."

She texted me an address and I pulled over long enough to plug it into Pasty Face's smart phone. Siri told me how to get where I was going. I didn't let myself think too much while I was following her directions.

I don't know what I was expecting. What I got was a pretty nice-looking house on the edge of the city and not far from the Chicago Yacht Club on Lakeshore Drive. I think you could safely call it a mansion. You could also call it a fortress. There was a big damn brick wall and a state-of-the-art security system. Okay, maybe it wasn't state of the art, but the cameras and the guys walking around and checking the perimeter made it look that way to me.

I pulled up in my broken-down-piece-of-shit-mobile and I think the property values dropped. Even the camera seemed to sneer contemptuously.

Nothing talks about your success as well as seeing how well your little sister is doing in comparison. I had a thousand bucks to my name, and she was living on an estate that probably cost more than the average Hollywood film budget.

Not that I was keeping tabs, but still…

I left the junker behind, and two goons with guns and Professional Badass sneers walked me inside.

Past the artfully decorated foyer I found Anna sitting at a desk. She was dressed in designer jeans and a white silk shirt with billowy sleeves. The desk was about the size of my clunker. She should have looked tiny behind it, but she didn't. She looked like she was born to be there. It's weird how that works. She was my little sister. I knew that, but she didn't feel like she was my little sister. She felt like she was a crime boss.

I felt Pasty Face's phone ping in my pocket. I supposed he was sending me a text message. I decided it could wait. Marko might be a nice guy, he might be trying to lead me down the path to vampiric salvation, but right then I was dealing with my sister.

Anna didn't look all that pleased to see me. Know who else didn't look happy? Tattoo. Last time I'd seen him he'd been kicking my ass. He'd gutted me and bled me and tortured me.

We weren't going to be friends.

Tattoo gave me the stink eye, and I ignored him. I wanted to give him the finger, but I figured, diplomacy being what it was, I should hold off.

Turns out sometimes diplomacy is harder than it should be.

I looked at my little sister and said, "Are you still fucking with me? I've got cops in half the country trying to shoot my ass and I'm sick of it."

"I didn't do anything!" Just that fast she was my little sister, popping out of her chair and pointing a finger, her voice rising in defense of my accusations. It was surreal. I accused, and she defended, and neither of us could have stopped it. It should have been funny, but it wasn't.

"Bullshit! You set me up for Blevins, and everything else came straight out of that!"

Anna looked at me for a moment, and I saw her force herself to relax. That was the end of our family moment. Any sudden need to defend herself from her big brother was gone, and the crime lord in charge of Chicago's Asian piece of the pie was looking me in the eyes and showing nothing at all.

"I did what was necessary." Her voice was even colder than the look on her face.

Tattoo was looking at my sister and then looking at me, obviously waiting for a sign.

I looked away from Anna and stared hard into his eyes. He was maybe feeling a bit cocky about that last time we fought. There were differences this time. Like I hadn't been hanging by my wrists for a couple of hours, and I'd done my stretches, so my legs weren't nearly as crippled.

Anna's voice was soft and cold and sent chills down my spine. "By the way. Johnny, what did I say I would do the next time you came to town if you weren't joining me?"

It took a minute. It did. I feel bad about that, but in my defense my life had been in nearly constant upheaval for a while. Last time I was in Chicago, my sister found me by using bait. The bait was a girl I used to be sweet on named Lisa Kresswell. Lisa helped her out to make sure that she and her unborn baby got to live to see the next day. Last time I saw Lisa she was crying and apologizing even as I hit the floor.

I turned back to look at Anna so fast I pulled muscles in my neck. "Leave her out of this!"

"Are you with me, or are you against me, Johnny?" She was in the process of taking off her shirt. I felt myself blush, because she wasn't wearing a bra and you just don't want to see your sister that way, even if she's hot. Back in the day Anna was always shy. I guess being a monster changed that part of her personality.

"Jesus, put your shirt on."

She shook her head and her body started growing.

I might be having trouble hiding my monster face, but for her it was as easy as could be. My body stays the same when I change. I might get furrier, but I don't grow much. Anna was not the same. I don't know the mechanics. I just know that when she becomes the green ogre she puts on a lot of weight and a lot of height.

She also gets uglier than hell.

I was busy watching her change, so I barely noticed the two darts that rammed into my thigh. I felt them, but I never saw Tattoo reaching for the taser.

I looked down just in time to see the metal wires running from the gun in his hand to my leg and then the prick pulled the trigger.

Dropped me like a ton of bricks. I couldn't think. I couldn't move. All I could do was tense up and let out little girly squeaks as long as that current was going through me.

He let up the juice and I started to get back up, furious and ready to tear him a new asshole.

And then he nailed me again, and I kissed the floor again.

And while I was twitching, my sister, the Hsi-Hsue-Kuei, jacked the hell out of my jaw and then beat me into the ground. The prongs popped out of my leg, and I tried to fight back. She slapped my claws out of her way and then drove her elbow into my chest hard enough to break something. I bit the crap out of her bicep for her troubles, and she went a little crazy on me. I'm stronger, faster, and tougher than most people. I can even say I had an edge on Pasty Face Marko and his guys. Anna made me feel like a five-year-old trying to beat the crap out of a pro football linebacker. Somewhere along the way, I felt a nasty pain in my neck, and my body stopped responding.

Sometimes, family sucks.

I didn't go out completely. Instead I got to flop around like a rag doll while my sister, the towering green ogre, flung me over one shoulder and went up the stairs of the beautifully appointed house she lived in.

I got to see all the nice furnishings from angles most people never consider—upside down—and I got to drool all over myself in the process.

I was trying to move, honest. Really strong, really fast, really tough. Not bulletproof. Not immune to having my neck broken, either. I guess you learn something new every day.

"You were getting angry, Johnny. I have too much to do for that. I can't kill you." She paused a moment and threw me onto a very large, comfy bed. I bounced and rolled and landed with my face pointed in her general direction. I almost blacked out again and I know something crunched in my neck, but I managed to stay awake. "Well, I can, but I don't want to. I will if I have to, though, so don't make me."

I thought of a lot of smart-ass responses. My mouth refused to let me say them.

She and Tattoo started chatting it up in Cantonese. Listen, I know some Mandarin. I don't know any Cantonese. It's just the way it is. I've said it before: I'm a mutt and I'm American. My sister had been studying our roots, I guess. Anyway, I had almost no idea what they were saying. I heard the word "jiangshi." That's what Tattoo called me the first time we met. Hopping ghost.

Finally Anna looked at me. "You're stepping into a mess, Johnny. I've been doing things here in town. Important things. And you're getting in the way."

What was I supposed to say? My mouth wasn't working so good. I managed a bit more drooling to counter her argument.

I tried very, very hard to move my body. My hand did a little twitch. It was a start.

I was suppressing my instincts.

They were saying that I should pull in a little life force. Take a nip from Tattoo and from my sister.

If I did that, I knew as sure as I can tie my shoes that Anna would have finished what she started when she rammed my face into the nice hardwood floors a few minutes earlier.

So I sat there and I let my body mend itself.

And while I was mending, I felt Pasty Face Marko's phone ping a few more times in my pocket. I guessed he really wanted to talk. That wasn't going to happen anytime soon.

I closed my eyes and drifted.

At least I thought I was drifting. Turned out I was passing out.

When I woke up it was later in the day and there were screams coming from outside the window.

I sat up and felt a few aches and pains, but I hadn't even been out long enough to make my legs lock up with their customary agonies. I'd been napping just long enough to mend myself up to being able to move. Yay for small victories.

I got off the bed as quietly as I could and looked around. Nice bedroom. Not my sister's. My first hint was all the men's suits in the closet. That was all that was in there, by the way. No guns, no seven-foot-tall ogres.

I thought about sneaking out of the house, moving from room to room until I could finally creep past all of the douchebags working for Anna.

Then I went out the window. I opened it, pushed the screen out of my way, and dropped down into the yard. I was only on the second story so it wasn't much of a fall. Landed like a cat for a change of pace, instead of landing like a potato.

I guess you live and learn, right? Remember how I said I heard noises outside. You know, screams?

Yeah. I could have probably walked right out the front door and no one would have noticed, because there was already a big fight going on outside. There were guys in all kinds of clothes out there and they were busy feeding their faces on the guys my sister was paying to work with her.

Vampires. About a dozen of them. They were on a killing spree and doing a damn good job of it. I know for a fact my sister had a lot more guys than I'd seen at the house. I saw a lot more of them when I was tied up and getting tortured a while back. But the ones she had in her front yard were bloodied, and most of them were dead. The guys doing the killing were a lot like my buddy Marko—that is, pale and fangy. Most of them dressed like his buddies back in Seattle, with leather jackets and jeans, or with hoodies covering up most of what made them stand out.

One of them came for me, grinning, with blood running down both sides of his mouth and smeared into a red goatee across his chin. I hit him as hard as I could in the chest and sent him staggering back. He wobbled a second or two and fell on his ass. By the time his butt hit the turf I was halfway across the perfect lawn and heading for the wall.

I was done with this. Seriously. I was beginning to think going into lockup would be better. It wasn't a feeling that would have lasted long enough for me to turn myself in, but I was giving it some thought.

Two more of the Pasty Gang nailed me. One of them came from the right and in front of me, and while I was getting ready to defend myself from him, another one smashed into me from the left rear quadrant and made me plant my face in the grass.

I was up a second later and seriously pissed off. The day was not going how I'd figured. I thought there might have been a touching moment of family reunion, I guess. Maybe part of me thought the loss of our folks would have somehow calmed Anna down. Maybe I just forgot what the ogre was like. Whatever the case, it wasn't working out right, and I was ready for a good fight.

The one that sneak attacked me got my boot in his knee. He let out a proper scream when the joint bent the wrong way, and while he was falling I let my claws talk to the other dude's throat.

I said I don't like killing. I never said I wouldn't do it. The one I throated fell back with both hands covering his neck. The other one was whimpering on the ground when I punted his jaw as hard as I could.

Off to my left I heard the deep roar of Anna's ogre form. I also heard someone let out a shriek in counterpoint. When I looked that way she was tearing a man in half—literally. She had a hand on one leg and the other oversized paw was wrapped around his stomach with the fingertips sunk deep into flesh. She has claws too, and they're bigger than mine.

She pulled, and he separated in an explosion of internal organs and blood.

Just like that, the fighting stopped. Maybe one or two of them missed the point, but damn near every combatant on both sides was looking at Anna with wide eyes and horrified expressions. Say what you want to about a good fight, but you see a man get ripped in half, it kind of takes the wind out of your sails.

"Enough!" Anna's voice was loud enough to shake the windows. "This ends now! Get out of Chicago! It belongs to me!"

Most of the pasty boys got the hint and took a few steps back. A few of them looked over at one of their own, and I recognized Marko. He was looking even paler than before, and he had blood on his hands and on his face, and his teeth were nice and long.

"You've been killing us! It stops now!"

I had absolutely no idea what the hell he was talking about.

Anna took a step toward him, and most of the guys around him took a step back. Marko held his ground.

"I told you before, Chicago is mine. No vampires allowed. I won't have this town fall apart like all the rest." They were Anna's words. I still had trouble believing that green thing was my sister, but I knew the way she spoke. "No one gets to come in here and lock us away, take away what I've been building. You assholes are causing riots in the streets. It stops!"

Listen, there were attacks going on all over the place. You couldn't turn on the news and not hear about the shit going down everywhere. You know what? I hadn't heard very much from Chicago. I mean, yeah, some stuff, but nothing on the same scale as New York or even San Francisco. And don't get me started on Calcutta. I am never, ever visiting India.

"We live here! We ain't leaving just because you say so." To make his point, he reached into his jacket and pulled out a very large revolver. I wasn't at the best angle, but I'm guessing .357.

Anna shook her head. "Don't be stupid. You fire at me, I kill you."

"You were waiting in my house to kill me. It ain't like you're giving me a choice."

I'm not a rocket scientist, but I got it right then.

Kang is in charge of San Francisco. I worked for him. I never told him everything that went down in Chicago, but I told him some. Enough, maybe, that he figured out that my sister was the Hsi-Hsue-Kuei. That meant he knew I'd lied. He didn't punish me, because family is family. I was as loyal to him as I was to my blood, but no more loyal. So instead he set me up.

Marko wanted to take out my sister. Apparently she decided the only good vampires either worked for her or they were dead. Maybe there were rules for peacefully living in her territory, but I didn't know them.

She'd been at Marko's place, what I assumed was her place, because she was waiting for him. Maybe he was Italian mob, and she was waiting to take him out. But I don't think so. I think she decided he was a threat to her peace.

So Marko went looking for a way to find my sister, and I made it easy for him. I had his phone on me. The phone he told me had an app that let him find it. I guess he could have actually been looking to set me up with a meeting with the Crimson Queen, but just as likely he was looking to take out my sister.

Any way you looked at it, I was in the middle of their shit storm.

"You guys want to maybe talk this shit out?" I had to try, right?

Yeah, they looked at me like I was brain damaged.

Anna looked my way. "Stay out of it, Johnny."

And Marko shot her.

The gun was damned loud, like almost as loud as a cannon, and a big piece of my sister's chest exploded from her back.

Anna let out a grunt and staggered back and sat on her ass, and I looked right at Marko and felt my face changing. My monster-face made itself clear. No halfway shit. He'd just shot my sister, maybe killed her.

Damnedest thing. He looked kind of surprised that she fell down.

I took two steps toward him, and he aimed at me. The barrel was even bigger when I was staring down its length. It stared back, and unlike me it didn't seem much like it needed to blink.

"Don't do it, Lei. Stay where you are."

"I'm gonna fuck you up." I don't think I meant to say that out loud, but I did, and Marko's face got all kinds of serious.

"I mean it, Lei. Just stay put. My issue was never with you."

While we were staring each other down, my sister, the ogre, came up roaring, and one of those impossibly long arms of hers slapped the gun right out of his hand and broke his arm in the process. Marko's entire body went sideways with the impact and he stopped looking at me and worried about the mean one in my family.

Anna was not amused.

I backed up fast, because I'd already been on the receiving end of a Hsi-Hsue-Kuei slap down and I wanted nothing more to do with that.

For that one second or so I thought the fight was over, but then it got started again.

Anna plowed into Marko like a bus hitting a moped. Marko wasn't weak and he wasn't slow, but my sister was in a whole different league. She grabbed his whole head in her hand and hauled him into the air that way, his legs and arms thrashing, and the gun going off as he squeezed the trigger. I have no idea where the bullet went. I heard screams, but by then everyone was getting back into it.

The crew with Anna was better equipped than I gave them credit for. I would've thought they'd go down fast and hard, but I was wrong. They were well armed and not afraid of proving it. Forget all that shit you see in Hong Kong action flicks. It was automatic weapons and marksmanship that counted here, not kung fu.

They aimed, they fired, and what they hit got hurt in a bad way. Maybe hollow point bullets; maybe something worse. Whatever the case, I saw one of the Pasty Gang basically explode when a bullet hit him in the chest. His torso went everywhere, and so did his blood.

Marko went up in the air and came down hard, his body bullwhipping into the ground, and his gun sailing away.

Another of the vampires charged at Anna, and then a second, a third. They were moving in to protect Marko, but it was too late for that. Anna was not in the mood to play with her food this time around.

One of them tried to tackle her as she was in the process of turning. He may as well have tried to push over a pissed off bull. Anna just sort of shrugged him into the air.

I got that in bits and pieces, because same as they were trying to take down Anna, they were aiming to finish me. In their defense I'd have done the same thing. I didn't have a gun, and I wasn't capable of literally tearing them in half.

On the other hand, I was angry, and I have to say, I was kind of looking to kick someone's ass.

First one got my knee in his junk. I guess I should be glad that stuff works on vampires. Well, at least the pasty ones that I've met so far. He let out a grunt and dropped. While he was falling I turned to the next one and drove the palm of my hand into his face as hard as I could. His face broke, and he fell back, but not before he planted a blade in my ribs. Lucky man that I am, it just got wedged in the bone instead of punching through my lung.

Third one was all ready to bite me in the neck, but changed his mind when I bared my teeth at him and snarled. Maybe he was thinking about how he didn't want all that fur wedged in his teeth. Whatever the case, he backed up and hesitated, and I broke his jaw with my elbow.

By the time I was done with that, Anna was done with Marko. Bullet hole in her chest or no, she beat him to death. Really, that's the only way to put it. She pounded him into the ground until what was left of him was squishy, and there didn't seem to be any solid bones left in his body.

And that was enough. When Anna threw him aside and roared, "Who's next?" there were no volunteers. Not far away we could hear the sounds of sirens. No one likes to hear sirens in the middle of a turf war. Doesn't matter if you're a vampire, a monster, or a person, sirens are a sign of Authority with a capital A.

Anna left Marko where he was and called for her people. She looked my way, and through the butt-ugly face of the Hsi-Hsue-Kuei I couldn't tell what she was thinking. I just knew that whatever it was, it didn't involve welcoming me to hang around and catch up on old times. I saw her people leaving. I didn't see any sign of Tattoo. I can't say as I was hurt that he forgot to say goodbye. Those that were still capable of movement were on their way, and the same was true of the Pasty Brigade.

That just left me with a few dead bodies and a lot of very broken living ones.

I decided that it was a good time to leave. There was nothing for me in Chicago. Near as I could figure, if I wasn't with Anna I wasn't going to stay in town anyway, and I couldn't be with her. The virus that had changed us had maybe changed more than our bodies. I still resisted the hunger. Anna reveled in it.

I left the junker. It didn't much matter, and—in comparison to the blood and guts spilled everywhere else—it was just one more thing to mess up an impossible crime scene. The cops would be working on that one for a long time to come. The only thing I took from it was my new backpack, complete with a collection of bullets. As I walked I worked the knife out of my ribs—with a lot of whimpering and whining—and I dropped that in with the bullets. I was hurt, but I was already healing.

I could feel the hunger in me trying to get itself fed. I made sure I was gone before the cops arrived. I might have been able to fight them off, but I also might have given in to that need to feed.

Still trying to be a vegetarian these days. Still mostly succeeding.

About two hours after I left the area, while I was well on my way out of Chicago and once again hidden in a hoodie and dark glasses, my phone pinged.

Well, not my phone.

It was Marko's.

When I looked at it, there was a text message that read: *John Lei, we need to talk.* It was signed "The Crimson Queen."

I put the phone away, but the message lingered in my mind.

And I guessed that maybe I had some place I needed to go after all.

But before I responded, I decided I needed a good night's sleep, and maybe even a beer or two.

"BREAKING NEWS" PT. 5

Jonathan Maberry

New York Harbor

Mr. Ballard and Mr. Billings sat in the crippled boat and watched Rancid vanish into the night in their eight hundred thousand dollar cigarette.

Their clothes were torn from the thorough pat-down their client had given them. Pockets torn out, linings slashed. Both of their Rolexes had been thrown overboard. All Rancid had left them was one cell phone, but he'd dismantled it, and it took ten minutes to find the parts and put it back together so they could call for a pickup.

"My father gave me that watch," said Ballard. It was the third time he'd said it.

Billings nodded. His watch had been part of a Christmas bonus from the law firm where he'd worked for the last ten years.

Everything in their wallets was laid out on towels. Rancid had dumped it all looking for one of those credit card-sized transmitters. He'd dumped driver's licenses, credit cards, and the rest onto the deck. Into the puddles of blood.

Ballard nudged his Amex card with a bare toe. His shoes had gone overboard, too. It was easy to put mikes in the soles or heels. Rancid had been right about that, and even though he hadn't torn the shoes apart to see if there were electronics built in, the bastard's instincts were good. The shoes—and the hidden mikes—had gone down into the black water. They had no evidence and had once again failed to obtain useful leverage on the man.

"You know we have to get rid of all this stuff, right?" asked Ballard. "You can't guarantee that they'll be clear of DNA."

Billings nodded again.

"I'd love to kill that son of a bitch," he muttered.

But, even out here, even with Rancid miles away by now, he looked around before he said it, and he spoke in a terrified whisper.

Ballard did not even nod in agreement. Just in case.

They sat on the bobbing boat and waited to be rescued.

"LOCK, LOAD, AND FIRE" PT. 1

Jeremy Robinson

LOCK

Blood.

It has always quietly ruled the world. It sustains, animates, and defends. Life, from the microscopic virus to the macroscopic blue whale, cannot exist without it. Size doesn't matter. Blood has always been a necessary ingredient for life. But like oil in a cake, it has never truly been appreciated. Soldiers on the battlefield are keenly aware of its power to sustain or rob life, but the average person doesn't give it a second thought—

—until it's taken away.

Then, with wide-eyed horror, they realize that this thing inside them, this precious fluid, is what they crave most in the world.

Trouble is, I crave it more.

Like most Bloods, I hunger for the life-giving fluid, but my desires go beyond simple consumption. At first, after the change, my newfound lust confused me. I didn't understand exactly what I was doing, rolling around in puddles of blood like a dog in fresh cut grass. Research provided the key. A book titled *Vampires: A Cultural and Sociological Perspective*—which is as dry and yawn inducing as it sounds—by the now infamous Luther Swann, revealed my pedigree. My ancestors were mostly Polish, making me an Upier, not to be confused with my Polish cousins, the Upierzy. I think the "zy" stands for "crazy." They're absolutely vicious, and left to their own devices, they'll wipe out entire populations. While I share their strength and thirst, I am in control. Calculating.

When I see people, *human beings,* I don't see one giant candy bar ripe for the taking. I see a herd. To be cultivated. Culled. And replenished. That doesn't mean I'm always in control. The bloodlust is hard to curb. Not only do Upier thirst for blood—ravenously—we also have a penchant for bathing in it.

It takes a lot of people to fill a tub with blood.

"Can I have that?" The voice is small, almost frail, still like a little girl.

I turn to Lucy, one of my recently "adopted" twin daughters. She's got long black hair. Shiny, straight, and perfect. Beyond that, there is very little about her that looks human. Her blood-red eyes are surrounded by twisted black skin. Her nose…is gone, sliced away by the long, dark teeth that protrude from her mouth, piercing her charred lips. She's never looked more beautiful; not that I knew her before the first V-War. Before the change.

I follow her long, pointed finger to an egg-sized globule of white blood cells floating on the surface of my blood bath. It's cooling down. Separating. Decaying. I've kept this collection of blood, taken from the bodies of nineteen people—soon to be twenty—in a liquid state by running it through the whirlpool tub's heating system. But I can't do that with company in the apartment. The sound would raise suspicion, and I'm not sure about my latest "volunteer." Mostly because I like her.

I pluck the squishy orb, spongy thick with white blood cells, and hand it to Lucy. She's perched on the far end of the tub, her clawed feet digging into the grout between the bathroom's now-stained white tiles. Her long teeth chatter as she raises the glob to her mouth and tries to bite it. When that fails, she crams the stuff between her teeth, like meat out of a grinder.

"Aaron?" Lace calls out from the living room. "Everything okay?"

I had intended on paying a quick visit to the girls, updating them on the night's meal, but the lure of the blood-filled tub proved too great.

"Fine," I say. "Something's not agreeing with me."

"Take your time," she says, and walks away from the door, the sound of her feet fading to silence.

"You don't want to fucking do it," Dee says. Her voice warbles, like she's speaking through liquid. She's in the small toilet room attached to the main bathroom, sitting atop the closed lid. Both girls are dressed in plaid Catholic school dresses, but have removed their tops, wearing only training bras—at my insistence. I think they'd run around feral and naked if I let them. They are barefoot, but there's nothing I can do about that. Their sharp talons make any kind of shoe wearing impossible.

In the partial darkness of the small space, Dee's translucent skin reveals luminous organs. According to Swann's guide, she is a *Penanggalan*, Malaysian by descent. While she doesn't tear off her head and spinal column at night, or use her internal organs like a whip, she does have a very long, very sharp tongue. She's ten feet away, but she's sipping from the tub with her tubular tongue. She prefers her blood fresh, so she must be thirsty, hence the foul mood. "You think she's nice."

"She is nice," I say.

"She's a *Beat*."

"Doesn't mean she can't be nice."

"Nice like you care, or nice like a cow you're going to make into burgers?" Lucy asks. "Because, you know, they're food. You shouldn't play with it."

"We're hungry," Dee adds.

I found these two in the ruins of a battle, three days after those V-8 assholes leveled a city block on Boston's south side. The girls were frightened and hungry. I took them in and have been caring for them since, hiding them in my 10th floor, East Chelsea apartment that overlooks North Point Park and the Museum of Science, over in Boston. Our view of the city is unparalleled. Normally this is a good thing, but the city, on the far side of the bridge extending across the Charles River, is a war zone now.

While life progresses on this side of the bridge, Bloods and Beats wage war on the far side. Bloods sneak across bridges, arrive by boat at night, and swim when necessary. The Beats arrive from the air, coming on waves of helicopters, like apocalyptic locusts, or they leap from the backs of planes, dropping into the city. The Hancock Building has been burning all week, like a massive candle. Fires light the smoke-filled night sky. The sounds of gunfire, explosions, and screams provide a soundtrack to the light show.

And yet, the intelligentsia residing in Chelsea, separated from war by a single river, choose to ignore the conflict. Art shows open on schedule. Poetry slams continue unabated. Book signings are less common (some authors have the good sense to stay away), but the city's residents seem willingly ignorant of the danger they are in—should the Bloods take Boston.

It makes things easy for me. With some people fleeing, and new people arriving all the time, finding victims—for lack of a better word— is simple. And the girls' appetites, which dwarf my own, make hiding the remains easy. Most of what's left gets flushed.

"She's a sympathizer," I say. "Understands what we're fighting for."

"*We're* not fighting for anything," Dee says from the toilet, snapping her tongue back into her mouth. This has been an ongoing argument since the "Battle for Boston" began five days ago. The girls, as young as they are, want to fight. They might be different breeds of Blood, but they're equally aggressive. Fearless. While I crave blood and willingly take it, I still feel fear. More for the girls, who I promised to protect, than for myself.

Before settling down in Chelsea as a graphic designer, I was an Army Ranger. When it came to war, we were the first boots on the ground and often the last to leave. A good number of my brothers met their end on the battlefield, but I sometimes wonder if they were the lucky ones. I've seen the worst battlefields there are. I know what war does to people, Blood or Beat. I know what it did to me… These kids don't deserve that kind of darkness, no matter how justified the fight might be.

"You're not our dad," Lucy points out. "We can leave whenever we want."

"You *ate* your dad," I say, putting my finger in the emotional wound. The girls' father was a Greek man. Their mother was Malaysian. Lucy and Dee are fraternal twins. Lucy's dominant DNA came from her mother. Dee, her father, making her a *Callicantzaro*; good luck pronouncing that. After the change, Lucy ate her father while Dee drank their mother to a dry husk. Their words. They're only ten, but they're bright. And passionate.

"If not her, I'll get someone else." I whisper the words, sensing Lace just outside the door. A gentle knock confirms it.

"Out in a sec," I say.

"Hey, sorry," she says, sounding sweet. "The fighting in the city has picked up again. I think I should probably go, in case it gets dangerous."

Both girls look ready to dive through the door.

I nudge a deep red globule of congealed blood in Lucy's direction. She snatches it from the tub and scarfs it down.

My boxers drip blood as I stand. "I'll walk you home. Just one more minute."

"Thanks," Lace says, and I hear her walk away.

Leaving a trail of blood, I tiptoe into the freestanding shower and blast my body with high pressure water, quickly rinsing the tacky gore from my skin and close cropped hair. Despite leaving the military seven years ago, I maintain the look and body of a soldier. Just not the mind... though I clearly haven't forgotten how to kill.

I wrap a towel around my waist, step out of the shower, and take one last, long sip of blood, until my belly feels over full. The blood is nearly room temperature. I tap the tub's heat control knob. "Don't forget to run this after—"

Dee clears her throat, sensing I might actually walk Lace home.

I match her hungry stare. "We'll see."

"Don't think with your dick," Dee says.

I nearly slip and fall. "The hell, Dee? Did you talk to your parents like that?"

"We *ate* our parents," Lucy says with a smile. "Remember?"

Holy shit, I think, *they're nearly out of control*. Not that I can blame them. The thirst for blood is powerful in me, but I've got a lifetime of experience, wisdom, and military discipline holding my cravings in check. These two are still young. Impulsive. And growing. Whatever hunger I'm feeling, it's probably dwarfed by their own. But still... "Just watch your language."

I wait for the girls' snickering to subside before leaving the bathroom, still wrapped in a towel, letting my body make the argument for Lace to stick around. I close the door behind me and stroll into the living room, hoping that Lace will say something to make me not like her, because I don't think there is anything I can do to get her out of this apartment, unless it's via a drain or sewer pipe.

LOAD

Lace stands at the living room window, her hands raised against the glass. She doesn't turn around when I enter. The view outside, across the river, is far more compelling. The city glows with fire, more than I've seen before. The muffled sound of gunshots and explosions can be heard. "You can feel it, can't you?"

I stop. *Does she know?*

"Put your hands on the glass," she says.

Feeling a twinge of relief, despite the fact that I am, in the girls' opinion, worrying about a cow, I step up to the glass. It's cool under my hands. And then I feel it. Each gunshot. Every explosion. The vibrations are subtle, but the battle moves through the glass like an unfolding story.

The desperation of the Bloods fighting—for me, and the girls—shakes through my hands, up my arms, and settles in my chest.

"How horrible it must be," she says.

"War is always horrible," I say.

She glances over at me, head tilting down, noticing my state of undress. And then my scars. Two bullet wounds in my right side. They ended my military career. She says nothing, but moves her left hand atop my right, kicking off a mental debate. She's beautiful. Gorgeous. And I do like her. When my belly is full, the hungers of my previous self rear up.

But the girls...

Don't think with your dick.

They know me too well already.

An explosion lights up a building on the far side of the bridge. The sound and pressure waves chase the flash, rattling the window. Lace gasps and clutches my fingers. I barely notice. My eyes remain focused on the building, now listing at an angle.

Then it goes, all at once, the base crumbling, and all fifteen stories toppling over, crashing across the street, and blocking the bridge. Farther to the east, a series of popping sounds reveals more explosions. Four bridges, including the iconic Bunker Hill Bridge, are demolished, professionally. Explosions on either side sever steel and concrete, dropping the bridges into the river.

"What's happening?" Lace asks.

"They're containing the fight. Blocking access."

"Or retreat," she notes. "But who would—"

"The Beats," I say. "The military. They tried it before. In Philly."

"That didn't work."

"Mistakes that cost lives make for powerful lessons."

She takes a step away from the glass. "Then what, they're going to nuke the city?"

I shake my head. That kind of action only made sense when they thought it could end the war. This is a battle. One of many being fought around the world. They're making a push from the south, that's for sure, and they don't want any Bloods escaping north. Once they reach Salem, it will be easy to blend with the locals, many of whom embrace the Bloods.

"But they're going to kill them all?" she asks, sounding genuinely concerned for the fates of the Bloods now trapped in the city. Her worry shames me. Those are my people dying in the city. Brothers and sisters in blood. And I'm here, hiding like a Beat, watching from a distance. Safe and comfortable.

"Oww," Lace says.

I've squeezed her hand.

"Sorry," I say.

"For my hand or for not helping?" she asks.

"You need help?

She turns toward the view. "They need help, don't they?"

"The Beats?"

She grins. "Only Bloods called regular people Beats."

I turn fully toward her, reassessing. "You knew?"

She nods.

"How long?" I ask.

"I'm a detective," she says. "Your trail was easier to follow than you think."

She makes no move for a weapon. Not that she has one. The tight dress she's wearing leaves little room for the imagination and even less for a weapon without getting uncomfortably creative.

"You're not here to arrest me," I say.

"Offending Bloods aren't arrested," she says, referring to the fact that many police forces now shoot to kill Bloods on sight. She could have killed me, but didn't. Instead, she bumped into me, casual and flirtatious. Accepted my invitation to dinner. For coffee at my place. It was all one long setup, but… *shit*.

I know why she's here.

Explosions on the far side of the bridge draw our attention. The bridge below my building isn't just a bridge. It also supports several buildings. Not easily dropped into the river. Despite the building fallen across the road, it is still a viable escape route, and it's being used.

Bloods, identifiable by their non-uniform appearance, climb through and over the rubble on the far side, shooting back at the black-clad enemy. *My* enemy, if I were brave enough. My body tenses as men and women making a stand on my behalf fall to gunfire. When the flames kick on, belching over the bodies of fleeing Bloods, I look away. I can't stand the sight of it.

"You know how to fight," Lace says. "I've seen your records. You can turn these kinds of things around. You must have a drawer full of medals."

"Shoebox," I say, clarifying, but not arguing with the rest. She's right. Impossible situations are—were—my forte. But I've already got an impossible situation. The girls would have been hunted down and killed if I hadn't been bringing them meals.

"No matter where you keep them, they're part of who you are." She makes sure I'm looking her in the eyes. "I think you should fight."

"Why?"

"Just because you're different, doesn't mean you're not people. You don't deserve extermination, and I can't stand what we've become. Since when are the actions of guys like Stalin, Pol Pot, and Hitler the right thing to do?"

It's a compelling argument. And she's managed to stir old convictions. But there is a problem. "It's not going to work out the way you think."

"It's a virus," she says. "Bite me. Have a drink. I'm good in a fight."

"It takes time," I tell her. "The change. This fight is happening now."

Gunfire erupts from the base of my building. A group of Bloods has hidden behind the courtyard wall and is firing across the river. It's a safe place to hide for the moment, but they're wasting time and ammunition. They're sloppy and unorganized.

"So I'll fight as a human tonight and as a Blood the next time. I've done the research. My family is a bunch of Vikings. I'll be *Draugr*. Powerful. I could make a difference."

I sigh. If only that's how it would work.

Fervent gunshots from below mark the arrival of more Bloods, fleeing, afraid, and on the verge of defeat. If we lose Boston, a fight it appeared the Bloods would win, morale around the country could sag. I'm embarrassed that it took a passionate Beat to remind me of who I am, but her strength will soon be mine.

"If we're going to do this," I say, "you need to do exactly what I say, when I say it. No arguments. One fuck up, and I'll drag you back here. Understood?"

Lace appears a little taken aback by the forcefulness of my words, but her reply is cut short by the two voices behind us, replying in unison. "Okay."

Lace spins around, gasping. The window gongs as she throws herself backward, smacking her head. "Oh my God!"

"Didn't know about them, did you?" I ask.

"I—I thought it was just you."

I pat my firm belly. "I couldn't eat that much on my own."

Her wide eyes turn to me. "You can still…"

My shaking head stops her. "I drink blood." I point to Dee, whose luminous insides are pulsing with anticipation. "Dee drinks blood."

Dee waves and smiles, revealing sharp teeth. "Hi."

"But Lucy… She's the problem."

Lucy wiggles her fingers at Lace—if that's even her name.

"Why is Lucy the problem?" Lace asks.

"Some of us drink." I frown. "Some of us eat. And if I'm taking them into that mess—" I hitch my thumb over my shoulder. "I need both of them at full strength." I put my hand on Lace's shoulder and turn her toward me. "I wish there was another way."

As tears fill her eyes, I lean in close to her neck and flick out my tongue. She gasps as the dart at the tip of my tongue punctures her skin and the wall of her jugular. The neurotoxin injected into her still-pulsing blood quickly reaches her brain and locks it down tight. She's not feeling a thing now, which is good, because the moment I step back, the girls are on top of her. Dee slips that long tongue into Lace's open vein, and Lucy makes a mess of the soft gut organs. They'll be strong and ready to fight by the time I'm done draining the tub, or as much of it as my belly can hold.

FIRE

"What's happening?" I ask, crouching down next to one of the Bloods taking cover behind the front wall of my apartment building.

He flinches away and looks at me with wide, red eyes. He's bald with pointy ears and rows of sharp teeth that would be impossible to hide. I look human enough that he's probably thrown by my sudden appearance and non-threatening nature. He's also a bit shell-shocked. Then he sees the girls—who are instantly identifiable as Bloods—and he understands that I'm with them, that I'm *one* of them. He looks me up and down, confused.

I'm dressed in the clothes I wore on my date with Lace, before my bath—black slacks, shiny shoes, and a clean white button down. The choice was strategic. Even soldiers will think twice before shooting the nicely dressed white man who doesn't look like a Blood. Up close, my nearly translucent pale skin would be a giveaway, but I'm wearing makeup.

"You just get here?" he asks.

I nod. "Just now. I can help."

"Ain't nobody who can help," he says, his accent thick Bostonian, a local fighting for his city back. "If you got people you care about, get out now."

"So you're bugging out?"

"I have a wife, and a kid on the way, man."

"A…baby?"

82
T

He nods. "Wife's a Beat. My son will be too. But I don't hold that against them, you know? And I wouldn't be out here fighting without her support. She's good people." He motions toward Boston. "Not like the assholes in there."

"What's your name?" I ask.

"Peter," he says, and it comes out sounding like Lois Griffin from *Family Guy*: "Petah."

I roll up my sleeve, revealing the Army Rangers tattoo on my forearm. "You know what this means?"

He shakes his head.

"It means I can help." I slide the M4 hanging from my back around to the front, punctuating the point. My apartment building shakes from an explosion; must have been a tank or mortar round fired from within the city. I peek up over the wall. Bloods continue to flee the city by the dozens, many of them cut down before they can run past the Museum of Science and the adjacent parking lot. *How many more are drowning in the river?* I duck back down. "Now, what happened? How did things go FUBAR?"

"I—I…"

Lucy, moving with surprising swiftness, steps up and takes Peter's throat. Her massive black teeth, which dwarf a normal man's, are millimeters from slicing off his nose. "Answer. The goddamn. Question."

"F—Federal Reserve Bank. It's the military HQ inside the city. Thirty-two stories. Concrete and steel."

I nod. "Government issue. Built solid. I know the type."

"Right. They've locked down the Financial District and the surrounding blocks from that building. They've kept us on the fringes of the city. But we controlled the underground. The subway tunnels. Fucking sewers."

"Controlled?" I say, emphasis on the past tense.

"They flushed us out. Cost them a shit ton of men to do it. More than we thought they'd sacrifice, but they…they must have found out…"

"About what?"

"We were under the Federal Reserve when they breached the underground. We…" He looks around, at the Bloods nearby, none of whom are paying us any attention. They've been chased out. The fight is over. Survival clouds their minds. "There's enough C-4 on the building's foundation for the ground to swallow it whole." He pulls a small device out of his pocket. "There's just one problem."

I recognize the device in his hands. It's a receiver, the kind that takes a cell phone call and detonates blasting caps buried in C4. They must have been interrupted before planting it.

"You were trying to cut the head off the snake," I say. "A good plan."

"This was supposed to be our night," Peter says. "Our victory."

"Still can be," I say. "But I'll need you to show us the way."

"Us?" he asks.

Dee stands up, her internal organs glowing with energy. She's wearing a long-sleeve, black, zip-up, hoodie sweatshirt at my insistence, but she's left it hanging open. Her tongue flicks out, catches hold of the receiver, and snaps it from Peter's hands. She deposits the device in my hands and says, "All of us."

After a moment, Peter nods, turns to the nearby Bloods, and cups his mouth to shout, but my hand covers his lips before he can speak. "Just us. Any more will attract attention."

I yank Peter to his feet and pull him toward the gate. Stray bullets eat up the terrain around us. Mortars and tank rounds pummel the bridge ahead of us and the buildings behind us. The military isn't worrying about collateral damage.

This is war.

Peter starts to struggle, his instincts telling him to take cover. "We can't just run out there and—"

I lift him off the ground so we're eye to eye. "Can and will. You're a fucking Blood, Peter. You're faster. You're stronger. My girls have more balls than you. It's no wonder you lost Boston."

I'm saying this as much to myself as I am to Peter. I've been the bigger coward, after all, hiding with my view of the city, pretending it was the girls keeping me from the fight and not my own painful history.

He reacts as I hoped, snarling with anger. "Boston isn't lost yet."

"That's better. Now let's take it back." I shove Peter toward the bridge. The girls, running on all fours, have a head start. We chase after them, passing confused-looking Bloods, many of them wounded, running in the opposite direction. "Head for the garage!"

The girls veer toward the large parking garage that services the Museum of Science. We chase after them and are soon out of the line of fire, hidden behind tons of concrete and rebar. There are Bloods here as well, taking shelter behind the building, but I pay them no heed as I kick in the locked, metal side door and enter the dark garage. I lead the group across the garage and up a level, heading for the far side at a sprint, the girls to either side, twisted smiles on their faces. Peter is close behind.

"Can everyone swim?" I ask.

The girls nod and run ahead, understanding my intention. It's hard to believe how these two twins can know me so well. We've only been together for a short time, but they seem to understand my intentions almost as well as they understand each other's. We have a bond. Like family. Hell, maybe they have more in common with me, at this point, than they do with their parents. Or *did*, before they ate them.

"I can't," Peter says as the girls leap up onto the side wall and dive off into open space. Two splashes from far below echo up, nearly lost in the sound of the gunfire ravaging the streets.

We stop by the side wall. I pull the receiver from my pocket. "Is this waterproof?"

He nods. "I can't swim."

"Better learn," I say, picking Peter up and hurling him into the Charles River. I follow him into the chilly waters. When I surface, it's clear he wasn't lying. He's about to go under and stay under. I wrap one arm around him and say, "If you don't stop thrashing, I will drown you myself."

The girls slide through the water like kids who spent a good number of hours at the YMCA. They're natural swimmers and seem to be enjoying themselves. We kick across the river, and beneath the bridge.

"What are we doing?" Peter asks, between sputters. I turn him around so he can see our destination, just ten feet away. "Storm drain."

The metal grate that blocks the large storm drain that empties into the Charles River is substantial, but heavily rusted. The water here ebbs and flows with the tide, the salt water corroding everything it touches. Three hard yanks and four popped bolts later, the grate is bent back enough for us to squeeze past. The sounds of battle fade once we're inside, though the tunnel vibrates and hums from the larger explosions. Absolute darkness envelopes us.

Knee-deep water sloshes around my legs as I move forward. But the water isn't clear. My feet roll over sometimes hard, sometimes squishy debris. Chunks of who-knows-what build up around my legs, clinging to me, forming a damn that's slowing me down. And then there's the smell, ancient rot mixed with sewer and a smell we're all intimately familiar with now—blood. With a shiver I'm glad the others can't see, I realize we're not the only Bloods in this tunnel, and I'm not the only one feeling it.

"Should have brought a flashlight," Peter says.

While some of our kind, like Lucy, can see well in the dark, I am not one of them. Neither is Peter. "Dee. Help us out."

The sound of a zipper coming apart syncs in time with a brightening light. Dee's luminous insides reveal the tunnel ahead. It's straight, gray, and full of knee-deep water, not to mention the occasional clumps of leaves, branches, and... I look down at the mass of debris wrapped around my legs. It's a body, torn in half lengthwise, it's organs wriggling back and forth with the water's current, it's transparent skin identifying it as a Blood. I look forward, viewing the debris with new eyes. Bloods litter the water, though very few of them are recognizable as human beings, or rather, used-to-be human beings. Did the water carry them here? Did they die here, looking for an exit? *Doesn't matter*, I decide, pushing forward with an air of indifference I hope will infect the others. Peter groans, but says nothing. The girls show no reaction.

We push past the dead into an underground network of tunnels, some of them more ancient than the city above. It's confounding, an unmarked maze that I could stay lost in for weeks, but Peter seems to know his way around. Or maybe he has a good sense of direction. Or he's bullshitting. But the farther we go, the more nervous he gets.

When he starts shaking, I take his arm and pull him to a stop, "What's wrong?"

"We're near one of the tunnel exits to the subway," Peter explains, taking a deep breath. "It was supposed to be one of our exit points. Instead, it's where they came in. With flame throwers. We had too many people backed in, ready to storm the surface. Instead, they got stuck. And cooked."

I force myself to look away from the bodies. To forget them like I've spent the last seven years forgetting the others. "That's not going to happen again."

"H-how do you know?"

"Aside from the fact that they wouldn't waste resources guarding thousands of tunnels while they've got us on the run on the surface, you're with *me* now."

"And us," Lucy says. She's clinging to the ceiling while Dee moves along the walls. They've both got super sharp, barbed claws that let them climb almost any surface. Despite the tough front both girls put up, it's clear that they're avoiding the water for the same reason Peter is shaking. All these dead Bloods have freaked them out. As they should.

As though to prove me wrong, something ripples through the water ahead, coming from an adjoining tunnel.

"Dee," I whisper. She clenches the hoodie together, plunging us into darkness.

"Who's there?" a man says. I'm not sure if he's Beat or a Blood until he continues. "Identify yourself." He's speaking with the authority of an active-duty military man. The real trouble is that he doesn't sound afraid.

I answer honestly. "Staff Sergeant Aaron Weedon. Second Battalion, 75th Ranger Regiment."

"We lead the way," the man replies, telling me he's a fellow Ranger.

I'm torn by split loyalties, but it lasts only a moment. The man in the tunnel ahead will torch me and the girls, whether or not I'm a fellow Ranger. I hear the man slide through the water ahead. "Hands up. All four of you."

Night vision. Shit.

"Even you, *Ranger*," he says "Ranger" with contempt.

"Throw me," the whispered words are so close to my ear that I flinch. Lucy climbs over my right shoulder, clinging to my arms with her claws, drawing blood. I tense and she says it again. "Throw. Me."

I raise my hands. Lucy slowly, painfully, scales my arm and plants her butt in my open hand. I nudge Dee with my foot. I whisper, "Three seconds."

"So Rangers are killing U.S. citizens now?" I ask.

The distinct sound of arms rising up slides through the darkness. Without seeing, I know he's taking aim with his weapon. "Man, you're not even human. And if you were a Ranger once, I'm sorry, but I'm doing you a favor."

I nudge Dee again. She stands and opens her hoodie. Bright light flares out from her revealed organs. The Ranger, just thirty feet away, shouts in pain, twisting away as the light is amplified by his night-vision monocle and shot into his retina. A single shot coughs from his weapon before I heave Lucy through the air with all of my now formidable strength.

The Ranger, still blind, but recovering his senses, swings his weapon in our direction again, no doubt planning to spray and pray his entire magazine. But he's still blind, and totally unaware of the fact that I have fired a round in his direction.

He finds out a second later when Lucy reaches him. Her mouth is open wide, the lower jaw dislocating like a snake's. The long, black teeth envelope the man's face. As a scream rises up, the powerful jaws lock and snap shut, carving away his eyes, nose, and mouth. As blood gurgles up from his throat, I hear him breathing, still alive. Still able to hear and see.

"*Sua Sponte*," I tell him. *Of their own accord.* It's a Ranger saying highlighting our ability to finish tasks, or missions, without prompting. We take actions into our own hands. He offers no reply—he's unable—but he goes still, understanding what's coming.

I aim my weapon at his forhead, but don't pull the trigger. I don't need to. He's either going to bleed out the old-fashioned way, or… His eyes widen, pleading to be put down, when he realizes I'm not going to shoot him. I lower the weapon and turn to Peter. "Are we far?"

He shakes his head. "Half a block." He rushes ahead, propelled by a newfound boldness.

After I check the girls for bullet wounds and find none, we follow.

It's actually less than a hundred yards to the tunnel exit, a simple drainage grate in the ceiling. We climb up and find ourselves in a basement, surrounded by thick concrete posts—the foundation of a skyscraper. Each and every post is absolutely laden with C4. When this goes up, it's not just going to pull down the building, it's going to take the whole block, maybe the whole Financial District if buildings topple to the side. This one attack will not only wipe out the command structure for the Beats in Boston, it will seriously impact their numbers and tactical capabilities. It will turn the tide.

I take the receiver from my pocket and hand it to Peter, who takes it and puts it in place. "They're networked," he says, and I notice he's holding his side. "When the signal comes through, they'll all go up… except… "

"Except what?" I ask.

"I don't remember the number." He chuckles at the ridiculousness of what he's just said.

"Is he serious?" Dee says, her insides luminous with frustration. She turns to Peter. "Are you serious?"

"If he is," Lucy says, taking a step toward the man. "I'm going to take him apart."

While many Bloods want to live normal lives, resisting the craving for blood and violence, the girls have taken to it like they were born for it.

"Shit, kid," Peter says, flinching away. "You eat a lot of red meat growing up?"

"Our parents were vegetarians," Lucy growls, hooking her fingers.

Peter holds up a hand. It's covered in blood. His own. "Just chill, kid. Fuck."

"You were shot," I say.

"No kidding." He leans against the support beam holding the receiver and a shit-ton of C-4. His blood trickles down the concrete. "But here's the good news. I can detonate locally. One button will do it."

"Are you sure you can't remember the number?" I ask.

"I'm going to die, either way, man," he says. "'Sua Sponte,' right?"

I smile. "You don't even know what that means, do you?"

He grunts and grins. "*Carpe diem* then. Fuck. Just go. Let me do this. Get your girls out of here."

"Can I give your wife a message?" When I ask the question, his resolve falters for a moment, but then returns twofold.

"Yeah," he says. "You can tell her to make sure he doesn't become like us."

I'm momentarily offended, but understand. The life of a Blood is… bloody. There's no escaping it. Maybe someday, but for now… what father would want this life for his son? It's too late for the girls, but I wouldn't have willed this life on them, either.

He rattles off seven digits that I realize are a phone number. I commit the numbers to memory and signal my acceptance of his sacrifice by backing away. The girls spring into action, diving back down the open drain.

"How long can you give me?" I ask.

"As long as I can stand," he says, but that doesn't look like very long.

I nod my goodbye and crawl through the hole in the floor.

Back in the tunnels, the girls and I run. They take the lead, outpacing me along the walls as I slog through the water. They take a sudden right and I'm about to shout at them to stop, but I see a small glowing streak on the wall. Dee left a trail of bread crumbs, though in this case it's drops of luminous secretions. Gross, but effective.

I no longer worry about the girls. They know where they're going, and they're faster than me. So I focus on moving, recognizing bits of the tunnel, pausing for just a moment when I realize the Ranger's defaced body is now missing. Winded and tired, I start to slow, but then I find myself at the final straightaway leading back to the storm drain beneath the Museum of Science. The walls shake from explosions. The distant popping of automatic weapons flits down the tunnel. The battle still rages above.

And then, a breeze. Slow at first, but then hard and fast, whipping grit across my face. Peter detonated the C4.

I know what's coming. I run, pushing through the water even as it builds up around me. A roar unlike anything I've heard before grows louder at my back. Massive amounts of pressure are pushing all the air, water, bodies, and everything else in these tunnels out.

Me included.

I reach the tunnel's end as the roar becomes unbearable. I climb the rusted grate toward the opening and against my better judgment, I look back. A raging wall of debris, bodies, and white water slams down the tunnel.

A pain, like rows of fishing hooks impaling my flesh, tears through my arms. And then I'm hoisted up, pulled free of the tunnel by the girls, who have buried their fingers into my arms.

The bent metal grate launches from the tunnel exit, shoots across the river, and embeds itself in the concrete wall. Water sprays out, sending a cloud of debris into the river. Up and down the river, drainage grates burst, spraying their contents into the night.

The battle above falls silent. A more distant din takes its place. Rumbling. A sharp shearing of glass. Thousands of windows shattering at once. The ground shakes from an impact, the footfall of a kaiju. And then another. And another.

The girls and I scale up the side of the river and watch the city topple in on itself, towers of smoke rising into the air. The military units nearby are panicking. Retreating. Chaos sweeps through them as those issuing commands are suddenly silenced.

The Bloods on the far side of the river understand what is happening. The plan, thought forgotten, has gone through. And they charge, as one, across the river, firing at the now confused military units. The sudden reversal is inspiring, but I'm too tired to join in the fight. My job, the job I thought I didn't want again, is done. All around the city, the screams of Beats rise up, mixed with the howls of Bloods returning to the fight. To victory.

I sit on a riverside bench, a girl to each side. Their bloodlust seems to have been quenched as well.

Lucy leans her black head against my side, and I loop an arm around her. "That was fun," she says.

I chuckle a little and put my other arm around Dee. "That, my girls, is how the Rangers get things done."

"Blood Rangers," Dee says. "That's what we are."

Blood Rangers. I can't help but smile. "I like it."

"So," Dee says slowly, teasing the word out, and I know the tone. "I'm thirsty."

"I'm hungry," Lucy adds.

"Are you ever not?" I ask, and then I wave my hands. "Go. The night belongs to you."

Both girls stop and wait for me to stand.

"Belongs to us," Dee says.

Lucy's red eyes brim with excitement. "Blood Rangers."

The nearby cry of some Beat perks our ears. "Blood Rangers," I say, and the three of us run into the night, ready to feed. Ready to fight.

"BREAKING NEWS" PT. 6

Jonathan Maberry

The Situation Room
The White House
Washington D.C.

I t was chaos.
Dozens of people, some in uniform, some not, everyone yelling into phones. Cells and landlines. A barrage of orders and demands for answers. The big screens flush-mounted on the walls showed a dozen different views of New York City.

The president was the only silent person in the room. Everyone he would need to call was already here. Everything he needed to put in motion flowed around him. All he could do was sit and wait and watch.

The images looked like something from a horror movie. It was like watching a live-action interpretation of one of the inner rings of hell.

Someone had started a tally on a whiteboard.

Number of confirmed detonations: 22
Number of buildings/structures on fire: .. 35
Number of confirmed fatalities: 191
Number of confirmed wounded: 1118
Projected fatalities: .... 2k *(as of 11:27 pm)*
Projected wounded at current rate: 6k

The National Security Advisor covered the mouthpiece of his phone and leaned toward the director of the FBI. They conferred briefly, then the FBI director turned to the president.

"Sir, we just heard from Feliz at Cyber Crimes, and she thinks we'll be able to trace the message back to its source. It's a residence, though, which means we need a federal judge to—"

"To hell with warrants," interrupted the attorney general. "This is a clear and indisputable terrorist attack. The Patriot Act covers it."

Everyone looked at the president, who nodded gravely. "Find these people," he said. "Move Heaven and Earth, but find them. No other option is acceptable."

"LOVE LOST" PT. 1

John Everson

Vampires were just as easy to kill as regular people.

Sometimes they ran a little faster, or fought a little fiercer… but whether you put a bullet to the brain or a stake to the heart, they laid down and died the same.

Mila pulled back on her bow and waited. There was no need to put a "stake through the heart"… but she found the silent stealth of the bow far more desirable than the too-obvious pop of a bullet. Her watch read 6:27. She knew the monster would be home soon. She'd followed his schedule for the past three nights.

Predictable.

He parked the Honda outside the garage at about 6:30 p.m. each evening after work and then entered the house through the front door. She didn't know why he never put the car in the garage, but he hadn't so far. She assumed that his Thursday would be the same as his Monday to Wednesday. So at 5 p.m. she had picked the lock on his back door and let herself into his house to wait. She'd wandered the rooms for a few minutes, examining the framed photos that showed him grinning, with his arms around a woman with large eyes and an even larger smile. She didn't know who the woman was, but she did know it was not someone in his life now. There appeared to be nobody in his life right now. And he was keeping it that way.

Gregory Hills had made a habit lately of draining the life from women. There was nobody home waiting for him.

Mila hated men who thought they had the right to take, just because they were men. She especially hated it when the men were vampires, and not only took women… but killed them. Since the explosion of the Ninety-Nine Bombs, the vampires had come out of the woodwork. At first, once she had discovered what her sister Danika had become—a *wurdulac*, which fed only on those it loved—she had simply hunted down everyone that Danika had touched. Mila felt a family responsibility to stop what Danika had started. But now… Danika's trail was cold and buried. It was no longer about her sister. She hunted down vampires because she felt she had to. If they continued to spread…

The key rattled in the lock of the front door, and Mila stiffened. She drew her hand back on the bow and held it ready. If this went well, he'd be down in one shot, and she'd be out the door a minute from now, one more problem solved.

The hinges creaked, just a bit, and Mila held her breath. Then the door opened, and she tensed, ready to let go of her steel-tipped arrow as soon as she saw his chest… but instead…

The chest that the door revealed… had breasts.

Large ones.

Their flesh overflowed the lace of a fancy white bra and rolled around the V of a pink blouse. There was a man's hand just below them. Hairy fingers. Holding the woman's midriff firm.

A second later, the door kicked closed, and Gregory Hills pushed his latest conquest through the living room. The woman struggled, and Mila held her aim, waiting for a clean shot. The woman was not making it easy. She flung her head back and forth, long auburn curls whipping across Gregory's face, while she tried to lock her legs in place to prevent him from taking her any farther inside.

The air snapped as he backhanded the woman.

"Stop it," he demanded.

"Please, just let me go," she begged.

Mila had no shot. The girl had strained so hard against Gregory's grip that she now faced the end of the room where Mila crouched behind a reclining chair, waiting to loose the vampire's death. Gregory dragged the woman across the room. Her body shielded his, preventing Mila from having a shot. The woman twisted, and pounded him with her fists. An ineffective attack, since the vampire had tied her wrists.

Then they were through the room and gone.

"Shit," Mila whispered under her breath. "What do I do now?"

The sounds of struggle ended with the slamming of a door in the kitchen. Mila eased out of her crouch and tiptoed to the kitchen. There was a white door on the far end.

She hadn't scoped that out when she had let herself into the house. Where did that door lead? Would he see her instantly if she opened it, or was it shielded from whatever was beyond?

Mila touched the doorknob and hesitated. What if she couldn't get her hand back on the bow in time to shoot, if he was right there when she opened it?

She could sit here and wait for him to come out. Then the shot would be clear, just as she'd planned it in the front room.

Door opens, bow pulls back, arrow punctures heart.

One. Two. Three.

The woman beyond the door screamed. No waiting this time. Mila took a breath, twisted the knob, and pushed.

The woman was hanging from a rafter beam, a chain around her wrists. They were in the garage that Gregory never pulled his car into. Now Mila saw—and smelled—why. The stench of the room hit her full force, and she felt her stomach clench. There were other women here.

Dead ones.

Their faces ranged from strangled purple to sickly green, but all of them were chained and hung from the center rafter beam that typically only held an automatic garage door opener. At the moment that Mila took all this in, Gregory was in the process of sinking his teeth into the tender flesh of the chained woman's neck. Some sixth sense alerted him, and he turned to see Mila.

She didn't hesitate.

"Who—?" he said.

The arrow punctured his shirt and sank below his third rib, just missing the sternum. He never got his next word out. The garage echoed the wet *splunk* of the arrow's passage. Gregory's eyes widened. His hands went to his chest, finding the unexpected, long wooden shaft there. His mouth opened to shriek, but only a wheeze emerged.

"This has to end," Mila announced, and stepped down onto the garage floor. She waited, but it only took a few seconds. Gregory's legs gave out and he collapsed to the concrete. He twitched and gasped, but never got out a word.

Vampires were easy to kill.

Mila slung the bow over her shoulder and walked to the woman on the chain. She unhooked the simple metal clasp he'd used to hold the chain fast, and released the woman's wrists.

"Thank you," the woman said, tears streaming down her cheeks. Blood pooled in the hollow of her clavicle from the wound the vampire's teeth had made.

"What's your name?" Mila asked.

"Genevieve," she said. Her voice caught as she said it. "I can't believe I was so stupid."

"You don't usually expect a guy to take you home for dinner… and then find out you're the main course," Mila said.

Genevieve shook her head angrily and picked up the blouse that Gregory had discarded on the floor. She slipped one arm into a sleeve, but Mila grabbed her arm.

"Wait," she said.

Genevieve looked at her strangely, but stopped dressing.

"You're bleeding," Mila explained, touching a finger to the woman's neck and holding it up, showing the slick red of blood. "Let's find a bathroom and clean you up before you ruin that."

Genevieve's eyes widened, then she nodded.

Mila took her hand and led her back through the kitchen to a small bathroom in the hall. The blood had already stopped running, but she wiped the wound down with damp toilet paper, then rummaged around in Gregory's vanity drawers for bandages. She found a box and quickly pulled one out, stripped it from its paper wrapping and pulled it tight over the slow-oozing wound.

"That should be good for now," she said.

"Thanks," Genevieve said, and pulled the blouse on at last, covering her lacy bra. "Let's get out of here," she said, and began walking quickly toward the front door.

"Hang on a sec," Mila said, and ducked back into the kitchen. Genevieve waited, and a moment later, Mila returned, wiping the head of a long arrow on a cloth. She slipped both back into a small satchel that hung across her back.

"Leave no soldier behind," Mila said with a grim smile.

Genevieve nodded. "I get it," she said. "I really do."

Mila led her out the front door and down the street to her car. She looked back and forth, up and down the sidewalks and windows of the other homes on the residential street, but saw nobody watching.

"Nobody will ever know we were here," she said, mostly to herself.

Genevieve nodded. "I'd like to forget I was here," she said. She stepped around the car and slipped into the passenger's seat as Mila closed the driver's door.

"Thank you," she said after Mila started the engine.

"No problem," Mila said. "Glad I could help."

"What's your name?" Genevieve said.

"Mila."

"Do you typically go about killing vampires in suburban garages?" Genevieve asked.

Mila nodded. "Something like that."

Genevieve smiled. "I like you."

Mila drove to the address Genevieve provided: a nondescript old brick ranch, just outside downtown. When she pulled up and left the engine running as she waited for her passenger to get out, Genevieve laughed.

"Are you kidding? C'mon. The least I can do is buy you a drink. Come in."

Mila hesitated, then agreed.

The place was old. Hardwood floors and walls painted twenty-five coats of white. Genevieve led her past a foyer into a living room with a couch and a worn oak wet bar. It all looked well used but comfortable. Mila perched on the end of the couch as Genevieve stepped behind the bar.

"What would you like?" Genevieve asked. "Wine? Vodka? Beer?"

"Do you have any whiskey?" she asked. "I would kill for a seven and seven."

"I think you have already fulfilled your half of that bargain," Genevieve said with a grin. She picked up a bottle of whiskey. "Anything for my savior—as long as you don't mind Sprite in place of 7-Up."

"That works," Mila said, settling back finally on the couch. She let out a deep breath and felt the tension of the past couple hours finally fade. "As long as I can taste the whiskey, it's all good. I can really use it after that."

Genevieve poured a healthy shot of Seagram's over ice. She topped it off—just barely—with a can of Sprite retrieved from the small fridge behind the bar.

"You're not alone," Genevieve said as she poured herself a vodka, neat. "I can't believe I was so stupid."

"What do you mean?"

Genevieve brought the drinks to the couch and handed the glass of bubbling liquid gold to Mila before sitting.

"I let him turn the tables on me," Genevieve said. "I knew he was a vampire. And I knew he was a killer, one of the bad ones. That's why I agreed to meet him."

"You tried to hook up with a murderer?" Mila said. Incredulity colored her voice. She took a sip and sighed as the warmth spread down her throat. Genevieve poured well.

"Well, I wouldn't say 'hook up,'" Genevieve said, closing her eyes as she took a long sip of her vodka. After a moment, she finished her thought. "More like… hunted."

Mila raised an eyebrow. "Sounds a bit unwise."

Genevieve smiled. "What were you doing at his house with a bow? Playing Cupid?"

Mila grinned. "Touché."

"You're not the only vampire hunter," Genevieve said. "Although you're the first one I've met outside of our little band."

"Band?"

Genevieve nodded. "There are three of us who live here. We all hunt vampires. Safety in numbers." Her face suddenly took on a look of panic, and she grabbed Mila's arm. "You can't tell Bryce or Jason what happened today, when you meet them."

"Why not?"

"They'll never let me live it down if they know I had to be rescued," she said. "Especially by a woman!"

Mila bristled. "They have a problem with women?"

Genevieve smiled. "No… but you know guys. They have a little of that macho thing. And they're always telling me I should stay behind while they do the *dangerous* work."

"Nice," Mila said. "And you are still friends?"

Genevieve smiled. "I know how it sounds, but they're good guys. They look out for me."

"Are you dating one of them?"

"No, no, not like that. We're just friends. We have been since college. I'm like their little sister."

Mila emptied her glass and reached out to set it on the coffee table, but Genevieve intercepted it, and began to rise.

"Refill?" she said.

Mila shook her head. "No, I should probably go."

"Don't, please!" Genevieve said. Alarm colored her voice. "I want to hear about you. All I know is that you're good with a bow and you drink seven and sevens. I want to know more about the girl who rescued me, before the guys get home."

Genevieve made her eyes grow wide and craned her head forward, then asked in an overly dramatic voice, "How did you… become… a vampire slayer?"

Mila laughed and then shrugged. "There's not a lot to tell. My sister turned into a vampire a few months ago." She hesitated, not sure how much of Danika's story to tell. Genevieve walked their glasses to the bar and busied herself refilling them.

"Oh geez," Genevieve said, as ice clinked into a glass. "What did you do?"

"I killed her," Mila said. Her voice was as cold as the drink Genevieve handed her. "She was doing horrible things."

Genevieve's eyes widened, then she nodded. "I can imagine what that must have been like. I mean, to have to kill your own sister… "

"She wasn't my sister anymore," Mila said. "I had to stop her from hurting more people."

Genevieve nodded. "Why did you keep going? I mean… I'm guessing that you killed more vampires after her, since you were there today."

Mila smiled, sadly. "I did. The gene that changed my sister… " She stopped and took a sip of her drink before continuing. "Basically, she turned into one of the Russian vampires of our ancestors. A *Wurdulac*. And the thing with *Wurdulacs* is, they can only feed on their family, or people they love. So basically, Danika started a little commune where she kept people that she was fond of. A blood farm. And some of them… well… they were also of Russian descent and had the same gene. Her bite was able to trigger some of them, and voila… there were more *Wurdulacs* running around."

"And you hunted them down."

"Exactly."

"How many have you killed?"

"Eighteen," Mila said, without pause.

Genevieve shook her head. Whether in anger or disgust was unclear. "It's just wrong," she said. "But if we don't do this… "

"The vampires will inherit the Earth," Mila asked.

"Something like that," Genevieve said. "You've heard that Luther Swann guy on the news going on about how we can all live together, same as the Mexicans and white kids in Texas and California do. Two similar breeds co-existing in peace. But it's not that easy. It's just not." When Mila nodded, Genevieve continued. "Sometimes it's dog-eat-dog out there, and we keep forgetting that."

"What got you started?" Mila asked, switching the subject back to Genevieve. "You can rationalize about this all you want, but in the end, it's killing. They may be vampires, but the courts still say they're people. You could go to jail for life if they catch you."

Genevieve took a sip of her vodka, and then looked Mila hard in the eye.

"A vampire killed my brother while he was walking home from 7-Eleven one night about six moths ago. The police never found the asshole who did it, but I saw the marks. They couldn't cover them up when they put him in the casket. I knelt there in the church at his body, and I knew right then that I had to stop this from happening to anyone else. They're *not* humans," Genevieve said. "They're monsters. And they all should die, not just the one who killed Ricky."

Mila felt a cold flicker at the base of her spine. But she nodded agreement with her new friend. "Sometimes, you just have to go all the way."

Genevieve smiled. "Exactly." She reached out an arm, and slipped it around Mila's shoulder. "Speaking of which… "

The warmth of Genevieve's arm synced up in Mila's spine with the warmth of the liquor, and she leaned her head back, enjoying the sensation.

"I'm really glad you came in," Genevieve said. Her voice was a whisper.

The whiskey was going to Mila's head, and the room suffused with a golden glow. She saw an aura around the ceiling light as she answered. "Yeah, me too. I haven't had anyone to talk to in a long time."

Things got even more warm and golden then, when Genevieve pulled closer and snuggled her face against Mila's shoulder. The action sent a jolt through Mila's spine. It was weird and unexpected… but Mila didn't push her away. Somehow, being close to Genevieve seemed like the most right thing in the world. She wrapped her arm around the other woman's back and hugged her closer.

"I can't believe I found you," Genevieve whispered. Her breath was warm against Mila's neck, and a lock of auburn hair tickled Mila's nose.

"Actually, I found you," Mila corrected, stroking Genevieve's hair as she moved it from her face.

Genevieve looked up then; her eyes blazed hazel emotion as they stared into Mila's. "Yeah, you did," she said, and then suddenly pressed her lips to Mila's. The sensation was warm and wet and wildly unexpected. Mila flinched, but didn't jump away. She didn't understand *why* she didn't, actually, but instead she opened her mouth to Genevieve's ardor and sighed beneath the press of her new friend's lips. Her chest filled with a strange heat. She felt paralyzed, wanting to stop Genevieve, but then again, *not*. The world had just tilted crazily sideways…

"I don't… " she tried to say, beneath the press of the kiss.

Genevieve's catlike eyes stared deep into her own, and the other woman raised her head, just a few inches, and asked, "You don't what?"

"I don't… know what to do," Mila whispered. She was both excited and afraid of Genevieve's advances. She'd never been interested in women, yet, somehow, the kiss of this one was like crack. Instantly addictive. Hot, liquid, dangerous… crack.

"Don't do anything," Genevieve whispered. "Just lay back and let me thank you."

Mila closed her eyes and let the sensations all wash over her, a mingle of beauty and buzz. She had not felt safe and trusting of anyone since the day she had awoken after her sister's bite. The bite that had awakened the gene that made her into the same creature that she hunted. Mila was a monster, just like Gregory Hills. But Genevieve never needed to know that. Her breath caught in her throat as she felt the other woman's hands slip under her shirt and trace the lines of her ribs.

Mila closed her eyes, as if the act of *not* seeing somehow meant she was not complicit in the act of love itself.

She surrendered.

———◆———

Mila awoke in the dark, beneath strange sheets. The air held the faint scent of lavender. This was not her room. And then it all came back to her when a warm shape beside her suddenly shifted and rose.

"Shhhh," a woman's voice whispered. "You're safe. You're here with me."

A stab of… something… cut through her chest and into the depths of her gut. Fear? Guilt? Weirded-out-ness? All of the above. Mila's eyes widened, struggling to see in the dark. She wasn't sure if she should jump out of bed and grab for her clothes, or…

Two lips fastened on her own, and the warm scent of Genevieve's breath was in her nose, calming her with its sweet heat. She let out a held breath of her own and answered the kiss. In moments, she was stifling moans as Genevieve's lips moved down her neck and sipped at every sensitive spot from her chin to her toes. Her orgasm in the dark was unlike any she'd ever felt, and after she had reciprocated and brought Genevieve to loud, staccato bleats of pleasure, they both settled back to the pillows and gasped for air. Finally, Genevieve rolled over and grinned. The faint light of dawn was now beginning to seep through the windows, so Mila could see her smile. "I guess the boys know now that I brought someone home," she said.

Mila's eyes widened. "Is that going to be a problem?"

"Nah, they'll probably be happy about it. But they will tease me."

"Maybe I should go now," Mila said.

Genevieve's hands gripped her shoulders. "No. I have just found you… I'm not letting you slip off into the night."

"Actually, it's morning," Mila said.

Genevieve pounced on her and pressed her head back to the pillow with a fierce kiss.

Breakfast was… awkward. Genevieve loaned her a fuzzy green robe to wear, and then put on a silky one herself, before leading Mila down the short hallway to the kitchen. The two men were already up, lounging on the couch in sweats and t-shirts. One was reading the newspaper while the other was sipping coffee, but he set the paper down when they entered the room.

"Well, well," he said. "I thought we had a couple cats in heat trapped in the back bedroom, but now I see it was you."

"Ignore him," Genevieve advised. "It's not like he's never woken me up with noises that sound like we've got a stuck pig trapped in here. This is Jason, by the way."

He moved the paper aside and stood up to extend his hand. Jason was tall and thin, with a faint fuzz of beard on his chin and a mop of unruly black curls on his head. His smile telegraphed mischief. Mila instantly found herself liking him. She took his proffered hand while holding her robe firmly closed with her other. "I'm Mila," she said. His grip was firm, and she could see his eyes sizing her up behind his smile. He was protective of Genevieve, she could tell without a word.

"And this is Bryce," Genevieve said, motioning to the red-headed man on the other side of the couch. Bryce didn't jump up, but nodded with a polite smile and said, "Good morning."

"Yes it was," Genevieve said, and Mila felt her face blush.

"Where did you girls meet?" Bryce asked, stopping any unsavory comebacks from Jason.

Mila looked at Genevieve; they hadn't discussed what to say, but Genevieve had been clear that she didn't want the truth out there.

"On a hunt," Genevieve answered, flashing a white smile. She slipped an arm around Mila's shoulders and pulled her close.

Mila saw both men frown in unison.

"Turns out we were both hunting the same vampire," Genevieve said. "Before I got a chance to take him out, she put an arrow in his chest."

"An arrow?" Jason said. His voice sounded incredulous.

"Quieter and more difficult to trace than guns and bullets," Mila said. Her voice was quiet, and the room stayed silent for a moment after her answer.

Bryce broke the pause. "Interesting choice," he said.

"You're not supposed to hunt without backup," Jason said. His voice did not sound happy.

"I know," Genevieve said, hanging her head slightly and exaggerating a pout. "But it all worked out, because I ended up with backup anyway."

"Hmmm. From the sounds of it, she really did get your back up," Jason said. Mila felt her face blush again, but Genevieve didn't let her show it. Instead, she grabbed her hand and pulled her towards the kitchen. "C'mon," she said. "I'm starving. Do you want some coffee?"

"A pot!" Mila said.

"You know, maybe this worked out just right," Jason said, when the girls returned to the family room and sat down with steaming mugs. "You're a vampire hunter," he said, looking directly at Mila, "and we've been getting ready for a big hit tonight. A warren."

Bryce's eyes lit. "I don't think that's a good idea."

"No, it's perfect!" Genevieve said. "She's really good, and we could use help with this one. What do you think, Mila?"

Bryce put up a hand. "We know nothing about her, we've never worked with her before and this is potentially the most dangerous hunt we've ever talked about doing. There are at least a dozen of them working out of that house. This is not the time to change the team."

"You've been nervous about us getting overpowered before we could take enough of them out. This way we could separate into two teams. You and me, Genevieve and Mila. If she is really a vampire killer, we could use her. We'd all be safer."

"How do you know they're vampires?" Mila asked. "I mean all of them. I usually hunt one at a time… and I'm double sure before I ever stake one out. If you're going in at night, you don't know who you're taking out."

"We're not murderers," Bryce said. His voice was taut. "I'm sure you've followed all the stories from Yuki Nitobe. The vampires are no longer simply turning and trying to live their lives without being discovered.

They're organizing. That makes them more dangerous, but also easier to track. Genevieve discovered this group a few weeks ago."

"It helps to work in a telecommunications data center," she interjected.

"Once we identify, we watch them for a while," Jason said. "We've been following this group closely, both in person and through the net. Every one of them in that house has killed in the past two weeks."

"They're really good at covering their tracks," Genevieve said, "and they're not just quietly hunting. They are planning something. They keep one of the most secure home networks I've ever seen, but I have been able to track encrypted emails to France and Germany."

"And they've been stockpiling weapons," Jason said. "I've been able to trace more than twenty purchases of guns and ammunition over the past couple weeks alone—all single purchases, so nothing is suspicious on its own... but they're stockpiling."

"So why not just report them?" Mila asked. "If you can prove they are setting up like that, it should be a no-brainer for the police or the FBI to come in and clean them out."

Bryce shook his head. "This is our neighborhood. We keep it clean. I won't risk the cops screwing it up and letting the whole nest get away."

"Plus there's a lot of messaging going between that house and Washington, D.C.," Genevieve said. "They're tapped into something bigger. If we report them... *we* may disappear, instead of them."

"You really think it's that bad?" Mila said.

Bryce gave her a long look. "It's every man for himself right now," he said. "You can't trust anyone. And you have to be ready to kill if you find a vampire. Whether it's your sister, mother, best friend... we have to stop this now, or in another year, it will all be over. The human race will be headed the way of the dinosaur."

"Why don't *you* call the police, instead of taking vampires out yourself?" Jason asked. There was a thin smile behind his question.

"It's personal," Mila said.

Jason smiled. "Exactly."

"BREAKING NEWS" PT. 7

Jonathan Maberry

New York Harbor

Ballard and Billings sat in the cabin of a fishing boat, blankets draped over their shoulders, cups of hot coffee in their trembling hands. A mile behind them the crippled boat from which they'd been rescued burned like a torch above the rippling black waters. Ten gallons of gasoline make a great fire.

They knew that it would burn to the waterline and sink without anyone coming from shore to either investigate or fight the blaze. Everyone who mattered was looking inland. From out here on the water, it looked like all of Manhattan was burning.

A distortion of what was happening, but not that extreme. There were so many fires.

Ballard and Billings stared through the windows at the city.

"'Set a few fires,'" said Billings softly. "'Blow a few things up. Make sure they notice.'"

He was quoting the original orders from Rancid.

Ballard shook his head. "Well, I think they'll notice that."

"Jesus fuck."

"I know."

"After the Ninety-Nine Bombs, I thought they were never going to use him again," muttered Billings. "Didn't we tell them? I mean, we were really clear on it, weren't we?"

"Clear as glass."

"This isn't what we asked for."

"No shit."

Billings turned to his companion. "You know this is going to fall apart, right?"

Ballard took a breath. "I… don't know. Maybe not."

"What?"

"Well, I can almost see where Rancid was going with this."

"Really?" Billings stared at him. "Now this shit I *have* to hear, because from where I'm sitting it looks like we did a lot more than screw the pooch. We knocked it up and named the pups after us."

"Like I said, maybe not. Look, you were never in the military, never in combat. I was and—"

"You were military legal counsel."

"I was in the 'Stan. I worked with them. With guys like General May. I know how they think. There's a philosophy that covers this."

Billings arched an eyebrow. "Oh, please enlighten me, o' Sun Tzu."

"There's a way of thinking that, if you can't win a stand-up fight, you either go big or go home. No, let me put it another way. Say someone breaks into your house and they're going to kill you. You can't stop them because there's too many of them and they're too good. What do you do?"

"Get killed."

"Or… maybe you set fire to the house."

"How the fuck does that save your ass?"

"Because, if the house is burning everyone panics. You create a threat they have to react to. Maybe you'll burn, but maybe you'll escape in the smoke because you know the house and how to get around, and maybe the intruders will trip over furniture and burn."

"That's a stupid fucking analogy."

Ballard shrugged. "Maybe it's not."

"LOVE LOST" PT. 2

John Everson

Where are you going?" Bryce asked a half hour later. Mila had put on her clothes from yesterday and picked up her bow. "I need to go home, shower, and change," she said. "What time do you want to get ready tonight?"

He shook his head. "I'm sorry. Genevieve may be sweet on you, but I don't know anything about you. You're not walking out of here after finding out our plans for tonight. You can borrow some of Genevieve's clothes."

"That's ridiculous," Mila began, but Genevieve interrupted.

"I'll take her home," she said. "That way I can see her place!"

"I don't think that's a good idea," Bryce said.

"You can't hold her prisoner," Jason laughed. "Let them go."

Bryce shot his friend a dour look, but then shrugged.

"I'll get my keys," Genevieve said, and dashed out of the room.

Bryce caught Mila's eye. "If you hurt her… " he said. His voice was low. Threatening.

Mila opened her mouth. She wanted to retort, "Hurt her? I saved her life!" but she closed her mouth without saying a word. Instead, she only nodded. And then Genevieve was back, a bounce in her step and a smile on her face. She'd pulled her hair back in a ponytail and slipped on flip-flops. She couldn't have looked any more "girl next door" with her grey sweats and baggy white and pink t-shirt. "Love Pink" it said, and Mila flashed on their moments in bed together this morning. The phrase suddenly took on a whole new meaning for her. Her stomach felt as if someone had just pumped helium into it. Light… and uncomfortable.

The past twenty-four hours had been the strangest day of her life. Even stranger than the day Danika had come to her apartment for soup and instead taken a bite out of her neck before leaving her unconscious on the floor. Presumed dead.

Mila unlocked the door to her apartment, and Genevieve slipped past her and pirouetted in the front room. "I like it!" she pronounced. "It's cute!"

Mila laughed. "It's tiny. But it's quiet. I think everyone upstairs and below is retired. Do you want something to drink?"

Genevieve shook her head.

"All right then. Here's the remote." She picked up the TV channel changer and turned the power on before handing it over. "I'll try to be quick in the shower."

Genevieve smiled and leaned back on the couch. Mila left her and stepped into the bedroom. She quickly stripped off yesterday's clothes and threw them in the hamper. It felt very strange to be getting ready to shower with another woman sitting on the couch just on the other side of the wall. *A woman she had recently kissed,* she reminded herself, as she put toothpaste on her brush.

Not just kissed, a voice in her head said, as she brushed her teeth and stared at her naked image in the mirror. *A woman she had made love to.* What the hell…

Once she stood under the hot spray of the water and began to soap herself up, she shook her head. This morning, and last night, another woman had run her hands up and down her thighs like this. Mila groaned. What had she gotten herself into?

A cold breeze suddenly cut the steam of the shower, and suddenly two hands were holding her midriff. Mila jumped, and the hands slipped around her belly to hold her tight. She felt the bristle of Genevieve's pubes against her backside, and the other woman laughed softly at her obvious discomfiture.

"I hope you don't mind, but I haven't had a shower today either," Genevieve said. She whispered conspiratorially. "Plus, I really wanted to be naked with you again." She moved a hand up to stroke Mila's left breast from behind.

Mila turned around, and Genevieve grinned as she ran her fingers lightly up and down Mila's chest, tracing the small rivulets of the shower down to her belly button and below. Mila shivered at the touch.

"Bryce wants me to keep an eye on you for one reason, but I want to do it for another," she said.

She raised her mouth and Mila met it with her lips. The heat that followed jolted from her tongue to her groin and then radiated out to every pore. She felt flush and faint and instantly horny as hell.

As Genevieve's tongue grew more daring, Mila also felt something else. She felt hungry.

Ravenous.

Oh shit, she moaned internally. Genevieve had knelt before her in the shower and Mila held the other woman's head as water streamed over and around her to drench Genevieve and her kisses. Genevieve couldn't tell the difference between the hot water and the hot tears that flowed over her.

What am I going to do? Mila asked herself. For a few hours, she'd been able to forget the fact that she herself was a vampire. A vampire who could only feed on those that it loved. A hideous Russian joke of Darwinism. No wonder the gene had gone dormant so quickly all those centuries ago, though not before legends sprang up about the *Wurdulacs* and their bloody slaughter of entire families in a night. The typical end to a *Wurdulac* had not been starvation, as you might expect, once an end came to the string of loved ones, but rather, suicide. Because how could anyone live with killing everyone they loved?

"What's the matter?" Genevieve asked, somehow feeling the emotional change going on above. She stood up and slipped her arms around Mila, pulling her close in an intimate embrace. The action made Mila gasp at the resulting heat in the back of her throat. She was suddenly so hungry she thought she might faint. She'd learned how to fight it off. She'd managed to keep a boyfriend without sucking him dry. But it had never been this strong. So hideously, provocatively strong.

"Nothing," Mila finally answered. "This is all just so weird for me. I'm sorry."

Genevieve pushed a lock of wet hair away from Mila's face and her eyes widened. "Are you saying you've never been with a woman before?"

Mila shook her head.

Genevieve grinned. "I've got your cherry!" Her hand slipped between Mila's legs. "And I'm never giving it back."

Mila snorted. For a little while, the hunger subsided as pleasure overtook all.

"Here we go," Jason whispered. They sat with the lights off in a car just a block away from their destination. It was 12:30 a.m., and the sky was dark with clouds. No moonlight would guide their way.

"Genevieve will use the code to turn off the alarm at the back door. If no lights go on, she'll text me and then enter, letting us in the front door. We'll split up then—Bryce and I will take the front room and the upstairs. You handle the kitchen and lower level. If anything goes wrong, get out fast and meet back here."

They met each other's eyes in one silent, serious moment. Then the car doors opened and they were walking through the suburban night, footsteps the only sound besides crickets. Genevieve led Mila away from the men. They cut through two backyards and then they were in place. The vampires' house looked the same as all the others in the neighborhood. A nondescript frame, two levels, with a concrete patio just outside the kitchen door. They crept up to it quickly, and Genevieve retrieved the access code from her phone. She typed it in to the small plastic box next to the door and hit the "enter" button.

Her eyes met Mila's then, large and expectant. If the code was wrong, they had likely triggered an alarm. If not... in thirty seconds they would use a skeleton key to open the door.

Mila looked around the dark shadows of the yard and imagined someone hiding behind every pool of darkness. All of them poised.

Next to her, Genevieve typed two letters on her phone: "GO."

Then she nodded at Mila and stabbed a bit of metal into the doorknob. She twisted it slowly, and Mila held her breath until Genevieve flashed a smile of triumph and the door cracked open. They were in.

Mila pulled her bow to position, and Genevieve pointed the way. Mila stepped as softly as she could and crossed the room, while Genevieve crept to the opposite side.

Genevieve peered around the doorjamb, jerked back, and put up her index finger to Mila. "One."

There was one vampire in the next room, and, from the blue shadows playing across the walls and low sounds of chatter and music, Mila assumed whoever it was was watching TV. Genevieve motioned for her to enter on one side while she took the other.

Mila slipped around the doorjamb and hugged the wall as she tiptoed towards the front room. She was in a small dining room, with a formal dark wood table and chairs in the center and a bureau on the end. The room was tight.

At the far end, she finally saw the television in the next room. And the couch where a man—no, a vampire—sat, head back on the cushions.

Mila raised her bow and nocked an arrow. But before she could loose a shot, there was a faint *pffft* in the air, and the vampire's head jolted to one side.

In the cascade of television light, Mila saw that the cushions around his head were now splattered with dark blood.

She rounded the corner and met Genevieve, still holding the silenced pistol before her. Genevieve winked and nodded toward the front hall. Then she darted to the front door. She turned the deadbolt, and then the doorknob, slowly easing it open to allow the men to slip inside. When Jason and Bryce were in, Genevieve nodded towards the front room, where the TV still played softly, and held up her index finger.

The men nodded and looked up the stairs. Genevieve gave the thumbs up, and then tapped Mila's shoulder. She led them down a short hall to a stairway. The home had a lower level, which the vampires had presumably turned into bedrooms, given the number reported to be in residence.

The stairs were carpeted, but that didn't stop them from creaking as they crept down, stepping as softly as they could. Genevieve led, and they stopped on every step, waiting to see if the noise brought anyone to investigate. The downstairs remained dark and quiet ahead.

The stairs T-ed into a hall; you could walk either left or right. Genevieve pulled out her cellphone and clicked it on, cupping her hand over it to moderate the light. They needed to see where they were going, but they didn't need to tip off those that they were coming to see. She led them left, and after five steps they found a door. There were five doors in a row, actually, and Genevieve nodded with a smile. Mila understood. This was the sleeping quarters. This was the moment of truth.

Kill or be killed.

Mila squeezed Genevieve's shoulder… and then left her and walked to the next door. Mila pulled out her own cellphone and flicked it on; a convenient low-light flash. Then she met Genevieve's eyes down the hall and nodded. Together, they pushed open their separate doors.

The room Mila found herself in was small; barely enough room for a double bed and a dresser. A man lay on the bed, wound up in a cascade of sheets and blanket. Only his head was visible, tucked into the crook of a pillow.

He looked absolutely harmless.

Mila raised her bow anyway.

She held the phone in the same hand as the bow. Using its faint glow as a guide, she aimed and loosed an arrow into the back of the man's neck.

He only jerked a couple times before he was still. She wasn't sure he ever even really woke.

She waited a moment, then yanked the arrow out.

Genevieve was waiting in the hall with a smile.

They nodded at each other and continued to the next two doors. This time, when Mila slipped inside, she found herself with a double challenge.

A man and a woman were in bed. And one of them shifted under the covers as soon as she stepped inside. Mila had learned how to hunt with her father, in the fields. Animals didn't lie there waiting to be shot, they moved. She had learned long ago how to shoot fast. And accurately. She let the first arrow go within ten seconds of entering the room.

As it buried itself in the neck of her first target, the second one sat up in bed. The woman.

"Paul, what was… " the woman began. Then she saw the outline of Mila in the doorway and the shuddering form of her partner bleeding out next to her. A wheezing sound came from her, a growing whistle that promised to turn into a bloody scream.

The second arrow passed through the woman's open mouth before she managed her fourth word, and lodged in the back of her throat.

The third arrow punched through the back of the man's skull and before the body was still, Mila had loosed the fourth arrow. It jammed into the woman's eye socket. The force of the impact drove her backwards and she joined her husband on the bed. Mila loosed two more arrows just to make sure, and then after waiting a minute in silence, moved forward to retrieve them.

The arrows came easily out of the vampires' necks, but the first one she tried to pull from the man's skull was lodged tight. It must have passed all the way through one side of the skull to be stuck in so hard. Mila shook her head and put one foot against his face as she yanked hard on the arrow near its fletching. She twisted until it finally gave.

She was having the same difficulty with the arrow that stuck out of the woman's now gruesome gash of an eye socket when Genevieve stepped in.

"What are you *doing* in here?" she whispered, before she saw Mila's foot on the head of the dead woman. "Oh, good god," she added.

"Sometimes they don't just slip right out," Mila said, grimacing as she pulled one last time. The arrow popped out, with a chunk of gore and the remnant of an iris dripping from its metal tip. She pulled out her kill rag and wiped it clean as Genevieve shook her head.

"That is disgusting. We really need to get you a gun."

Mila cleaned her other arrows and shrugged. "I used to use a gun," she said. "I like my bow better. But I don't usually have to take out an entire house in one go," she whispered.

They stepped out of the room and back to the hall. "Just one room left down here," Genevieve said, pointing at the sole remaining closed doorway.

Something thumped upstairs.

"Should we go help?" Mila whispered.

Genevieve shook her head. "We clear our floor first, or we'll have them behind and ahead of us if the guys have run into trouble. Let's do this fast."

Mila nodded and readied her bow. Genevieve turned the knob on the door, and they stepped inside. The light from the open door cut across two beds. Genevieve took the first one, extending her hand and aiming at the center of the tousle of hair that cascaded across the pillow and sheet. The pop was soft, but enough. Before Mila could loose her arrow at the shadowed form in the next bed, it was no longer there.

A hideous shriek erupted, like the wail of a banshee. Something hard bashed into the back of Mila's knees, knocking her off balance. A small figure hopped across the space between the beds, arms outstretched. For a moment, Mila's heart shrank; it was a child, and they had just slaughtered its mother right before its eyes. The poor kid's arms appeared outstretched to embrace the dead woman in the other bed. But that wasn't its intent.

Genevieve yelped, and her second shot caught the ceiling as she fell. Chunks of drywall caught Mila in the face.

"Jesus, shoot it, Mila!" Genevieve called from the carpet. The shriek took on the aspects of a siren, rising and falling.

Mila stepped around the bed and saw the kid on top of Genevieve, pummeling her with tiny hands. "It's just a kid," she complained.

"She is stabbing me!"

That's when Mila finally saw the glint of the knife in one of the outstretched hands. Genevieve let out a small scream, and Mila took a deep breath. She pulled back on the bow, but the kid leapt to her feet… there was blood on the girl's mouth. It streaked the ratted curls of her blond hair. She charged at Mila brandishing the knife, and Mila's self-preservation reflex abruptly trumped her aversion to shooting children. She let an arrow fly straight at the girl's chest. Before the girl was flat on the ground, a third gunshot whoofed and the threatening arms stilled.

Genevieve had gotten her gun back, though she still lay on the ground.

"What the hell," Genevieve said. "Why didn't you shoot it?"

"You didn't say there would be kids here," Mila complained.

"Not a kid," Genevieve said, struggling to sit up. "A vampire."

"It was a kid, and you just killed her mom," Mila said, offering Genevieve a hand up.

"I doubt if it was her mom," Genevieve said. "Look at them closer. White women don't usually have Asian kids."

Mila looked at the still creature on the floor. It lay on its back, but its arms remained outstretched, pointed at the ceiling. The features were heavily Asian, though its skin looked strange, more green than brown, almost like parchment.

"What is wrong with it?" she whispered, half to herself.

"*Jiangshi,*" Genevieve said, with a faint gasp of pain. "A hopping vampire. When they turn, they get crazy stiff and their skin begins to change, almost like armor. They can't move the best, but they make up for it in meanness."

"Oh jeez, you're bleeding bad," Mila said as Genevieve struggled to stand. Red soaked through her shirt in several places.

"I'm alright," Genevieve insisted, and then almost immediately stumbled, grabbing at Mila for balance.

Mila slipped her arm around Genevieve's shoulder. "C'mon," she said. "Let me help you."

"We need to help Bryce and Jason," Genevieve insisted. As if in answer, something thumped on the ceiling above.

"We need to get you out of this house. Before they find us."

Mila urged her forward, guiding them out the door and down the hall. She tried to keep her bow ready, in case they met interference, but the main floor still appeared deserted. Upstairs was a different story. Things were falling. Glass breaking. A male voice yelled in frustration.

"Go help them," Genevieve insisted. "I'll stay here."

"Not until you're in the car."

They exited the back door and retraced their steps, staggering down the block. As Mila eased her into the passenger seat, Genevieve wrapped her arms around Mila's neck and pulled her close. Mila smelled the blood on her and grew dizzy. Her canines ached; she could feel her jaw adjusting. And then Genevieve's lips were on hers. Mila felt her own mouth instinctively opening, readying for the leap, the twist. The bite.

The hunter slid up her spine like a snake. Her eyes opened, fastened on Genevieve's. The other woman held her, drawing strength. Drawing love.

Drawing Mila's teeth.

The ache grew in the back of her throat, the heat behind her teeth. She broke the kiss.

"I better hurry," she mumbled, her words slurred. She pushed herself out of the car and closed the door. "I'll be back," she mouthed through the window, and then forced herself to walk away, before the hunger consumed her.

She found the remnants of a battle at the top of the stairs. A lamp lay without its shade in the middle of the hall. A bookshelf was tipped to the floor in a bedroom. Bryce and Jason were holed up in the last bedroom. They crouched behind a bed, holding off three vampires with periodic bullets.

Welcome to the OK Corral, Mila thought as she appraised the situation, still unseen. Then she readied an arrow, took aim, and brought down a vampire from behind. The arrow entered just at the base of his skull, and he pitched forward instantly, without even a gasp. One of the other vampires turned, seeking the source of the arrow that rose from the back of his friend's neck. His eyes widened in surprise when he saw Mila. Before he could get out a word, an arrow entered his brain from the tunnel of his left nostril.

Bryce and Jason took the opportunity to leap out from their makeshift barricade. One of them put a bullet in the head of Mila's second kill to make sure he was dead, while the other focused on firing at the remaining vampire. In seconds they joined her in the hallway.

"Where's Genevieve?" Bryce asked. She could hear the dread in his voice. He assumed the worst.

"In the car," she said, and quickly explained what had happened. Bryce never blinked as she told the story, and when she was done, he brushed past her.

"That was the last of them," he said. "I'll get the computer from the office, and we can get out of here."

Jason put a hand on her shoulder and squeezed. "You did good," he said. "This was a rough one." His smile looked lopsided and exhausted. There was blood on his shirt; she couldn't tell if it was his or someone else's.

———•———

"Does this hurt?" Mila ran her fingers across the bandage on Genevieve's chest. She'd been stabbed seven times, but this was the worst cut. Jason knew a nurse who would ask no questions, and in the middle of the night, she'd sewn Genevieve up and gotten antibiotics, avoiding any difficult questions at the hospital.

They lay now in Genevieve's bed, the late morning light pouring in strong through the windows. Genevieve looked pale, but smiled. "A little. But it feels good too, having your hand rubbing me."

"Pleasure and pain?"

She nodded.

Mila laughed softly. "Story of my life." She ran her fingers across Genevieve's bare breasts, marveling at the softness and smiling when the nipples hardened beneath her palm. She had never touched another woman before Genevieve, and she was taken with the ways in which they were similar, and the ways they were different. Genevieve's skin seemed softer than her own, with almost no body hair.

"We are lucky we got out of there alive," she said.

"That was the biggest hit we've ever done," Genevieve said. "I don't think we would have gotten out of there alive if you hadn't been with us."

Mila shook her head. "You might not have gotten turned into a pincushion if it wasn't for me."

Genevieve grinned. "No, maybe I would have just been turned into a chew toy."

"I'm sorry," Mila said. "I just wasn't ready for... a kid."

"Just another vampire," Genevieve corrected.

"What if that had been your little sister who had turned?" Mila asked.

Genevieve's face grew tight. She took a breath. And then she said, "I'd kill her."

Genevieve looked hard at Mila. "I did kill her," she said. "My sister was just nine years old, when she went through the change. We didn't know what was wrong with her at first, and then she bit one of her friends who was over playing computer games. I went and found my dad's revolver and I took care of it." Genevieve looked at her beseechingly. "My parents wouldn't do it, but she wasn't human anymore. She wasn't my sister anymore. She was just a monster."

"I'm sorry," Mila said again. But her heart had a spear of ice through it. "My sister changed too, but she wasn't a kid anymore."

"What did you do?" Genevieve asked.

"I killed her," Mila said. She didn't elaborate.

Genevieve nodded. "We can't let them spread. If we do... "

There was silence for a minute, and then Mila asked the question that had frozen her heart.

"What would you do if I changed?"

"I'd kill you," Genevieve said. "I'd have to."

Mila nodded, and bent down to hug her so that Genevieve couldn't see her eyes. They were welling with tears. She had felt more happiness in the past few days than she had in the past year or more. But she knew that she could not stay here. She could not have this. In a way, she and Genevieve weren't so far apart; she had spent the past few weeks doing nothing but killing vampires. But that track record, that allegiance to humanity, would not erase the fact that she was, herself, a vampire. She could deny what she was to herself... but not to her lover. Not for long.

As she embraced Genevieve, she felt the ache in her jaw, the thirst. She wanted desperately with her heart to make love with Genevieve. At the same time, she wanted to drink her life.

Mila took a deep breath and rolled onto her back, swallowing the hunger. "What's next?" she asked, staring at the ceiling.

"What do you mean?" Genevieve said. "Like, what vampire nest is next?"

Mila nodded.

"Not sure," Genevieve said. "I think Bryce wants to try to use their computer to track down some of their connections. Bryce usually tracks them down, and then Jason and I handle the 'stakeout' stuff, figuring out when the best time is to go in. Usually it's just one or two at a time, not like last night at all. Sometimes we've even handled it solo, but we aren't supposed to do that. It's just too dangerous."

"So that's why you were going home alone with Gregory Hills."

Genevieve smiled ruefully. "I said 'aren't supposed to.' Doesn't mean... won't."

———— • ————

"She's in an apartment on Fifth Street," Bryce said.

Mila and Genevieve had just sat down in the family room with coffee. Genevieve was moving slow, but Mila helped her. Each brush of her arm across Genevieve's shoulders sent a charge of excitement to the core of her groin… and the base of her jaw. She didn't know how she was going to leave this girl with the beautiful laugh and hypnotic eyes. But she had to. Or one of them would die.

"Jason picked up on her," Bryce explained. "She should be an easy hit—we don't think she's connected with any others of her kind yet."

"Genevieve can't go out yet!" Mila protested.

"She'll be fine," Jason said. He shook his head. "You two can be our backups, but this should a quick in-and-out."

Genevieve nodded and said something… but Mila couldn't hear it. Her skin was flushed. Her ears burned. Her jaw throbbed. She was dying for food. It had been too long. And every beat of Genevieve's heart next to her was like a neon sign. "Suck me… suck me… " it advertised.

She had to eat. Soon.

"What time are we leaving?" she asked.

"Got a hot date?" Jason asked. "Oh wait… you've got a shot date."

"I was stabbed, not shot, asshole," Genevieve said.

Mila shook her head. "I just want to stop home for a couple hours. Catch up on some stuff. I haven't been home most of the week."

Two hands slipped up her arm. "And it's been mostly an amazing week."

"It has," Mila said.

———◆———

"So I guess you missed me," Trevor said, as Mila knelt at his feet. Her mouth instantly fastened to the soft flesh just above his wrist. No foreplay. No words.

"That's okay, you don't have to say anything. Just drink my blood… that tells me everything I needed to know."

She didn't acknowledge his words. Couldn't. All she saw was a haze of red warmth. Her spine burned; her groin tingled. The blood brought her to a silent orgasm as the hunger subsided. She felt a hand grab at her hair, and finally, she did look up. Trevor looked shell-shocked.

"Thanks," she said. "I didn't think I was going to be able to stop."

His face was white. "Me either," he said slowly. His words were slurred with the euphoria that all of her victims seemed to get when she drank their blood. Some kind of enzyme she excreted that made the food docile…

"Where have you been?" he asked. "I thought you'd lost your sweet tooth."

Mila stood. "For you? Never!" She kissed him on the forehead. "I've just been a little busy."

"Who is he?" Trevor asked. His eyes were fastened on her.

"Not a he," she said.

His eyes widened. "Playing the field *and* switching teams? Damn. Does she taste better than me?"

"I don't know," Mila said. "If I touch her, I'm dead. She has guys looking out for her."

"Sounds like a regular Shakespeare play."

Mila shook her head. "I need to stop it… I just don't really want to."

"I've been saying that about girls for years."

Mila went to the kitchen and brought him back a glass of orange juice. As he drank it, she covered his bite marks in bandages.

"I've missed you," he said.

"I can't stay," she said.

He nodded and said nothing.

———•———

"So you guys are… what… air-conditioning repairmen?" Mila looked Bryce and Jason up and down. They each wore gray jumpsuits, with the words COMFORT INC. on the breast.

"Whatever she needs us to be," Jason said. "We look legit, that's all that matters."

Genevieve was dressed normally, in jeans and a grey t-shirt. Totally low-key, "don't notice me" garb. "Let's get it done," she said, and opened the rear car door for Mila.

"What's the plan?" Mila asked once they had gotten on the road.

"Bryce and I will go to the front door. We'll tell her we're there to check the furnace, and I'm sure she won't let us in… but while she's at the door, you and Genevieve can go to the back and let yourselves in. Whoever takes her out first wins!"

The ride was short, but quiet. Genevieve apologized for being tired, and put her head back and closed her eyes. Bryce, not atypically, said nothing. Mila looked out the window, watching the blur of strip malls and subdivisions pass by, and wondered when she would tell Genevieve she was going back home for good.

Jason dropped them around the block, so that they weren't seen exiting the car together. Mila slung the bow over her shoulder and followed Genevieve down a side yard until they were in place. Genevieve texted Jason "Ready, Set… " and a moment later, she got the reply. "Go."

Genevieve showed Mila the text and then motioned for her to follow. The back door was tucked in a corner and opened on a small concrete patio. Genevieve and Mila ducked below the windows, and then Mila held the screen door open while Genevieve picked the lock. It only took a few seconds, and then Genevieve nodded, easing open the white wood door.

They stepped into a small foyer that opened into the kitchen. Genevieve pointed towards the hall and then cupped a hand around her ear.

Mila cocked her head to listen and could just barely hear Jason's voice. The guys already had the vampire at the door.

Genevieve motioned for her to follow. They crept through the kitchen and halfway down the hall. The woman's back was to them; she held the door with one hand. Young, thirty-ish, long black hair. Genevieve pulled her pistol from where she'd kept it tucked in the waistband of her jeans. She didn't hesitate. Five seconds later, there was a bloom of red in that black hair, and the woman teetered and fell as Bryce and Jason let themselves inside and quickly closed the front door.

"Well, that's one," Bryce said quietly.

"There are more?" Mila said, looking over her shoulder. "I thought she lived here alone?"

"She did," Bryce said.

Jason looked at Genevieve, but said nothing. Mila felt her stomach shrink. Nervously her fingers tightened on her bow. Something wasn't right.

Genevieve turned her eyes to Mila's. There was no hint of the love or lust of the past few days.

"Where did you go this afternoon," Genevieve asked. Her voice was cold as arctic steel.

"I went home… " Mila began.

Genevieve shook her head. "You lied to me." She pulled out a folded piece of paper from her front pocket and held it out. Mila took it, but didn't need to open it to know what she'd find. The paper unfolded to show a picture of her on her knees in Trevor's apartment, her mouth on his arm.

"You followed me?" Mila said. Her voice was incredulous… and hurt. Genevieve had not trusted her.

"I can't believe I kissed you," Genevieve said. "You're just another one of them."

"I'm the same person I was yesterday," Mila said. "I was good enough to love then."

Genevieve shook her head. "A lie. You lied to me."

"What's your game?" Jason asked softly. "Were you going to drink Genevieve dry tonight? Tomorrow?"

Mila shook her head. "I'm on your side," she said. "Don't you get it? I hunt vampires because I think they're a disease. An abomination. I never wanted to be this. But I also don't give in to it. Trevor lets me have some of his blood to keep me going. He's like family to me. I'm not like those vampires who go out killing. I don't want to see vampires inherit the earth. I don't want to be this."

Bryce nodded. "You've come to the right place then."

Genevieve leveled her gun at Mila. "I'm sorry," she said.

Behind her, Jason and Bryce both raised their own guns.

Mila dropped to the floor and rolled as a muffled shot hit the wall where she'd just stood. She came up in a crouch and ran three steps towards the kitchen. Something cold punched her thigh, and she saw the blood on the tile floor before she saw it on her leg.

She didn't stop.

Mila dove around the corner just as the pain finally hit her brain. She slipped behind the kitchen island just as Genevieve and Bryce crossed into the kitchen. Both of them were firing, trying to keep her from answering. A chunk of tile exploded near her, and the thin slivers that exploded from the floor bit her in the side.

"There are three of us and one of you," Bryce said from just a few feet away. "And you've got a bow and arrow. Just give up, and we'll make this quick for you."

Mila put her fingers on the nock, readied a shot, and took a breath. Then she popped up above the kitchen island and loosed the arrow at the first face she saw. Bryce. She heard the faint *pffffft* impact as she ducked again beneath the counter. A bullet cracked a cabinet behind her.

Bryce went down hard, with a loud cry and a louder thud.

"It doesn't have to be like this," Mila yelled. "I am on your side."

"Doesn't feel that way to me," Genevieve said from just around the corner.

Mila readied the bow and pushed it out around the corner of the wooden island. As soon as the tip of the arrow poked out, it was answered by a bullet. Another cabinet splintered. Mila pulled the bow back and then surged forward, turning around the island. Genevieve was on her knees there, gun at the ready.

The arrow caught Genevieve in the ribs and the gun clattered to the tile. Mila grabbed the weapon and shot to her feet, firing as soon as her eyes cleared the counter. Jason was there behind the couch, and her first bullet loosed more couch cushion than blood. But the second and third bullets caught him in the head and shoulder, and he toppled to the floor.

She dropped back to the floor, where Genevieve was holding onto the shaft of the arrow that stuck out from her chest. "Oh my god," she whispered. "That hurts… "

"Not as much as you hurt me," Mila whispered.

Genevieve's eyes looked at her with disdain. "You're a vampire," she said.

"I'm a woman," Mila corrected.

"You just want my blood," Genevieve said, choking on wet air.

"I wanted your love," Mila answered, moving closer. She stroked Genevieve's hair to the side of her face, and felt the familiar hunger rise like a lion. Mila raised Genevieve's head and slipped an arm behind her, avoiding the point of the arrow that rose from her middle.

"But at this point, I'll take your blood."

Genevieve tried to shift away, but Mila allowed the hunger to come again. Allowed it to consume her. *Vampires aren't the enemy*, she thought. *Small minds are…*

In a heartbeat, her mouth found her lover's neck. She took Genevieve's life viciously, no longer concerned with anything but food.

She drank hard, angrily. And when the initial thirst was slaked, she drew back, feeling Genevieve's pulse slowing.

"I would never have hurt you," she said. "I just want you to know that."

Genevieve's eyes widened, and then she was still.

People were just as easy to kill as vampires.

Mila felt her heartbeat slow, as the hunger and anger of her emotions drained away.

Genevieve's mouth hung open, slack, one auburn curl twisted across her cheek. Her eyes stared, unblinking, at nothing.

Love was dead.

Love was lost.

"BREAKING NEWS" PT. 8

Jonathan Maberry

Upper East Side
New York City

The doorman of her building tried to block Yuki and Martyn as they sought to leave.

"Miss," he said, "maybe you shouldn't. It's pretty crazy out there."

"It's okay, Moses," she said, touching his arm, "I'll be fine."

Moses Howard stood his ground. "No, miss, I don't think you will. It's not just those bombs."

"What is it?" asked Martyn. "What else could be—"

"Looters, sir," said Moses. "People are going nuts out there."

Behind him some of the hotel's staff were carrying steel shutters outside and rigging them in front of the big plate glass windows. In the six years since moving into the hotel, Yuki had never once see those shutters put up. Not even during the first waves of violence following the outbreak of the V-Wars. Through the glass she could see the red-and-blue of police lights and the continuous flicker of the towering fires. But through the lights she could see figures running.

Mostly young. All colors.

Laughing.

Not screaming in fear.

Laughing.

Carrying TVs and boxed video game consoles.

Looters.

It made her sad. So sad.

"Why do they always take TVs?" murmured Martyn.

Moses just shook his head. "Seen a lot of this stuff in my time. If any of it ever made sense, no one ever told me."

Yuki nodded. "Look, Moses, I appreciate your concern, I really do, but my camera crew is waiting for me. I have to get out there. I need to report this."

Even to her own ears it sounded like she was pleading a case. She was a media star these days and she no longer *had* to be anywhere. She could do standups on her balcony with the city burning behind her. That would give it a sense of majesty, like Christian Amanpour in Baghdad in the early days of the second Gulf War. Lesser field reporters would already be out on the streets, risking their lives to send footage to feed the news cycle. Yuki did not have to get her hands dirty in the trenches anymore.

And yet… her city was burning, and she had slept through part of it. She and Martyn had made love through some of it.

But Martyn's words upstairs had more than explained her ennui to her. They had carved a red line through it, digging into the flesh of her indifference until they found a nerve that had not yet become desensitized by having too much news to report. That pain had awakened something.

Made her *feel* something.

She knew that she had no choice but to get out there.

Outside, beyond the heavy glass, she saw the Global Satellite News truck idling at the curb. Her cameraman, Lonnie Barlow, stood fidgeting, waving at her, ready to jump in with both feet.

Moses turned to follow her gaze and saw Lonnie. He sighed and stepped out of her way.

"Please be careful, Miss Nitobe," he cautioned, regret and disappointment heavy in his voice.

"I will. And keep a light on for us, okay?"

She gave him a smile, but he only managed a wince.

Yuki and Martyn hurried out.

On the street Lonnie jerked the van door open. "This is some radical shit going on out here," he muttered. "President's going to address the nation in twenty, so everybody'll be tuning in. Saul wants your face on every screen when they do the cutaway to the address."

She nodded, understanding. If she announced the president's remarks, then she'd be seen as the conveyer of that information. She'd be the perceived conduit to official information, and it would be cemented if they cut back to her for commentary and on-the-scene updates directly afterward. Standard manipulation of public perception designed to make a reporter appear to be part of the official flow of information. Yuki had done it before and understood how it worked. It was cynical, but it also provided a measure of stability in the flow of information, and therefore a measure of subjective comfort.

"Okay," she said as she slid into her seat, "where are we going?"

Martyn sat behind her, silent and skeptical. His dislike of the inner workings of mainstream media was well known, but he never interfered. And if there was trouble, Yuki wanted him there. Martyn was a handsome man with medium brown skin, gold eyes, and a shaved head. He looked like an artist or dancer, with the hint of athletic power in his movements and posture. The true extent of his power was hidden. Like many vampires who could "pass" for human, Martyn had none of the outward physiological changes some of his brethren endured. No facial fur, no excessively large fangs, no bat ears or rotting flesh. What he had, though, was exceptional muscle density. He looked like he weighed about two hundred pounds; really, he weighed closer to three-fifty. Ultra dense muscle, denser bones, and stronger tendons that were a gift from his maternal Chilean grandfather, and incredible speed and reflexes from his West African ancestors. The combination of *cherufe* and *asansabonsam* made Martyn superhumanly powerful. Yuki had once seen him tear a two thousand pound steel vault door out of a stone wall, and she was sure that it hadn't pushed him all the way to his limits. Those abilities, and his natural grace and intelligence, made him the perfect field operative for the Crimson Queen. If any street thugs tried to hurt Yuki, she had no doubts that Martyn could keep her safe.

However, there were greater dangers than looters.

Even Martyn could not stop a thousand panicked people. Even he could not withstand the blast of a bomb or the collapse of a flaming skyscraper.

Yuki pulled her door shut.

"Let's go," she said.

"STREETS OF FİRE" PT.1

✝

Keith R.A. DeCandido

Alberto Soriano held his hand out to indicate the neighborhood around Bryan Park, a bit of green wedged in at the intersection of Fordham and Kingsbridge Roads. In Spanish, he said, "This all is yours now, my brother."

Rafael nodded. "I won't be lettin' you down. I ain't like Sammy Junior."

Alberto pointed a finger at Rafael. "Don't go dissin' Sammy. When he got his ass busted, he coulda given us up to the DA, but he keepin' his mouth shut. He's a good soldier."

Again, Rafael nodded.

Alberto led Rafael up Kingsbridge Road, past the big new library. It was after midnight and most of the shops were shuttered. As they walked up the hill, Alberto pointed at Poe Park where Kingsbridge intersected with Grand Concourse. "Remember, don't be dealin' at the park. Cops be all up in that, 'specially since they put in that visitor's center."

They walked under a tree in front of the library.

"What about that crew from down the Concourse? I hear they be movin' up."

With a snort, Alberto said, "Don't you be worryin' about those *pendejo*s. Now, the stash houses move from—*urk*!"

That last was after a sharp object rammed into his neck. He couldn't talk, could barely breathe.

Looking up, he saw a big black dude sitting in the tree overhead. He mostly looked like your average banger, with a ballcap on sideways, baggy pants, t-shirt, and hoodie.

"Mostly" because he wasn't wearing sneakers. Or any other kind of shoes, because he had big-ass hooks instead of feet. And one of those hooks had impaled Alberto's neck.

Rafael cried out in English, "A fuckin' bonsie!"

Alberto knew that the crew down the Concourse had hired *asansabonsams* for muscle. A lot of black dudes with the V-Virus turned into bonsies, and besides the hook feet, they had iron teeth and mad strength.

It was getting harder and harder to breathe. Alberto flailed, trying to get his hands on the hooked foot to pull it out of his throat.

"Fuck you, bonsie!" Rafael ran straight for the tree.

Eyes widening, Alberto tried to yell for Rafael not to get his stupid ass killed, but he couldn't do more than just gurgle. His mouth tasted salty and wet with blood.

And then his eyes widened further when he saw Rafael's hands and face alter shape. A snout grew on his nose, and his fingers turned into what looked like giant suction cups.

Carajo, he's a vamp! Alberto had no idea that Rafael had the vampire virus, and that he was a damn *chupacabra*. If he'd known the boy was a choop, he'd have put him in security instead of dealing.

Rafael leapt up into the tree and boxed the bonsie's ears. The bonsie screamed and snarled, thrashing against Rafael's grip. Alberto's crew had a few choops, and they sucked the blood right out of you with their hands.

All three of them fell out of the tree in a heap. Alberto barely even noticed the impact, even though it scraped up his arm, as he was having a harder and harder time breathing. There were spots in front of his eyes. Alberto tried to scream as the hooked foot ripped out of his throat, but he couldn't.

His vision started to blur, but he saw the bonsie bite down on Rafael's shoulder with his iron teeth. Rafael screamed, but kept his grip on the bonsie's head.

Alberto's eyes went dark, and a moment later, he couldn't hear anything either.

Squinting against the early morning sunlight shining in her face as she walked down 106th Street toward the East River, Mia Fitzsimmons stared at the entrance to the tenement building she was approaching, and wondered if someone was playing a joke.

Double-checking her phone, shielding the display with her hand against the sun, she verified that this was the address that Detective Trujillo had texted her after her editor, Bart Mosby, told her that the mayor's office had approved her request.

The top three floors of the dark-brown stone building had boarded-up windows, but the second-floor windows were uncovered and had fluorescent bulbs alight on the ceiling and evidence of people moving around.

When she walked up the small stoop to the front entrance, she saw that a metal box had been placed next to the doorbells, with an NYPD sticker and another sticker with the letters VCU scrawled in Sharpie under it, on either side of a big red button. Gamely, Mia pushed the button.

A burst of static exploded at her, which Mia as a lifelong New Yorker easily translated as "Who is it?" as heard over a crummy intercom system.

"Mia Fitzsimmons from the *Daily News*."

A moment later, a low buzz emitted from the wooden door to the tenement, and Mia pushed it open. She entered a very narrow hallway, at the end of which sat a bored-looking middle-aged black woman in a sergeant's uniform with a nameplate that read BUCKLAND. Without even looking up from her romance novel, the sergeant said, "They're waitin' for you upstairs." As Mia approached, Buckland held out a visitor badge on a clip, still not looking up from her book.

Mia flashed her driver's license, just so she could say that she did, and took the badge, clipping it to the collar of her blouse.

The wooden stairs creaked as she climbed them. At the landing, she found an opening to a huge room dotted with support posts that took up almost the entirety of the second floor. Scattered about was metal desks and metal chairs on wheels. On the far side of the room were a series of whiteboards with pictures and writing, and on both sides there were makeshift floor-to-ceiling walls that created an illusion of privacy.

A tall, lanky African-American detective saw her and asked, "Can I help you?"

"I'm Mia Fitzsimmons, I was—"

The detective nodded. "The reporter, right. We're getting ready for the top-of-shift confab, so c'mon over."

Several cops in plain clothes were rolling their chairs toward the set of whiteboards. One was leaning on a cane and looked like he was in pain; Mia wondered why he didn't sit down.

There was only one other woman in the room, a surprisingly slight Latina. The rest were men, many with thick, short mustaches, as cops were the only subset of humanity who never got the memo that those mustaches went out in 1979.

One of those was the only person she recognized by face: Hector Trujillo, who had been a detective in the 24th Precinct before being reassigned to the Vampire Crimes Unit.

The one with the cane said, "Okay, let's come to—Mullinax, who is this?" That last was said as the tall detective led her toward him.

Trujillo stepped forward before Detective Mullinax could respond. "This is the reporter, Sarge. Mia Fitzsimmons from the *News*."

"Right." He reached out a hand. "I'm Sergeant Mike Yanoff, commander of the VCU. You are going to do every single thing I tell you, or that any of my people tell you. Failure to do exactly what anybody in this room tells you will result in your privileges being revoked, and you being kicked out of the VCU. Clear?"

Being sure to return the handshake as firmly as her small hands were able, Mia said, "My editor and I already worked out the terms with the commissioner and the mayor, Sergeant. I'm here to write an article about the VCU and what it does. The NYPD has the right to read the article before it's printed." Mia left out the part about how the NYPD had no control over the content, only the ability to object, and the *News* was under no obligation to do anything about those objections. She thought mentioning that might just piss the sergeant off.

"That might be a problem. Most of these guys can't read." Yanoff said those words in the same clipped tone he'd been using all along, and Mia couldn't tell if he was kidding or not.

But then Trujillo grinned. "Hey, c'mon, Esposito just finished *Dick and Jane* yesterday."

Mia shook her head. "That means he's already more literate than most *News* subscribers."

That earned her chuckles from both Trujillo and Mullinax, but Yanoff just stared at her. "Don't try to be funny, Fitzsimmons."

"My apologies, Sergeant, it won't happen again," Mia said gravely.

Pointing with his cane at a chair that was on the periphery of the gathering cops, Yanoff said, "Sit over there. Take all the notes you want, but don't record—"

Mia interrupted. "I can only record a one-on-one conversation and then only if the other person gives prior permission. I *really did* work this all out with the commissioner."

"And now you're working it out with me. Go sit down."

Nodding, Mia went to the indicated chair.

Looking away from Mia, he raised his voice only slightly. "All right, people, let's get to work!"

Within moments, all the cops were seated. Yanoff pointed with his cane at Mia. "First off, we have a guest: Mia Fitzsimmons. The commissioner and the mayor and the editors of the *Daily News* have decided to embed a reporter with the VCU for a month so the general public will have an idea of what we do here."

A red-haired detective raised his hand and said, "So she's gonna write about how we sit on our asses all day writing reports that read like Bran fucking Stoker?"

Yanoff fixed the detective with the same look he'd given Mia when she'd tried to engage in witty banter. "First of all, Sullivan, it's *Bram* fucking Stoker, short for Abraham, not something you eat for fiber. Second of all, that's only what she'll write if she only talks to you. Which I may make her do, if I feel like punishing her."

Everyone in the room chuckled, including Sullivan.

"Try not to make us look *too* bad," Yanoff said dryly, "on the off chance that someone out there actually reads her article."

Now Yanoff pointed his cane at one of the pictures on the whiteboard, which showed three people lying in a bloody heap on a sidewalk. One had an odd face that indicated that he had I1V1, but Mia couldn't tell from the angle what he was. Another was very obviously an *asansabonsam* based on the hooks where his feet used to be.

"This," the sergeant said, "is the triple at Poe Park last night. What do we have there, Thorndike?"

A massive white guy who barely fit in his chair—the thing squeaked in protest every time he shifted his considerable weight—said, "Got us a bonsie, a choop, and a normal. The choop is Rafael Guesa, the normal's Alberto Soriano, and the bonsie's Jason Johnson, street name 'Chops.'"

Trujillo asked, "He called that before or after he got vamped?"

Mia smiled. "Chops" would be an understandable nickname for someone who had metal teeth.

Thorndike shrugged his massive shoulders. "Fucked if I know, that's just what's on his sheet. Anyhow, M.E. on the scene says Guesa killed Johnson, and Johnson killed both Guesa and Soriano, but the bodies got sent to Muck to be sure."

Mia frowned, wondering who "Muck" was, but knowing better than to interrupt.

Yanoff said to Thorndike, "You said he had a sheet?"

"Yeah, Johnson's known associates include half the bangers on the Concourse, and Vice says that Soriano's in charge of most of University Heights' drug trade. Guesa's got no record, so we don't know if he's in the game, or just got caught up in a drug hit."

"Could be two vamps clashing, too," Mullinax said. "Fighting over who gets to suck Soriano's blood."

Mia started tapping her pen on her notebook.

Everyone turned to look at her.

Yanoff asked, "You have something to add, Fitzsimmons?"

Suddenly self-conscious, Mia considered saying "Nothing," but figured she had the opening. "It's just that *chupacabras* absorb blood, they don't suck it, and *asansabonsams* aren't interested in blood at all. There's nothing to clash over here; they *both* could've taken what they wanted from Soriano."

Yanoff stared at her for a second, then looked at Thorndike. "You said Muck has the bodies?"

Thorndike nodded, which, given that he had no discernible neck—he seemed to just go from chin to shoulder—looked really bizarre.

"Fine, take Sullivan to the morgue. Take the reporter with you too."

"Sure," Thorndike said, at the same time that Sullivan leaned back, ran a hand through his red hair, and actually whined like a teenager: "Aw, c'mon, Sarge, why me?"

Yanoff pointedly ignored Sullivan's plaintive request. "Now, next up… "

———•———

Simon Ousmanov slowly walked down the street that was labelled with the sign "Brighton 11th Street," but which everyone in Brighton Beach just called "11th Street." The distinction was necessary because Brooklyn had several 11th Streets: Bay 11th Street in Bay Ridge, West 11th Street in Gravesend, East 11th Street in Sheepshead Bay, North and South 11th Streets in Williamsburg, plus the regular old 11th Street in Park Slope.

Simon thought it was stupid. Just name the streets, or normalize the numbers like they did in Manhattan.

Mostly he focused on the inanity of the multiple 11th Streets because it was a handy way to avoid what he was facing.

About halfway between Oceanview Avenue and Cass Place sat a small diner, wedged in between a medical center and a place that sold floor tiles. In the four years since he'd emigrated to the States, he'd never been invited to set foot in the diner, and he'd been hoping to go at least four more years without having done so. The eatery was labelled only with a battered, off-white sign that had the word DINER in both English and Russian, stenciled in red. The dirt-streaked glass door deliberately hadn't been cleaned any time recently, as it kept anyone from seeing inside.

Simon pushed the glass door inward, to be greeted by a small counter on the left and four booths on the right. A very large man with a very visible sidearm sat at the counter sipping a cup of coffee. Someone sat to his right, but Simon's view of the person was obscured. As Simon entered, a man in a white apron moved from behind the counter to the back room.

Only one booth was occupied, by the man Simon was here to see. He was unassuming, with a pudgy middle negating the effect of his broad shoulders. His button-down shirt was open to form a v-neck and display both a salt-and-pepper hairy chest and a gold chain around his neck. He had a cigarette dangling from his mouth, which violated New York City's indoor smoking ordinances, and a samovar on his left.

As Simon entered the diner, the man at the booth poured more tea from the samovar into his glass cup while flipping through this week's edition of *Russkaya Reklama*.

Simon did not know the man's name. Everyone just referred to him as Drakon.

After flipping a few more pages, Drakon finally spoke in Russian, without looking up. "Okay, Simon, where is my heroin?"

"I am sorry, but—"

Now Drakon looked up, waving an upraised finger back and forth. "No. I am not interested in apologies. I asked a question, I expect an answer. Where is my heroin?"

Simon blew out a breath. "It was stolen."

"Yes. Yes, it was. That is the fourth shipment from Afghanistan I have lost. No, I misspeak. The fourth shipment *you* have lost."

"I have changed the routine each time, but it is as if they can read my mind."

"I doubt there is much to read. You've failed, Simon, and I am running a multimillion-dollar business. Also, who are 'they'?"

Shifting his weight from foot to foot, Simon said, "I do not know. I think Armenians, at first, but the heroin they're putting on the streets is from Mexico. Maybe the Dominicans? The Chinese?"

After sipping his tea, Drakon said, "You have no idea, do you?"

Simon lowered his head. He'd honestly thought it was the Armenians, but his people had checked into it. "No."

"That is what I thought." He looked over at the counter.

The big man nodded and got up from the stool. Now Simon could see the person next to him: a very old woman, wearing a shabby gray dress.

She turned on the stool, and Simon got a good look. Her face was incredibly pale and wrinkled, her nose huge and bulbous, her lips so thin it looked like someone had drawn a line in pencil under the nose.

But what stood out were her eyes. At first she had them closed, which was just bizarre, but when she opened them, Simon understood why.

Simon Ousmanov would spend the rest of his life trying to figure out how to describe the deep wells of horrendous darkness that he saw behind the old woman's eyelids.

As soon as she looked at him, a sharp pain started in his abdomen, even as a migraine struck him with the force of a freight train.

Buckling to his knees, he tried to breathe and snuffled, as blood was now pouring from his nose. Bracing himself on the dirty formica floor, he found it hard to inhale.

Somehow, he realized as the pain spread to every part of his body, it wasn't a surprise that Drakon employed an *eretica*.

It took Simon a very long time to die, and every moment of it was wracked with agony.

"BREAKING NEWS" PT. 9

Jonathan Maberry

44th Street near Ninth Avenue
New York City

I can't," said Swann.

"What?" asked Derkin, his head swiveling around like a praying mantis's. Hector turned, too.

"Doc, please… "

But Luther was already reaching for the door handle. He pushed it open against the hot wind and the smoke and his own cowardice. And as he stepped out, he wondered how much of this was compassion and basic humanity, and how much was his inability to bear the weight of more shame?

There were people everywhere.

Many were already dead, or so far gone that they were probably unaware of the depth of their own destruction, their minds blown dark by the loss of too much of themselves.

But that still left the others.

Hundreds of them.

Crying, begging, mewling.

Swann tore off his sport coat, jerked his necktie from around his throat, and dropped down beside the nearest, a woman whose left arm had been torn away at the elbow. He began winding the tie around her upper arm as a tourniquet. He wanted to yell at Derkin and the driver to get out of the fucking car, to help. But he had no right, no moral authority. He'd hidden in the car for nearly fifteen minutes. How many people had died in that time? How many could have been saved with basic first aid?

How many lives were marked against his own soul?

The woman moaned, and tears ran down her cheeks, carving paths through the soot. Her lips moved, and Swann had to bend close to hear.

"My baby... my baby... my baby... "

A plea, a question, but an unanswerable one. Swann looked around and saw children, some of them little more than hunched shapes. Were any of them her child? There was no way to tell. No way at all.

Her eyes were blind and stared sightlessly up as if wondering why heaven didn't open to release its angels. Swann had been wondering that since the outbreak. Where was God in all of this? Was He anywhere at all?

The words of the madman who'd called in to take proud responsibility rang in Swann's ears.

I am God's Soldier.

Had it come to that? Had the cultural paradigm shifted completely from an ethnic war to a purely religious one? If so, then the V-Wars might never end.

Never.

Wars of any kind tended to either drive people from the church or make them flock to fill every pew. Faith was the most savage whip any leader could wield. Without it, no one would ever strap on a bomb vest. Without it, the Middle East might have seen something less than the oceans of blood that had washed those sands for four thousand years.

If God's Soldier was able to orchestrate a terrorist act as massive as this, then it spoke to an organization that had to be large, well funded, and well organized. Since 9-11, it had become virtually impossible for such an organization to effectively strike within U.S. borders.

However, the V-Wars had been changing that. Vampire cells had launched dozens of strikes throughout the nation, claiming tens of thousands of lives. Human extremist groups had struck back. Then the Ninety-Nine Bombs had exploded all chances of a peace and launched the second V-War. Although a person claiming to be a vampire had taken public credit for that attack, the Crimson Queen's intelligence network had virtually proved that it was not the case. At least one of those bombs had been planted by a man—if man he was—known as Rancid.

Rancid was believed to be a new species. Not human, not vampire. Possibly not even a lycanthrope, because werewolves—that rarest of genetic flukes—had been proven to be previously misidentified species of necrophageous vampires. Flesh eaters instead of blood drinkers.

Rancid was something else. Forensic evidence collected at a dozen crime scenes had revealed something entirely new. Something not seen in any of the more than three hundred known vampire species or fifty-eight hundred hybrids. There was absolutely no trace of an active V-Gene in the tissue collected from the man known only as Rancid. None. He was not a vampire and he was not any version of lycanthrope known to the new post-Ice Virus science. No one had an answer to what Rancid was except a monster.

And now there was God's Soldier. Clearly human, if his statement was true—and Swann had no reason to doubt it—but he was every bit as much of a monster as Rancid. And he had managed to launch a coordinated strike fifty times more devastating than the Twin Towers. On par with the Ninety-Nine Bombs, though at the moment confined to New York.

And in the distance, Swann could hear fresh explosions. He'd seen the telltale streaks of rocket-propelled grenades punching into the sky to blow National Guard helicopters to bits and sow their human occupants to the winds. The scope and precision of all of this was military. That's how it seemed to Swann as he moved away from the dying woman to try and help another person.

And another.

And another.

This was an attack as sophisticated as anything put into operation by a seasoned general.

Which meant what, in terms of who God's Soldier was?

He knelt beside a teenage boy who kept calling for his mother. His nose and left cheek were gone, and one eye was torn to pulp. Swann wondered what his mother could possibly have done for her son had she been here.

The boy coughed, arched his back, and then flopped down.

Dead.

Just like that.

Swann almost launched for him, almost grabbed him, as if somehow he could pull the boy back from that long drop into eternity. But a voice rose out in a shrill scream of immediate need, and Swann turned, crawled, got to his fingers and toes and ran like a dog across twenty feet of debris to a middle-aged woman who was trying to pull a splinter from her stomach. The splinter must have been torn from a window casement; it was a fourteen-inch spike of aluminum. He cupped his hands around hers to try and help.

"No," said a voice, and Swann looked up to see a fat Asian man come hurrying over. He dropped to his knees and pushed Swann's hands gently away. "Don't. That splinter's the only thing keeping her from bleeding out. Give me something to pack it. Tear some of her skirt. We need to create a pressure bandage around the splinter. Come on, man, move."

Swann blinked twice, then his hands were moving, taking hold of the torn hem of the woman's skirt, tearing it, having to bend and bite the cloth to rip the piece from the rest. The Asian man took it, nodded thanks, and began to carefully wind the cloth around the point of entry.

Swann watched him work. Saw how deft and clever the man's hands were. Saw the lines of concern etched into the man's face, the fear and compassion glittering in his eyes. When the woman screamed, the man winced, and Swann saw something else. The gleaming points of incisors. Long. So long.

"She's not a vampire," said Swann.

The Asian man looked at him. He closed his mouth to hide his fangs.

"She's not a vampire," repeated Swann.

The man frowned. Almost another wince. "So what?"

Swann had no way to respond to that. So he didn't.

Instead, he looked around for someone else to help and moved off without saying a word. He pulled his shirt off and began tearing it into strips for pressure bandages, for tourniquets. He wished he could strip off his own skin, and would have if it could have helped.

Then he saw more figures move out of the smoke.

A few last victims, but others, too. People who were uninjured. Coming to help.

Not one or two.

Many.

Car doors opened along the choked street and people began stepping out, drawn by the example of this newcomer, their fear of involvement metamorphosing into action.

The Asian vampire stood and began yelling orders. He was clearly a doctor or EMT. He grabbed people and gave them simple instructions, giving them tasks they could accomplish and the power that came from knowing they could make a difference.

Like an infection, it spread.

And spread.

When Swann rose from bandaging an old woman, he saw Derkin on his knees beside Hector, assisting inexpertly as the driver bandaged a head wound.

Some of the injured were vampires. Many were not.

Some of the people from the cars were vampires. Most were not.

All of the people who had come out of the smoke *were* vampires.

Swann stared in wonder. He wished Yuki Nitobe was here to film this. To record this moment.

If it could air, if the raw footage of this could get out, then so much might yet be saved.

But Yuki was not here.

So Swann took his cell phone out, set it to video, and began recording it himself.

"STREETS OF FÏRE" PT. 2

Keith R.A. DeCandido

Mia tumbled out of the back seat of the department-issue Chevy trying to get her bearings. Giving Sullivan an accusatory look as he got out of the driver's seat, she then turned to Thorndike, who unfolded his massive frame from the passenger seat. "He *always* drive like that?"

Thorndike grinned, showing yellow teeth. "Nah, usually he's reckless."

Sullivan shrugged. "What? You gotta drive on the FDR like that."

They had taken the FDR Drive from 106th Street down to 34th Street, then traveled over to 1st Avenue and 30th Street, parking the car in a no-parking zone while placing their NYPD credentials on the dashboard. Mia had lost track of the sudden lane changes and the number of cars Sullivan had cut off by the time they passed 96th Street.

"My old man," Sullivan said as he headed toward the entrance, "he always said that you knew you'd be okay drivin' in New York if you could navigate the FDR without shittin' in your socks."

"In that case, I wanna see your socks," Mia said.

Both cops laughed, and they headed inside, eventually reaching the office of Dr. Mukta Patwardhan, which explained the "Muck" nickname, though not why the doctor put up with it. Thorndike knocked on the door, and an accented voice said, "Come in!"

Opening the door, Mia saw a slender Indian woman with dark hair tied in a bun, a pointed nose, and very dark eyes. Looking up, she said, "Red, Fatso, it is good to see you both."

"How you doin', Muck?" Sullivan asked.

Mia managed to hold in a laugh. She wondered if Patwardhan's nicknames for the cops were a response to being called "Muck" or if she was the one who started it.

"I am very busy, but you are already aware of that. Who is this?" She asked that last with a nod at Mia.

Jerking a thumb at her, Thorndike said, "This is Mia Fitzsimmons from the *News*. She's following the VCU around for a month. Sarge figured she should meet you."

Patwardhan rose to her feet and offered a hand. "Oh, really? It's a pleasure, Ms. Fitzsimmons, and may I say, you don't look a thing like the picture that accompanies your articles."

"I'll take that as a compliment." Mia had been bitching to Bart about that photo for a year now. She returned the handshake.

"Well, I'm quite the devoted reader. You are one of the few voices of reason on I1V1 in the press."

"Thank you. I appreciate that."

"You're welcome. Of course, I've a vested interest. I don't know if Sergeant Gimpy told you or not, but I've been tasked with doing the autopsies for all the I1V1 cases, which means it is my curse to have to deal with the VCU."

"Ah, c'mon," Thorndike said with a grin, "you love us, Muck."

Patwardhan just gave the detective a look before saying, "I assume you came down for the triple in the Bronx?"

Sullivan nodded. "Yeah, we caught that."

"Well, you are about to catch a good deal more. Come with me."

Getting up from behind the desk, Patwardhan led the two detectives and Mia out of her office and toward the morgue.

Sullivan hesitated. "Do we have to—"

Thorndike snorted. "Nut up, Johnny. It's just a couple three stiffs."

"Actually," Patwardhan said, "it is more than that."

She led them down the hall and through large swinging metal doors.

As soon as they entered the chilly room decorated entirely in cold metals and harsh plastics, Sullivan's mouth burbled.

"Fuck," Thorndike said, "you gotta be kiddin' me."

"'Scuse," Sullivan managed to utter before running out of the morgue.

Patwardhan shook her head. "Every time. You would think he would grow accustomed."

"He's third grade—he didn't do homicides before he got shifted over to VCU." Thorndike shrugged. "Some people ain't got the stomach. Anyhow, Trujillo owes me twenty bucks now."

Mia frowned. "Huh?"

Thorndike grinned. "Hector said Sullivan wouldn't yak until the sheets came off the bodies. I didn't think he'd make it through the door." Then Thorndike's face fell. "You ain't gonna put that in the article, right?"

That prompted a smile from Mia. "We'll see."

"Fuck." Thorndike shook his head and then looked at Patwardhan. "So whatcha got for us?"

The M.E. and two other orderlies all pulled the sheets away from the heads of the three victims, side by side on three gurneys. Rafael Guesa had the snout that was characteristic of *chupacabras*, Jason Johnson had teeth made of metal, and Alberto Soriano sadly looked just like a young man whose throat was ripped to pieces.

"The cause of death is fairly straightforward in all three cases. They all died of severe blood loss. In Soriano's case, it was through the carotid artery after it was torn apart by a metal hook that happens to match Johnson's foot. Said appendage had multiple traces of Soriano's blood on it. As for Johnson, he has multiple small puncture wounds on his face and considerable blood loss. In fact, it's approximately the amount we found in the sacs on the tips of Guesa's fingers. Johnson also has blood on his teeth, which matches that of Guesa, who has a bite on his clavicle with metal shavings in it that match those of Johnson's teeth."

Thorndike frowned. "So the bonsie killed Soriano and the choop both, and the choop killed the bonsie?"

Holding both hands palms up, Patwardhan smiled, showing perfect teeth. "Congratulations, Detective Fatso, I have just handed you three closed cases at once."

"Whoopee dingle. The sarge can show that off at the next COMPSTAT meeting."

Mia was scribbling furiously. There were plenty of instances of vampire-on-human violence and vice versa, but this sort of fight between two vampires with a human in the middle was unusual. A lot of vampires were huddling together. Some were your basic support-group type things, others more nasty, like the New Red Coalition that had been engaging in terrorist attacks all over North America. But there was a lot less of that in large cities like New York. Sure, some groups of vampires stuck together, but plenty were off on their own. Much easier to lose yourself in the crowded big city after all.

Now Patwardhan held up a single finger. "However, there is more. I have had several bodies sent to me over the past forty-eight hours that fall under the purview of your unit." She walked over to another set of three pallets, this time uncovering the feet, which were desiccated husks.

Mia looked at the M.E., recognizing the handiwork of a vampire from Armenian folklore. "*Dakhanavar?*"

Patwardhan nodded.

"Where'd you find these guys, Sunnyside? Belmont? Murray Hill?" Thorndike listed three neighborhoods that had a heavy Armenian population.

"That's the bizarre part, I'm afraid. They were found in Brighton Beach. And two of them have I1V1, and stingers under their tongues, so probably *upierczy.*" She walked over to another pallet, where she revealed the face of a man who looked Russian. "This gentleman was also found dead in Brighton Beach. Cause of death is massive and comprehensive organ failure from no cause that I can determine. Given the neighborhood where he was found, my guess is an *eretica.* All four of our victims have ties to the Russian mob."

Making more notes, Mia pondered. Scientists had spent a lot of time recently trying to figure out exactly *how* the *eretica* could just stare at someone and cause them to die. Most I1V1 mutations had *some* kind of scientific explanation, but the *eretica* had continued to baffle.

Patwardhan pointed at another two pallets. "Those two have no cause of death that I can determine whatsoever, and they were found on the Lower East Side, not far from Chinatown."

"You're thinkin' hopping ghosts?" Thorndike asked.

Another nod from Patwardhan. "But they were *not* found in Chinatown, and these two victims are of Jamaican descent, with criminal records indicating they are involved in the drug trade."

Mia looked up.

Thorndike, though, was shaking his head. "Fuck. All right, Muck, get us the reports on all these guys." He pulled a cell phone out of his jacket pocket. It was almost lost in the detective's massive hand. After manipulating the touchscreen, he put it to his ear. "Hey, Sarge, it don't look good here. We need to get somebody from Vice onna line. We may be lookin' at a drug war usin' vamps."

148
✝

———————

Transcript of interview with Sergeant Michael Yanoff

MIA FITZSIMMONS: And we're now recording.

SERGEANT MICHAEL YANOFF: Let me be clear about something: I will *not* discuss Michael Fayne. I talk to a department psychiatrist once a week whether I need it or not, and between that and my cane and my Percocet prescription, I have *plenty* of reminders of Fayne. Clear?

FITZSIMMONS: Uhm, okay, well, that kinda messes up my first question, which was going to be about how you got this post.

YANOFF: Everyone knows that. Jerry Schmidt—God rest his soul—and I caught the Katelyn Montgomery murder. Two weeks later, we're overrun with vampires, my partner's dead, and I'm laid up in the hospital. A piece of unbreakable glass broke and tore into my leg. For this, the department decides I'm a "vampire expert," they promote me, and put me in charge of this stupid unit.

FITZSIMMONS: Stupid?

YANOFF: Look, they probably don't want you putting this in the article, but this unit is just spitting in the wind. The V-Teams, they get resources, hardware, an actual budget. Meanwhile, we're lucky we have a whiteboard and spotty wifi. Yes, we can call on ESU, assuming they're not busy somewhere else.

FITZSIMMONS: You said that you're considered a vampire expert after encountering Fayne, but you and your partner actually called in a vampire expert.

YANOFF: Yeah. That was actually *my* idea. Jerry and I went to Luther Swann's office at NYU and asked him to consult. Thanks to us, he's on TV every night, going on raids, testifying before Congress. He's the most famous person on the planet right now, all because I saw him a few times on those Discovery Channel shows my kids watch. Now he won't even return my phone calls.

FITZSIMMONS: What exactly is the mandate of the Vampire Crimes Unit, Sergeant?

YANOFF: Honestly? To keep the stats in the precincts and the other units from getting out of hand. We've got more and more vampire crimes, and we can't close the cases. Either we don't have the manpower to take them down or we can't even *find* them—or the V-Teams take them into federal custody, leaving us with an open case, since the feds generally can't be bothered to include us. But, since all vampire-related crimes get kicked over to us as a special unit, our stats are counted separately. As a result, NYPD can say that they're keeping a lid on crime even with all the vampires.

FITZSIMMONS: Sergeant, do you really want me to put all this in the article?

YANOFF: What I really want is a Scotch. So we're done here. If you want to ask me anything else, do it at the Bronx Alehouse in an hour and lose the recorder.

* * *

The entire time he sat in the queue of trucks waiting for clearance to depart the Red Hook Container Terminal, Jerome Whitmore kept staring at his passenger. Jerome hadn't been told the man's name, but his unusual feet and metal teeth made it clear that he was a bonsie. Jerome had heard that Antwon had some on the payroll, but this was his first time seeing one up close.

Finally, the bonsie turned to look back. "The *fuck* you lookin' at?" His voice sounded funny because of the teeth.

Jerome turned back to stare at the truck that was ahead of him. "Nothing."

"Just drive the motherfuckin' truck, a'ight?"

"I *am* driving it." Jerome bent his head back to crack his neck, the bottom of his dreads tickling his back as he did so. "I *been* driving it for two years now. Antwon ain't never put security with me before. Why don't he trust me now?"

"Ain't about *you*, motherfucker."

Jerome glanced down at his passenger's large metal hooks that served as feet. "So what's it about?"

"Ain't your problem, neither."

"My truck, my problem."

"Antwon's drugs in your truck, which means you shut the fuck up or we tell po-po who's been smuggling shit."

Jerome shook his head. He'd been driving trucks in the city for twenty years, taking containers that arrived at the Red Hook port and bringing them to the various clients who hired the company he worked for.

Plus one client he'd taken on two years ago when the child-support payments went up because LaShonda decided to send little Tyreese to private school. The good news was he got more visitations out of the deal, but the bad news was that he could only make the payments if he didn't pay rent. The landlord frowned on that, so he took his cousin up on the offer he'd made several times to haul stuff for his boss. Jerome had figured it was illegal, but he didn't realize how illegal until his truck hit a huge sinkhole on the Van Wyck Expressway. He pulled off at the next exit to make sure the cargo was okay, only to find heroin in one of the boxes.

He was drug muling. Not exactly what you'd call a good example for Tyreese, but what the hell else was he supposed to do?

But now he had a bonsie riding shotgun, with the only explanation being a text message from Antwon's burner phone saying, "It's security, don't worry about it."

Sure enough, the head gate guy, José, took one look at the bonsie and said, "Who's that?" He noticed the teeth, and then looked down to see the hooked feet. "What's he doin' here?"

"Trainee," Jerome said without missing a beat. "Bosses are doing some kind of affirmative action nonsense, hiring vamps. Honestly, I think they just want someone they can pay less to and get away with it."

José made a *tch* noise. "Yeah."

The rest of the exit procedure went smoothly, with nobody ever noticing that one of his boxes was filled with black-tar heroin. Jerome then proceeded down Hamilton Avenue under the Gowanus Expressway overpass. Traffic on the Gowanus was always a mess, and it was easier to drive on Hamilton, which ran under the elevated highway.

As Jerome drove through the intersection of Hamilton and Bush Street, an SUV came zooming down Bush and plowed right into his truck.

Jerome had thrown himself to the floor of the cab and put his arms up to protect his face before he consciously realized what was happening. The rat-tat-tat of gunfire, combined with the shattering of glass, created an ugly cacophony as the bullets slammed into the windshield, the window, and the mirrors.

I'm never gonna see Tyreese again, was all he could think as bullets flew over his head.

The hail of bullets stopped, and Jerome glanced up to see that the bonsie had also taken cover on the floor of the cab.

But once the bullets stopped, and Jerome heard a voice say something in Russian, the bonsie broke into a huge grin. Since his teeth were metal, it was the single scariest grin Jerome had ever seen in thirty-six years of life.

The bonsie threw the bullet-riddled passenger door open and rolled out of the cab. Raising himself up a bit to see more clearly, Jerome watched as the bonsie rolled around the pavement on his shoulders and arms while his legs whipped back and forth. There were about half a dozen white guys all holding AK-47s. Four black SUVs were blocking traffic on Hamilton in either direction, while Jerome's damaged truck was now blocking Bush.

Razor sharp hook feet started slicing through the legs, torsos, and arms of the Russians. While the bonsie twirled around on the ground like a breakdancer, the Russians tried to get their bearings and shoot him, but their shots all missed or went wild, as the bonsie was just too damn fast.

After only a couple of seconds, the Russians were all bleeding on the street, dead or dying. The bonsie clambered upright, sunlight glinting off his metal grin. He started walking slowly and awkwardly toward the truck, like he was on stilts.

Jerome was about to get out of the truck when he saw that the bonsie hadn't actually killed all the Russians. Just the ones with AKs.

A wrinkled little old lady wearing a gray sweater and matching skirt came walking slowly out from behind one of the SUVs, her eyes closed for some reason.

Then she opened her eyes and looked right at the bonsie. Jerome had never seen eyes like that before. God willing, he never would again.

"Shit!" The bonsie dove to the pavement and did his breakdancing act, twirling on his head and shoulders and arms toward the old woman. For her part, she was taken aback, apparently not expecting so bizarre an assault.

Then the bonsie's left foot cut the old lady's neck open and she fell to the street. More blood gushed out onto Hamilton Avenue, joining the ever-growing pool.

Jerome fumbled for his cell phone. The bonsie didn't get back to his feet, instead crawling toward the truck. Jerome saw a rictus of agony on his face and wondered what happened to him. Nobody had actually *touched* him.

He pointed at Jerome. "Do *not* call the fuckin' cops, you feel me, motherfucker?"

For a second Jerome just stared at his phone. Then he looked back at the bonsie. "I was gonna call Antwon."

The bonsie winced in pain. "You do *not* tell *nothin'* to *nobody*, motherfucker!" Then he fell facedown on the pavement.

Jerome heard sirens. He wondered what the hell was going to happen now. No matter what, though, he had the feeling that Tyreese wasn't going to be going to private school for much longer…

Mia sat next to Detective Medawe Bieo on the Roosevelt Island tram as the cable car wended its way across the East River, the 59th Street Bridge on the right, several newly constructed apartment buildings on the left. Mia wondered idly if the owners of the building warned prospective tenants on the upper floors that tram riders would be able to see *right* into their homes.

Bieo had invited her on this trip, but had been tight-lipped about specifics, only saying that he was visiting a confidential informant.

As they went out over the river, Mia said, "I'm surprised that you've been able to develop CIs so quickly. The unit's only a few months old."

The detective, an African-American man in his forties, smiled to reveal a very expensive dental appliance. "Good police always have CIs. That's where the real work's done. You don't talk to people, you don't develop relationships, you ain't police; you're just some thug who arrests people sometimes." He shook his head. "Least that's what Pop always said. 'You walk a beat, you got to know everyone on every corner, or you ain't doin' nothin' but showin' off your fancy uniform. But you know the people, then you can keep the peace.' And maybe we can't always do that, but at the very least we can get things *back* to peace when it gets broke."

The tram started downward toward the Roosevelt Island terminus. A long strip of land between Manhattan and Queens, the island was mostly residential these days, though it started out life as a prison and as the location of several hospitals and insane asylums.

She looked at Bieo. "Your father was a cop?"

"And my grandfather. Not my great-grandfather, though, 'cause they weren't too keen on black folks being cops back then." The smile came out again. "Actually, they weren't too keen on Grandpa, neither."

"I'm surprised; I figured, with a name like yours, you were a second-generation immigrant."

"I am on my mom's side. She was born in Kenya, and I was named after *her* pop. I never knew him, he died on the boat coming over here. But my father's side has been here since before the Civil War."

Mia nodded, making notes.

Watching her do so, Bieo said, "Look, I want you to understand something. If *any* specifics of this meeting go in your article, I will hunt you down, you understand? The 'C' in 'CI' is for 'confidential,' and I take that *very* seriously. Keep it very, very vague."

She made a show of putting her notebook away. "So why did you ask me along?"

"Because all everyone's talking about is the war against the monsters, but these aren't monsters, they're *people*. I figured you should meet one."

The tram came to a stop, and one set of doors opened to allow the passengers to disembark. The other set of doors to let on passengers headed to Manhattan didn't open until the island-bound folks cleared out. If you wanted to ride the tram right back, you had to go out and come back in, paying the full $2.50 fare.

As they walked down the ramp toward West Road, Bieo said, "NYPD's always been about maintaining order. It's really all you can do in a city this big. It's funny, every commissioner they appoint has all these grandiose plans about how they're going to run the force right and fix things, and then nothing significant changes, and then they quit or get fired. Teddy Roosevelt, you ever look at his life? This is a man who succeeded at *everything* he ever did, from San Juan Hill to the Natural History Museum, all the way up to being president, but even *he* couldn't handle being NYPD commissioner. It's the only job he ever quit."

They walked down West, Mia occasionally glancing to her right to take in the bright lights and varied architecture of the Manhattan skyline. The Citicorp Building, with its slanted roof, stood out amid a hodgepodge of buildings that were constructed in a multitude of eras, from the nineteenth century to last week.

"Right now, the vamps are just like every other immigrant group that's come into town. You know, when the Irish and Italians first arrived, all the Dutch and English types would turn their noses up and not want to give them jobs and wish they'd go back where they came from. Nothing changes." He shook his head. "Only this time, the immigrants got superpowers, at least some of them, and the whole damn U.S. military's out to kill them. But that's the feds' problem. For us, we got to keep doing what police are supposed to do: make the peace."

Eventually they worked their way to the demolished campus of the Coler-Goldwater Specialty Hospital, which had closed its doors and was scheduled to make way for a Cornell University campus. Construction had halted a few months ago for reasons that were never made public, though one of Mia's colleagues had been trying to dig into it.

A huge bird flew overhead, buzzing the pair of them. Mia was no kind of expert, but she knew that they didn't generally breed birds to be two hundred pounds.

Which meant it had to be someone with I1V1. Sure enough, the bird landed behind one of the half-demolished walls of the former hospital.

As it came in for a landing, Mia noticed a satchel around the bird's neck.

"Ow, *fuck* that always hurts," came a voice a few moments later from behind the wall.

A few more moments, and a very attractive African-American man walked out from behind the wall, buttoning a shirt.

Bieo fumbled in his backpack, and then pulled out a pouch that contained blood. He tossed it to the gentleman, who caught it unerringly and, after glancing down at it, regarded the detective with a raised eyebrow.

"Cattle blood," Bieo said, "straight from the butcher."

The gentleman grinned. "My man." He ripped open the pouch and gulped down all the blood therein.

Mia blinked, and realized something disquieting. She'd been reporting vampire-related stories for the *News* since the Bronx District Attorney candidate she'd been covering announced to the world that he was a *loup garou*. Yet this was her first time actually watching somebody drink blood.

What struck her as odd was how, well, *ordinary* it looked, like someone drinking from a canteen during a hike.

"Hits the *spot*." He tossed the pouch aside, where it was quickly lost in the other detritus that had collected in the construction site.

She looked at him and said, "*Impundulu*?"

"The fuck do I care? Just call me Bird." He stared at Bieo while holding out a hand toward Mia. "Who's this?"

"Mia Fitzsimmons from the *Daily News*. She's embedded with the VCU, and I wanted her to meet a real—"

But Bird was backing off. "What the *hell*, motherfucker? What you doin' bringin' a *reporter* here?"

"She's one of the good ones. She's the one who covered Big Charlie."

Bird stopped backing off and looked at her. "You wrote that one, what's it—*Ladies and Gentlemen, the Bronx is Burning*?"

Mia nodded, both relieved and flattered. She actually got nominated for a couple of awards for that piece, though it didn't win anything, deemed too controversial because it didn't out-and-out condemn the vampires. "That was me."

"That was some righteous shit you wrote. Okay, fine, so what's up?"

"We've been seeing a lot of vamp-on-vamp violence, and it's looking like it's connected to the drug crews."

Bird nodded. "Yeah, that's some fucked-up shit right there. Look, I got my people, okay? We just be hangin' out and stayin' outta trouble and tryin' to find us some blood. We don't go for that New Red Coalition terrorist *bull*shit."

"So no terrorists, but you'll enforce for drug crews?"

"How we supposed to get *paid*, motherfucker?" Bird held up his hands. "Hey, I ain't goin' for that shit, but that don't mean my brothers and sisters won't. There's some *mad* cash in the game."

"Look, Bird, we've got multiple drug-related homicides committed by your brothers and sisters. I've got a bonsie and a choop killing each other in the Bronx, working for rival crews. I've got Jamaican dealers killed by hopping ghosts, two yoops killed by daks, and another bonsie and an *eretica* killing each other in Brooklyn."

Mia shot a look at Bieo, vaguely amused that nobody had come up with a good nickname for *eretica*.

Bird shrugged. "C'mon, yo, we need to eat like everybody else."

Indicating the discarded blood pouch with her head, Mia said, "Well, not *exactly* like everybody else."

"Yeah, you're funny, but shit still *costs*."

"So the pay's good enough to kill their own kind?" Mia asked.

Bird just stared at her, and Bieo also fixed her with a confused look. The latter said, "Drug dealers have been killing 'their own kind' for as long as there've been drug dealers."

"Yeah, I *know* that, Detective, that wasn't an expression of surprise. I was asking a question. Reporter, remember?"

Bird grinned. "I like her, she funny. And she gotta point. We ain't usually takin' up arms 'less it's against you motherfuckers, not our own kind. And we don't usually shit on our own. Thing is? I used to be in the game, back in the day. This ain't no drive-bys. This is up close and personal, and that only happens when the killer knows where the kill-ee's gonna be, know what I mean?"

"Intelligence leaks," Bieo said. "Happens all the time."

"Nah, not like this. What you talkin' 'bout happens every once in a while, but this? This shit's all wrong. Happenin' way too much, 'specially when crews is usin' our kind, you feel me?"

Bieo nodded. "Okay."

"That it? 'Cause I gotta bounce. Nice meetin' you, reporter lady. Keep writin' that good shit." He turned and started unbuttoning his shirt, moving back to the broken wall so he could finish undressing in private before turning back into a huge bird.

As soon as Mia arrived at the second-floor landing of the VCU tenement, Yanoff called out from across the floor. "Fitzsimmons, my office, *now!*"

All the detectives—even Trujillo, Bieo, and Thorndike, who all actually seemed to *like* her—were eyeing her as she walked across the floor toward one of the cubicle walls that separated Yanoff's desk from everyone else's, giving him a makeshift office.

As soon as Fitzsimmons entered, Yanoff pointed at a copy of today's *New York Post* on his desk. The front-page headline read GANG WAR with a picture of the crime scene from Hamilton Avenue. The subhead read, "Drug Lords Use Vampires for Mayhem."

"What do you have to say about *this*?"

Mia glanced at Yanoff, who was glaring at her with intense brown eyes. "Well, I'm surprised they didn't go for a bad pun in the headline, and I think headline writers are the only people in the world who still use *mayhem* in a sentence."

Yanoff pointed an accusatory finger at Mia. "Cut the bullshit, please. Are you responsible for this?"

"Seriously?"

"We've managed to keep this out of the press. Narcotics has been having a field day since we brought that truck driver in, and we've got several closed cases thanks to vampires killing each other. Nobody's noticed the pattern yet, so nothing in the papers—until this." He tapped his cane on the desk on top of the paper.

"Okay, first of all, did you not read the memo that says that I work for the *News*? That's the *Post*, which isn't so much a newspaper as something handy to line the litterbox with."

"Your deal says you can't reveal anything until the article's out, but that's only for your paper."

Mia just shook her head. "So I took it to my biggest competitor? On what planet does *that* make sense? Sergeant, let me be clear: I'd sooner drive a white-hot poker through my eyeball than give the *Post* an exclusive."

"So tell me how they found out about it."

"Well, they do have reporters working for them, and I have it on good authority that some of them have even achieved sentience. It's possible that one of them figured it out."

Yanoff shook his head. "Either way, this just turned into a press case. Our deal still stands. Your paper can send someone else to cover this and ask me questions I won't answer. What you see here does *not* leave your notebook until your month is up. Clear?"

"Crystal."

Mia went into the bullpen, heading for the counter that had all the caffeine fixings. Trujillo was dumping a scoopful of sugar into a coffee mug with the NYPD logo on it.

As Mia reached for a similar mug, she smirked at the detective. "You want some coffee with that sugar?"

Trujillo snorted. "Used to drink coffee black. Then I became a cop." He shook his head. "So you remind the sarge that you don't work for the *Post*?"

Mia chuckled as she poured her coffee into the mug, which she had taken the time to rinse out just in case. "Yeah, he doesn't get the whole rivals thing, does he?"

"More like he doesn't give a shit. A reporter broke the case open, which always pisses the bosses off. When the bosses get pissed, the commanders get reamed."

Nodding, Mia said, "And the abused kick downward."

Trujillo grinned under his thick black mustache. "Right. Which means you get to go home and kick your cat tonight."

Mia took a thoughtful sip of her coffee, then made a face, thinking that Trujillo had the right idea with his sugar additive. "So anybody figure out where the leak is?"

"What?"

"The leak." Mia shook her head. "Didn't Bieo tell you? Someone's letting the crews know where to strike."

"Yeah, he told me. Who gives a shit?"

Mia's eyes widened. "Excuse me?"

Trujillo shook his head. "Look, nobody in the real world gives two shits about *why*. Motive has never once helped me close a case, except maybe to point me at someone to talk to. What we do is *who* and *how*. *Why* is the perp's shrink's problem. I don't know why the vamps are killing each other in drug raids. I also don't give a shit."

"Yeah, well, I'm not a cop, I'm a journalist."

"No shit?" Trujillo grinned. "Thought you were the new secretary."

Rolling her eyes, Mia took another sip of the awful coffee.

Yanoff said, "All right, people, let's get to work!"

After the top-of-shift briefing was over, Mia went over to one of the spare computer terminals and connected to the NYPD's intranet. She had been given a temporary account with limited access—basically only to things that would be available to the general public anyhow. The intranet access mostly just meant she could see some of that stuff before it was released.

The VCU had been working with Narcotics on tracking all the violence between crews. They had seized an impressive amount of heroin and cocaine amid the dead bodies, and a lot of crews were hurting. They'd made bunches of arrests, too.

For the rest of the day, Mia made a methodical search of all the case files. She found corpses that were *impundulu* and *asansanbonsam* (both from African vampire lore), *eretica* (which was mistyped as "erotica" in more than one report) and *upierczy* (both from Russia), *chupacabra* and *loup garou* (from Latin America), *jiangshi* (China), and *dakhanavar* (Armenia).

Mia abhorred racial profiling. However, a lot of the drug dealing in town was divided up by race. The crews tended to stick with their own kind, and most of the dealing was done by African Americans, Latinos, Russians, and Chinese, with a bit by Armenians.

There was one ethnic group, however, peculiarly missing from all the reports…

Mia stared down at her tablet, scrolling through her e-mail, the late afternoon breeze blowing through her short brown hair as she sat at a table in front of the café on East 187th Street in the Bronx. An espresso sat cooling at her side, as yet untouched.

An older gentleman wearing a gray fedora, a checked button-down shirt, and a gray cardigan sat across from her. "How's your espresso?" he asked in a friendly tone.

Mia smiled and took a sip. It was not only cool enough to drink, but also akin to the nectar of the gods after swilling the sludge at VCU. "Delicious. How are you, Secondo?"

With a shrug, Secondo Amalfitano said, "Ah, the doctor keeps telling me not to smoke what I like to smoke or eat what I like to eat. I tell him, my *nonna* lived to be 102 eating what I eat."

Mia chuckled. "But not smoking what you smoke?"

Secondo chuckled right back. "No, I suppose not. So what is it you want from an old man, Mia?"

"I know you're retired, Secondo, but I'm wondering if you can tell me how business has been lately?"

"Business is business." Secondo got the attention of one of the young women waiting tables. "Cappuccino?"

The woman nodded. "You bet."

"*Grazie.*"

The waitress dashed back inside.

"My family's business has not changed, Mia. Our construction company—"

"C'mon, Secondo, cut the shit."

Secondo frowned, his wrinkled face growing a few more wrinkles. "Such language from a lady."

Mia winced. She'd been hanging out with cops too long. "I'm sorry. Look, Secondo, I know what your family business really is. I know how you got the information you gave me for those stories about corruption in the City Council and the zoning commission. I know it's because they took somebody else's bribes instead of yours—or was it that they took yours and still didn't give you the contracts?"

The frown deepened. "Mia, you are asking questions you should not ask."

"I'm a journalist, Secondo; there are no questions I shouldn't ask. And even if there were, the ones I absolutely *have* to ask are the ones that the person I'm asking doesn't want to answer." She took a sip of her espresso, and reminded herself to be careful, as this was a man who was ordering people assassinated before Mia was born. Allegedly.

"You didn't ask questions then."

"I didn't need to. And maybe I should have."

Secondo leaned back in his chair, and took the fedora off, revealing a bald crown with wisps of white hair. He set the hat down on the table and ran his hand over his head to pat down the hair that was now flying out in all directions. "In that case, Mia, perhaps you should ask the actual question you want to ask."

"Fine. There's a gang war going on, crews stealing other crews' stashes, and their vampire enforcers are killing each other. Blacks killing Latinos, Armenians killing Russians, Chinese killing Jamaicans, and so on. But I'm noticing a distinct lack of the *Cosa Nostra* there."

Shaking his head, Secondo said, "You think we're too weak to get involved, is that it?"

"That's not what I'm saying at all. I mean, you guys *are* weak, or at least weakened. *The Godfather* made you guys hip, *The Sopranos* made you obvious, and reality made you less and less relevant. But *somebody* has been feeding information to all the crews and telling them where to strike their rivals. It's chaos out there now, and I'm wondering who would benefit from that the most. And—"

A throaty chuckle built in Secondo's throat, and then it exploded into full on laughter. Then it modulated into a coughing fit, and Mia leaned forward, concerned. Secondo held up a hand, got his coughing under control, and sat back upright.

The waitress brought his cappuccino and asked, "You all right?"

He nodded. "I am fine, but could you please bring me some ice water?"

"Of course." She dashed off again.

Secondo poured a bit of sugar into his cappuccino and stirred it, making the foam atop it swirl around. "I laugh because you see but do not see. We do not wish to increase our trade in filthy poison."

Mia frowned. "But that doesn't make sense. Why cripple the crews if you don't... " She trailed off as she remembered that there were two common elements to all of what she'd seen lately. One was drugs.

She stared at Secondo. "You're going after the vampires."

"Of course. It is what we have always done. The legends of crosses and holy water defeating vampires—they are because the *Cosa Nostra* served as the warriors who battled the *strega* and *vampiro* for the Vatican."

Mia shook her head. "Sonofabitch."

"But, as you so rudely put it, we are weak. We cannot wage a full-scale war on *vampiro*, as the government has been with their soldiers. However, we may fight smaller battles along the way." Secondo stopped stirring his cappuccino and sipped it, then licked the foam off his upper lip. "You will, of course, not write of this." It wasn't a question.

"My editor is persnickety about on-the-record sources, and I'm gonna go out on a limb and say you're not willing to be quoted?"

Secondo just stared at her from over the lip of his mug, taking another sip.

"Right." She finished her espresso off. "Thanks, Secondo. It's good to see you again."

"The pleasure was mine, Mia. I have always enjoyed your company." Secondo put his mug down and stared at her intently. "I would very much hate to never enjoy it again." As Mia reached for her purse, Secondo added, "No, I will pay."

"Thank you." Rising, she offered her hand. "Take care, Secondo."

The old man took her hand and kissed the top of it. His lips felt like sandpaper, but Mia smiled gamely anyhow and pretended that Secondo didn't just threaten her life.

She walked down Arthur Avenue toward Fordham Road and the bus that would take her home. While she waited at the bus stop, she started making notes on her tablet.

The article on the VCU would get written, and it would talk about the cops she'd been hanging around with and the job they had to do, and it would talk about the gang war. And she wouldn't specify why this was happening. After all, it wasn't sourced, and besides, it would spoil the narrative. Trujillo's rant on motive would make good copy, maybe a sidebar for the article, and actually providing motive would undercut that.

Besides, the article was about a unit of the NYPD. What Secondo just told her was deep background for a news story. One she intended to write, no matter what Secondo wanted.

Or threatened.

"BLOODS"

Sam Orion Nova West-Mensch

This was playing on the radio in the burning house. The hip-hop artist was a rapper named Syphone.

This is gonna get ugly… truuust me
I'm your worst fear, brought to life right here,
    right from your nightmares
No crucifixes or holy water
Will stop me from going after your only daughter
She won't let me in, I'll muscle in
Rip blood, bone, muscle, skin
Dismember Beats limb from limb
If that's your stake, you need to raise the stakes
    to get me pinned
No man alive can cage this beast within
Blood soaked lips and machine gun clips drip with the life
    of the righteous and sinful alike
You want a monster? I'm the archetype
From darkness comes light
    and then a plunge back into darkness again
Was a starving artist until my teeths sharpness
    devoured the heartless leaving a forest
    packed with carcasses of men

The song continued to play, the pulsing beat hammering at the walls and the floors and the broken glass in all of the windows. The singer argued his point, growled his message, threw his warnings out with anger and force.

But everyone in the house was dead.

Outside, the mob ran away, laughing.

"THE LOW MAN" PT. 1

☾

Hank Schwaeble

The small float plane banked into the wind, and Faron looked down to see a brown bear on the rocky gray shore raise its snout and stare before it turned and lumbered into the dense wall of forest. His uncle's words came whispering back to him, joined by details he may or may not have filled in—the sound of the blade scraping against stone as the man spoke, lapping splashes of water behind them: *Always remember, Little Mosquito... nature thrives on violence.*

"You don't look like a professor," the pilot said, her voice loud and crackling through his headset.

"I left my corduroy sport coat with the elbow patches back in Sitka."

She seemed to smile at that, but it was hard to tell, as she wore one of those hard-to-read expressions only a woman could pull off. A little curious, a little amused. The flight had been barely twenty minutes, but the pilot had certainly made the most of it with her questions. A few comments about ferry traffic, then questions about where he lived and what he did. He only wished this leg had been the long one. An unmarked government transport had flown him from Seattle, with no other passengers on board. No commercial flights since the quarantine, so that wasn't surprising. Over three hours in a jumpseat, listening to the roar of the engines and the rush of wind, alone with his thoughts in a yawning fuselage. The military pilots stayed hidden in the cockpit, and except for a brief glimpse as they boarded, he'd never even seen them.

"I meant, you seem... young."

"So do you," he said. And she did. Red hair, some freckles across her nose. Skin very pale compared to his. A blue flight suit. War brings out the patriot in everyone.

"But I'm allowed to look young," she said. "I'm not a professor."

No, he thought. And not military, either. Private contractor of some sort. It occurred to him that maybe the small talk was a ploy, but then he pushed the notion aside. Didn't seem like there would be any point. He was asked to provide assistance, he said yes. Of course, the rules had changed. Maybe points had, too.

"Are you from here, originally? This area, I mean," the pilot asked.

"Because this is Alaska and I look like an Eskimo?"

The woman swallowed, swiveled her head. "No! I'm sorry, I didn't mean—"

"Relax. I'm just giving you a hard time. Yes. One of my great-grandfathers was a tribal chieftain who fought the Russians less than a mile from the runway where we took off."

"It wasn't how you look, I mean, you look good, what I'm trying to say is it had nothing to do with that. It's your name. Is that an Eskimo name? Is Eskimo even the right word? Is it considered offensive?"

"No, Eskimo is fine, when it applies. It's just not accurate. I'm actually Tlingit. And only half, at that. My mother was a native, but my father was from the lower forty-eight. He came here to start over, worked as a commercial fisherman."

Faron turned, peered out the window. *And to dodge the draft*, he thought to himself. A guy who'd met his mother a few years after arriving, then took off when he was still in diapers. *Well*, he mused, watching the scenery float by, *if you were going to escape, this was the place to do it*. Hills and mountains rising out of the water, rows and rows of green, white caps painting the highest peaks. A good place to get lost.

He started to say something about the countryside, realized he was in danger of being chatty, a kid on a first date. He thought about how much he'd already said, how eagerly he'd volunteered information, and felt a bit goofy about it. But he couldn't help it. Redheads did that to him. There was one in high school he'd followed around like a puppy. Same curly hair, same nose freckles. So unlike his light mocha complexion and straight dark hair. Opposites attract, he supposed. Sometimes.

"And you're a professor. What do you teach? Or is your college one that's been closed?"

"It's been zoned, but there is still a light schedule of classes. My field is ethno-archaeology."

"Oh, you're definitely too young for whatever that is."

The plane began to descend. The pilot pulled the throttle back to idle and eased the plane down, pulling back on the yoke a few feet above the water and holding a glide until the pontoons skimmed the surface. The plane settled and slowed, and the pilot gave some power to the propeller to steer it toward a clearing with a dock where Faron saw at least two men waiting near a black SUV. White men, the both of them, and given the way they dressed, he was pretty sure they weren't Alaskans: their jackets overpriced tourist brands, brightly colored, probably bought that morning. He wasn't sure why he had been expecting someone native to be there to greet him, but he had been.

"And you really don't know what this is about?" he said, repeating the first question he'd asked her, shortly after takeoff.

She shook her head. "My job is to deliver you. They don't tell me much more than where and when. I'm lucky if I get the who."

Faron nodded. The men near the dock stood watching as the plane coasted the last few yards, engine noise reduced to a sputtering hum with the throttle pulled back again. No sign of conversation between them, two sets of eyes, one behind sunglasses, following the plane and nothing else. The guy on the left was tall, balding; the other average, with wavy brown hair. Matching windbreakers and dark slacks. Large black shades on the tall one, tortoise shell eyeglasses on the other. Nothing threatening about their demeanor, but nothing friendly, either. All business.

The right pontoon bumped against the dock, and the pilot flipped a few switches before pulling back on the fuel mixture. The engine cut out, and the propeller stuttered to a stop.

"But, you know," the pilot said, "I'm supposed to make another pick-up, then I'm probably going to be giving you another ride. So maybe you can tell me all about it when we get back to civilization."

Faron smiled. "What's your name?"

"Katrina," she said.

"You got it, Katrina," he said, thinking, *even if I have to make something up so it sounds interesting.*

An eagle soared past, barely a hundred feet overhead. The tall man stayed near the SUV and watched it as the shorter one made his way toward the plane. He was holding a container of bottled water in one hand, still full. Faron opened the side door and used the pontoon to step onto the dock.

"Professor Younger," the man said. It wasn't a question.

"Yunge. And I was the last time I checked."

The man tucked the bottle of water under his arm, slipped his hand into the pocket of his coat, and removed a small cellophane bag. He clawed a finger into the bag and pulled out a large white capsule. He pinched the capsule between his thumb and forefinger, replaced the bag in his pocket, then held out the bottle and the pill, one in each hand.

"Please take this."

Faron stared at the pill, then at the bottle, then at the pill again. "Why?"

"Because I'm telling you to."

He looked back over his shoulder at the pilot, who looked interested in what was going on but didn't show any indication there was much she could do if she wanted to. "And if I refuse?"

The man said nothing, arms still extended. Beyond him, the tall man continued to lean back against the SUV, eyes on the sky. It was, Faron noted, the kind of forced disinterest one might expect from someone contemplating a kill. No attempt at intimidation, no threat. It was the pill, or a bullet, and neither gave any hint they cared which one he picked.

He took the pill using the same two fingers the man giving it to him had, rolled it over to get a look at it, then popped it into his mouth. It had the texture of a vitamin, tasted like a penny. He unscrewed the bottle cap, swigged a mouthful of water, and swallowed. The lump took its time making its way down his throat.

"Offering me the choice of blue or red would have at least shown a sense of humor."

The man reached into a different pocket, this one in his trousers, and removed a penlight. He stepped forward, gestured to Faron with it to show his intentions, then shone it in Faron's eyes, first one, then the other.

"Have you ever been diagnosed with a gastric ulcer?

Faron blinked away the flashbulbs popping in his eyes. "No."

"Have you taken any aspirin in the last twelve hours?"

"No."

The man checked his watch, counting off digits in his head, and after a prolonged pause, used the light on Faron's eyes all over again.

"Come with me," the man said, placing the penlight back into his pocket and gesturing to the pilot that she could go.

Faron watched him start toward the SUV, then began to follow. He glanced back once at the pilot, who smiled and shrugged before nodding a good-bye.

The tall man opened the rear driver side door to the SUV and waited as his colleague circled the vehicle and got in the front.

Faron paused before getting in, peered into the black ovals of the tall man's sunglasses. They stared back without any indication the eyes behind them were even looking at him.

The door shut after him, and the tall man got in behind the steering wheel and pushed a button to start the ignition.

"Would you mind—"

"Seat belt," the man in the passenger seat said, vaguely gesturing with his finger over the seat.

Faron pulled the seat belt over his shoulder. The driver shifted the transmission, and the vehicle crunched forward over a gravelly unpaved road. "Would you mind telling me what this is about? I've traveled quite a long way. I don't think it's asking too much."

"You volunteered."

"But not to be kept in the dark this long. If the request hadn't come from Luther Swann, I wouldn't have agreed."

"Your cooperation is appreciated, Professor, if that's what you want to know. You'll see why you're here soon enough."

"That's it? That's all I'm going to get?"

The man said nothing. He adjusted his glasses and shifted his gaze toward the windshield.

Cooperation, he thought. This hadn't been a request—it had been an order to report, couched in government politeness. If he hadn't agreed, the guy with the car and armored escort that met him on campus would have brought him by force. It had been foolish not to have realized it right away, to have deceived himself like that. This was war. The catch-all justification for everything. The bigger the war, the bigger the everything. And this one was global. Everything was the biggest it had ever been.

Faron looked out at the water, watched it recede behind trees as the SUV veered through dense woodland. They hit a bump, and the bottle sloshed in his lap.

"Can you at least tell me what that pill was?"

The man with the glasses turned to look over the seat, stared a few seconds before speaking. "A concentrated dosage of a chemical agent. It acts as a catalytic when paired with the appropriate catalyst, targeting the medullary chemoreceptor trigger zone."

"Medullary trigger zone? You were trying to induce a seizure?"

"Vomiting, Professor, merely vomiting. And only when paired with the specific catalyst."

"What catalyst?"

The man studied him, expression blank, but incredulous. "I hope you're not really that obtuse, doctor." He turned to face the windshield. "Blood. What else?"

———•———

The gravel road followed the shoreline for almost a half mile before winding inland. Faron inhaled the scent of pine, the briny odor of kelp, and the earthy aroma of the moss that blanketed the standing armies of spruce that quickly gave way to towering monuments of cedar. He'd almost forgotten how it felt to be immersed in these bastions of calm: the throngs of enormous old growth; the cool, misty layers of flora; the gentle trickle of rainwater cascading downhill from pool to pool. This was the Alaska he knew, the Alaska that was a part of him. Sacred rainforest. A temple of plenty. The one he'd left behind. The one he'd never allowed himself to miss.

The path grew rougher, snaking around hulking trunks, crossing shallow streams. The SUV crunched and splashed for over a mile, the speedometer barely reaching ten, then it curled around a giant yellow cedar. Ahead, straddling the path, or what was left of one, was an enormous tent. Another SUV similar to the one Faron was in sat in front of it, parked sideways, like a road block. Two men stood before it, each wearing identical tac gear—helmet with tinted visor, flak jacket over a black, long-sleeve uniform shirt, black jump pants and black boots. Both held what appeared to Faron as rather sophisticated-looking military rifles across their chest.

A little too sophisticated.

"Exactly what branch of government are you with?" Faron said.

Neither of his escorts responded. The SUV slowed to a stop, and the driver shifted it into park and shut it off. He got out and opened the door for Faron, who hesitated, glancing at the armed sentries, before figuring at this point he didn't have much choice. Both men accompanying him exchanged nods with the guards as they passed, and one of them pulled aside a section of canvas to make an entrance for him.

The inside of the tent was cavernous, but every square foot looked like it was being put to use. There were rows of tables set up with laptops and what Faron took to be communication equipment, maybe radar, though he couldn't be sure. A large piece of clear plexiglass stood near the center of the tent, with a diagram of Alaska and parts of Canada on one half, the chain of islands surrounding where they were on the other. Stickers and symbols and concentric rings drawn with colored markers were in abundance, along with some scribbling along the edges that Faron couldn't read. He counted six people on their feet, four men and two women, plain blue shirts with empty epaulets, darker blue pants, all milling about, leaning over shoulders, pointing at screens. Another eight in similar garb were seated at the tables, taking direction and punching keyboards. In the center of the activity, staring at the plexiglass map, was a man in a uniform. He was medium height, a bit sinewy, but solid, with broad shoulders. Salt and pepper hair. Light skin, and bone structure that smacked of Scandinavian blood somewhere in the mix. The uniform was gray, with matching shirt and trousers, but bore no insignia. Black boots buffed to a high gloss. From the moment Faron saw him, there was no doubt who was in charge.

"What's the story behind your name?" the man said.

It took Faron a moment to realize the man was talking to him. He hadn't turned around, hadn't stopped studying the diagram in front of him. But no one else reacted, and Faron's escorts stared mutely as if also awaiting his response.

"Excuse me?"

"Your name." The man scrutinized the panel for another moment, committing something to memory, then turned and made eye contact. "Surely you don't expect me to believe you've never had anyone ask?"

Gray eyes, same as the uniform. Not cold, or cruel, but there was something about them that made Faron's breath almost catch. It wasn't what they hid, more like what they didn't seem to hide. He had to shift his gaze to avoid peering directly into them.

"My mother," he said. "She loved country music. I guess with my father's name being pronounced the way it is… " He shrugged. "She was a fan."

The man appraised him briefly, mulling over the information. He nodded. "I suppose some things are as obvious as they seem. Even if that wasn't his real name. Your father, I mean."

Faron let that settle in. He'd considered the possibility many times, but had never had anyone else suggest it.

"It was real enough to my mom."

"His actual name was Younger. Edward Younger. He killed a man in a bar fight in Cleveland. Managed to flee the jurisdiction. It was a lot easier to disappear back then, start fresh. He used the name Earl Yunge because he remembered it from a classmate in grade school who was killed in a car accident one summer break. Probably heard it in alphabetical roll calls, never forgot. Same initials. He died not too long ago. In Philadelphia. Was using a different name by then."

Faron looked around the tent, held the gaze of the men who brought him there for a moment. "Will someone please tell me what's going on? Who are you people?"

The man with the gray eyes stepped closer, held out a hand. Faron watched it, like a bayonet aimed at his midsection. He shook it warily. The grip was firm, like a vice.

"My name is Prescott. I could apologize, pretend I'm concerned with what you think, comment about my lack of manners, but none of that would be sincere. I am going to guess you'd prefer I respect you with directness, rather than soothe you with blandishments."

"I'd settle for you answering my question."

"Let's just say I command a rapid response unit. Civilian, of course. Sort of a forward operational reconnaissance team. We deploy, assess, report."

"And what are you responding to?"

"In a moment." He reached over and picked up a clipboard, flipped up a cover sheet. "There's one piece of information we haven't been able to come by. Or, I should say, one missing piece that bugs me. You went straight into the army out of high school, received a commandant's award in boot camp, breezed through Basic Airborne. Base Combatants Champion two years in a row. Your RASP score was... impressive, to say the least. Graduated at the top your class in RIP, and were number two at Ranger School. By all accounts, a superstar in the making, if not already one."

Prescott lowered the clipboard, raised his eyes. A penetrating gaze, straight into Faron's.

"So tell me, why did you get out when your hitch was up? You were offered a chance to finish your degree on the Army's dime, promised OCS if you wanted it. And with the particular demographic qualities you brought to the table, you were looking at a very promising career. Below-the-zone promotions at least until light colonel."

"With all due respect, Mr. Prescott, what the hell does it matter to you? You expect me to answer a question like that when I don't even know why I'm here?"

"Yes, as a matter of fact, I do. I'll say 'please' if it will help."

Faron took in a breath. The tent smelled. Mildewy, gamy, fumy. A whiff of fuel. Something else, too, something rotten. He glanced at some of the other faces, a few of them briefly looking his way. His two escorts watched him with the same apathetic gazes they had from the beginning, though the one with the glasses did show a hint of curiosity in the tilt of his head.

"I reassessed my priorities. Decided just because I was good at it, didn't mean it was what I wanted to do. And I suppose I didn't appreciate being a political trophy, either. The Eskimo soldier command wanted to show off to everyone, whether I was Eskimo or not."

"So you became the Eskimo professor who wasn't really an Eskimo that your university administration showed off to everyone instead." Prescott tapped the clipboard, flipped the cover sheet closed. "Am I supposed to believe a man of your background, someone in the prime of his life, has watched an existential conflict involving the fate of mankind unfold around him and just decided he was going to sit it out?"

"Even if I had the power to control what you believe, I don't care enough to try."

"Good answer! For the record, I think you're full of crap, but I also think you've told me what I wanted to know."

Faron said nothing. He hadn't lied. Not exactly. He still remembered the day his sense of self shifted, the day another member of his battalion made a remark that jarred him, a comment about how the brass always talked about leadership and management skills, when really all they were doing was training men to kill people. He didn't know why it had struck him, a statement so obvious, but it had. Okay, so maybe he had lied. The truth just didn't seem believable.

And as for the war, he had his reasons, and he'd be damned if he was going to explain them.

Prescott gestured to the tall man who'd driven the SUV, handed him the clipboard. "Now, I believe you expressed some interest in knowing why you're here."

The man turned and headed to the far side of the tent. He stopped and looked back, an expectant set to his face. He reached toward the hanging edge of canvas, waiting until Faron approached before pulling it back.

"This, Professor. *This* is why you're here."

A flash of daylight in Faron's eyes, and he clenched his lids a few times until his vision adjusted. Beyond the tent, the path opened into a circular clearing. Before he could focus, a breeze swirled, and the smell hit him.

Gagging, he covered his mouth and looked. Not much made sense. He found himself wandering closer. Slow, staggering steps into the clearing.

Armed men, more helmeted soldiers in black tac gear—not soldiers, really, more like paramilitary sentries—held positions along the edge, scanning the woods, rifles at the ready. There were bodies, maybe a dozen. The skins were removed, the hides stretched across traditional wooden hunting frames and placed at rough intervals along the perimeter of the clearing. The skulls, eyes round and staring, meat and tendons still overlaying the cheeks and jaws, formed stacks in the shape of a pyramid, while torsos, exposed ribcages still housing organs, sat upon pikes. On the far side of the clearing, detached limbs zigzagged end to end from one side to the other in some sort of pattern. Beyond that, a small cabin was recessed along the tree line.

The sight was so overwhelming, he almost didn't notice the centerpiece. When he did, his eyes climbed it's length.

"A totem," he whispered.

"Yes," Prescott said.

Faron flinched, not realizing the man was right next to him, practically brushing his arm.

"Who did this?"

"Well, Professor, I was hoping we might explore that question together."

"I thought this part of Alaska was a VF zone," Faron said, mopping his face, squinting in the light as the sun hovered over the forest in front of him. "Isn't it the only state with more free zones than red zones?"

"Yes, that's what they say. Although the state as a whole is still under general quarantine. That's why I'm here." He took a few steps forward, held out a palm toward the huge carved pole in the center of the clearing. "What can you tell me about this?"

"It's a traditional totem. Large, meaning it's intended to denote something significant. Probably a story pole, but it's hard to be sure."

"What does it mean to you, when you read it?"

Faron shook his head. "That's not how it works. Totems aren't readable. These images aren't like hieroglyphics. The symbols can usually be discerned, but what they symbolize was historically private. Known only to the artisan and the people at the dedication ceremony."

"Come now, surely this must mean something to you?"

"I don't… Typically, they tell family histories, stories. Sometimes they're a means to relate myths, or to serve as a memorial for someone. Occasionally, they're used to ridicule people, to shame them. They were sort of like billboards, ways for families to brag or posture or warn others. Commemorate an event, maybe."

"You're telling me that even for you, an academic of native Alaskan descent who grew up here and teaches the stuff, this holds no particular meaning? I suggest you take a closer look."

"I'm not an expert on totems, Mr. Prescott. There are dozens, probably many dozens, of people in Sitka or Juneau who know far more about them than me. I doubt anyone—" Faron let the thought evaporate before finishing, his next words dissipating under the intensity of Prescott's stare. He buried his face in his coat to take a few breaths and closed his eyes before stepping forward to more closely inspect the graven shapes in the wood.

"The top is a raven. That would indicate the particular clan to which the family or person commissioning it belonged. Below that is a woman, with child. Traditional depiction. You can see her arms enfolding her womb. Below that, an unknown creature. A bat, maybe. Or an otter. Mythological creatures, even made-up ones, were often included. The fish is undoubtedly a salmon. And then there's a man's face. It looks Tlingit."

"That's your tribe, isn't it, Dr. Younger? Your mother's?"

"The name is Yunge. And yes, it is. Was hers, too. As is the case with a fairly large percentage of the population in this region; a region where I haven't lived in almost fifteen years, I might add."

"And your mother's family, your family… the symbol of your house is a raven, correct?"

"Yes, but—"

"How many Tlingit are there, Professor? How many live in this stretch of territory? Fifteen thousand? Twenty? Given your ancestry, surely you're aware that there has not been a single case of vampirism reported among them. Not one. Doesn't that strike you as odd? Odd enough to warrant attention?"

"What the hell are you getting at?"

"Tell me about the low man on the totem pole, Professor. What does he signify?"

Faron held the man's look, wanting to say enough was enough and demand answers, but sensing it was best to tread carefully for the moment.

"It's hard to say," he said, forcing himself to loosen his jaw. "The idea of the totem pole low man being the least important, or of low status, is a myth, the result of Westerners confusing ridicule or shame poles with more common types. In actuality, the low man is most likely to be the most important of all, the person of honor or status, the one the pole is about or is dedicated to."

"You misunderstood. I meant, tell me about *this* low man on this pole."

Faron scratched the back of his head, eyeballed Prescott for a long moment before looking at the pole again. He took another step toward it.

"It's obviously a man's face. A bit more detailed than normal, more life-like than others I've seen, but it would be imposs—"

The face peered back. Faron slid to a point squarely in front of it, stopping when it seemed to be looking directly at him.

"That can't be."

"Really? Even though it clearly is? Why do you think we tracked you down?"

The words came out more like an admission of defeat than an answer. "Because Swann recommended me."

"Come now, Professor. You're too smart to have actually believed that, aren't you? You've met the man, what? Twice? Three times, over the course of how long? Seven years? Academic conferences?"

"You're saying you were able to identify me from that?" Faron said, pointing at the carving. "Even if there's a resemblance, it's not like a photograph. And there's no way that's me, anyway."

"Oh, you're right, we'd have never been able to track you down from just that, even though I'd say the likeness is quite good. But as to whether it really is you, not all the clues are so subtle."

Prescott dipped his head, and Faron followed the line of his sight beyond the pole to where the limbs were strewn. He shot another look at Prescott, who nodded for him to take a look, then he moved toward them. He stopped when he was almost past the pole, the closer vantage point making the shapes more obvious. He swallowed, rubbed his eyes.

The limbs were bent to varying degrees at the elbows or knees, arranged to make letters. The letters were arranged to make words. Two words.

Faron Younger.

"Doesn't exactly require a Ph.D.," Prescott said.

Faron kept staring. "I didn't even know that was my father's real name until you told me a few minutes ago."

"Ah, but that doesn't change who you are, does it?"

"Why are you acting like I have something to do with this? I have no idea who put this here, or why."

"I'm going to venture that you do, Professor. At least the second part. You just may not realize it."

Faron held the man's eyes for a long moment, then turned his head to scan the clearing. "Why here? Why now?"

"That's what we'd like to know."

"No. I mean you. Why are you here? This island, it's remote, used for hunting and fishing, just like myriad others up and down the coast, most within sight of others, and none of them populated. But with the quarantine, travel in Alaska has been limited to locals. No one is likely to have found this for weeks, months, maybe longer. These are fresh kills, a day old at the most, and you have to have been camped here almost as long. So my question is, why? Why here? Why now?"

"You're very perceptive. Observant. Not all academics are."

"Perceptive enough to know you're not going to tell me, is that it?"

"Something like that. You know the drill. Operational security, etc., etc."

"Yes, I know the drill. I also know that you should be more worried than you are."

"My detail is well armed."

"But that didn't stop this from happening, did it?"

Prescott said nothing. He stared back, one arched eyebrow offered as an invitation to continue.

"That's the only thing I can think of that explains your presence so quickly—you, or some of your men—were already here. And well armed is an understatement. If I'm not mistaken, your security is carrying

XM25s. That's next-generation military hardware, and as far as I know, it's only been issued as prototypes, for field testing. The fact that your guys are toting around stuff like that before anyone else has them, combined with the anonymous uniforms, tells me you're a Memo 7 contractor. Which we all know just means many of your team are spec ops that have been technically discharged so the government can maintain they haven't deployed active-duty military personnel to wherever you're doing your thing. Sort of like bombing Laos."

The breeze carried the stench again, but this time Faron didn't gag. He kept a steady gaze, letting his words sink in. He wasn't as certain about the allegation as he was pretending, but he was certain enough. There had been a number of executive orders issued by the president since the V-Event, orders delegating power to the DHS Secretary to issue directives blandly called Memorandums of Authority. Memo 7 was the one people in the know whispered about. While many governors had declared martial law for certain regions, and National Guard troops had been federalized in several states, there was increasing pressure from Congress to limit actual military teams to places where a federal security emergency had been declared. Many considered Memo 7 to be martial law by other means.

"Okay, so you're even more clever than I gave you credit for. I applaud your wits. But frankly, Professor, you need to start thinking outside the box."

"I told you, I have no idea what this means."

"Try harder. Let's start with the totem. Your best interpretation, given what you see."

"There's no real way to… " Faron paused.

"What? What is it?"

"I just… "

"Tell me what you're thinking."

"This looks like it may have been a potlatch. Or was going to be."

"Now we're getting somewhere. Keep going."

"A potlatch is a ceremony, which I'm guessing by the look on your face you already knew."

"Consider me your pupil."

"They're sort of a like a festival. A community gathering. Totems were often dedicated at them, if the family was wealthy enough. They were ways of commemorating events, the upper classes used them to give gifts, sometimes lavish ones, to others. As a display of status."

"And the bodies?"

"I don't know." He turned his head, taking in the mounted torsos one at a time. There were canvas tarps near each of them. "Sometimes animals were involved, but never for slaughter. These weren't religious ceremonies. They were more like birthday or graduation parties. Those tarps were likely meant to cover them, until the unveiling."

"A way to celebrate, then. And why do you suppose death would be celebrated?"

"Like I said, I don't know."

"Ah, but you say it like you do know."

"No, I really don't."

"But you have an idea."

"I have a thought. And one I have a hard time thinking is possible."

"Don't be shy, spit it out."

"The bodies."

"Yes?"

"If it was supposed to be a potlatch, or a mock potlatch—" He swept his gaze around the clearing. "—maybe the bodies are the gifts."

———•◦•———

"We should call Swann."

Faron was sitting at a table in the tent, staring at a device in the corner. It looked robotic, a flat machine with aerodynamic lines, a twin set of turbines. It sat atop some sort of canister.

He shifted his attention to the men around him, skipping from face to face. Prescott sat directly across from him, the two men who'd met him at the plane behind Prescott, standing. A pair of those sentries in black tac gear on each side. The rest of Prescott's personnel—the men and women in bland blue—kept working at their tasks, some at screens, others looking like they were comparing data. All of them seemed a bit scared. Furtive glances, controlled expressions. People immersing themselves in a job to avoid thinking too much about what they were doing.

Or to make sure it *looked* like they weren't thinking too much about what they were doing.

"He may be able to lend some insight," he continued. "He knows more about this stuff than anyone, I'm sure."

Half of Prescott's mouth curled down, undecided as to whether to frown all the way. "You're supposed to be the expert on native peoples, aren't you?"

"This goes way beyond any expertise I may have. What was Swann's take? I mean, what did he say when you told him about my… about the name Younger being spelled out and everything?"

"I think it's best we focus on you and what you know, Professor."

Faron slumped back in his seat. "He doesn't know anything about this, does he? You never even spoke to him."

"Come now, Dr. Younger. Don't look so indignant. We're involved in a war for the survival of our species, yours and mine. In case you hadn't noticed."

"It's *Yunge*. And I guess dropping his name seemed like an easy way to get me to come."

"Would you have preferred we apprehended you? Put a bag over your head and thrown you in the back of a van?"

"The truth would have been a novel approach."

"Well, this isn't a novel. This is the real world. And in the real world, any VRMH in a quarantine zone makes it a Memo 7 issue, which means my team has authority to investigate."

"VRMH?"

"Vampire-Related Mass Homicide."

The term seemed to repeat itself in Faron's head. "How do you know?"

"Excuse me?"

"How do you know it's vampire-related? I saw nothing out there that couldn't have been done by a handful of people. Maybe just one, if he or she were ambitious. Ambitious, and sick." He leaned forward across the table and peered directly into Prescott's eyes, fighting the feeling those eyes conjured. "There are still plenty of garden-variety human beings like that in the world."

Prescott spread his lips into a flat, thin smile, one that didn't reach his eyes. "What I would like from you, Professor, is fewer questions and more answers. Let's start by you telling me your impressions of that totem, knowing what you do now about your name, so colorfully arranged next to it."

"I told you, totem poles are not like cryptograms, or ideographs adorning the walls of a pyramid. You either know what it is, because you were there at the ceremony when it was explained, or you don't."

"Think, Professor. Let your mind search for what you're not seeing."

Faron inhaled deeply, the pungent smell of gasoline stinging his nostrils. His eyes drifted over to the machine in the corner. A large fuel tank sat not too far away. At least it was better than the putrid stink on the other side of the canvas.

"The raven on top," he said. "We can assume that refers to the clan, the family."

"Okay."

"The woman beneath it, she is with child. So it might be celebrating a birth."

The man clapped his hands together, rubbing them against each other audibly. "This is more like it. Go on."

"The creature below her, it could possibly be a land otter."

"Land otter?"

"It's a mythical treatment. The Tlingit word is 'kushtaka.' Roughly translated, it means 'otter man of the land.'"

"See? Now we're getting somewhere. What do you know about them?"

"I said that image *might* portray one. They're just a popular native legend. Stories vary. In some tales, they're shapeshifters, but the people who've actually claimed to see them describe them as hairy people. The hair, I suppose, reminds them of an otter. But a lot of it is suggestion. People see a bear stand up through some distant trees. In northern California, the first thought might be Bigfoot. In southeastern Alaska, they might think *kushtaka*. They're just legends."

"Do I really need to point out why that kind of thinking no longer applies, Doctor?"

Faron sighed. Hard to deny that one.

"No. I suppose not. But everything we know about the… about what's going on in the world indicates it's genetic. The *kushtaka* myth doesn't lend itself to that kind of thing. The stories are all over the place, and quite fantastical. At the core, they're sort of hairy monsters who lure people to secluded areas and attack them or imprison them."

"Imprison them? Now, why would they go and do a thing like that?"

"It's not clear. The legends were always vague. You have to remember, these were cautionary tales, like something out of the Brothers Grimm. Used by parents to warn children not to venture deep into the woods by themselves, or to stay clear of the water."

"So, you could say they're predators. That regular human beings are their prey."

"I suppose. In a manner of speaking."

"Which means they could have imprisoned people as a food source."

"Why do I get the impression you know something you're not telling me?"

"Any other legends like that, Professor? Do the Tlingit or maybe some neighboring tribes have any other creatures in their mythology of that sort?"

"You're asking me if there is a Tlingit vampire myth." He paused. "I can only think of one."

Prescott spread his hands, palms up, before lowering them to the table.

"The sister of a tribal chief once wanted a child, but could not have one. So she—"

"Why?" Prescott said.

"Excuse me?"

"You said she couldn't have one. Why not?"

"It was never made clear."

Prescott nodded, thinking for a moment, then gestured for him to continue.

"So she gave up hope of being a mother, the thing she wanted more than anything, but one day was delighted to have found herself pregnant."

"How?"

"Do I really need to explain the process?"

"I think you'd be surprised at how well I understand reproduction. But what I want to know is, what made her suddenly able to become pregnant?"

"It's never revealed. These are just tribal folktales, handed down as part of an oral tradition, not works of literature. And certainly not historical accounts to be taken literally."

Prescott eased back in his seat, drumming his fingertips against the table. "Go on."

"According to the story, the child grew unnaturally fast. He was born within weeks, covered with hair, a mouthful of fangs for teeth."

"Interesting. Not to be taken literally, of course, but fascinating nonetheless. What happened then?"

"Word of the child's peculiarities swept through the village as he grew. There were whispers of him hunting forest creatures and killing them just for the thrill. Accusations that he was responsible for the disappearance of other children, allegations that he not only killed them, but drank their blood. The villagers claimed he was not a child at all, but an evil spirit. A spirit that relished the taste of human blood more than anything else."

Faron noticed his audience had grown. The pseudo-military technocrats had slowed to a halt, listening to his story.

"But he was the chief's nephew, so no one dared touch him. Eventually, however, too many people disappeared, and the child was no longer a child, but a fully grown man, and the chief knew he must cast him from the tribe. But the man-child refused to leave, baring his fangs in a smile, and looked like he was about to attack. The chief drew a knife and tried to cut him, but he would not bleed.

"The child was too big and too strong for the chief to defeat, but the chief managed to keep him from sinking those fangs into his neck. They struggled all night, until finally they rolled near a raging campfire, and the chief managed to push him into it."

Prescott stared past him, over a shoulder, thinking. "A baptism," he said.

"I don't understand," Faron said. "What do you mean?"

"Nothing. The chief threw his nephew into the fire. Then what?"

"The child burst into flames, crackling like wood, and yelled that he could not be gotten rid of so easily. '*I'll drink your blood for a thousand years,*' is what he supposedly said. Then the flames consumed him and a huge cloud of smoke rose from the fire, and every ash that floated away became a mosquito, which is why they drink blood to this day."

"And what happens at the end of the thousand years?"

"Excuse me?"

"He said, 'I'll drink your blood for a thousand years.' What then?"

"Look, mister or colonel or commander or whatever you go by, this is just the native equivalent of a bedtime story. It's like telling children thunder is the angels bowling. Insects have been around for a hell of a lot longer than a thousand years, in case you hadn't noticed."

Prescott nodded, lips pressed tight. "Little Mosquito."

"What?"

"That was your nickname growing up, wasn't it? 'Little Mosquito'?"

Faron paused. His mind raced, trying to process too much. The air inside the tent suddenly grew thick, the surrounding sounds distant, like he was submerged.

"How could you possibly know that?"

Before Prescott could respond—if he was going to, Faron wasn't sure—one of the men clad in tac gear came into the tent. The man approached the table and leaned close, mouth not far from Prescott's ear, covering the flexible boom mike on his helmet with his gloved hand.

A few nods, eyes narrowing intermittently, then Prescott dropped his hands onto the table and pushed away.

"Alright, Professor. Hold that thought." The man stood and gestured for Faron to do the same. "There's something else I want you to see. It will answer a lot of your questions." He looked around at the people populating the tent. "The rest of you, keep things on schedule."

A second ticked past, then another, then finally Faron rose, taking his time, eyes snapping mental pictures of everyone in the room, what their positions were, how far away, general state of readiness. The guys in tac gear were the ones he made sure to mark in his head, exactly what combination of moves he'd need to apply, in what order. It had taken him years to break himself of that habit, but now he welcomed it, felt the warmth fill him, like an old but well-preserved cigarette in the pocket of a coat. A small measure of control, or at least the illusion of it.

"If you're ready to begin sharing, let's start with how you know so much about me," he said.

"We'll get to that. And other things." Prescott moved toward the split in the tent canopy, but turned back when he reached it, stepping aside like a maitre d' as he held the flap back. "Like how I know this is VR."

The breeze had picked up, and Faron felt the first chill against his face since arriving. The sun was low, dipping below the tree line. He scanned the surrounding forest. It had to be after nine p.m.

Someone had picked up the tarps and draped them over the bodies, hiding them from view.

"With carrion like that, your men need to keep an eye out for bears. Covering them won't help. A brown bear has a better nose than a bloodhound."

"I can assure you, Professor, the danger is manageable."

Faron said nothing. He followed Prescott across the clearing, his two escorts from earlier, tall and short, falling in behind them, along with one of the tac gear mercs he started mentally tagging as sentries. They headed toward the cabin.

"A hunting lodge," Faron said. "Gone to seed. They're not uncommon on these islands."

It was heavy log construction, the forest surrounding it a mix of lush growth and felled, rotting logs, furred with moss. The cycle of life, Faron reminded himself. Hundreds of years of growth, decades of decomposition, new germination dependent on the decay. Life, death, and renewal. No life without death. No death without life.

Prescott bounced his eyebrows. "Yes. If not used, things can be easily forgotten."

In front of the structure, a large tripod of thick branches, ten feet across at the base, and taller than Faron, pointed to the sky. The center was packed with smaller branches, twigs, and woodshavings. A fire stack.

"That looks new," Faron said, slowing. "Like it was made today."

"So it would seem."

They stepped onto the porch. Faron's eyes drifted back to the teepee-shaped collection of wood. Prescott exchanged a few words with one of the men standing guard, who handed him a small jar. He twisted the jar open and scraped a finger through its contents. He made a wiping gesture with his finger under his nose like a demonstration, not actually touching anything, and held the jar out to Faron.

"You may want to try a dab of this."

Faron took the jar and peered into it. The fumes assaulted his nostrils, forcing him to pull it away. Menthol. Very concentrated.

"I'm good."

"Humor me," Prescott said, hand on the door, waiting for Faron to follow his instruction. "This will go much more smoothly if you do."

Faron stepped across the threshold. His head grew light from the vapors invading his nostrils. He braced himself for a stench. Nothing. Just the menthol fumes, exciting his nasal passages, burning his sinuses.

His vision adjusted, and Faron saw the cabin was all but empty of furniture. A bare, single room. A lone man sat in the middle. He was strapped to a wooden chair with buckled leather restraints. The man was wizened, elderly. He raised tired eyes that flashed briefly to life when he blinked. Familiar eyes. Familiar flash.

"I am sorry, nephew," the man said. "These men are insane."

There were two sentries in the room, rifles across their chests. Behind him, the tall man and the one with glasses, the ones he still thought of as his escorts, filed in. The one with glasses circled around the small room and came to a stop near the farthest sentry.

"We secured the prisoner as instructed," the sentry closest to Prescott said.

"I can see that. And the guests?"

"Ferries should begin arriving in three hours. Sir, I'd like to talk to you in private."

"Yes, yes—about your concerns." Prescott turned to Faron, eyes practically rolling. "Newbies. Always questioning authority. Check-in with so-and-so this, regulations that, chain of command, blah blah blah. Makes you wonder how you're supposed to ever get anything done, doesn't it?"

"Just what the hell is going on here?" Faron said.

Prescott raised an arm, extending it like a curator in front of a prized exhibit, and smiled. "What's going on is the future."

Still smiling, he spun himself around, whipping his arm in a level arc, fingers tight together and flat. The end of his hand slashed the throat of the sentry he'd been speaking with. The sentry's hands shot to his neck, blood pumping out between his fingers, wet sounds gurgling out his mouth.

Before Faron could react, the short guy with the glasses grabbed the other sentry from behind, pulling his head to the side and ripping a chunk of his neck out with his teeth. Long, sharp teeth.

The first sentry dropped to his knees, hands still crossed over his throat, then toppled onto his face. The other one made a series of muffled cries, flinging his fists back, grasping and clawing at the face latched onto his neck.

Knowing the other was beyond help, Faron sprang toward the sentry being bitten. But he found his body stuck in place when he tried to move, stopped cold. The taller of his escorts had clamped an arm down across his neck, a large hand locked around his bicep. The grip was strong, immobilizing. His mind groped for what to do, how to react. Something was wrong, something more than rust.

Heel stomp down the shin, elbow to the ribs, inside of palm to opponent's elbow, step and twist.

The heel of his shoe flailed to find the other man's knee, his leg stabbing to each side of it. The elbow strike was slow and weak. Faron pressed his palm up against the man's arm at the bend, failed to budge it. It felt like iron.

"A DAY IN THE LIFE" PT. 1

Jonathan Maberry

Cedar Streams, New Jersey

V era Brookins always wore a kerchief and sunglasses to the supermarket. She knew it made her look funny. Like Don Draper's wife on *Mad Men*, except not skinny, blonde, or pretty. Retro, she supposed. A sixties housewife out to do some shopping. The kerchief hiding a fresh hairdo or curlers, the sunglasses hiding a black eye or bloodshot vodka eyes.

None of which was really the case. Not for Vera.

She had no husband or boyfriend. Not even an abusive jackass, one with a heavy hand. She was alone and had been for two years. The sunglasses hid something else. So did the kerchief.

Not style changes or shame.

Shameful changes. Not her words. That was how the minister at Third Presbyterian referred to it. Speaking not to her, but in general to anyone in the community who had been marked by the Devil. Anyone who had transformed into sons or daughters of Cain.

Like that.

Bullshit, but said with a lot of fire and brimstone. And believed by nearly everyone in church. Which was a big chunk of the people in Cedar Streams.

So, Vera hid the tufted ears and the red eyes and did what she could to pass for the person she'd been before the minister told her she was a monster.

"THE LOW MAN" PT.2

☾

Hank Schwaeble

Don't bother," Prescott said. "Carver here is quite strong; stronger than he looks, for sure. As many of us are. And knowing your background, I took precautions. Just in case."

Pulse racing, Faron felt his head swim a bit more with each breath. He reached his free hand to his upper lip, scraped at the thin smear of balm. Something in the menthol. He wiped off as much as he could, forced himself to breathe only through his mouth, which wasn't hard, given how out of breath he already was. But the fumes were hard to escape.

"Yes, it acts quickly. The mentholatum opens up the airways, increases the sensitivity of the blood vessels. And if by chance you were wondering why I didn't just spike the cocktail you were given when you landed, I needed you alert until now. I also needed to make sure you weren't already turned, one of those awful sympathizers, a traitor to your kind. Not a foolproof method, but there isn't any, at the moment."

Faron tried to hook a leg behind Carver's knee, use a leverage move, felt himself wrenched sideways before he could manage it. Manhandled.

"Really, if you'll just hear me out, I think you'll see there's no need to struggle. I'm trying to help you."

Faron raised his legs, swinging them, slamming them down and pushing himself back, squirming and bucking with everything he had. Nothing.

"Haven't you always felt out of place? Held back? Forced to be something you weren't? That's because you were."

The man in the chair spoke, his voice weak but projecting. "Don't listen to them, Nephew. Their words are madness."

Prescott clucked his tongue, shook his head. He looked down at his bloody fingertips then stuck them into his mouth one by one.

"Oh, come now, *Uncle Jeremiah*. There's no need to be insulting. I'd thought we'd grown close these last few days. I hardly had to torture you at all toward the end. And why don't you call him by his nickname? Little Mosquito?"

"What do you want?" Faron said, jerking a few more times to no avail.

Stop, he told himself. *Catch your breath, breath through your mouth. The more you struggle, the more you're drugging yourself.*

"You see these?" Prescott held up his hand. His fingernails were long, each coming to a point. Traces of blood still in the crevices, a tendril of flesh curling off one of them. "Half an inch or so. I can extend them at will. One of the anatomical changes, a reconfiguration of the tendons and small muscle fibers. The miracle of evolution. Took some practice, though. Training. Discipline."

Faron said nothing. He focused on his breathing. *Through the mouth. Steady, controlled. In, out. Oxygenate.*

"And really, that's the point. Whatever this… this *gift* is, you see, it needs to be cultivated. Nurtured. Encouraged. But those who don't possess it, those who are jealous, afraid, unwilling to accept change, they want to wipe it out. Wipe us out. Oppress and subdue and neuter us, then absorb what's left into little well-behaved clones of themselves. Stick us on reservations, you might say. Deny us who we are. Again."

Each breath started to come more easily now. Faron tucked his chin in, retracting his lower jaw as far back as it would go, pulling in air from below, avoiding the menthol as best he could. Only breathing through his mouth.

"But this, Professor Faron Younger, anglicized descendant of a proud line of people invaded and oppressed first by the Russians, then by the Americans, a man named not after any chieftain ancestor, but some country-western crooner. This… *this* is your chance to overcome all that. To lead a movement that will transform your own people from within. I dare say, this is what you were meant for. Your destiny. Your people's destiny. Don't you see it?"

He could feel the strength returning, the heaviness of his limbs giving way to tension in his muscles. But the progress was slow. Exasperatingly slow.

"I have no idea what you're talking about."

"Surely you don't think your folklore is just a collection of silly myths, legends, and superstitions, do you? You, of all people, should champion the idea that this is the collective wisdom of a race in touch with themselves, in touch with nature, wisdom distilled into an essence, portrayed in allegories."

"This is insane. What wisdom?"

"Open your eyes, Little Mosquito! That tale you told is not some absurd yarn about how blood-sucking insects came into the world—it's a prophecy! A clue about one aspect of the mysteries surrounding the glorious evolution sweeping the planet! A woman gets pregnant from a man who is not one of her people, and a child is born. He is cast into the fire and gives birth to a thousand years of vampirism!"

"You're fucking psychotic. It's just a *myth*."

"We shall see. The Tlingit people. Fifteen to twenty thousand strong as a tribe, and not one reported vampire among you. That's all about to change."

Prescott flicked his chin toward the door, and Carver began to move in that direction, dragging Faron with him. Carver pushed the door open and stepped out. Faron managed to hook his hand over the door frame enough to jerk the both of them to a stop.

"Can you even hear yourself? How crazy you sound? All the science points to recessive genes, dormant vestiges, manifesting themselves like infections. My pe—the Tlingit have no control over their DNA. There could be any number of components in the genetic makeup that suppress it."

"Ah! That's an interesting word to use, isn't it? Suppress. By all means, let's talk about suppressing our nature. You were a star soldier, an elite member of the Rangers, a certified killing machine. But you dropped out. Why? Because you suddenly woke up one day and realized you didn't enjoy it? No, I don't believe that. I think it's because you had never actually killed anyone, and the more you thought about it, the more you realized that once you did, you would very much enjoy it. Instead of embracing who you were, who you are, you ran from it. Frightened, conditioned to believe such feelings and inclinations are bad. So you hid in the safe ivory tower of academia, where the battles are so fierce because the stakes are so low."

"What do I have to do with any of this?"

"You? You're the key, of course! Little Mosquito! The thousand years are up! Yes, yes, I'm sure that was not meant literally, just a measure to suggest an incomprehensible amount of time. But that time has passed, and now you will become the vessel that awakens the vampire destiny of your people. And once that is demonstrated, once our brothers and sisters are released from this state of suppression—to apply the term you so aptly volunteered—then other tribes will see that this is not an affliction, but an eschaton. A fulfillment. Prophesied, foreseen, ineluctable!"

Prescott turned to the other man, who was on one knee, mouth still attached to the sentry's throat.

"Arthur, please bring our friend's uncle outside," he said with a nod toward the chair.

"Hey!"

Faron's grip yanked free, and he felt himself being dragged onto the porch, down the steps, into the grassy, rocky area near the firestack. The body of one of the sentries who'd been on the porch was prostrate, the stump of his neck spilling blood over the edge onto the ground where his still-helmeted head lay, a few feet away. The other sentry stood near the stack, a stick with cloth wrapped at the end of it in one hand, a lighter in the other. He smiled beneath his helmet, revealing twin sets of curved fangs.

Prescott stepped off the porch and gave a signal. The sentry flicked the lighter, moved the flame so that it licked a dangling strip off cloth. The flame scampered up the strip and quickly covered the wrappings.

"Since I don't suppose it would do any good to request that you and your uncle act out the process voluntarily, we'll have to make due. The guests will be arriving soon."

"Guests?" Faron said, trying to dig his heels against the ground, stalling. "What guests? What are you talking about?"

"Tlingit. Hundreds of them, if all goes according to plan. The largest potlatch in generations. Thousands of invitations, ferries dispatched to what was promised to be the event of the century. A much needed escape from the horrors gripping the world. They will arrive here just in time for the transformation to begin. Of course, I can't actually do the fire part with you in front of them, since there's little chance you'd play your role. So we'll have to relate the story as it is supposed to be. He who controls the story controls the moral."

Faron squirmed, testing Carver's grip, gave up quickly. Still too strong. And him still too weak. "You want to burn me? What in God's name is that going to accomplish?"

"In God's name? Nothing. But in the name of the Crimson Queen, much. Unlike you, I have faith in the lore of your tribe. I believe the flames will unlock what's lurking inside you, the key to erasing whatever it is suppressing the next stage of evolution of your people. And the symbolism! The story will spread like the fire that gave it birth. The uncle here, descendant of a chief, the nephew, likewise. The vampire man-child, rising out of the ashes, his true self emerging."

"True self? A monster?"

"That's the beauty of it! Not a monster to anyone with vision, but rather something miraculous, something wonderful to behold! And whatever you shall become, it will be what brings out the vampires in your tribe, in your related tribes. It will be the symbol of the struggle, proof that science doesn't hold all the answers! That we're not a disease, but a revolution!"

"And when I do nothing but die? What then?"

"In the unlikely event that were to happen, you would serve as an allegory. Why do you think I had the totem made? Everyone will see what happened here, and they will believe. Not just Tlingit, but Haida, Eskimo, all those who have been suppressing their inner selves. It will serve as the clarion call for them to wake up, rise up, take what is rightfully theirs! Of course, a healthy dose of a viral exacerbator, delivered in an aerosol form, should help defeat whatever quirk of the Tlingit immune system has managed to suppress the effects of the virus to date. Those who aren't turned will serve as meals for those who are."

"Aerosol? The drone? You're going to use a biological weapon to infect innocent people? And you wonder why they see you as a threat?"

"Isn't there an old saying about the lion not caring what the lamb thinks of him?"

"Wait. In the legend, the uncle doesn't die."

"Ah, but, alas, here, he must. In order for the people to believe, for this to have the desired effect as it spreads throughout the tribal nations, we can't have the man going around with a negative attitude, giving a conflicting account of what took place. No, we had to bring him here so that there would be no holes in the tale. The circle is complete. Uncle kills Nephew, creating a thousand years of hidden vampires, symbolized by the mosquito; now Nephew kills Uncle, and emerges from the fire as a god, an emblem of transformation, something to be revered. Something to be emulated."

Another gesture by Prescott, and the sentry lowered the torch to the stack, shoving it into the packed center. The fire from the torch climbed and flowed out, slowly at first, then pieces started to crackle, sap began to pop. Within a few seconds, tall orange flames clawed at the sky, which was beginning to grow pale at the edges, signs of darkness falling.

"But why me?" Faron said. "Even if the legend were some prophecy, what makes you so certain it has anything to do with me?"

Prescott didn't answer. Only a furrowed brow and a tilt of his head indicated he'd even heard the words.

The heat from the fire began to sting Faron's cheeks. The cracks and snaps grew louder, as did the groan of the flames. His strength was returning, coming back faster now, a little with each breath. He knew he would have to make a move, that he didn't have much time left, but before he could come up with a course of action he felt his feet lift off the ground, saw the fire and the woods and his uncle and the cabin tumble sideways, and he was high off the ground, seven feet or so, looking down, hoisted over Carver's head.

"As I said, Carver is quite strong."

That, Faron thought, was an understatement. Fingers like steel rods, squeezing tight enough to pinch off nerves, making movement almost impossible.

Then he heard the screams. Some high, some more like yells, people shouting. He twisted his head, looked back across the clearing. Some of Prescott's personnel, mostly the men and women in the plain blue uniforms, were running from the tent, being overtaken easily by others, mostly the ones in black. One guy made it pretty far, a dead beeline for the woods, only for his head to snap forward, a burst of red misting the air where it had been, a shot ringing out.

"I do so wish there was a way to do this in front of the crowd. But isn't it exciting? I cannot wait to see how you emerge. Will you be a cloud of infectious ash? Breathed in by your people? Will you be thousands of actual mosquitoes, biting and infecting your own kind in a way that removes their stubborn resistance? Or will you simply reveal your true form? The fire stripping away the artifice, awakening the viral reactions that stimulate the genes, triggering the metamorphosis?"

Faron looked over to his uncle, so small and frail compared to how he'd seemed twenty years ago. He wanted to tell him he was sorry, sorry for so many things—this especially, but for leaving, for distancing, for always playing the role of the outsider, reveling in the notoriety, when really there'd been no call for it. He wanted to shout some sort of apology, only he couldn't. That would mean giving up, admitting defeat, and he was not going to give anyone the satisfaction of that. Ever.

His jaw popped as he clenched it tightly. The most he would allow was a small dip of his head, hoping it would say what needed to be said. Before he could even do that, the vamp next to his uncle, the one he'd heard Prescott call Arthur, jerked up straight, eyes wide, mouth open. His arms dropped to his side, releasing Faron's uncle, then he collapsed forward onto his knees. He stayed like that for a moment, then another, then fell onto his face, the handle of a large knife standing straight up, buried to the hilt in the back of his skull.

A figure landed on top of him, crouching on the flattened man's back, hand clenching the knife and giving it a yank. It was a woman. Red hair, blue flight suit. Pale, freckled skin.

Katrina?

The knife popped free, and she cocked her arm, and threw it, all in one motion. The large blade tumbled once, then embedded squarely in Carver's chest.

There was a brief instant where everything seemed to go still, Carver lowering his head to stare at his chest, Faron still suspended above his head, then Faron felt the arms supporting him buckle and everything collapsed. He crashed straight down on top of the angular vampire's body, Carver's limbs twisting and bending in unnatural ways and offering no resistance. Faron was so close to the fire by the time he stopped tumbling that one of his shoes caught. He scrabbled back from the flames and stamped it out.

Too much to take in all at once. Two of them down. The fire growing in front of him, howling with anger. The sentry to his left raising his rifle toward the pilot. His uncle, confused, standing his ground, but uncertain what to do. Not the kind of man, Faron knew, to run and leave his nephew in danger, even in old age, but not in a position to be much help, either.

Movement. Faron snapped his gaze over in time to see Prescott pounce on the woman who'd just saved him, arms hammering down, those talons of his raking toward her face. She rolled backward, timing his contact, using her legs to vault his body over her, flipping him a good meter past.

She spun and bounced into a stance, knees bent, arms slightly out, hands shoulder-width apart, palms out. Ready to fight.

Faron snapped his eyes back to the sentry with the rifle. He saw the flutter of the barrel as it tightened to a stop.

"No!"

He threw himself forward, exploding into a sprint. Shoulder lowered, arm flexed and tucked tight against his ribs. He smashed against the sentry's midsection, could hear a grunt of air escape, just before the clap of the rifle crashed in his ears and made everything go silent except for a high ringing.

The vampire dropped onto his back, ass first. Faron was still weak, but was now fueled by waves of adrenalin, and without a thought he was on the thing's chest, pinning the rifle across it's torso with a knee, thrusting a palm under the chin to expose the windpipe with one hand, then pounding his fist into the Adam's apple with the other. Once, twice, three times, rapid repetitions, maximizing leverage with his weight, snapping each blow at just the right time for optimal velocity at impact, like the cracking of a whip.

Then, without thinking, he closed his thumb and three fingers around the larynx, shooting his hand down just as the vampire's hands arrived, feeling the icy grip on his wrist. Knowing that would happen, knowing the creature would try to pull his arm away, banking on it, tightening at just the right moment, using its strength to multiply his own.

The front of its throat shredded loose. He felt his fingers tear into the flesh, felt the cartilage separate. He let go and pushed himself off, kicking his feet and crabbing away to let the thing drown in its own blood.

A flash of motion. *Katrina.* He looked in time to see her land a good front kick to Prescott's chest, but watched as she mistimed a spinning side kick, allowing him to step inside it. Prescott was fast, not so much in his movements as his reactions. He managed to hook an arm around her extended leg and slam her onto her chest.

The vampire grabbed a fistful of her red hair and pulled her head back. He hissed, opening his jaws wide, too wide, like they were dislocating at the hinges.

Half a second to think, less to act. Faron scrambled back to the vamp he'd just killed, its body still in spasms, throat still bubbling foamy blood. He grabbed the rifle slung over the creature's body and fired it from a prone position, resting it on the thing's chest, shooting through the flames, the image of Prescott, face veined and bestial, jaws unhinged, wavy and distorted through boiling air.

A puff of cloth and blood on the shoulder. Prescott's head cocked around, feline eyes widening, then narrowing. Faron took a steadier aim this time, but before he could fire, Prescott clenched both hands around Katrina's throat and held her up between them. She kicked him in the midsection and was about to a second time when he shoved her into the fire.

Sparks and embers flared in all directions. The stack collapsed around her, and her suit caught. She rolled out, slapping at herself frantically. Faron scrambled over to help, pulling his jacket off and smothering patches of flame.

In seconds, the flames were out. Her suit was charred in spots, a few holes burned right through. The ends of her hair were singed, but she seemed alright.

Faron looked up. Prescott was gone. He panned the dark tree line for a sign of him.

That's when he saw his uncle. Lying on his side, slumped. A round bullet hole in one cheek. The realization was a gut punch. That errant shot of the vampire. The one Faron had caused to go off target.

Katrina grabbed him by the arm. She hustled him into the woods until they were out of sight of the clearing.

"I'm sorry," Katrina said. She listened for a moment before wiping dirt and ash from her clothing. She paused to let out a sigh and looked at him. "Your uncle was more vulnerable. That's why I saved him first. You, I figured, could take care of yourself. If given the chance."

A few seconds passed in silence, confused noises making it through the ringing in his ears. The faint popping of the fire, distant movement around the tent, moans and grunts and faraway yells.

He turned to her, his voice low. "Is anyone ever going to tell me just what the hell is going on?"

"Yes, of course. But not right now. Now we have to move. He'll have reinforcements close by. And the vamps on his team have killed the others by now. We have to get out of here."

He didn't argue. His gaze drifted back to the glow of the fire, barely visible through the foliage. His mind still held on to the last image of his uncle. Lifeless eyes staring into the void, dying flames dancing in the reflection.

"By now, I mean *now*," she said, bending over to finish dusting off the pant legs of her flight suit. She started to move away, urging him to follow with an impatient wave of her hand.

He jerked a thumb toward the cabin. "Weapons?"

"Leave them. My plane is this way."

He followed her into the forest, her body moving swiftly and smoothly. She was graceful and quick. It took some effort to keep up. How she managed to know her footing so well was a mystery.

"So, is now a good time?"

"Shhh!" She said, her voice a harsh whisper. "Look around you. We're not out of the woods yet. And I'm being literal, in case you didn't notice."

Almost ten minutes later they finally were out of the woods, the sky a purpling bruise overhead, the water gently slapping against the thousands of smooth rocks, tiny whitecaps glistening in the light of the rising moon. The plane was on the beach, pontoons half out of the water.

"Help me push it out," she said. "Just so it's loose of the shore."

He did, the cold water filling his shoes and quickening his pulse. Then the plane was fully floating, and they climbed in, his feet squishing in his socks. Katrina wasted no time flipping switches, adjusting throttles, and turning the ignition. The propeller cranked a few times and then chugged to life, whining loudly in his ears.

She opened the throttle a bit and steered the plane around, then pushed the stick all the way in. The plane moved along the top of the water, accelerating until it began to skim the surface. She pulled back on the yoke, and Faron felt gravity press him into his seat as they became airborne.

Faron looked out the window in time to see Prescott emerge from the trees, rifle in hand, two sentries behind him. Shots rang out as the figures shrank into the distance. The whistling rounds could be heard even through the drone of the propeller and engine, causing Faron to flinch. One punched through a pontoon, but if Katrina was concerned, she didn't show it.

"They probably have a chopper on the island," she said, shouting over the groan of the engine. "Maybe two or three, but we'll be too far and too fast by the time they can get in the air. I suppose you'd like those answers now."

"That would be nice," he yelled back.

She reached behind the seat and produced a headset, handed it to him. She grabbed another for herself.

"Prescott," she said, adjusting the volume on the com unit. She turned to face him, her voice switching tone. "Can you hear me?"

Faron nodded.

"He's bad news. Had an idea he was, but wasn't sure how bad. Now I know."

"Slow down. In fact, throw it into reverse for a second. I'm still in the dark here."

"Right. Well, some of us have suspected—well, *known* is more like it—that many critical levels of the government have been infiltrated."

"'Us'? Who is 'us'?"

"Concerned citizens. Vampire and human. We're sort of watchdogs. Strictly private, though. Can't be too careful who you trust."

"Private? You're serious. A group of concerned citizens. Fighting against vampires?"

"Fighting against the bad guys, whoever they are, vamp or human. Prescott, he's a bad guy, in case you hadn't noticed."

"Yeah, I noticed. What's his deal?"

"Besides being bat-shit crazy? It's hard to say for sure, but we believe he's part of a strategy to seed chaos using official channels. If this had gone the way he'd wanted it, no one would have known he and his crew were the cause. He'd have been the one writing the official version of events."

"And what did he expect was going to happen?"

"You heard him. He thought fire was the key to getting your vampirism to manifest, and that you would then be the catalyst to bring it out in the rest of your tribe, and maybe others. With a weaponized viral accelerator as a back-up plan."

"But why? Why me?"

"For almost two decades now, everyone in the military has had blood samples stored for DNA use. It's in the fine print. When this whole thing erupted, and theories started focusing on the genetic aspect, the government started trying to crossmatch samples they had with known cases of vampirism. We're talking about desperate, frenetic research. Various genetic markers were flagged for different reasons. The idea was to keep track, see if they lined up with outbreaks or whatever."

"And my DNA sample showed something?"

"Not necessarily. But your father was killed by a V-8 raid. Prescott must have been handed a file on him, traced him to you, seen your military record, and decided something was keeping you from turning. That's the best guess."

"You're saying my father, he was a vampire?"

"Yes. Sort of a nasty guy. Sorry."

Faron stared out the window. The water below was dark now, much darker than the sky. "What would have happened if he'd thrown me in the fire?"

"I don't know. Prescott clearly believed something would. But, again, bat-shit crazy. That aerosol agent? Something his chemist-geek-vampire Arthur whipped up. It's all about the chaos; maybe it would work, maybe it wouldn't, but one way or another a bunch of people would be dead."

"What about the ferries? He said people were coming by the score. Tlingit people. They're heading for a massacre."

"Some of my associates were already heading to intercept them. We scrambled and found some speedboats. They should all be turning back by now, warned off. I wasn't able to understand enough at first, but I radioed when I made the connection."

"And you came back. For me?"

"Yes."

Faron nodded. "I suppose you needed to be there to take care of me, if Prescott turned out to be right."

The plane poked through a cloud, and the lights of Sitka were suddenly visible, twinkling far ahead in the twilight.

"Hey," she said. "I came back to help you, not kill you. And don't think of it that way. No matter what you are, you're *you*. *You're* in control. You, me, all of us, even that crazy fuck Prescott—we have free will. Monsters exist because some choose to embrace the devils of their nature. And, like I said, it doesn't matter what you are."

"What do you mean, what I am? What am I?"

She shrugged. "I'm familiar with your military record, your training. And I saw how you handled yourself back there. Not too shabby for a guy who hasn't been active for a decade. We could use a guy like you. Seriously. There's no greater cause. We set our own agenda, fight the battles we choose. If this war is to be won, it will be groups like us that win it."

"You want me to join you? Some vigilante group of… what? Resistance fighters?"

"Think of us more as a citizen militia, of sorts. Isn't that why you got out? Because you didn't trust the government to do the right thing? To not sell you out? Not betray the cause you were fighting for? Not be riddled with treacherous psychos like Prescott?"

"I want to know what would have happened if he'd gotten me into that fire."

"Who knows? Maybe it would have released something, some vampire part of you; maybe he just thought it would piss you off so much, whatever subconscious repression you have going on would finally let go. But whatever it is, don't forget what I told you. You're you. Here's your chance to fight for what you believe in."

"I don't know." He looked out, watching the deepening colors below, the shadowy forest passing by, scaling mountains with peaks as far as the eye could see. A wilderness vast beyond comprehension, still keeping its secrets. Only showing what it wanted you to know. "When I killed that guard of his, it was just like I always worried it would be."

"You enjoyed it?"

"No. I simply didn't care. Still don't. That's what I became afraid of. That behind the ribbons and trophies and promotions, I was nothing but a stone-cold killer."

"So, you're saying you're worried that there's an internal struggle? That the moral and ethical part of you has to keep the reptilian part in check? That there's something bestial inside you that you need to control, to channel?"

She looked at him, her lips drawing back to reveal two large canines that extended well below her bottom row of teeth. For an instant, her eyes bulged, and her brows pulled back into straight lines, her cheeks rising to form a sinister triangle with the point of her chin. Then she cocked her head to the side, cracking her neck. When she faced him again, she had the same girlish face she'd had before: pale, with freckles across her nose, a friendly smile on her lips.

"In that case, welcome to the club."

She pushed the yoke forward, and the plane began to descend.

"The one where you're no different than anyone else," she added, the expanding darkness beneath them spreading out in all directions, the lights of Sitka bright but lonely on the horizon.

"A DAY IN THE LIFE" PT. 2

Jonathan Maberry

Chicago, Illinois

"**S**tay down."

First Joe said it, then the other kids began chanting it. "Stay down! Stay down! Stay down!"

Though they all wanted Trey to get back up again. That was the game. He got up, and Joe knocked him down.

Trey lay on his chest, blood dripping from his lips and nose. Fireballs seemed to be bursting in the air around him, and there was some darkness creeping in at the edges of his vision. A strange darkness. Dark red.

It scared him.

"Stay down! Stay down! Stay down!"

Trey placed his hands on the cracked pavement and took a breath. He wanted to stay down. That would be fine. That would be smart. Stay down, maybe take a few kicks. He could endure it. It wouldn't be the worst thing that could happen, and not nearly as bad as some of the stuff that the kids had done to him over the last six months.

Trey knew that all he had to do was stay down.

Down.

He spat blood onto the ground. It was as red as theirs. As red as anyone's.

"Stay down! Stay down! Stay down!"

He gritted his teeth and pushed.

Raising himself off the ground was so hard.

Shame was such a heavy thing.

Humiliation was every bit as ponderous.

Trey pushed himself up. First to his hands and knees. Then he sat back and looked at Joe. And around at the circle of kids. Seemed like most of the damn ninth grade was there. Surrounding him. Laughing. Chanting. Some of them so into the moment they looked high.

He dragged the back of his hand across his mouth, looked at the red smear.

"Stay down! Stay down! Stay down!"

Yeah, well.

Trey got a foot under him. He took another breath, then pushed, standing slowly, knees protesting, joints creaking.

Joe stared at him with a mixture of surprise and wonder. And some doubt. They both knew how hard Joe had hit him. Way too hard. Harder than the ninth graders thought. Joe had overdone it, and the kid knew it. He was big, too, with chest and shoulders that spoke to the brute he'd become by twelfth grade. A cornerback on the team who might even have a shot at a college scholarship. All muscle, very little brains. Some heart, but a conscience that bent under any pressure.

"Stay down! Stay down! Stay down!"

Trey stood up and turned to face the boy. He had to look up at the ninth grader, even though they were thirty-seven years apart in age. The kid balled his fists and took a tentative step toward him, ready for the next round. The next hit.

"Don't," he said to Joe. It wasn't a plea. Not a request. It was merely that word, letting Joe take from it whatever he was capable of grabbing.

He saw the flicker of doubt in Joe's eyes, and it confirmed something Trey had guessed before. Joe didn't really want to do this. Given any kind of chance he'd walk away.

But even though Joe was stronger than his peers, and tougher than any five of them, he wasn't nearly as tough as all of them. In combative terms, yes, but not in weight of disapproval. Not in weight of need.

The chant changed, as it always changed.

"Knock him down, put him down, way down!"

A sing-song rhythm. All those voices. All those faces.

"Knock him down, put him down, way down!"

"Don't," said Trey once more.

He saw Joe's mouth twitch, saw the words form, but the boy put no power behind them. Merely mouthed them.

I have to.

Trey made eye contact with him, and for a split second they stood alone. The battered school janitor and the hero of the masses. Trey was assigned the role of villain in this drama, not because of the color of his skin—nine-tenths of Ford High School was black or Latino—but because of the structure of his genes. Joe was given his role as the fist of human aggression. As simple and cliché as that. As predictable and trite as that.

As painful as that.

Trey saw the pain and fear in Joe's eyes. The trapped-animal look. The desperate terror that burned like a cinder inside the boy.

It moved him. He felt his own eyes burn. He knew that if he shed even a single tear, then the chant would likely change again. *Cry-baby.* Something like that.

"Knock him down, put him down, way down!"

Joe pleaded with him in that silent, shared moment, and Trey understood the power of that last blow. It wasn't meant to hurt. Not in any meaningful way. It was meant to stop.

To stop the chanting. To stop the fight. To end the drama.

Trey saw it and understood. And Joe saw that he saw it. And understood. The boy's eyes glistened, too.

Trey gave him the smallest of nods.

A permission.

And sewn into the fabric of it, forgiveness.

Joe's fist was a blur. It was a hammer at the end of a whipping branch.

Trey did nothing to block it or evade it. He took it. And, as his role demanded, he went down. Way down.

And this time when they chanted for him to stay down, he disappointed the children by doing just that. Even though he could have killed them all.

But that would have been wrong.

"THE MONSTER INSIDE"

♈

Scott Nicholson

"I can't let you kill them."

As soon as Sheriff Jimmy Templeton said the words, he wanted to take them back. He stood on the steps leading to the Unitarian Universalist Fellowship Hall, a sanctuary for the citizens he was here to protect. The bar lights of his parked cruiser threw a blue strobe over the steamy August night. The dozen or so men assembled in front of him were heavily armed, bearing everything from shotguns to semi-automatic rifles, and their faces did not show the least bit of back-down.

The sheriff mused that in a different era they might be carrying torches and pitchforks. With this crowd, he wouldn't be surprised if hand grenades were hidden away in those Carhartt vest pockets.

"You're not doing any letting, Sheriff," said Dale Shook, the self-appointed leader of the rabid pack. "If you're too chickenshit to join us, then step aside."

"Sorry," Templeton said. "This is my county, and we're still following the law as long as I'm breathing."

"You won't be breathing once these heart-stealers tear open your rib cage and drink like it's happy hour in hell." Shook rubbed the sleeve of his plaid shirt across his bearded mouth, his manic eyes bright in the street lights. The other men shifted restlessly behind him, muttering and sliding their hands over their weapons. Templeton wouldn't be able to control them for long.

But he had to try.

"Go back home to your families," Templeton said. "Leave this to the National Guard and the proper authorities. Let justice be served."

"What, so another hundred can get bled dry while we wait? They're all holed up there in the church. We can end this right now."

"Yeah, let's clean out the vermin while we have them cornered," shouted Walter Aldridge, who ran the tractor supply shop in Peck's Mill. A deacon at the First Baptist Church and a board member of the Chamber of Commerce, Aldridge was almost the stereotype of a "solid citizen." He was a big backer of the local Democratic Party that had almost defeated Templeton in the last election. To see him in the mob was alarming—the partisan poison had seeped deep into the veins of this community.

Templeton found it hard to believe the vampire war had found its way here. It was one thing when the weird diseases had hit the big cities and scientists went on television to talk about junk DNA and ice viruses and stuff right out of the movies. Those mutant bloodsuckers they called the "Bloods" emerged in ever greater numbers, but their behaviors were different in each area of the world. It was hard to identify the threat, much less isolate it. Even when those hundred bombs erupted across the country, the conflict seemed distant and surreal—an urban problem.

But the pigeons had come home to roost. When the Mathesons and McFalls had turned up dead—not just dead, but horribly mutilated—Templeton knew the affliction had arrived in their peaceful little pocket of the Blue Ridge Mountains.

Worse, the killers were Cherokee, descendants of the natives who had lived here long before the European settlers fled their kings and brought their moonshine and myths to the mountains. A consultant with the CDC had explained to county officials that Cherokee DNA contained a buried time bomb that gave them extreme physical strength and a violent instinct that had helped them survive many centuries before. A new virus had caused them to devolve back to that primordial state, and they'd killed eight people before anyone really knew what was going on.

White people. They'd killed white people.

Which made the situation even more explosive.

Templeton had arrested Billy Standingdeer, who claimed stone-faced responsibility for the deaths. Billy was currently in the federal penitentiary in Atlanta, or else this mob would be storming the county jail right now instead of gathering outside a Unitarian church. But other Cherokee were huddled inside, granted shelter by the Unitarians for their protection. Not all of the confined were carriers of the virus, but Dale Shook's militia didn't know or care about the difference.

Dark faces appeared in the church windows, and Templeton knew if even a single shot was fired, he'd be dealing with a massacre—one way or another.

"This is not the way we're handling it," Templeton said. "Billy Standingdeer will pay for his crimes if he's found guilty. This is still America. We still follow due process."

"I got your due process right here," someone said, chambering a round with an audible click. The parking lot felt like a stage beneath the lights. Other civilians watched from inside the houses that surrounded the church, and traffic whizzed by on the adjacent street, a car occasionally braking for a look or honking in support.

Templeton's hand itched to close around the butt of his holstered Glock, but he couldn't afford provocation. "It's not just Cherokee inside," he said, forcing his voice to remain steady and strong. "Some of the church folk are taking care of them. Your friends and neighbors and customers."

"They ain't my friend if they're giving aid to heart-stealers," Shook said.

"Just because they carry the virus doesn't mean they pose any threat. No one else has been attacked."

"And we want to keep it that way." Shook took several steps forward, his makeshift militia on his heels.

"Not on my watch," the sheriff said, feeling stupid because it sounded like something the star of a TV cop show would say. He just wanted this to be over. No reruns.

"I can't believe you're sticking up for the goddamned vampires," Shook said. "What's wrong, you got some Indian blood in you or something?"

Templeton did have a Cherokee great-grandfather, since interbreeding wasn't that unusual among the early settlers. But he had no claim to the tribal heritage, and he certainly didn't go around letting that fact slip out in Pickett County, with its ninety percent Caucasian population. He was able to separate his own lineage from his job.

At least, that's what he liked to tell himself.

"Everybody in this county has equal right to the law, regardless of race, creed, or color," he said to the restless crowd. A few residents had come out of their front doors to watch. Templeton noted with dismay that a couple of them were armed.

"'Vampire' ain't a creed or color," Shook said. "It's a monster. Even the president's calling them 'Bloods,' and if that jug-eared son-of-a-bitch can pass judgment, anybody can. They're different, and that's good enough for us." Some of his posse muttered their agreement.

"They're citizens under the law," Templeton insisted.

"Animals don't have any rights," Walter Aldridge said.

Templeton wished he'd called in one of his deputies as backup, but with tensions running high, he'd ordered heavy patrols of the rural areas. He never suspected his community would turn vigilante so fast. First it was rocks thrown through front windows, followed by some KKK-style cross burnings, and then Wayne Beaver had been beaten while trying to order an after-work beer in the County Line Tavern. Beaver hadn't pressed charges and refused to identify the men, but since then, the Cherokee had banded together, almost like it was the late 1700s and pale-skinned strangers had first invaded their lands.

If the Cherokee had been infected with this virus back then, history might have turned out a whole lot differently, the sheriff thought grimly.

"I'm standing guard," Templeton said. "So I have them under surveillance at all times. They can't pose any danger if they stay in the church until this gets settled and health officials can come up with a treatment. The government will be issuing guidance on this thing. So we wait."

Shook lifted the barrel of his rifle so that it no longer pointed at the ground. Not *at* Templeton, exactly, but suggestive of a business position. "How many of us gotta die before then?"

"Nobody's going to—"

The gunshot cut through the night, shattering glass and setting off a car alarm.

Templeton and most of Shook's crowd ducked instinctively. The shot hadn't come from any of them. Templeton drew his Glock and glanced around. The people in their doorways had gone back inside. The shot could have come from one of them, or even from a passing car.

"That came from the church," Shook said.

"No way," Templeton said, although it wasn't beyond the realm of possibility. The Unitarian minister, Edward Leeds, had vowed to protect the tribal members unto death, and he might have taken his own mandate to the extreme.

Great. That's all I need, for every church to start its own army.

"Shit, they shot the side window of my pickup," one of Shook's gang said.

A voice boomed from the church alcove, its owner hidden in shadows. "You're all trespassing. Go home."

Leeds. Having an ally gave Templeton no comfort. This was going to escalate quickly if he didn't get control of the situation.

"Mr. Leeds," Templeton called, still crouching low. "Please put down your firearm and go back inside."

"I'm not going anywhere until all of you get off our church property."

Templeton wanted to explain that he wasn't with Shook's mob, but he didn't want to antagonize the armed men any more than necessary. When this was all over, they'd be neighbors, voters, and taxpayers again.

"Send out those heart-stealers, and we'll go," Aldridge shouted back. Shook waved at the group to fan out, like soldiers positioning to make a run at a bunker.

"No," Templeton said, standing and slipping his Glock back into its holster, although he left the leather restraint strap unbuttoned. "I'll handle this."

He walked slowly toward the dark alcove sixty feet away, arms outstretched to show he wasn't a threat. As he moved away from the harsh greenish glare of the streetlights, he could make out the minister's form in the darkness. He wondered how many volunteers the church had on hand, and whether they were likewise armed.

For that matter, he wondered if any of the two dozen Cherokee inside were armed. He wouldn't blame them if they were. They'd already learned their lesson on the Trail of Tears, when the U.S. government had marched their ancestors westward in a genocidal march of disease and starvation.

But now they didn't need guns, if they were capable of the damage Billy Standingdeer had inflicted. His victims had their rib cages torn open, their hearts removed, and much of their blood drained, although Templeton didn't quite buy the eyewitness accounts of Standingdeer drinking the blood.

Still, he was almost as afraid of the Cherokee as he was the armed mob in the parking lot. And now he was caught in between them, with nothing to do but swallow his fear and stand tall. There was no shield to hide behind out here on the front lines.

"Put down your weapon, Mr. Leeds," Templeton said, feeling the eyes of Shook's mob on his back.

"Are you for us or against us, Sheriff?" the minister asked, still veiled in shadows.

"I'm for peace and order," Templeton said, reaching the concrete landing that led to the alcove. "And I mean to keep it that way."

A pause. "Okay, then. Come on in."

A door opened, revealing a sliding quadrangle of yellow light, and the minister slipped inside. Templeton took a look back to make sure Shook and his buddies were staying put. They fidgeted and mumbled, but none of them had advanced on the church.

"Give me ten minutes, fellahs," he said, in his folksiest "man of the people" manner.

"Better make it five," Shook called back.

As Templeton entered, Leeds stood there in jeans and a sweater, looking not at all like a preacher. Of course, Unitarians didn't really preach, as far as Templeton could tell. This building housed meetings for Jews, Buddhists, and even pagans, one size fitting all, but it was more like a community center for liberal activists. That alone was enough to arouse suspicion among Shook, Aldridge, and the others, but Templeton's department had never responded to a call or complaint here.

Leeds was in his late fifties, with wild white eyebrows and a trimmed goatee, a fervent gleam in his eyes. He obviously believed in his mission. He rested his rifle against a bookshelf and locked the door behind them. "Welcome, Sheriff."

"I'm going to have to issue you a citation for discharging a firearm within city limits," Templeton said. "But I think it can wait until tomorrow. I don't want to cause any more anxiety than necessary."

Leeds gave a tired smile. "You don't want to inflame the lynch mob, or you would have cited them for disturbing the peace, communicating threats, and probably a dozen other creative charges."

"They're scared, Mr. Leeds. Just like your guests are, I'm sure."

"We figured the good old boys would want blood sooner or later. That's why we offered sanctuary to tribe members."

"How many do you have here?" Templeton strained to peer down the hall but no one was in sight. The lights in the church were low, and it was difficult to discern the layout.

"Nineteen, plus a volunteer. We've been here for a week, cooking meals in the kitchen and bedding them down in the fellowship hall."

"No signs of, uh… unusual symptoms among them?"

"I can tell you'd like to see for yourself. This way." Leeds took up his rifle before motioning Templeton down the hallway.

Entering a set of double doors, Templeton found twenty sets of eyes fixed upon him. He recognized a few of the people—one woman worked in the cafeteria of his son's elementary school, John Longwater operated a successful landscaping service, and the slender Longwater girl was a starter on the high school basketball team. Not all of them were full-blooded Cherokee, either. Some of the spouses were white, one was Asian, and several of the mixed-breed children were blonde and blue-eyed.

Just people. Good citizens. Not monsters.

Longwater had apparently taken a leadership role, because he asked, "What were you expecting, Sheriff? Fangs and cloaks?" He gestured to the sleeping bags and rumpled blankets scattered across the floor. "Thought we'd be sleeping in coffins?"

"People are jumpy. After what Billy Standingdeer did, you can understand. Not to mention what's happening around the world."

"So the witch hunt is on," Longwater said, the burnt-sienna skin crinkling around his raven-black eyes.

"No hunting on my watch," Templeton said. "But I need to know how many of you are armed."

"None of us except Mr. Leeds," Longwater said.

"Okay. Just hang tight for a while—even if it's another day or two—and I'll get this cleared up. I know you folks are worried and scared, but I promise I'm going to settle it. No one's going to harm you."

"We're not the ones with fear in our hearts, Sheriff. We know what it's like to be hated."

Templeton nodded and then addressed Leeds. "That rifle doesn't require any registration to be lawful, but I'd appreciate it if you kept it out of sight. Those men out there are right on the edge, and I'd rather not push them over."

"Then why are you in here instead of out there?" Longwater asked, maddeningly calm. A couple of the children drew closer to their mothers.

"I'll reassure them that everything's okay and talk them into going home. If that doesn't work, I'll place Shook under arrest. Cut off the head, and the snake usually dies."

"But a snake's head can still bite, even after it's removed."

"Not all white men are evil," Templeton said, glancing at Leeds.

"Neither are all vampires," Longwater said. "We didn't ask for this virus."

Templeton was surprised, because he'd assumed none of them were infected. Billy Standingdeer seemed more muscular and agile due to his virus, with heightened reflexes, but the main visible symptom was his oversized pupils, as if moist black beads had been pressed into his eye sockets. His fingernails had thickened, and evidence suggested he'd torn into his victims with his bare hands, which would have taken superhuman strength.

No one here seemed capable of such raw violence. One of the kids looked up from a comic book and yawned.

"We can handle this, Sheriff," Leeds said.

"I'm sure you can. I'll go have a talk with—"

He was interrupted by shattering glass and a *whoof*, accompanied by a sharp petroleum smell.

"*Fire!*" Leeds shouted.

As shrieks erupted, Templeton dashed to the hallway. A narrow window beside the front door was broken, flames dancing up the casing. The arsonists had used an accelerant of some kind, paint thinner maybe, and the fire grabbed hold of the curtains and bookshelf. Hot, oily smoked billowed from the blaze.

"Front door's blocked," Templeton called. "Better try the back way. Get those kids out, now!"

Leeds and the other volunteer frantically ushered the group to a door behind the lectern. The power blinked as Templeton sealed the hallway doors, hoping to contain the flames and buy some time.

"Locked from outside," Leeds shouted, pounding on the back door while shaking the handle.

The windows in the fellowship hall were set high off the floor, near the top of the vaulted ceiling. As Leeds climbed atop a table in an attempt to reach one, a couple of shots rang out, piercing the window and slamming into the far wall.

"Down, so they don't see your silhouette," Templeton ordered. "All of you."

Leeds climbed down as the mothers huddled with their children. Longwater and the other men didn't move as several more shots rang out.

"Any other way out?" Templeton asked over the crying children.

John Longwater didn't look scared or even really surprised. He glared at Templeton for a moment, and then nodded grimly. "There is a way out. Unfortunately, it is the wrong way."

As Templeton watched, and shouts poured in from beyond the church, Longwater changed.

The effect was subtle at first—a tightening of the skin around his eyes, a fading luster in his pupils, a slight flexing of his shoulders. His posture stiffened as he leaned forward, seeming to grow a couple of inches. He looked down at his hands, and the fingernails elongated with a cracking and splitting sound.

Jesus Christ, it's real.

He'd believed the accounts of those who watched Billy Standingdeer kill, but to see this mutation for himself…

And it wasn't just Longwater—the others, at least those with Cherokee features, changed as well. Even two of the children.

"Mr. Longwater," Templeton said, instinctively drawing his pistol. "Easy now."

What did he expect the man to do? Stop the change? It was a virus, or at least that's what the government claimed. Longwater could no more stop being a vampire than he could stop being Native American.

"We didn't ask for this," Longwater said. "We wanted to be left in peace."

Longwater and several of the other men scrambled up the wall with agility and obscene grace, driving their fingernails into the plaster. When they reached the high windows, Longwater threw back his head, and a chilling ululation poured from his throat. The shouts outside the building fell silent, and Templeton could hear the crackle of flames licking at the door.

Then Longwater threw himself through the window, glass raining down into the fellowship hall. One by one the others followed. Several children scrabbled up the wall with eerie, spidery movements and then disappeared into the night.

"I... I didn't know," Leeds sputtered.

Templeton dashed to the door that Leeds had already tried. He threw his shoulder against it, but it didn't budge. The vigilantes must have planned to burn them all.

"Come on," Templeton said, waving at a heavy oak church pew. "Help me lift."

Leeds and the volunteer joined it, but they could barely budge it. Templeton glared at the children and spouses of the Cherokee that had been left behind. "Do you all want to die in here?"

The women glanced at one another, and then they stooped down to help lift. Even with the oldest children pitching in, they could barely raise the pew off the floor.

The fire boiled from the front entrance, smoke already darkening the interior of the sanctuary and causing the children to cough. They'd only get one chance, so Templeton skipped the countdown. "Go!" he shouted, running the pew toward the steel door.

They nearly dropped the heavy pew, but they hit their target. The wood splintered on impact, but the door creaked open maybe fifteen inches. The fresh air was welcome, but the burst of oxygen fed the flames. Templeton ushered the youngest children through the gap, then waited for the other adults to escape. By the time he pushed his way outside, he was nearly blind. He rolled into the landscaping, sucking in the humid night air as steam rose from his uniform.

By the time he rose to his feet, the screams had started. He waved at Leeds to move the children out of harm's way and hurried to the front of the church.

A shotgun exploded, and figures fled across the parking lot. Something dashed out of the darkness beyond the streetlights and took down a man from behind.

Before Templeton could react, the figure lifted its face into the light of the burning structure.

Longwater.

The Cherokee ululated again and raised his curled hand, driving it down into the fallen man's rib cage. Templeton wouldn't have believed it possible if he hadn't seen those fingernails. Above the gusty rush of flames drawing oxygen and eating wood, Templeton heard a distinct crunching *slooosh*.

Longwater yanked the heart from the man's chest and held it aloft, fluid streaming from dangling shreds of meat. Templeton could have sworn the organ pumped a couple of times, squirting blood from a fleshy bit of hose.

"Drop it!" Templeton bellowed, dropping into firing position and pointing his Glock.

Around him, a smattering of gunfire punctuated the screams and shrieks. Another car alarm sounded, and distant sirens wailed across the valley. But Templeton couldn't wait for the cavalry—or the National Guard—on this one. At least half a dozen bodies already lay sprawled on the asphalt.

Longwater turned to face Templeton. His black eyes now bore a reddish glint, or maybe that was the reflection of the conflagration. The Cherokee lifted the heart to his mouth and licked it with a pointed, protruding tongue. His teeth, like his nails, had grown.

Freak. Monster.

Templeton squeezed off two shots. One struck Longwater in the shoulder, causing him to drop the organ. The other shot went wild.

At least he's bleeding. At least they can be killed.

"Now do you believe me?" someone yelled.

Dale Shook.

Shook crouched behind a pickup, sighting his rifle across the hood. He fired, and Longwater's abdomen exploded.

As Longwater folded and collapsed to the ground, Shook swung his barrel and took down another fleeing form.

In the chaos, Templeton was unable to tell the vampires from the vigilantes. But maybe they weren't vigilantes dispensing justice. Maybe they were soldiers in the first real world war.

Doors opened in the houses along the street and neighboring the church. The good citizens who had been hiding now stepped outside, their curiosity replaced by a contagious desire to exercise their Second Amendment rights.

And destroy some vampires.

Or maybe just some Cherokee.

Just like old times.

Templeton didn't even know where to begin to restore order. There was no law anymore, just a primal desire to destroy the Other.

His goal instantly shifted to protecting the innocent—if he could find any.

There.

Leeds and the church volunteer still stood near the rear of the sanctuary with a parade of coughing, teary-eyed children, along with the spouses who had not contracted the genetic virus. It was as if none of them understood the danger they were in, or else they were succumbing to shock.

"Mr. Leeds, get them out of here!" Templeton shouted, hunching and dashing toward the group. He'd only taken four steps when a shadow dropped in front of him. He barely recognized the twisted face as Melvin Beaver's. The speed of the vampire was stunning, and Templeton didn't even have time to raise his Glock before one long claw swept toward him.

Templeton closed his eyes, bracing for the fatal blow.

Kuhh-rakkk!

The concussive roar sent a warm, wet spatter across his face, followed by the thud of a falling form.

He blinked blood from his eyes, wondering if his distant Cherokee ancestry would convey the infection to his own bloodstream.

Wondering if he'd become one of *them.*

No. If he were a monster, he wouldn't be compelled to protect those children.

The staccato popping of guns was like the Fourth of July. Leeds doubled over, holding his belly. Several of the children collapsed, and a young woman moaned in pain and anguish.

"Stop!" Templeton screamed, but nobody listened. The sheriff had no authority here. The mob ruled.

Within a minute, the gunfire abruptly died, the acrid scent of gunpowder melding with the heavy smoke boiling from the skeletal remains of the church. The parking lot was littered with corpses, pools of darkness seeping out around each, resembling motor oil under the streetlights. Most were the mutated Cherokee, but some were members of Shook's posse, including Walter Aldridge.

Shook, rifle nesting in the crook of his elbow, walked over to Leeds. He kicked the minister and reloaded, checking each of the bodies. One child raised a trembling hand for help, and Shook dispatched her with a single round to the skull.

Templeton fell to his knees and vomited. Around him, the posse members whooped in adrenaline-soaked exhilaration. Shook helped the sheriff to his feet.

"They were… innocent," Templeton shouted over the approaching sirens.

"They weren't us. That makes them guilty." Shook managed a smile that never reached his eyes. "We won."

You're right, Templeton thought, wiping blood from his lips, hoping he hated the taste. Hoping he wasn't a carrier. Not wanting to be one of them.

Not wanting to be *any* of them.

The monsters won.

Either way, the monsters always win.

"A DAY İN THE LİFE" PT. 3

Jonathan Maberry

With rap by Sam Orion Nova West-Mensch

Gary, Indiana

"**W**hat's this shit called, yo?" asked Pico.

"Yo, man, this is Krush," said Slip. "This is the shit, man."

"I ain't no pipe. How the fuck we supposed to —"

"Don't need no pipe, man. You smoke it like douja. Come on, let's go inside."

The two of them had been standing in the hall outside of Pico's apartment. There was no one else around, or at least no one looking, but they both scoped up and down to make sure. Same hall. Same nothing. Slip pushed his friend inside and closed the door behind him. The apartment was gray with dust and yellow with light filtered through sunfaded curtains and a pulled-down shade. The TV was on because the TV was always on. It was a nice box, too. Forty-six-inch Sony flatscreen with high def and 3D. The couch was thirty-two years old. Some of the plates in the sink had been there since January, and there was a small red-brown roach crawling up the wall. Trash everywhere, and the lingering stink of unwashed clothes and slowly decaying pizza.

The girl on the couch was asleep and she wore only black underpants and a bra. No tits, or at least not enough to fill the B cups, but Slip looked at her anyway. He'd let her blow him if the lights were out. She'd done it before when Pico was too stoned to give much of a cold shit. Which was most of the time.

The radio was on, blasting a rap by Syphone, a vampire rapper out of Compton.

Beats fear me, before they see my teeth
A black man in a hoodie, they don't care what's underneath
Me and all my clan, man I swear we're under siege
Like a pack of wild dogs, we really run these streets
Even when it's placid, they think we're running rabid
So like the pound, they try to put us down
Blood on their hands, blood on our crowns
Even on white hands, dried blood looks brown
They murder sons
You heard what happened out in Ferguson
Police with itchy fingas,
    just can't wait to pull a trigga
And now me and my street team
    have activated V-Genes
Just one more reason they have the heebeegeebees
Ain't nothing changed
Cops still anxious to bang
Instead of the color of my skin, it's the length of my fangs
They trade one bias for another
Come and try us mothafuckers
Thought we were dangerous before?
We'll take injustice no more
You pushed us to the limit, now we're prepping for war
So, if it's a must that they bust,
Just know
It's ashes to ashes, dust to dust

Slip hadn't heard that song before and he liked it. He sat with Pico, both of them bobbing their heads to the beat. Pico perched on the edge of the couch and waved Slip to the red vinyl kitchen chair that was the only other piece of furniture in the room apart from a coffee table made from two cinderblocks and a door. A bong sat on the table, and Slip could tell that Pico was baked.

"When'd you get weed, man?" he asked.

Pico shrugged. "Layla got some."

That was Pico's way of saying that Layla had either fucked somebody for a nickel bag or she'd done a few five-dollar BJs out by the interstate. Truckers didn't give a fuck if it was a crack whore or a wide-mouth snake as long as they could bust a nut. And what was five dollars to them?

Pico shoved the bong across to Slip. "Some left."

"Nah, man, I brought us some *real* shit."

"Krush? I ain't never heard of that."

Slip removed a thin joint from his shirt pocket and held it up. "This is the total shit."

Pico looked crestfallen. "Fuck, man, that's even smaller than your dick. What the fuck? I thought you were going to set us up, yo."

Slip grinned and shook his head. "Yeah, well, that's you being stupid, man. You ever heard that saying? It's not the size of the boat, but the motion on the ocean?"

"Yeah, and chicks tell me it's bullshit."

"How 'bout big things come in small packages?"

"You fucking with me, yo?"

"Nah, this is straight up." He wiggled the joint between two fingers. "Ticket to paradise, yo. No joke. This stuff will light you all the way up."

Pico still looked dubious, but he shrugged and picked the lighter up from the coffee table. "You better not be fucking with me, yo."

"God's honest."

"You tried it?"

"Not yet. I got it from Salamander."

Pico looked suddenly wary. "Sal's a Blood, yo. What the fuck?"

"Sal's Sal. Being a Blood don't change nothing."

"Yeah, but they got their own shit, yo. That new stuff? Spike? Fuck, you hear what that does to the fang gang? Man, some of those fuckers go ape-shit."

Slip shook his head. "So what, yo, I don't see no fangs on you."

"Not what I mean, man. How do you know this shit's even going to be safe? I heard that Beats can't take Spike cause it's a weird fucking high."

"Who told you that shit?"

"I dunno, man. You hear shit around town. People talking. Heard that Spike's not safe."

"Safe? *Safe?* Since when the fuck'd you ever care about that shit? You going pussy on me, yo?"

"Nah… I'm just saying."

"Fuck, Pico, if you don't want it then say so, and I'll go get high with Brock or Tyreese. Last I heard they still had dicks."

"Nah, nah, don't be like that," Pico said quickly… "It's all cool. I was just talkin', yo."

"Besides," said Slip, "this is Krush. Ain't no Spike bullshit."

"You sure, man?"

"Why would Salamander lie to me, yo? He's my boy."

Pico licked his lips, then waved his hand for the joint. "Yeah… okay, man. Long as this Krush jam isn't Spike, we're good, we're good. I was just fucking around. It's all good. Let's burn that motherfucker."

"That's what I'm talking about," said Slip as he put the joint between his lips and leaned toward the lighter.

The apartment fell silent except for the hiss of long inhalations, the small grunts as they held the smoke deep in their lungs, and the longer, softer sigh as they exhaled. Over and over again. They grinned at each other as the high began uncurling like a sleeping serpent.

The screaming didn't start for at least ten minutes.

"THE RUSH" PT. 1

Marcus Pelegrimas

64 kilometers west of St. John's
Newfoundland

J on McNabb was a pretty good guy… right until he drove our fifteen-passenger van into the only tree visible for a hundred yards. And it wasn't even much of a tree. More of a stump, really. Small enough for most of us to overlook until it was too late. Big enough to bring the engine block about a foot closer to the dash and drive the steering column through Jon's chest on impact. Strange, but one of the first things that went through my mind when I saw Jon's bloody face and the broken column protruding from his back was that the airbag should have gone off. That sort of thing was more of a concern back in the days when anyone gave a shit about safety regs. Now, it's a good day when you wake up to see another sunrise.

For a few seconds, my head was filled with a hazy collection of random notions swimming in a soup of disembodied voices. Some of those voices were familiar. Some were gnarled claws scraping at my eardrums, growling in foreign languages.

"*Trooooiieed,*" it snarled to my inner ear. "*Niii mor do eet ahhh troooi-ieed.*"

That's what it sounded like, anyway, as I was yanked quickly back into the present. All of those voices rushed out of my brain to be replaced by the grinding of broken gears, moans of pain from the seats behind me, and the horn's fading, warped wail.

"… the FUCK happened?"

I peeled my eyes open, blinked a few times, and tried reaching up to wipe something away from my face. That's when I heard a wet scraping sound, followed by another scream. This time, the scream came from me.

"Ray, you all right?"

A hand reached from the seat directly behind me to pat my shoulder. "You all right, Ray? Can you hear me?"

My head was spinning from the stabbing pain that had sucked all the breath from my lungs. After taking a second to pull myself together, I managed to say, "Yeah. I'll make it. I think my arm's broke."

"How's Jon? Is he all right?"

"He's hurt bad," I said while looking at the man who'd been rudely introduced to the steering column. His eyes were milky white, their pupils wiped away just like the rest of him. "He's gone. Jon's gone."

Unlike the smooth and silky voice that had come from directly behind me, the next one to rise above the chaos was a grating rasp. It came from a big Lithuanian named Stan Petkus, and when he gave orders, people's first instinct was to follow them. "If this van ain't mobile," Petkus said, "we gotta get out! Who needs help to move?"

Two of the other passengers responded that they needed a hand. I wasn't sure exactly which ones because my senses were starting to fade. Doing my best to keep from passing out while unbuckling my safety belt, I used my good arm to reach for my door handle while pushing against it with my shoulder.

As soon as the door came open, I realized I was too unsteady to swing my feet out all the way and toppled out of the van. Bracing for the pain that was sure to follow landing on my freshly broken arm, I sucked in a quick breath. That impact didn't come. Instead, a pair of strong hands grabbed hold of my jacket to pull me up again.

"On your feet," said Trace Bilson, a tall guy with a rumpled mess of brownish red hair hanging down to his shoulders.

Once I was upright again, my vision began to clear. A cool breeze went a long way in keeping me alert, but didn't keep me from moving like a sloppy drunk.

"Can you see?" Trace asked. "Your eyes look strange."

"They're better than Jon's," I said. "He drove straight into that tree!"

"Right. What about your legs?"

"They're fine," I replied. "I can walk."

Trace didn't say anything else. He simply draped my good arm over his shoulders and moved us away from the van.

"What happened? Is someone gonna answer me or not?"

That was Kate Timmons asking for the update, and it was Pete Hester who answered her. "We crashed, all right?" he said. "Let's get somewhere safe and ask questions later."

I thought I heard some of the others speak up to agree with that sentiment. Then again, it could have also been the voices creeping back into my head. Darkness slowly overtook my field of vision, choking out the wide open expanse of thick dead weeds and rocky soil spread out in front of me. Trace kept moving toward a large rock, telling me I could sit down once we got there. I was out well before that.

————◦————

Liiig dom iiiii.

Those words smeared across my brain, shredding the peaceful dark that had wrapped around me.

Liig dom iii. Taa say aahhg teach.

Again and again, they rolled through my head like the invasive thrusts of a rapist's hips to take away any solace I might have found while my body slept.

When I woke up again, I didn't know what time it was. That was something else that seemed to have fallen by the wayside now that the whole world was dealing with the Ice Virus. Trace didn't even bother wearing a watch any longer. When I'd asked him why, he told me that once a man's taking his last breaths, he doesn't bother counting them.

That's always stuck with me.

It was getting dark, and the wrecked van was far behind us. The air was colder than before. A wind blew across the top of all that dead grass on either side of the road, making it sway and whisper. At least, I'd hoped that sound was the grass. These days, you never could tell.

The first person to realize that I was trying to sit up was Yancy Darmond. She scooted over to me from her seat near the others by a little campfire, while favoring her right side. When she got closer, she stretched both muscular legs in front of her and propped herself up. Long, thick black hair fell down to cover half of a beautiful face covered in smooth, coffee-colored skin. "You're awake," she said.

"How long was I out?"

"Just an hour or so."

"What happened to your leg?" I asked.

Yancy pushed her hair back, then prodded her knee gingerly. "Dislocated my knee," she said in an Icelandic accent that I always thought sounded like a cross between Norse and Elvish. "It doesn't hurt very badly. What about you? Is your arm still painful?"

"Not as much as before. I thought it was broken."

"It was. Still is." Holding up a small bottle made of clear brown plastic, she added, "Percocet."

"Ahh. The good stuff. No wonder." My smile was caused partly by the drugs and partly by the close-up view of Yancy's light blue eyes. The smirk faded quickly enough once I got a better look at the others clustered nearby.

There'd been eight of us crammed into that van. Sure, it could hold fifteen passengers, but a good chunk of that space had been filled with weapons, food, survival gear, and some communications equipment we'd scavenged from a rinky-dink electronics store outside of Placentia. Over the course of several hard days of driving, enough space emerged to add another couple of stray passengers. I could only see three figures huddled around the sputtering fire. Petkus was one. Pete Hester was another. Trace was doing something to Pete's foot, and judging by the occasional yelps that would come from him, Pete wasn't floating on the same prescription cloud as me.

"Where's the rest?" I asked, even though I wasn't quite sure if I was ready for the answer.

"Jon's dead," Yancy told me. "But you know that. Mix is lying over there."

Tammy Crocker was the one responsible for my exceptionally good mood. She'd been an emergency room nurse back when the world still made sense, and always knew where to look for medical supplies. About three days after the crash of Flight 472, Petkus caught a round in the hip from an overzealous gas station attendant. When Tammy fixed him up and shot him full of morphine, he'd wanted to call her Doctor Feelgood. Yancy came up with Mix instead, citing her inspiration from a box of name brand cake mix. Since Tammy Crocker wasn't a fan of drug dealer references or smash hits of the '80s, the second name was the one that had stuck.

"Is she okay?" I asked.

"Bumped her head," Yancy told me. "I think she'll be fine. Pete broke his ankle. I think we are all very lucky after being in such a crash. What happened back there, anyway? You were sitting next to Jon when he was driving. Why did he crash? Was he trying to swerve away from something?"

I narrowed my eyes, focusing on that moment in the past. "No," I said. "There wasn't anything in the road. I didn't even know that tree was there until we were about to plow into it. Damn." I winced in pain as a wave of cold sweat broke at the top of my forehead and trickled down my face. Then I felt Yancy's hand on my cheek.

"You need to rest," she told me.

Who was I to argue with eyes like that?

———◆———

I dreamt of Flight 472. Up there, it felt like we'd escaped the war for a while. No more disease. No more shooting. No more crazed lunatics trying to eat us alive or rip us apart. There were just us people in that little passenger jet trying to get somewhere safer than the States.

I dreamt of landing in Deer Lake near the Gulf of St. Lawrence, dragging my bag through the airport while trying to figure out where to catch my connecting flight, thinking about why international travel still had to be such a colossal pain in the ass. I'd been looking at the menu of a coffee stand, wondering if I had enough money to buy a brownie, when the plane that had brought me this far slammed into the ground. It was less than an hour after I'd gotten off of it. There'd been fire. Screaming. Death.

Always screaming.

Always death.

All the time.

Not just here.

Everywhere.

I couldn't open my eyes fast enough. The drugs had worn off, leaving me with a slight dizziness and a shitload of pain. My left arm was in a sling wrapped tightly around my torso to keep it in place. For a moment or two, I stayed still, waiting for all those echoes to stop ringing in my ears.

Then I saw it.

Movement.

Something was trying to circle around me from the right. I twisted to look in that direction, but whatever it was darted away.

"Ray's up," Trace said from the campfire. He stood up and took a step toward me. "Something wrong, Ray?"

"I saw something in the air," I said. "It was black. Floated like smoke."

"There's plenty of smoke," Petkus said. "From the fire."

No matter how much it hurt, I pulled myself to my feet. "It's more than that. It was trying to sneak up on me."

A few years ago, a statement like that would have been laughed at. Now, it brought everyone to their feet. Our group had collected two shotguns and three pistols, which came up as well.

Kate Timmons was one of the only ones to have brought her own gun to the fight. It was a .40 caliber Glock that was as much a part of her as the little red tattoo on her ankle. "Vampires?" she snapped. "Where?" Even without the gun in her hand, Kate was an intimidating sight. Her short, straw-colored hair and the slight upturn to her nose were attractive in a way, but there was an intensity in her eyes that hadn't dimmed in the slightest in the short time I'd known her.

"Wait," Petkus said in a harsh whisper. "I hear them. Whatever it is sure ain't floating. There's boots on the ground."

Ta say ansayo.

Whatever the hell the voice was saying to me now, I didn't have time for it. The damned thing must not have liked being ignored, because it growled, "*Ta say ansayo. Ni mor dooiit trooeeed!!!*"

I tried not to react to the voice I was hearing. We hadn't been together as a group for long, and I wasn't about to tell them I was in the middle of a psychotic break. My ears strained to pick up a snarling breath or a hungry wheeze, anything that would let me know what sort of bloodsuckers might be headed for the campfire.

Tension pulsed through the air like a collective breath taken by every one of us. About twelve to fifteen yards away from the fire was a man walking at a slow and steady pace. After a few more steps, he was close enough for me to see a few bits of metal attached to his clothing. Light from the stars and some from the fire glinted off a web belt around his waist as well as an insignia pinned to his chest.

Petkus stepped forward holding his shotgun in a loose grip. "What're you doing here, soldier?"

The figure stopped.

"Better answer me, boy," Petkus warned as he brought the shotgun to his shoulder.

Trace had a flashlight in his hand and pointed its beam at the approaching stranger. The newcomer was definitely a soldier, and when the light shone in his eyes, he shied away from it. His clothes were stained and tattered. He carried a rifle slung over one shoulder, which he switched to a two-handed grip.

Petkus took aim. "We're human! Take a look for yourself."

The soldier leaned his head to one side and stared at us with blank, pure white eyes. Lowering the weapon, he opened his mouth to speak. Saliva dripped from his bottom lip as he said, "I'll crawl into your SKINS!"

Without hesitation, Petkus squeezed his trigger. The shotgun roared in his hands, causing an eruption of crimson pulp to explode from the soldier's chest. Fire from the weapon's barrel acted like a flare, illuminating the faces of at least four more soldiers who'd been crawling toward the camp with their bellies pressed against the ground.

"They're crawling on the ground!" I shouted. "Aim low!"

"I got some over here too," Trace said. "Conserve your ammunition."

Some pistols were fired in the vicinity of the campfire. I could tell a few of those rounds hit due to the wheezing groans coming from ground level. Something was to my left, so I wheeled around to face that direction. The creature I found had also once been a soldier. His uniform was stained with blood and caked in mud. When he looked up at me with those solid white eyes and bared long, jagged teeth, I slammed my heel straight down into his face.

Bone crunched beneath my shoe. Even as the thing's head was snapped to one side, it reached up for my ankle with both hands. I tried to yank my foot away before the thing got a tight grip on me, but its fingers cinched in with the desperate strength of someone whose body was pushed past its limits by this goddamn plague. As it pulled my foot in closer, the vampire opened its mouth to display several teeth that were exposed almost down to the root due to the gums being shriveled away. Their tips were chipped and broken, sharpening them down to irregular points. The sight was more than enough to wipe away the last of the Percocet haze still lingering in my brain, allowing me to pull my leg free. When I swung it back to kick the vampire's ugly face, it was instantly captured by another crawler behind me.

Having my momentum stopped so suddenly robbed me of my balance. I tried to stay upright, but was quickly brought down to land hard on my side. It was all I could do to twist my body around to avoid slamming all of my weight down onto my broken arm. Although I succeeded with that, the impact still drove a good portion of the wind from my sails.

"I'm a friendly!" someone said. I didn't recognize the voice, but it sounded like a woman's. "I'm here to help!"

A shotgun roared. The groan that followed started off as an inhuman cry, but faded into something more familiar.

I heard all of this as I kicked and thrashed both legs to keep away the two vampires who'd set their sights on me. One of the creatures opened its mouth so wide that I could hear the wet snap of its jaw breaking. Every muscle in its face worked to try and get its teeth just a bit closer to my broken arm before clamping down. I managed to pull my arm away, but rolled onto the cast as I twisted around to keep my legs out of either creature's range.

The pain that flooded through my body sharpened my senses like a whetstone. I spotted a pistol in a holster clipped to the belt of one of the things crawling on the ground, and when I shifted my weight to reach for it, the pain from mashing my arm against the ground forced a scream from the back of my throat.

The vampires on the ground screamed as well, crying and wailing in a terrible chorus amid the sporadic gunfire. By the time I stretched out to grab the gun I'd spotted, my body was perpendicular to the vampire's. My fingers closed around the pistol's grip and I pulled it from its holster as the creature flopped around to come at me again. It was so close that I could smell the coppery stench of all that blood caking the inside of its mouth. I gave it something else to chew on when I jammed the pistol's barrel into its gaping maw with enough force to shatter most of its front teeth. I squeezed the trigger, but nothing happened.

It reached for me with both hands while gnawing on the gun barrel. Using my thumb, I flicked off the pistol's safety, and squeezed the trigger again. This time, the gun bucked against my palm while sending a very satisfying spray of blood and bone fragments out the back of the vampire's head. I should have been more careful about conserving ammo, but I kept pulling that trigger until the fucking thing stopped moving. Another one was crawling my way. Rather than take the time to free my newly acquired weapon, I angled it within the mostly hollow skull of the still-twitching vampire and fired another couple of rounds. Those bullets punched into the other vampire's body, but a third creature was coming at me with fire in its eyes. When that one's head exploded like a cherry bomb, I knew it wasn't because of divine intervention.

I looked up to see a tall woman dressed in the same kind of uniform as the vampires crawling on the ground. Hers was far from clean, but it wasn't as putrid as the rags wrapped around the things that had attacked us. The assault rifle in her hands looked like an older model AK-47. She had crudely buzzed hair and a long face, but was the sweetest thing I'd seen in a good long while. "Are you able to stand?" she asked.

"I think so."

She pulled me to my feet before sending a few more rounds into one of the vampires on the ground. After that, she swapped out the rifle's magazine for a fresh one and worked her way back to the campfire while shooting in short, controlled bursts.

There were bodies strewn everywhere. Most of them still clawed at the ground like broken toys without getting anywhere. The rest were so messed up that I couldn't tell if they were once a part of my group or one of the things that had raided our camp. Pretty soon, I caught sight of Pete Hester facing one of the vampires. He dropped to one knee, furiously working the pump action of a spent shotgun while pulling its trigger. No matter how many times he came up empty, he kept trying to find another shell.

I stepped in on his behalf using the gun I'd taken from the dead soldier. There was a time when shooting something, anything at all, would have been tough for me. Those were distant memories, and the only problem I had now was stopping after blowing too many holes through the back of this bloodsucker's skull. It dropped onto its side and let out a shuddering breath.

"You all right, Pete?" I asked. "Did it get you?"

"I'm fine," Pete replied.

That's when I saw the mess of blood on the front of Pete's shirt. It caught the flickering firelight to look like a thick oil spill over his stomach and waist. I reached out to help him up, and when he stretched out an arm toward me, the gaping hole in his belly yawned open. I still had a loose grip on his hand when he flopped to the ground like a piece of luggage that had been dropped into a mud puddle.

I'm not completely certain what happened after that. I grabbed the shotgun by the barrel, burning my hand against the hot metal, and swung it with everything I had. Having my left arm wrapped in a sling didn't keep me from smashing some of those fucking crawlers' heads like melons.

——•——

However long it took for the shooting to stop, it took longer for the screaming to fade away. Once it got quiet, and we found a new place to camp, I was reminded just how different Newfoundland was than the place I'd left behind. The night was darker somehow. Colder. Then again, that could have been the company I was forced to keep.

Petkus approached the campfire, emerging from the shadows while sliding one last shell into his shotgun. Looking around at those of us gathered in the paltry bit of warmth offered by the flames, he asked, "Is this all that's left?"

Besides me and him, the only ones I could see were Yancy, Trace, Kate, and the two soldiers who'd arrived at the same time as the invading crawlers. One of them was the woman carrying the assault rifle. The other was a younger guy with sunken features and tired eyes pulled straight from a nineteenth century photograph.

"Pete's dead," I announced.

Frowning, Petkus asked, "You sure?"

"Oh yeah."

Kate Timmons kept her hands on her hips as if she needed support just to keep from wilting in the middle. "Mix is gone too."

That one hit our group hard. Everyone liked Mix. There was something comforting about almost everything she did, right down to the tone in her voice. There was a vaguely haunted look in Kate's eyes when she added, "She didn't have a chance. One of those things got to her before she could get up."

"That knock to the head must have been pretty bad," I said. "Maybe she didn't even know what was coming."

Kate wanted to fire back at me, if only to have a target for her anger, but she choked it back down. "It was probably a peaceful way to go," she said unconvincingly.

"We don't have time for this," the soldier with the assault rifle said. She carried herself like someone who should have worn a lot more bars and medals on her uniform than what she had. "We need to regroup and head to the north end of Windsor Lake."

"Why?" Yancy asked. Her face was scraped up pretty good, and she favored her arm even more than the last time I'd spoken to her, but she seemed to have pulled through the fighting relatively well. "What's at the lake?"

"For that matter," Petkus snapped, "who the hell are you guys, and why should we listen to a damn word you say?"

I was expecting Kate to jump onto that bandwagon with both feet, but Trace was the one who spoke up first. He'd been gathering firewood in the darkness surrounding camp and stepped into the light with his arms full of twigs. "One thing's for certain. Before we discuss anything or even entertain the thought of following your orders, we need to know what those things were that attacked us."

The woman with the assault rifle scowled at each of us in turn. "They are vampires," she said. "And they're everywhere, unless I'm mistaken."

There was an accent coloring her words, blending the local dialect with a bit of Russian tossed in for spice.

"You're not mistaken," Trace said. "It also seemed these vampires were dressed in uniforms similar to yours."

She pulled in a deep breath. When she finally let it go, it took a good amount of her strength along with it. "They were part of my squadron. Some were stationed here. Others joined to replenish our ranks. Now, we are like many of the fighters who are not part of a larger military. We stay organized, keep mobile, and do what we can to survive while helping others whenever we can. Those things infected us. Tore us apart from the inside. Forced us to abandon the train station we'd fortified as a base."

"They weren't like the vampires I've seen before," I said. "Why were they crawling? One of them had white eyes."

She seemed confused as she looked at me and then to Trace. Finally, she said, "I thought maybe you've been here since the bombs fell."

"No. We were on a plane that went down not too long ago. When it crashed, it took out most of the airport at Deer Lake."

She nodded. "I heard of this. That was Flight 472."

"That's right. I was on that plane along with Yancy and another guy named Jon. Jon's dead. That's Yancy right over there."

Yancy gave her a tired wave.

"I'm Ray Bulloy, by the way. Over there is Stan Petkus. That's Trace Bilson right in front of you."

Trace stepped forward to extend his hand for both of the new arrivals to shake. Never one to let anyone do her talking for her, Kate approached them directly and introduced herself.

"I'm Anne Fleming," said the woman with the assault rifle. "I was a Corporal in the ICRU."

"What's that?" I asked.

Petkus answered my question before Fleming could say another word. "Icelandic Crisis Response Unit. They're a small group, but do a lot of good work. That explains why these two have been able to survive in a fortified location when so many others are scrambling for their next meal."

Shaking her head, Fleming replied. "Our transport landed at an airstrip about fifty clicks south of here. Before we could take off again, we were overrun. Since then we've barely been surviving. Tonight, most of us couldn't even accomplish that much."

"How many of you are left?"

"Besides me," Fleming said while motioning to the man to her right, "there is only Private Gundafssten. He was new to the ICRU before the first V-Cells made their presence known."

"That was a while ago," Trace said warily. "You guys must really be tight when it comes to handing out promotions."

"Our rank means nothing," Gundafssten said dryly. "It is a relic of the world as it was."

And I thought Petkus needed to lighten up every now and then.

"There were half a dozen more in our unit," Fleming continued. "Three times that in civilians who'd sought shelter within our barracks. Over the last day, all of the civilians were either turned or killed. Then my men began to fall. We evacuated, and now there is only what you see here."

"I'm real sorry to hear about the people you lost," I said, "but we stand to lose even more if we don't get somewhere safe. You mentioned Windsor Lake. What's out there?"

"I only heard about it two days ago. It's supposed to be an abandoned radio station with a functioning broadcast tower and a cellar underneath the main building. Sounds like a good place to lay low and call for help."

"I suppose so," Kate said with a shrug. "As long as the tower has a wide enough range to be much use, Ray might be able to do something with it."

Trace lowered himself to sit on the ground near the fire. Its flames were quickly petering out, so he fed it some of the wood he'd collected. "You still haven't told us about those vampires. They're different than the ones we've seen in the States."

Fleming's entire body tensed, and her eyes narrowed into slits. She was sifting through some fresh nightmares, trying to force them back into whatever cage she'd created for them in her mind before they got the best of her. I knew that look all too well from personal experience.

"They are called *adjyaseek*. Or that is what our liaison out here called them. It is a Beothuk term that means 'two made into one.'"

"Beothuk?" I asked.

Fleming nodded once. "They're a people who lived on these lands hundreds of years ago. Maybe more. Maybe a little less. I'm not a historian, but there were creatures similar to them back home in Iceland. We call them *draugr*. They possess the bodies of those close to death, turning them into the creatures you have seen tonight."

"They seemed more like animals," Trace said. "I saw a couple different kinds of vampires when I was working my way through Arizona and into Mexico, but nothing like that."

"That is because the souls of the people they were are still inside them," Fleming replied. Shaking her head, she added, "These are different than our *draugr*. More savage. I believe they have gone mad or reverted to a more primitive state."

"For not being a historian," I pointed out, "you sure seem to know a thing or two about these vampires."

When she spoke again, her voice was drawn taut. "Soldiers from my unit were sent here as reinforcements to aid in the war. I and one other of us were attached to this detail because we have faced the *draugr* before."

"Then you know how to kill them?" Trace asked hopefully.

Fleming's eyes went to him and then to each of us in turn. "It is as I said. These are different. They look out through eyes that have been wiped clean and attack like dogs that have been beaten and starved at the bottom of a pit. These *adjyaseek* are something terrible."

Coming from a soldier in this damn war, that meant something.

"Jon's eyes were like that," I said. Looking to Fleming and Gundafssten, I added, "He was driving us here when he got real quiet. His eyes rolled back or turned white or whatever. Then he just stepped on the gas and steered for the first thing he could find."

Gundafssten nodded solemnly. "The *adjyaseek* cause as much damage as they can because they feel no pain. They enjoy tearing us up, making us betray and hurt the people around us before they feed and move on."

"I don't know if these vampires are better or worse than what we had back home," Yancy said.

I had to agree with her. Also, I was getting a real good sense for the kind of nightmares that were drifting through Fleming's mind.

"A DAY IN THE LIFE" PT.4

Jonathan Maberry

Las Vegas, Nevada

On the set in fifteen," said the production assistant. "We're going to block out the dorm scene. Then Roger's going to want to do the first take right after."

Lacey Starr looked up from her book. "Okay."

When the PA left, Lacey leaned back against the couch cushions and closed the book. It was the trade-paperback edition of Tony Robbins' latest self-empowerment stuff. Most of it was geared toward people on the junior executive track in corporate America, but there was some stuff for her.

Even for her.

Her trailer was almost evenly divided between the world we lived in and the one she wanted to embrace. Around the couch were bookshelves filled with business books, spiritual upliftment books, personal development books, and a lot of New Age stuff about attuning oneself to the universal harmonic and how to draw success to you through the power of intention. Lacey gobbled it all up, and she clung to the promises in each of those books, and in the YouTube videos, the online seminars, and those live events she could afford.

The other half of the trailer—well, three quarters really—reminded her of the anchors that kept her in this life. Framed posters that had been installed as "gifts" by her producers. She was on every poster, just as she was on every DVD cover. In every poster she was partially or entirely naked. In every poster she was performing a sex act—fellatio, cunnilingus, anal or vaginal sex, or self-gratification with enormous dildos. In every picture she was dressed as she was now, in a black wig, with bat earrings, blood-red lipstick, and fangs.

Always the fangs.

The fangs were what sold the act.

Lacey Starr, vampire porn actress.

Real vampire. Real sex. No genuine passion, no dignity, no future, no nothing.

Money, though. Enough to pay for a lifestyle that was worlds better than what some of her friends had. There were vampires in homeless shelters. There were vampires working the streets giving BJs and getting fucked thirty times a night so they could feed their kids. Most of them had human kids. The V-Gene didn't turn everyone. Human women could give birth to vampire babies. Vampire women could give birth to human babies. It was weird. It was fucked up.

Like her life. Fucked, and fucked up.

The posters were so stupid, with titles like *Bloodlist*, *Eaters of the Dead*, *Dracula Sucks*, *Virgin Blood*, and *Staked*.

Fang porn.

Last year it was a niche market that only made money from underground sales. One Supreme Court battle later it was a legal mass market with an anticipated gross income of one-point-three billion. With a "b."

Her take was a sliver. A slice.

More than she made doing *faux* dorm room porn and *faux* casting call porn before the wars. After she turned, she spent sixteen months making no money at all except when she could get a call girl gig here in Vegas. Somehow that was more humiliating than fucking for the cameras.

Now Lacey was on her way to being a solid third-tier star. Second tier maybe, if she wanted to have her boobs done and let a dentist file her other teeth. The women who did that could earn in the mid six figures. This year she'd hit six, but only just.

She tossed the book onto the couch and stood up.

Her costume for this scene was typical of the new genre. Stockings with a spiderweb pattern, a black corset trimmed with red lace, short black and red satin cape with a high fan collar. So 1950s bullshit retro.

But it sold. The plot of the movie—such as it was—involved a pack of female vampires invading a college dorm. The entire story could be written in large letters on a three-by-five card with plenty of room for a comment like, "Are you fucking kidding me?"

The film would go straight to video, and with streaming it would be on the laptops of millions of lonely men by the end of next month. Lacey tried not to think of how many solitary orgasms had been engineered because of her. It did not make her feel sexy or special.

Or human.

Or anything.

The PA knocked twice on the door and yelled, "Five minutes."

Lacey stared at herself in the mirror. She was, according to the doctors at the clinic, a *white lady of fau*, a species of seductress vampire. And she had some chops with that. She could always get her costar hard and keep him focused. But she was also a mutt, like most American vampires. Her grandmother was half-French, which is where the *fau* gene came from. The rest of her was just a human-looking bloodsucker. Nothing special. Not without special effects, push-up bras and good lighting.

She closed her eyes for a moment and willed herself not to cry. Messing up her makeup would delay the shoot, and everyone would be mad at her. Lacey didn't want anyone to be mad.

She took a deep, steadying breath, switched off the lights, and left.

Another day, another dollar.

"THE RUSH" PT. 2

Marcus Pelegrimas

The camp was quiet.

It was late.

We were supposed to be getting some rest, but that was a whole lot easier said than done. These days, sleeping was mostly just what we called passing out under slightly controlled circumstances. The only other rest I got anymore was after being *knocked* out.

"You're not a soldier," Fleming said to me.

The two of us sat on the periphery of the firelight, keeping watch for anything crawling toward the camp from the shadows.

"No," I replied. "I'm not."

"How did you get to this place?"

"On a plane. Weren't you listening before?"

The expression that flickered across her hardened face may have been a smile, but I couldn't be sure. "You know what I mean," Fleming said. "Traveling anywhere is dangerous. Making such a long flight across so much open ground is a risk one would only take if they had to."

"I was working at a radio station in Albuquerque. That's in New Mexico."

"I know."

"My brother-in-law was a lieutenant in the Air Force."

"Was?" she asked.

Used to be that I felt something like a gut punch whenever I thought too hard about Terry. It was getting easier every day, though. Not much, but a little. Thinking about my sister was another story. "Yeah. He and a few others got a communications relay started at my station. It began as a way to help troops pass along intelligence reports, or allow anyone who needed it to get organized by hooking up with other groups. After a while, radio traffic got scarce."

"Did the military take over the station?"

"No. The bloodsuckers wiped out just about everyone close enough to get our signal." As images of all those bodies and all that blood rose to the surface, I took a breath and kept talking. "Eventually, the station became more of a beacon. It let people know there were still some humans around that could point them in the right direction."

"Like a lighthouse," Fleming said.

"Something like that. Pretty soon, Terry developed a working relationship with a guy named Luther Swann."

That caused Fleming to perk up. "Van Helsing?"

"That's his call sign. You know him?"

"I was trying to contact someone who might be able to put the rest of the pieces together on how to fight the *draugr* back in my country. It took a long time for messages to be passed along. The most recent one I received was from Van Helsing. He directed me to a man named Brian Childs, a researcher who either would know about the *adjyaseek* or could find something that would be of use." She shook her head. "I only got a few messages after making my request. Gundafssten thought that perhaps the Americans were holding out to strike some sort of bargain for the information."

"What did you hear from Childs?"

"He mentioned something about an airborne virus, along with a few legends about possession. We haven't heard anything from America for a while now."

"How did you contact Childs and Swann?" I asked. "Was there a series of relays that passed your message along to a final destination frequency of 105.7?"

"Yes! I found a list of frequencies to be used for such a purpose and 105.7 was the last one in the sequence. Have you used the same system?" Before I could answer that, she snapped her fingers and said, "That was where you were working?"

I put a hand to one ear as if to hold an imaginary set of headphones in place and slipped into a smooth yet smarmy voice as I said, "This is *One*

Oh Five Seven, The Ruuuush. Your best place for the best rock, day or night. Request lines are open."

Fleming couldn't have looked more confused if I'd thrown confetti in the air and started doing the Macarena.

"I was a DJ," I told her. "I worked all over the country and was at that station for less than a year before the Ice Virus popped up. Terry convinced me to stay when he needed a communications setup to aid the military, and put me to work. I helped keep the place running and manned the switchboard. Kind of the same job as before except with the occasional firefight and vampires roaming the streets."

"And that's how you wound up on that plane?"

"Things were getting bad. The fighting was getting worse. Terry said it was only a matter of time before the station got overrun and we had to clear out of there. I thought he meant going to California or maybe up into Canada, but he meant clearing out of the States altogether, and Canada wasn't far enough away. I've found that when someone in the military tells you something like that, you listen."

"This is an awfully long way to run, isn't it?" Fleming asked. "Or was this the first international flight you could find?"

"No," I said. "I'm pretty sure I've got some family in Sweden. I think it's still pretty safe over there."

"Only pretty sure? About family?"

"Yeah. What do you want from me?"

Fleming shrugged. "I don't mean to upset you. I just thought you would have had more information on the matter, especially since you worked at a station where information was relayed from across the globe."

"We didn't get information from the entire rest of the world, but we did get it from a lot of… "

After a few seconds, Fleming put a hand on my knee. "What is it? Are you all right? Look at me."

"I'm fine. I just haven't really taken a lot of time to think about all of this lately. Everything's been so hectic after the crash. All I remember is— "

"Shut up," she snapped. "I said look at me. Now!"

"Relax. I'm trying to think."

But I had a feeling that Fleming wasn't the sort who relaxed very much even under good circumstances. She grabbed my chin and forced me to look straight at her. That wasn't enough, so she used her free hand to open my eyes even more by peeling the lids up with her thumb. Since I didn't want to get blinded with a stray poke, I sat still and let her do her thing.

"Do you feel dizzy?" she asked. "Or lightheaded?"

"No. Why?"

"Because that's how someone feels when they are taken over by an *adjyaseek*. They feel dizzy, sick, and their eyes lose all color. Your eyes seemed strange for a moment, but they're fine now," she said while releasing my chin.

"I still feel kinda sick."

"I've felt sick since the first day this war started," Fleming sighed. "The truth is that I know very little about my country's *draugr* and even less about the parasites here."

"What about voices?" I reluctantly asked.

Her eyes had been tired, but showed more of a spark when she heard that. "What kind of voices?"

"It seemed that some of the people that were taken over by those things were hearing voices. Is that… a thing?"

She nodded. "That was in the reports sent to Iceland. I heard it from a few of the locals here as well. Some of those infected by the *adjyaseek* heard a voice in their head. A voice that wasn't their own."

"What did it say?"

"I couldn't make sense of what they told me, but I am not a linguist."

"You must have been able to put something together," I said, my lack of sleep becoming abundantly clear with every impatient word. "Isn't that why you're here?"

"Brian Childs thought the *adjyaseek* might have been some sort of airborne poison spreading that breed of vampire like a plague."

"A vampire consciousness that was carried to another country and then spread to different hosts." Saying it out loud didn't help the news go down any easier. "What about leeg dom aye?"

The abrupt subject change hit Fleming like a splash of cold water in the face. "What?"

"Whoever was hearing those voices," I explained, "mentioned them saying something like that."

I couldn't tell if she was buying the fact that I wasn't the one who was the crazy bastard listening to voices, but she gave it some thought before replying, "That was similar to something in the reports, but I don't know what it means."

"Do you think they were really hearing them and weren't just crazy?"

She let out a tired laugh. "It makes as much sense as the other shit that's been happening."

There wasn't a good way to fight that kind of logic, so I didn't even try. "So this facility at the lake," I said. "What are we talking about? What kind of setup is there?"

"We'll know when we get there."

"How do we know it's any better than where we're at?"

"We don't," Fleming replied. "We just have to keep moving before those *adjyaseek* find us. If they do, we will become those things you saw."

"Do you know anything else about them? Like why they crawl or why their eyes are like that?"

"All I know is that they inhabit the bodies of the dead, and shooting them doesn't put an end to them."

"The ones we shot seemed to be ended well enough," I said.

She looked at me like someone trying to decide whether or not to tell a child about who really put the presents under the tree every Christmas. Rather than burst my bubble, she nodded and found somewhere else to be.

———◦———

"How's your arm?" Trace asked the next morning.

It was early, but not so early that it still felt like night. Hell, it didn't really matter. It was time for breakfast. Trying not to move too much as I sucked in my next breath, I said, "Hurts like a bastard. What did you expect?"

Trace was kneeling on the ground beside me. For such a lanky guy, he had some muscle. When he took hold of my wrist and shoulder, I couldn't even come close to pulling away from him. "What about that?" he asked.

"What the fuck do you think? That hurts too! What do you want from me?"

"I want to see if your arm was set correctly."

"You're the group nurse now?"

"Now that Mix is dead, I suppose I am."

I felt bad about snapping like that. "Where are those Percocet?"

"You can't have any," Trace replied almost immediately.

"Why not?"

"First of all, you've been popping those things or some other kind of painkiller since the crash."

"Yeah? So? My eardrums popped on the flight over here, and I caught some shrapnel when the goddamn airport was exploding around us. Following recommended dosages for pain meds isn't exactly a priority, is it?"

As always, Trace stayed on track no matter how many diversions landed in front of him. "We need you to be sharp," he said. "So far, you've been helpful to the group, but if there's functioning radio equipment at that lake, you're the most qualified among us to operate it or recognize any repairs that need to be made." Looking to the soldiers, he asked, "Am I right?"

"We lost our technical specialists some time ago," Fleming replied. "I can operate standard communication gear, but that's about it."

"There you go," Trace said. "We need you at your best, Ray, and that means no more pain meds."

As I averted my eyes from Trace, something else caught my attention. "Gundafssten? What the hell do you think you're doing?"

Gundafssten had drawn his pistol. When I turned to get a better look, I could see that he was actually pointing it in Petkus's vicinity, if not directly at him. Stan didn't appreciate the distinction.

"Answer the question, soldier," Petkus said as his hand drifted toward his sidearm.

"I saw something," Gundafssten replied. The look of absolute certainty that had been on his face a moment ago was quickly slipping. "It was there."

I stepped closer to him, putting myself between Gundafssten and Petkus. "Did it speak to you?"

Gundafssten's eyes snapped over to me. In them was confusion and not a small amount of fear.

"Is it speaking to you right now?" I asked.

He blinked rapidly, like he'd just gotten something splashed onto his face. I was trying to maintain eye contact with him, which was how I saw the redness spread out from his pupils. In a strained voice, he said, "Seead ahg teacht. Lig dom i." When he blinked again, the redness was gone, along with every other bit of color that had been in his eyes, leaving nothing but milky white orbs in his sockets.

Before I could say a damn thing about what I saw, Gundafssten turned his gun toward the people having their breakfast around the fire and started shooting. Kate caught the first two in the chest. She was reaching for her Glock and even managed to fire off a round before her back hit the ground.

By this time, Petkus had opened fire as well. Gundafssten was close enough to me that I could hear each of Petkus' rounds slapping against flesh and bone. Even as he fell, Gundafssten kept shooting. After he hit the ground, he sent his last bullet through Petkus' neck.

All of this happened in less than three or four seconds. Since I didn't have a gun on me, I tried to get the hell away from all the shooting. Along the way, I noticed what had caught Gundafssten's attention in the first place. There were four people in tattered clothes pulling themselves toward the camp. Some wore the remains of military uniforms, and others were wrapped in simple jeans and sweatshirts. They didn't make a sound. They just stared at us with wide, pure white eyes.

"Here!" Fleming shouted at me. "Take this."

She was handing me the assault rifle, which I took and hefted to get a feel for its weight.

"Just get close to them and pull the trigger," she said. "I will… "

The rest of what she said was lost amid the roar that suddenly filled my ears. It was a sound that was part voice and part gust of wind coming from my left and rushing directly at me. As it got closer, I could hear words within the static filling my mind. *Leeg dom i. Leeg dom i.*

The blackness enveloped everything I saw, seeping in around the edges of my sight until my entire world was reduced to hazy images seen through black gauze. My heart pounded as if it was trying to escape through my shattered rib cage. With every thumping beat, the blackness grew thicker.

I couldn't see much of the outside world. All I could make out was a few scrambling bodies and one large figure looming directly in front of me. It was Fleming. She stared directly at me and said something, but her words were washed away by the voice spewing in my mind. All the other times, I'd tried to shut the voice out, push it back, do anything so I wouldn't need to hear it. Now, I was too distracted and just too damn tired to put up a mental fight along with the one involving guns.

As I stopped resisting the voice, it became less of a snarl and more of an insistent cry for attention. I still didn't know the language that was being pumped into me, but it slowly shifted into something I could understand.

They are coming.

Fleming took a swing at me and connected with something a lot harder than a fist.

The blackness became everything.

———•———

I woke up slowly, pulling myself from the mental muck like one of those vampires dragging their sorry asses across the cold dirt. Back in the days when I worked at the radio station, and life wasn't a continual shit storm, I used to do the occasional interview. Mostly, I spoke to local musicians who were inevitably asked about their inspirations or where their ideas came from. Many times, they referred to coming up with stuff in a dream or having epiphanies in the space between sleeping and being awake. I used to think that was some poorly veiled drug reference, but suddenly I wasn't so sure.

In that sliver of time between thinking I should open my eyes and actually moving a lid, I had an epiphany of my own, and it was a whopper.

"Let me in," the voice had told me. But more than that, it had spoken to me without taking control and without trying to turn me into a bloodthirsty animal. Maybe the one doing the talking wasn't a vampire, but something else. Someone else.

A voice from the past.

A victim crying out to be heard.

There was another fight happening nearby. Gunfire erupted in the distance, as well as my immediate vicinity. People were shouting. Some were growling. I didn't dare open my eyes all the way, so I cracked them just enough to get a peek at what was going on. The first thing I saw was a gray sky smudged with clouds that looked like dirty paint caught in the process of drying. When I turned to see where the closest voices were coming from, pain stabbed through my face and neck. The surge of adrenaline that came next acted like a spotlight inside of me that I hadn't meant to switch on. With a series of quick, choppy breaths, I did my best to bring that surge down to a trickle.

I was lying on the ground, so I turned my head and spotted a mess of brownish red hair. Trace was crawling toward me. A few gunshots exploded above me, and Trace's body thrashed with the impact of each bullet. He landed on the ground, his head turned to one side so he could stare at me with gaping, milky white eyes. One of his hands came to rest upon my torso, and when I tried to push it off, the fingers closed into a fist around the front of my shirt.

A dirty black boot swung past my face. I could see the laces and stitching as I braced for the impact of a kick against my jaw. Instead, the boot caught Trace's arm and knocked his grip loose from where he'd grabbed me. There was a solid thump against the ground a few inches away as the person wearing the boot took a knee and jammed a gun barrel against my temple.

"Open your eyes," a familiar voice demanded.

When I tried to shift my body and head to get a better angle, the barrel was pressed against my face so hard that it practically nailed me to the ground.

"I said open your eyes!"

"There," I said while opening them as much as I dared. "See?"

Corporal Fleming looked down at me over the top of her assault rifle. It was an AKSU-74, a relic as far as weaponry went, but still reliable, and one hell of a good companion in a fight. If I allowed myself to think a little harder, I probably could have come up with plenty more. "You were being turned," she said. "Your eyes were changing. I took my gun back and knocked you out before you were lost."

"That explains the headache."

"Get up," she told me. "We need to move."

"I can't."

"Do you need help?"

"It's not that," I said. "I've got to tell you something."

She squinted down at me, silently looking me over for wounds. "It needs to wait," she said. "The *adjyaseek* have overrun us on all sides. A mix of your people and mine."

"I... don't know how much longer I can hold it back."

Fleming looked up with a snap of her head and brought her assault rifle along with it. Gritting her teeth, she squeezed off a three-round burst to send one of our former acquaintances shrieking into hell. A few empty bullet casings rained down from the breach of her rifle, burning my cheek before rolling off my face.

Keeping her eyes up and scanning from side to side, she reached down with one hand to slap my shoulder impatiently. "We don't have time for this. If you want to lie here and babble, you can do it alone. If you want to see another morning, you'll suck it up and get to your goddamn feet!"

"This spirit or vampire or whatever the hell it is has been in me for a while," I said. "I don't even know how long."

That brought her attention back down to me. After firing a quick shot at something that rasped obscenities at her from about five meters away, she swapped magazines and chambered a fresh round. "How can that be?"

"I might have picked it up from one of the men in my brother-in-law's unit. Maybe he got it from overseas. I don't know. All I know is that it's not the only other presence in me. There's something else that's been talking to me.

"So you were the one hearing voices?"

"Yeah. It came from one of the first victims of the *draugr* that came over here from Iceland. It spoke to me in an old Irish dialect."

"How do you know this?" Fleming asked. "You've been hit in the head too many times. You're losing your grip."

"I won't argue about getting knocked around a bit too much lately, but

I know this is the truth. It was telling me to let it in. The whole time, it wanted me to let it in. Once it was strong enough to make me understand, I relaxed and… "

Fleming shook her head vigorously. "Whatever it is you're hearing, it's either a lie or a fever dream."

"No!" I snarled. "It's told me everything I need to know! The *adjyaseek* don't jump around from dead body to dead body. The more powerful vampires find one living host they like and stay there. They send out little bits of themselves into dead bodies to collect essence that they feed on. The one that's caused all of this trouble… it climbed into a body in one country and when it came out again, it was in another part of the world. Kind of like a fly in your car when you're taking a road trip. It doesn't realize the whole car was moving until it gets out again. One confused fly," I said with a tired smile.

"This makes no sense," Fleming said. "You are just dizzy."

"The *adjyaseek* wanted to get back home and used me to board Flight 472 to get there. It twisted my thoughts around. Influenced me. The damn thing is like some kind of fucking virus in my head, but when it bonds with its hosts it takes a part of those people with it. One of those former hosts has been trying to reach out to put an end to this, and I'm the one that's finally started to listen!"

Something nearby groaned, and Fleming answered back with a burst from her assault rifle. She swept her eyes once more in a wide pattern to search for incoming threats. "What did it tell you?" she asked.

"The *adjyaseek* burrows down deep inside someone and stays there. That's how it's lived for all the centuries before the Ice Virus. It feeds, creates its drones to gather food, and then wipes away the memory of what happened from its prey so it can repeat the cycle over and over again."

"So they were not created by the Ice Virus?"

"They ARE a virus," I said, pushing the words out while I still could. "What did you learn from Swann?"

"Just some old tales about the creatures feeding on human souls and that the only hunters to ever kill one of those demons had to use their bare hands."

There was less noise now. The shooting had pretty much stopped. Closing my eyes, I said, "Sounds like the fighting is over."

"It was almost over when you woke up," Fleming said. "It was a massacre, just like when my men and I were forced to evacuate our barracks. We've got to move, Ray. Whoever's left is already heading for safer ground. It will start again soon. The dead... I can already see them starting to twitch. We need to move before they rise."

"This thing that's inside me... it's still trying to get a firm hold. It's trying to feed. Trying to get stronger."

"You're delirious," Fleming grumbled. Slinging the assault rifle across her shoulder, she reached down to grab me under the arms and lift me up. "I'm taking you out of here, and we're going to that fortified position near Windsor Lake."

"No!"

My heart thumped solidly within my chest, sending blood through my veins in a strong and quickening pulse. As my senses cleared, and emergency energy was sent to my muscles, I could feel the thing inside me growing stronger. And with that strength came awareness.

"This thing," I said quickly, "it's draining the life out of me, just like the other vampires drink human blood. The voice... it says the *adjyaseek* feeds on life itself. I know that's true because I can feel it draining out of me."

"Enough," Fleming said. "I believe you. But we've got to get moving. The dead are waking up."

As I was lifted to my feet, I could hear the strained wheezing of resurrected lungs being forced to process air again. It was an eerily mechanical sound that made me appreciate how elegant a natural breath could be. My arm didn't hurt anymore. That whole half of my body was almost completely numb.

"This life energy the voice talked about," I continued while being pulled along, "I think it's adrenaline. The *adjyaseek* must drink that instead of blood... "

"Now I know you're babbling."

"Listen to me! It's the rush. Whatever it is, the chemical, our essence, adrenaline, or anything else it can be, that's what it wants. The monster inside me right now is curled up deep in my chest, sucking it out of me. I

253

can feel it. Like I'm bleeding out. I've seen the look on people's faces when a vampire is feeding on them. There's the rush of being bitten, and right before they die, there's a clarity in their eyes. They're understanding what's happening or what's about to happen."

"We have all seen such things," Fleming said gravely.

"Well I see what's happening now. Somehow this thing got passed to me just like it got passed to some of your men."

"You don't know that!" Fleming roared.

"Some of your people heard the voice too! It wasn't just me! These fucking things can't be seen. This might be our only chance to end it! If it gets past us, it'll tear through the next humans it finds, and it may be God knows how long before someone else listens to the goddamn voices in their head!"

"We need to—"

"Quiet!" I snapped.

Judging by the look on her face, Fleming wasn't used to being spoken to that way. Even so, she let me go on.

"I think these drones are weaker than the source," I said. "Too weak to stand on their own feet, but there're only a few stronger ones like the thing inside me now." As I spoke, memories that didn't belong to me flowed into my brain. I'd lowered the walls to make contact with the voice calling out to be heard, but that wasn't the only consciousness within me. The voice was gone, whether satisfied that it had done its job or torn apart by the thing that had brought it along for the ride. The images that screamed through my head were savage, brutal, and hungry. They were visceral and the furthest thing from human I'd ever known. "This goddamn monster caused the crash of Flight 427. One of its drones was left behind and killed the pilot during takeoff." Forcing myself to concentrate only on what I had to, I said, "It came back to me because I made a good host, and fed whenever it wanted. It jumped into one of my friends when he was driving. The fucking thing was hungry so it fed off of Jon and made him hit that tree!"

Whatever Fleming saw in my eyes, it was enough to make her stop in her tracks. I could already feel my heartbeat getting faster as I filled with desperation, anxiousness, and fear. The presence inside of me swelled up to consume the surging life energy created by those emotions, leaving a cold pit inside my chest.

"What do you want me to do?" she asked.

She knew what to do. She just needed to hear me ask for it.

"If you shoot me," I said, "the *draugr* can just move on to someone else. Probably you. If I brought this thing here, I should be the one to get rid of it."

"But it must have left you before if it infected others like you say."

"I don't think it could get back into me because I was either unconscious or doped up on pain medication after breaking my arm. With no adrenaline flowing, it had nothing to feed on. It's feeding now, though. I can feel it. Now that it's sunk in, it knows what's happening. If you don't put an end to it now, it'll end you. And if we put an end to the source creature, the drones won't survive for long."

"How?" Fleming asked.

"It's an airborne virus. That's what Swann said. Something airborne has to be breathed in, right?"

"Yes."

"Then that's got to be how the *adjyaseek* gets out again. Put an end to me by closing off my nose and mouth."

"That is what the legends mean," she whispered. Fleming set me down and knelt beside me. "The only hunters to kill the *adjyaseek* used their bare hands."

"Then do it, goddamn it," I snarled. My vision started to fade again, and the last few minutes of my life washed away with it. My eyes felt like they'd been frozen in their sockets, and the rush of panic filled my entire body where it was just as quickly drained away.

Fleming's hands clamped down over my nose and mouth, pressing down tightly. She had a soldier's resolve, committing fully to the horrible task she'd been given. There would be plenty of time for regrets later. Regrets and nightmares.

As for me, I used every bit of my remaining willpower to just lay back and let it happen. It was scary, but that thing, the blackness creeping in around my edges, was even more terrified than I was. That made everything else worth it.

Beneath Fleming's strong, callused hands, I think I was smiling.

I woke up some time after that on a cot next to about half a dozen other wounded folks. We were in a basement beneath a bunker on the northern edge of Windsor Lake. Turns out I'd been out for just over six days after receiving what the medics called "severe head trauma." Since I wasn't wild about the idea of being labeled a mental case, I left it at that without mentioning the voices. My energy was returning, but would never quite come all the way back.

Fleming had nearly killed me that night. Whatever was inside me had nothing left to feed on or might have even gotten an overdose of adrenaline as I was forced to the edge of death. Either way, it was too much for the *adjyaseek* to handle. Every day after that night, I've felt exhausted; almost like being forced to wake up too early after going to bed too late, only it's all the time, no matter how much sleep I get.

Since I get winded taking a piss these days, I've spent my waking hours working a switchboard or radio console passing on whatever information I can about every form of vampire there is.

Fleming didn't stick around long enough to see me wake up. I never got a chance to thank her, which was what bothered me the most. A month or so later, I passed along a message from a joint special-ops task force made up of U.S. Rangers and ICRU troops. I don't know what they're up to, but my prayers go out to them.

I'm praying now, huh?

Maybe I am crazy.

"A DAY IN THE LIFE" PT.5

Jonathan Maberry

Camden, New Jersey

The five of them looked like they'd come straight from central casting. Tall, broad-shouldered, deep-chested, with huge arms, no necks, shaved heads, and sunglasses. They might as well have had "thug" stenciled on team t-shirts.

Their point man was thinner, shorter, and had dreadlocks. Also cliché, but at least he was articulate. Caliban appreciated that.

"You came alone?" asked the guy with dreads on, who sat on the opposite side of a small card table from Caliban. His street name was Totem, because he was supposed to be part Cherokee and had all sorts of Native American tats on his body, ankles to neck.

"Sure," said Caliban. "Why not?"

Totem grinned. "You either have considerable testicular poundage or you are demonstrating a degree of trust uncommon in our particular trade."

Caliban loved this guy. Testicular poundage. Yeah, he'd be stealing that.

"Let's just say," he began, "that I think we both want this to be about business, not about fucking around."

"Fair enough," agreed Totem. "And how would you like to proceed?"

"That's up to you. You asked for a certain weight; I brought it. You've got a nice new Puma gym bag that I think is my Christmas shopping money, am I right?" Totem merely smiled. He had a good smile. Caliban wondered if it would be weird to ask him who his dentist was. And if the dentist ever took Bloods as patients.

"So, part one of this is good old-fashioned I-give-you, you-give-me stuff and yay for capitalism."

"Nice," said Totem, nodding his appreciation. "But here's the thing. I need to be absolutely sure that what I'm buying is *actually* the product in question." He closed his fist slowly, as if crushing something. Even in a building that had been swept for electronics, neither of them was inept enough to mention either Krush or Spike out loud.

"Why even ask?"

"Because," said Totem, "there have been an inordinate number of patients presenting at local ERs with symptoms consistent with substances less favorably tolerated by those of the non be-fanged persuasion. It's possible—even likely—that the product in question had been substituted—accidentally or deliberately—with a similar product intended for *your* kind of people."

Caliban said, "Ah."

Spike was the go-to drug for Bloods. It was a synthetic psychotropic that created intense hallucination, like amped-up LSD, and then ended with a feather-light comedown. It only worked on Bloods. Any Beat that took it experienced a psychic fracture that resulted in extreme violent behavior, and the comedown was so intensely negative that there were many cases of suicide.

The product Caliban dealt was different. It had begun as Spike, but had been further modified to allow it to give the same intense high and gentle drop as Spike, but was safe for Beats. Street name was Krush. Since both drugs had hit the streets a few months ago, there had been some tragic crossover use, batch contamination, and outright misdirection in terms of sales.

"I feel you," said Caliban, "but I don't provide weak product. Never have, never will. If you got a bad batch, then it wasn't from me."

Totem studied him for a long time. He still wore his smile, but any warmth in it was an illusion.

"What assurances can you provide?" he asked.

Caliban spread his hands. "Not my job. You want to test the merch, get one of your own, dose 'em and put him in a room. If he just smiles and tries to fuck a unicorn, then you're good. If he freaks out and tries to rip out his own spleen, then I give you full permission to come back here and shove a nine up my ass. But if you're asking for a product safety data sheet, then I suggest—and I mean this in a good way—you go fuck yourself."

They sat there and smiled at each other as seconds ticked by and burned to ash in the still air of the warehouse.

Then Totem raised his right hand and snapped his fingers. One of the thugs bent to pick up the gym bag. He walked it over and set it down beside Caliban's chair. Then he picked up the two heavy suitcases of product and retreated to stand with his fellows.

"I think we're done here," said Totem.

"I think we are," said Caliban.

"It was a pleasure doing business with you. As always."

Totem got to his feet and turned away. Caliban remained seated.

"Oh, one thing more," said Caliban mildly, "and I mean this in a good way."

Totem stopped and looked over his shoulder. "What?"

Caliban reached inside his shirt—doing it very gingerly, so as not to upset anyone—and pulled out the badge that hung on a lanyard. Instantly lights flared inside the warehouse, washing all shadows away. Doors banged open, and two dozen men in full SWAT gear rushed it, weapons raised.

Caliban grinned to show his fangs. "DEA, motherfucker. You're busted."

"HER CORNER OF THE SKY" PT. 1

Tim Waggoner

She dreamed of fire, of burning, of being reduced to ashes, only to rise healed and whole. And then flames engulfed her once more, and the cycle started anew. She dreamed this over and over, and each time she burned, she screamed. Oh God, how she screamed...

———•———

The dark seemed to last a long time, and she would've been content if the calm, quiet nothing had lasted forever. But then her eyes opened, and she found herself looking up at a middle-aged man with long black hair bound in a ponytail and a full salt-and-pepper beard.

"Glad to have you back among the living." He smiled, displaying slightly elongated canines. "So to speak."

Cybill tried to sit up, but she was too weak, and she only made it partway before her body gave up and she fell back onto the bed.

She looked around. The room was small—bed, nightstand, dresser, and a single window with heavy curtains drawn across it. The bearded man sat next to her on a simple wooden chair. He wore jeans and a blue pullover hoodie with MY BOSS IS A JEWISH CARPENTER printed on the front in white letters. His skin was pale, and his red-tinted eyes were set in dark hollows. He was obviously a Blood.

He must've seen her looking at the window, for he said, "Don't worry. All the windows here are painted black, boarded over, and curtained. We don't like to take chances."

"Where—" she started to ask, but then memories came flooding back. Sunlight pinking the eastern sky, pain crackling across every inch of her body like fire. Adrenaline washed away her weariness, and she bolted upright. She held her hands up to her face, expecting to see scraps of burnt flesh clinging to blackened bone. But her hands were intact, the skin pink and healthy. Almost too pink, actually, and so smooth, like a baby's skin. She reached up to touch her face, then ran her fingers over her hair, and found both intact.

"Your healing abilities are truly remarkable," the man said. "Even for a Blood."

She wore a different t-shirt than the one she'd had on when she'd left—no, *fled*—her mother and father's house, a plain white one. She shifted her legs beneath the blanket and realized the only other item of clothing she wore was a pair of panties. She assumed they, like the shirt, were loaners. Her original clothes—a University of Pittsburgh t-shirt, jeans, and running shoes—had doubtless been rendered unwearable during her human barbecue act.

As if reading her mind—and who knew, maybe he was—the man said, "Don't worry. Lucy, one of our members, dressed you."

Members. That was an interesting choice of words.

"My name's Morgan Fell. I used to be a pastor at a Lutheran church over in Greensburg. Until I changed."

"I can see how that would've made things awkward," she said, then smiled.

"Just a little. Do you have any memory of how you got here?"

"No. I don't even know where *here* is."

But a snippet of memory did come back to her then, just a snatch of sound...

She frowned. "I remember a horn blaring. And then I... hit something? Or maybe it hit me."

"That would've been a pick-up truck. One *I* was driving, as a matter of fact. Lucy and I were coming back from town when we saw you lying in the middle of the road. I swerved to miss you, but you jumped into the air and hit the truck's passenger door head-on. I stopped the truck, and when Lucy and I got out and saw that your skin was burning, we rushed to your side, gathered you up, and put you in the truck bed and covered you with a tarp. Lucy sat with you, while I drove as fast as I could to get you here where we could tend to your injuries. Not that we needed to do much. As I said earlier, your healing abilities are remarkable."

"Were you and Lucy badly hurt when you helped me?" she asked, feeling guilty.

Fell smiled. "We did get a trifle singed around the edges, but neither of us is as sensitive to sunlight as some Bloods are. I don't mean to pry, but what were you doing so far outside town at dawn? Did someone drive you there and leave you? It wouldn't be the first time a group of Beats decided to get rid of a Blood that way."

His expression was neutral and his voice calm, but Cybill detected a cold anger beneath his words.

It would've been simpler to let Fell believe that's what had happened—not to mention less embarrassing. But she'd never been much of a liar. Not so much because of moral principles, but because she wasn't any good at it.

"I walked there myself. No one forced me."

She remembered seeing Robbie's face, eyes closed, head on his pillow, blanket pulled up to his chin. She'd stood by her younger brother's bedside earlier that night, silent and motionless, for the better part of an hour. She'd been hungry, so much so that she could barely think. Finally, without being fully aware that she was doing so, she'd reached out to brush a lock of hair from his forehead, but she stopped when she saw that the fingernails on that hand had become long and curved. She'd realized that she'd been about to kill her brother. So she ran. And she kept running until she had left Arbordale far behind, and continued running as the sun rose. She'd hoped its rays would kill her, so she'd never be a threat to anyone again. And they might have—if Fell and his friends hadn't found her and brought her here.

Fell's eyes narrowed, and she had the feeling he was reappraising her. But then he smiled and said, "If you're up to it, would you like to meet the others?"

"Sure," Cybill said, then added, "Um, could I borrow some pants first?"

* * *

The room Cybill had recuperated in was located on the second floor of what Fell described as an "old farmhouse." He put a hand on her elbow to steady her as they descended the stairs, but while she appreciated the gesture, it wasn't necessary. She felt strong and clear-headed, nothing at all like a woman who had been on the verge of burning to death only a few hours ago.

She was surprised by how much more optimistic she felt. This morning she'd considered herself a monster and had been determined to die. Now she felt as if she could handle whatever challenges this new life of hers presented. It seemed that her time sleeping had healed more than her physical body, and she was grateful.

She heard voices as they drew near the bottom of the stairs, men and women talking in low tones. Fell led her to the dining room, and she saw a dozen people squeezed around the table. A laptop computer lay open on the tabletop, and a news video was playing on the screen. As soon as she and Fell entered the room, a young African-American woman reached out and tapped a key to pause the video. Cybill recognized the man on the screen as a news anchor from a Pittsburgh TV station. And she caught a single phrase before the sound cut off: "Home Guard."

The people ranged in age from late teens to early seventies, and while the numbers were divided evenly when it came to gender, race was a different matter. Most of them were white, while a couple were black and a couple more Hispanic. No Asians—other than Cybill herself, of course, and most of them were Bloods. The majority smiled at her, although a few regarded her without expression, as if they intended to withhold judgment until they got to know her better. But the woman who'd paused the video—about her own age, late twenties—smiled wider than the rest. Cybill thought she knew her from somewhere. She recognized her kind eyes and gentle smile, but a name wouldn't come to her.

The women said, "How are you feeling? You weren't in the best of shape when Morgan and I hauled you into the bed of the pickup."

You must be Lucy, she thought.

"I'm feeling much better." Cybill raised her hands palms out and turned them back and forth to display her new skin. "As you can see."

"I think introductions are in order," Fell said. People took turns giving their names. The woman was Lucy Darnell. Cybill had hoped hearing her full name might help her place the woman, but no luck.

When the last person was done giving her name, everyone looked expectantly at Cybill.

"You weren't carrying any ID," Fell said.

"Oh. Right. I'm Cybill Zhang."

She waited for the questions to start. *Why didn't you have any ID? Why did you try to kill yourself?* But no one said anything, and for that she was so grateful she almost cried.

"This isn't all of us," Fell said. "Several of our human members are out running errands."

"But we're the core group," Lucy said. "The proverbial inner circle, right, Morgan?"

Fell smiled. "That's fair to say—if a bit melodramatic."

"What is this place?" Cybill asked. "Are you all members of some kind of church or something?"

Fell put his hand on her shoulder. There was nothing especially creepy about his touch, but she did feel the gesture was a bit patronizing.

"Why don't you take a seat, and we'll tell you all about us."

———— • ————

"We call ourselves Unity," Fell said. "We're a group of both Bloods and Beats who want to create a world where vampires and humans can live in peace."

He'd taken a seat next to Cybill and nursed a cup of decaf coffee. He took small, infrequent sips, and Cybill wondered if he still tried to drink coffee out of habit more than anything else.

Fell continued. "We're small, but we're growing. We have a web presence and we're working on helping people elsewhere set up their own branches."

"Basically, we're franchising," Lucy said with a grin. "Or trying to, anyway."

Cybill liked the idea of a group comprised of both Bloods and Beats working together for mutual benefit. So much of what had happened since the resurgence of the vampire gene in the modern world had been about Beats versus Bloods. But they were all still human at their core, weren't they?

She thought of how she'd stood next to Ronnie's bed, fighting to keep from feeding on him, and she wondered just how human *she* was these days.

"We haven't done much yet," Lucy said. "Nothing big, anyway. We've produced some informative literature that we pass out, pamphlets that dispel some of the myths people have about Bloods. We've given some talks about the subject in Arbordale and the surrounding communities. Admittedly, with mixed results."

"We also organize protests," Fell said.

"*Peaceful* protests," Lucy added.

Fell nodded. "Naturally. But most of all what we do is try to help both Bloods and Beats in whatever ways we can. Sometimes it's through trying to promote mutual understanding and respect—"

"—and sometimes it's picking them up off the road after they catch on fire and slam into your truck," Lucy said.

Cybill lowered her gaze to the table, embarrassed.

"Sorry about that," she said. "I'll pay for the damage."

"No worries," Lucy said, then smiled. "I'm just glad you didn't ignite the gas tank. *That* would've been a rough start to the morning."

"You were watching something when I came down," she said. "Some kind of news report?"

"Yeah." Lucy reached out and started the video again.

They all watched as the anchor—a rather severe-looking man in his fifties—talked about a group calling itself the Home Guard. There were clips of an interview with the group's "commander," a round-faced man dressed in military camo fatigues, with thinning black hair and pencil mustache. Frank Walker, according to the on-screen letters beneath the picture.

"We're not saying that *all* Bloods are monsters," Walker said. "But it's common knowledge how dangerous they can be. They're like a dog with rabies. You don't hate the dog for something it can't help, but you make damn sure it doesn't bite you. That's what the Home Guard is all about: protecting innocent citizens from the rabid dogs among us."

Lucy reached out and tapped a key, and the video froze. Cybill looked at the still image of Walker's face, and she was drawn to his eyes. They weren't filled with anger or fear. On the contrary, they were completely empty of obvious emotion or thought, and she found that far more frightening.

Fell shook his head. "Sometimes I despair that humans—Beats *and* Bloods—just want to know who it's okay to hate, as if they have a deep need to hate *someone*, and they don't really care who it is."

"The Home Guard is coming to Arbordale tomorrow night," Lucy said. "They're going to hold a rally in Woodlawn Park."

"I've heard of them," Cybill said. "My father brought home a flier advertising the rally. My mom thought the group seemed kind of shady, but my dad... He's desperate to find some kind of cure for what he sees as my *condition*. He's a doctor, and he sees just about everything in medical terms."

"We're not a disease," Fell said. "We're a natural part of evolution."

The others around the table, Blood and Beat both, nodded.

"We're planning on mounting a protest at the rally," Fell said. He glanced at Lucy. "Nothing too confrontational, but we want to make our presence known. We need to counter their message of hate with one of—"

"Unity," Cybill said.

Fell broke into a grin.

"Precisely."

———•———

Cybill stood outside, between the farmhouse and a barn with a sagging roof. It was early April in western Pennsylvania, but it felt more like winter. She wore a borrowed sweater; it did little to fend off the chill, but that was okay. The cold didn't bother her like it had when she'd been a Beat. It was full night, but late. As it turned out, she had slept through the daylight hours and well into the evening as her body healed. She didn't know exactly what time it was, but she could feel that dawn wasn't far off. Bur rather than fill her with dread, she actually found the sun's imminent arrival comforting. Maybe she could no longer walk in its light, but the ancient cycle of night giving way to day continued. In other words, life—even the variety she currently found herself living— went on. The night air felt deliciously invigorating on her newly healed skin, and she was half tempted to remove her borrowed clothes and go running naked through the fields.

"Not thinking of trying to get a suntan again, are you?"

Cybill turned, startled despite herself. She'd been so caught up in her thoughts, she hadn't heard Lucy approach.

Lucy was smiling as she drew near, but when she saw Cybill's expression, her smile fell away.

"Too soon?" she asked.

Cybill couldn't help it; she laughed.

"I know you, don't I?" she said. "Did you go to Pitt?"

Lucy nodded. "We had a couple undergrad classes together. Intro to Anatomy, and Advanced Bio."

Now she remembered her.

"That's right," she said. "I was pre-med then. I don't remember what your major was, though."

"Biomechnical engineering."

"I'd made it to med school by the time the virus changed me. I can pass for human, so I tried to hide what I'd become and continue with my classes."

"I tried the same thing. I'm betting it didn't work any better for you than it did for me."

"No, so I left school and came back home to Arbordale."

"I ended up leaving school too. With everything that's been happening in the world, engineering just didn't seem so important anymore, you know? So . . . what flavor are you?"

"Excuse me?"

Now it was Lucy's turn to laugh. "What species of vampire are you? It's a standard Blood GTKY question."

Cybill looked at her blankly.

"Get To Know You," she explained.

"Ah! To be honest, I feel kind of weird talking about it. I've never discussed the matter before, not even with my family."

"Most of the Bloods in Unity are of the basic European variety, but we have some more exotic types. Morgan's Jewish—yeah, I know; he used to be a Christian pastor, but he's Jewish on his mother's side—and he's an *astryiah*. *Astryiah* was a vampire from Hebrew legend who used her hair to drain her victims' blood. Weird, huh?"

Cybill thought of how Fell wore his hair in a ponytail. To keep it under control until it was time to feed? Maybe.

"I'm an African variety of Blood called an *impundulu*," Lucy said. "You should see what I can turn into!" She paused, then asked. "Can you shape-shift?"

"Not really. I look more… vampirish when I feed, though. Does that count?"

"Sure, I guess."

"My dad's of Chinese descent, and my mom's family came from Germany. So I'm not only biracial, I'm… Bi-Blooded? I possess some traits of European vampires, but I also have qualities of *jiangshi*."

Lucy frowned. "Aren't they the hopping vampires? I've never seen one in real life, but they look pretty cool in the movies."

"I don't hop, exactly. But I *can* jump really far when I want to. And instead of feeding on blood, I feed on life force. I limit myself to feeding on small animals. White mice that I buy from pet stores, that kind of thing…" *But mice aren't enough to fill you up, are they, Cybill? That's why you snuck into your brother's room last night. You were starving for a taste of some* real *food.*

"I guess we're all weird in our own way, huh?" Lucy said. "Bloods *and* Beats. That's why I like this place and these people. It doesn't matter who you are or *what* you are. If you believe in peace, there's a place for you in Unity."

Cybill began to feel the first faint stirrings of hunger since she'd woken. Maybe talking about her vampire nature had stirred the hunger. Or maybe her system was beginning to come back into balance after the horrible shock of nearly being burned to death. The hunger's voice was little more than a whisper right now, but she knew it would get louder, until eventually it became deafening.

Cybill changed the subject. "Fell said the two of you were coming back from a trip into Arbordale when you found me. What were you doing?"

"Picking up some supplies," Lucy said. "But we also spent some time checking out the park where the Home Guard is going to hold its rally tonight. We wanted to get a feel for the place, you know? Not that we're expecting any trouble, but it's always good to know where the exits are."

She understood the practicality of what Lucy was saying, but even discussing the threat of violence in the abstract disturbed her. She changed the subject once again.

"From what I've seen so far, Unity seems great," Cybill said.

"Seems?"

She shrugged. "I've only just met everyone. Nothing personal, but I don't really know any of you yet."

"Sure. I get it. I felt the same way when I first came here. It took me a while to come around, but you will, too. If you want to, that is," she added quickly. "Unity gave me purpose. Direction. A chance to try to do something to help make the world a better place for vampires *and* humans. It can do the same for you."

Lucy shook her head and smiled ruefully. "Listen to me. I sound like a door-to-door evangelist. But I believe in these people and what they're doing. Give us a chance. That's all I really want to say."

She smiled. "Your corner of the sky, huh?"

Lucy frowned.

"It's part of a song," Cybill explained. "From the musical *Pippin.* I was in the drama club in high school, and one year we did it for our spring musical. In the play, the main character is trying to find his place in the world. Sounds like you found yours here."

"Yeah. But it's not like this is a paradise or anything. We have our problems, and sometimes we have to make compromises from time to time. But it's totally worth it. I mean, you have to focus on the big picture, right?"

She wasn't certain, but she thought she saw Lucy's gaze flick toward the barn, just for an instant. She was about to ask her what she meant by "compromises," but there was a whisper of wind, and an instant later Fell stood by Lucy's side, a hand on the younger woman's shoulder. Cybill hadn't heard the former pastor approach. One moment he wasn't there, the next he was.

Fell smiled, displaying elongated canines.

"Giving our new friend an orientation?" he asked Lucy.

Lucy smiled back, but Cybill thought her smile was strained.

"Just getting to know her better. Turns out we actually shared some classes at college."

"Really? Well, as a man of faith, I like to believe there are no coincidences and no accidents. Everything happens for a reason, even if we can't always understand that reason at first. But then, that's why they call it faith, right?"

Cybill saw Fell's hand tighten on Lucy's shoulder. Her smile faltered, but held.

"I guess."

Fell looked at her for another moment before finally relaxing his grip and removing his hand. He then turned to Cybill. His long hair was loose, and it hung over his shoulders. It rippled gently, as if stirred by an unfelt breeze. Cybill thought of what Lucy had said about Fell's "flavor," and shuddered.

"We should go inside and get you settled before the sun starts to rise," Fell said. "Your skin looks good, but it's still in the process of healing. It will react poorly to even the weakest sunlight."

Cybill agreed, and the three of them headed for the house. She couldn't escape the feeling that Fell was herding them inside, though, like a shepherd bringing in his flock from the field.

She felt an urge to glance back over her shoulder at the barn, but she resisted, and as they walked, she listened to the growing hunger whispering in her ear.

"A DAY IN THE LIFE" PT. 6

Jonathan Maberry

Philadelphia

The vampire's name was Ruthven.

It wasn't the name on his birth certificate or driver's license. It wasn't the name on his apron at Home Depot or on his Starbucks Rewards account. It wasn't what they called him at Denny's when he went in for his morning plate of eggs, bacon, and grits. And it wasn't the name his ex-wife and nine-year-old daughter called him.

It was the name he called himself, though, when he dressed to go out on the weekends. When he changed out of jeans and a button shirt, white socks and paint-stained Reboks. It was the name he put on with his black clothes. It was a name from a story he'd read when he was in high school. A name he wore like a cloak.

It changed him.

Having a name transformed him. More so than any virus could. He believed that.

Though, he was only guessing. Unlike in his two best friends, the V-Gene had not fired in Ruthven. He wanted it to. He wished it would. He even prayed that it would happen, but so far... nothing. Zilch. Zip.

Both of his friends had made the change. Danny was first. He grew two inches in nine months, lost nearly all his skin pigment, and got those cool-as-fuck red irises. He was one of what the press called a "melting-pot vampire," and what the haters called a blood-sucking mutt. A little of his Scandinavian mother's *draugr* and a whole lot of his English dad's *revenant*. Made Danny look like the guy who played Loki in those superhero movies, except he had more beef in his chest and shoulders. So, maybe more like an MMA dude with fangs. Cool fangs, too. Not so big they gave him a lisp, but definitely eye-catching. Danny wore it well, with blood-red shirts under black Armani knockoff jackets. Started calling himself "Lestat." He got laid more than industrial carpet. Bloods and Beats, too. And, if his stories were true, sometimes both at the same time.

His other friend, Greg, was gay, and he had a made-up name instead of one from fiction. Astoria. Ruthven wasn't sure that it was cool, because it came from the name of a hotel, but Astoria liked it. He was a *fau*, which was kind of funny since almost all *fau* were women. The folklore was all about *The White Ladies of Fau*. Not so much for the brothers, even those that liked dudes. But Astoria made it work and he was happy with every aspect of who he was. He was a pale-horse, pale-rider type. Blond hair, pale blue eyes, pale skin, hung like a fucking caribou—which Ruthven knew because of the showers in gym class back in school. Ruthven only swung one way. Astoria, though, he played hard for the other team, and there were a lot of gay Bloods in the clubs. Especially over at *Staked*, which had an S&M vibe that made Ruthven a little uncomfortable. He only went because there were so many chicks there. All leathered up and wicked. Ruthven had gotten a couple of them in the sack, though that was risky. Some of the vampire chicks had stamina like race horses; Ruthven could gallop along as well as any thirty-something, but he wasn't a porn star.

Even so, he always felt powerful when he dressed for the night and went out with his boys. His dogs. His pack.

He stepped back from the mirror and assessed his looks. He was already pale and made sure to always wear a hat outside. Tans turned off the vampire groupies faster than a cold sore. Funnily enough, it didn't skeeve the Bloods because they knew that a lot of vampires didn't turn pale. Some vampires were florid, some had fur, a few had lizard scales—which made Ruthven wonder how *they'd* be in the sack—but most of them looked normal. Some even took a pretty good tan. It varied. Like people varied. But the public were, on the whole, dumbasses and they believed the hype on the news.

Still, it got Ruthven laid more when he went pale, so he went pale. He'd had his hair darkened at the salon, like a lot of guys did. That had become a growth industry for the fringe crowd. For the mix and munch crowd, as they called it on *Daily Beast*.

The clothes made him look simply badass, and he'd become diligent with his Bowflex. Even had a six pack—though right now it was more like a sixer of lite beer, but he was working on it. More crunches, less pizza. And Ruthven had to admit that it was a major, major turn-on to look past his own muscular torso at a head bobbing up and down on his dick. That was an insane rush. It must be what real vampires felt like when they were getting it on.

Oh hell yes.

Ruthven spritzed on some cologne, making sure to put some in the armpits of his shirt in case he sweated.

Then he blew himself a kiss like he always did, turned, and went out.

Astoria was leaning against the fender of Lestat's Escalade, and Lestat was behind the wheel talking on his cell. Talking trash to some girls, trying to get them to come down to IV, the latest Blood hangout. They actually had IV drips of blood, too, though it was all cow blood. Ruthven tried it once and spent ten minutes on his knees in the bathroom, throwing up everything he'd eaten since Bush was president. He wondered how the fuck Bloods ever *enjoyed* that shit.

IV served all their regular drinks with red food coloring, too, so everyone looked like they were sipping blood from the plastic tubes. So badass.

"Hey, dawg," said Ruthven, doing the clasp-handshake half-hug that made him feel gangsta.

Astoria returned it, and even though his friend didn't muscle it, Ruthven could feel the power there. Astoria was the strongest of the three of them, even though Lestat had some *draugr.*

"'Sup," said Astoria, leaning back. "You look ready to kill."

"Always," laughed Ruthven. He leaned in and waved at Lestat, who was still on his call and responded by lifting his little finger from the phone. Lestat's face was drawn, almost tight, and there was pain in his eyes. Ruthven straightened and leaned toward Astoria. "What's up with him?"

Astoria sighed. "It's a family thing. He only has a sister here in Philly and a brother in Brooklyn, and they're both Beats. Hardline Beats, too. Real haters."

"Fuck."

"Tell me about it. His sister's kid has her first communion next week, and they don't want Lestat to come."

"Why not?"

"Why do you think?"

"Are you shitting me?"

"They say it wouldn't be right to have him in church."

"Oh, come on. He's a fucking CPA. It's not like he's a serial killer."

"You don't have to tell me. Lestat's the straightest motherfucker I've ever met. He actually gives a shit. He's never missed a birthday or Christmas, and he used to babysit his niece."

"When? Oh, you mean 'before'?"

"Before, yes."

They both sighed and tried not to be seen looking at Lestat. Ruthven could see the sparkle of tears in his friend's eyes—and even though the windows were closed for privacy, it was clear that Lestat was pleading. Sometimes yelling. Begging. It was written on every line in his face and in that terrible mix of shame and anger in his eyes.

Ruthven couldn't look at it, and he turned away.

"This is so fucked up," he growled.

"HER CORNER OF THE SKY" PT. 2

Tim Waggoner

She woke in the same bed she'd slept in when she'd been brought here. She'd dreamed again of being consumed by fire, over and over, and she hoped she hadn't screamed out loud. She didn't want to disturb the others' rest.

She got out of bed, feeling good despite the nightmares she'd suffered, if not quite as full of energy as she'd been the last time she'd wakened in this room. But she wasn't *really* alone, was she? The hunger was with her: no longer a whisper, but an insistent murmur.

She did her best to ignore it as she left the room and headed downstairs. She found Fell and Lucy—along with a dozen other men and women—in one of the front rooms. She figured it was used as a living room, since it held several comfy chairs and a big couch, along with a large flat-screen TV. A large cardboard box sat on the couch, filled with fliers that said BLOODS AND BEATS, WORKING TOGETHER in large letters at the top. There were a number of signs propped up on one of the chairs, various slogans written on them in colorful marker on white cardboard. WE'RE ALL "HUMAN," UNITY MEANS U + ME, HATE IS THE REAL MONSTER!

Fell stood in the center of the room, speaking with Lucy. Everyone turned to look at her as she entered.

"Sorry I slept so long," Cybill said. "Guess I'm not all the way back to full strength yet. Getting ready to head into town for the protest?"

"Yes," Fell said. "It's going to be the biggest event we've had a presence at, and we'd be honored if you'd join us."

Fell's invitation elicited nods of agreement from those assembled.

She wasn't sure what to say. Arbordale was her hometown. Like her, most of her friends had gone off to college, but her parents and younger brother still lived there. What if she embarrassed them by showing up at the Home Guard's rally tonight? Worse, what if the Home Guard found out who she was and decided to punish her for her association with Unity by singling out her family, harassing or perhaps even harming them? Violence between Bloods and Beats—initiated by both sides— had become all too common. And what had Lucy said last night? *It's always good to know where the exits are.* How could she risk involving her family in anything that might cause them harm?

But if she could do something to help stop the violence between Beats and Bloods—even if only on a local level—shouldn't she try? She'd been studying to be a doctor—a *healer*. Well, now she had a chance to help heal in a different—and perhaps even more important— way.

"Okay," she said "I'd like to come along." She scanned the room, meeting each person's gaze in turn. "If that's all right with all of you," she added, and then smiled.

Everyone smiled back.

———————⋅•⋅———————

Cybill rode in the pickup with Lucy while Fell and the others rode in the vans. As Lucy drove toward town, headlight beams cutting a path through darkness, Cybill turned to her.

"Have you ever done anything like this before?" she asked. "A protest, I mean."

Lucy smiled. Her canines were more pronounced than Cybill had seen them before.

"A few times, back in college. Political issues, mostly. But I was human then. This'll be the first time I've protested anything related to Blood issues—especially *as* a Blood. Truth to tell, I'm a bit nervous. I keep telling myself there's no reason to feel that way. You carry a few signs, pass out some fliers, chant a few slogans. Piece of cake, right?"

"It may not be that simple," Cybill said. "It all depends on how the Home Guard reacts to our presence."

"No need worry on that score," Lucy said. "If things get hairy, we can take care of ourselves. And *you* don't have any reason to be scared. Not with your needle riding on full. You got plenty of fight in you if it comes down to that."

The comment made Cybill uncomfortable. She understood that when Lucy had said the members of Unity could take care of themselves, she'd been speaking of those Blood members with enhanced strength and other capabilities. But something else Lucy had said—or almost said—bothered her deeply.

And you *don't have any reason to be scared. Not with your needle riding on FULL.*

She'd been near death when Fell and Lucy had found her. Several hours later she was healed, good as new, and the hunger—which had been her constant companion from the moment she'd changed—had been silent. Living beings, Bloods and Beats, weren't closed systems. They didn't heal spontaneously. They needed resources to draw on, and chief among those resources was food.

"Who was it?" she said softly.

Lucy glanced at her but didn't respond.

"Whoever it was didn't volunteer," Cybill continued. "As hurt as I was, I would've needed a *lot* of life energy, as much as one person could provide. He or she wouldn't have survived."

Lucy remained silent for several more moments. Cybill saw the lights of Arbordale in the distance, and she knew they'd be at Woodlawn Park—and the Home Guard rally—soon. She imagined the townspeople gathering in the park, her own father and mother among them, perhaps, waiting for the Home Guard to start speaking out against the monsters that lived among them. Monsters like her.

"He was nobody," Lucy said at last, "just some bastard we caught beating the hell out of a Blood teenager with some of his knuckle-dragging friends last week in Jeanette. We pounded the hell out of them and brought them to the farm. We trussed them up and gagged them, and we bring them out whenever there's a need."

She had no memory of feeding on anyone, but she was certain it had happened. Someone—Fell, or maybe even Lucy—had brought one of the captives into her room, and her survival instincts had done the rest. She probably hadn't even been fully conscious.

"They're kept in the barn, aren't they?" she asked. "The prisoners."

Lucy placed a gentle hand on her arm. "You were dying," she said. "We did what we had to do to save you. And before you ask why we don't feed on animals, you know it's not the same. We need the real stuff if we're to keep running at full strength. Morgan says it's only natural."

Cybill looked at her. "What makes my life more valuable than the life of the person you fed to me?"

Lucy had nothing to say to that, and a few moments later they entered Arbordale.

"Quite a turnout tonight," Fell said.

Cybill stood with him, Lucy, and the rest of the Unity members. They'd parked the pickup and the two vans near the park's entrance. They'd been unable to get any closer due to all the vehicles of the people who'd gotten there before them. People were still arriving, but now they were forced to park on the street outside.

"The media's here," Lucy said, nodding toward the amphitheater where the Home Guard had set up their mikes and sound system. Several news vans were parked close to the amphitheater, reporters and camera operators in position and ready to start recording. The news vans had their station and network affiliations printed on the sides of the vehicles.

"Local *and* national," Fell said. He smiled. "Good." He turned to face the others. "Let's start out at the rear of the crowd so we don't seem too confrontational. We'll stay together to present a stronger presence, and for God's sake, don't let your emotions get the better of you."

"But if things start to get rough…" Lucy said.

Fell bared his fangs. His hair was unbound, and it swayed at the tips, like an undersea plant stirred by the current.

"Then we'll do what we have to," he said.

Most of the Unity members carried handfuls of fliers, and held signs, and although Cybill saw no evidence that any of them were carrying weapons, she could smell a harsh tang of metal. She assumed some of them—if not most—carried handguns, Blood and Beat alike, concealed by their jackets.

Fell turned his attention to her.

"Are you ready for this, Cybill? It's okay if you're not up to it just yet. You can wait in the pickup."

Fell's tone contained only kindness and concern, but she detected the appraisal in his eyes. She hadn't been invited along so that she could determine whether or not she wanted to join Unity—at least, not only for that. This was an *audition*. And if she didn't pass, would Fell let her go on her way with no hard feelings? Or would he view her as a potential threat to his group and dispose of her, just as he'd disposed of the man he'd fed to her?

She tried to tell herself that she was being overly paranoid, but she couldn't bring herself to believe it.

"I think so," she said, if only to placate Fell.

He gazed at her for a few more seconds. Finally, he smiled.

"Great! Let's get in place before everything starts."

She nodded and accompanied Fell and the others as they started walking toward the crowd. Outwardly she appeared calm enough, but inside a storm of emotions roiled. She hadn't been around this many people since she'd changed, and she'd never been "out" as a Blood before. That alone would have made her nervous, but she was still reeling from the knowledge that she'd killed someone. Maybe she hadn't done so on purpose, but that didn't change the fact that she was ultimately responsible, and that she was now walking around with smooth, healed skin because she'd stolen someone else's life energy. Most of the people who'd come to hear the Home Guard tonight were humans afraid of beings they viewed as predators overtaking their towns and cities, reducing the human residents to little more than cattle to be fed upon. She'd originally agreed to come because she'd wanted to show the people of Arbordale that Bloods weren't all monsters, any more than all humans were. But after what she'd done to survive and heal—consciously or not—she wasn't certain she believed that anymore.

Maybe it would've been better if Fell and Lucy hadn't found her, and she'd been left alone to finish burning to death beneath the cleansing rays of the sun.

A number of Arbordale's finest had shown up for the rally, and they wandered through the crowd, gazing back and forth for any sign of trouble. The cops had guns. Fell and his followers had guns. And she was sure the Home Guard were armed as well, as perhaps were more than a few people in the crowd. And the emotional atmosphere in the park was so tense, it felt like the air right before a huge thunderstorm erupted. Whatever happened here tonight, she knew it wasn't going to end well.

The amphitheater was surrounded by trees—maple, elm, and ash, primarily, but with a few chestnuts and poplar. Cybill had come to the park many times while growing up, and she and her friends would run across the amphitheater's stage and dance on it, pretending they were putting on a play. The performance they were going to see tonight would be far less innocent, though.

Once they all chose a place to stand, those who had signs held them up, and some of the people standing near them scowled—or worse, looked alarmed—and moved off. But some nodded and smiled, and a few gave a thumbs-up, and Cybill found herself heartened by the show of support. Maybe things wouldn't be quite as bad as she feared.

Frank Walker was on the stage, along with three other men and two women, all wearing camo fatigues. They ranged in age from twenties to fifties, and one of them—a tall clean-shaven man with a crew cut—had obvious fangs.

She leaned close to Lucy and said, "What's a Blood doing up there?"

"There are a few in the Home Guard," she said. "They hate what they've become, but they've decided to use their 'evil' powers for good."

The stage was lit by several floodlights the Guard had erected, and Walker was well lit as he stepped up to the microphone stand. A number of the people in the crowd cheered, clapped, and whistled, but there were more than a few boos and hisses, and shouts of "Racist!", "Nazi!", and "Haters go home!"

Walker let the noise continue for a moment, and then he raised his hands for quiet. Not everyone became silent, but enough people shut up for him to be heard as he spoke.

"Good evening, people of Arbordale. I'd like to tell you that it's a pleasure to be here, but in all truth, I wish I wasn't. I wish I didn't have to be. But I *am* here, as are the other representatives of the Home Guard who've joined me here tonight. We're here because *they* are here." He paused, and then in a lower voice added, "The Bloods."

Shouts came from the crowd, cries of "Vampires!", "Monsters!", and "Bloodsuckers!" People waved homemade signs displaying anti-Blood sentiments, such as VAMPIRES SUCK! and STAKE EM ALL! But Cybill caught sight of one sign that made her stomach lurch. WE ARE NOT YOUR FOOD!

She estimated there were several hundred people present, but it was dark and the lights onstage only reached so far. She searched the crowd for her parents' faces, but she didn't see them. That didn't mean they weren't there, but she hoped they were safe at home.

Walker continued.

"There's an infection spreading throughout our country, a disease that could strike any one of us at any time. But it's more than that, because this disease creates monsters. Monsters that hunger for our *blood!*"

He shouted this last word, and the crowd responded with shouts of its own.

We're not the only monsters here, Cybill thought. *Not by a longshot.*

"We don't want your blood!" Fell shouted. "We only want to live in peace!"

Cybill was surprised by how far his voice carried. He wasn't standing in front of a microphone and he held no megaphone, but his voice echoed throughout the park. One of his Blood abilities, or a result of years spent speaking from a pulpit? Either way, Fell got everyone's attention—Blood and Beat—and the crowd turned to look at him.

Walker glared at Fell as he spoke into the microphone once more.

"What does your kind know about peace?" he said, sneering.

"I'll tell you!" Fell called back. He leaned close to Cybill and whispered in her ear.

"Come with me. I need you."

She had no idea what he wanted, and no way in hell did she want to go with him. But then he took hold of her left arm, and Lucy took hold of her right.

"It's okay," Lucy said softly. "I'll be right there beside you."

Cybill wanted to fight, to thrash back and forth in an attempt to break free. She felt her claws begin to emerge and her fangs extend as her body readied itself to fight. In other circumstances, she might've done it, but the atmosphere in the park was one of barely contained violence, and she feared that if she struggled with Fell and Lucy, she'd set off everyone else. If that happened, who knew how many people might get hurt—or even killed?

"All right," she said. She willed herself to be calm, and her fangs and claws retracted. Then she allowed Fell and Lucy to begin leading her toward the amphitheater, the crowd parting so they could get through. Most people remained silent as they made their way toward the stage. The few Bloods they passed gave them sympathetic looks and supportive smiles, but the humans' reactions were more mixed. Some nodded, and a few even clapped, but most drew away, as if afraid they might be contaminated by close proximity to Bloods. Some looked scared, some curious, some angry. If they'd been holding rocks, Cybill wouldn't have been surprised if they'd attempted to stone her, Lucy, and Fell.

She avoided meeting people's gazes as they walked, afraid that she'd see someone she recognized. Former teachers and classmates, childhood friends that she'd fallen out of touch with, boyfriends she'd long ago broken up with. She didn't want to see the looks in their eyes as they realized that one of their own had become a monster. But as much as she wanted to avoid that, what terrified her the most was that she might walk past...

And there they were, her mother and father. Both in their sixties, her father lean, her mother a bit on the plump side, but still attractive. They wore light coats and dark slacks, and Cybill knew that her father wore a tie beneath his jacket. He rarely left the house without one. There was no sign of Robbie. He was a good deal younger than Cybill, still in middle school, and their parents would've been reluctant to expose him to this sort of crowd. She wondered if they'd gotten a babysitter or if they'd left him home alone to look after himself. He was certainly old enough.

Her parents moved to the edge of the corridor the crowd had made for Cybill, Fell, and Lucy. When the three drew close. Cybill's mother—tears streaking her face—reached a hand toward her. But Cybill's father put his arms around his wife and held her back. Cybill both loved and hated him for doing that, and then Fell and Lucy escorted her past her parents and toward the steps leading to the amphitheater's stage.

As they climbed, the Home Guard members standing around the base of the stage kept close watch on them, and Cybill noticed more than a few held their hands near their sides, as if ready to draw weapons. Some had metal batons or stun guns holstered at their hips, but a good number carried pistols.

Walker's face held an expression of grim suspicion as they approached, but he made no move to reach for his own gun. His fellow Guard members on the stage displayed more hostility, glaring openly at them. The Home Guard member who was a Blood hissed, bared his fangs, and took a step toward them, claws growing from the tips of his fingers. Walker held up a hand to stop him, and although the man didn't look happy about it, he complied with his leader's orders and stayed where he was.

Fell and Lucy led Cybill to the microphone, and Walker joined them.

"You're all vampires, I take it?" Walker said.

"*Bloods*," Lucy corrected.

"We're also human," Fell said. "Just like you. We're just a different *kind* of human."

This remark earned Fell a smattering of applause among shouted invectives and cries of rage.

Walked smiled, but there was no humor in his gaze.

"If that's true, then I invite you and your fellow *Bloods* to stay here the rest of the night and greet the dawn with us."

Laughter from the crowd at this.

"You know not all of us are affected by sunlight," Fell countered. "But even if we were, would you ask someone with a peanut allergy to eat a whole jar of peanut butter to prove they were human?"

"If all your kind ate was peanut butter, the rest of us wouldn't have a problem with you," Walker said.

More laughter, followed by loud applause and cheers.

Cybill had no idea what Fell was up to, but whatever his plan was, it didn't appear to be going so well. Both he and Lucy still had hold of her arms, and she wished they would let her go. Why had they brought her up here with them? What could Fell possibly want from her?

Fell turned to address the crowd. "This woman here—" he gestured to Cybill with his free hand "—is a resident of this town. She grew up alongside many of you, went to school here, made friends, fell in love, graduated from high school, went on to college, and then, as it happened for so many of us, she changed. And yesterday, for reasons she hasn't shared with us yet, she attempted to kill herself. She would've succeeded, too, if I and my friend here hadn't come across her in time to rescue her."

Cybill was horrified at hearing her suicide attempt revealed in public like this—especially with her parents in the audience. She frantically scanned the crowed for them, and when she found them, she saw that her father had his arms around her mother, who was weeping with great, wracking sobs. It was all Cybill could do not to break into tears herself.

Fell continued.

"My name is Morgan Fell, and before my change, I was a pastor. I still believe in God and consider myself His servant as much as, if not more than, I ever did. I founded a group of Bloods and Beats called Unity, and we believe that all of us—*all*—need to live together. We don't want anyone to feel as conflicted as Cybill, as if they have no choice but to end their lives rather than continue struggling to find a way to keep going in a world that hates and fears them simply because their biology is different from what's considered 'normal.'"

Cybill felt sick inside. Had Fell saved her—sacrificing the life of a human captive in the process—only because he'd wanted to use her as a visual aid in a *speech*?

The audience—and especially the gathered media—were eating this up. News cameras recorded, cell phones took video and photos, and camera lights flashed like tiny explosions throughout the park. Walker looked at Cybill, his grim expression replaced with one of confusion mingled with alarm, as if he feared he was on the verge of losing control of the rally before it got fully underway. Before he could say anything, though, the Blood Home Guard member stepped forward and put a hand on Fell's shoulder. He spun Fell around to face him and bared fangs that had grown even longer than they had been a moment ago.

"You want to know what the difference between you and me is?" the man said.

He tightened his grip on Fell's shoulder, the claws of his hand sinking into Fell's flesh and drawing blood.

"I know *I'm* a monster. You're too damn dumb to realize—"

That's as far as he got before Fell's hand lashed out—claws fully extended—and slashed deep furrows across the man's throat. Blood fountained, and he clapped his hands to the wound, as if trying to hold the blood back. He staggered, but he didn't go down, and Cybill knew that he was already in the process of healing.

The scent of blood hung heavy and electric in the air, and even though Cybill didn't feed on blood—at least, not primarily—and especially not *vampire* blood, the smell caused the hunger in her to come roaring to life so strong that it hit her as like a physical blow.

Walker, initially stunned by Fell's attack on his companion, recovered and reached for his gun. Before he could draw it, however, Fell— moving lightning fast—reached around to the small of his back and drew his own weapon. He stepped forward and pressed the muzzle of a 9mm Glock against Walker's head.

"I don't want to hurt you," Fell said, loud enough for his voice to carry throughout the crowd. "But I'll pull the trigger if you—or any of your people—make me. It's your choice. Peace—or war."

Most of the other Home Guard members, as well as the police in attendance, had drawn their own weapons or were in the process of doing so. But when they saw Fell holding his gun to Walker's head, they lowered their weapons, although they didn't put them away.

The wounded vampire kept his hand pressed to his throat and glared at Fell with blazing hate. Lucy released Cybill's arm, drew her own Glock from her waistband, and leveled it at the vampire's head

"Don't move unless you want to get shot," Lucy said.

The man looked at Lucy, his hands curling into fists, but he made no attempt to attack again.

Fell kept his expression gravely neutral, but Cybill saw a tiny smile playing around the corners of his mouth. She wondered how much of what had happened so far had been planned by him and how much had been a matter of circumstance. Either way, Fell had taken over the event and he now had the news cameras trained on him. This story would go national, maybe even international, elevating Unity—and Fell—to the world stage. And he'd used her to make it happen.

Fell kept his gun pressed to Walker's head as he spoke to the audience. "I deeply regret the scene you've just witnessed, but it demonstrates the sincerity of Unity. We could kill these men, but we don't want to harm anyone, Blood *or* Beat. We believe in unity for *all* humans, and we'll do whatever it takes to make our vision of a unified humanity a reality."

Cybill couldn't remain quiet any longer.

"Does that count for the humans you keep prisoner?" she asked. "The ones you use to feed your own people? To feed *me*?"

The audience had become silent, riveted by the drama playing out in front of them, but now Cybill heard a woman cry out in despair, and she knew it was her mother.

Fell looked at Cybill, his expression unreadable. Finally, he shook his head sadly.

"Whether we like it or not, we're at war," he said. "But Unity fights for *all* Bloods and Beats who want to coexist peacefully. Our enemies are those who would prevent that peace from happening, whether vampire or human."

"So it's all right to use your enemies as food?" she demanded.

Fell looked at her for a long moment, then he smiled slowly, lips drawing back to reveal his long incisors.

"All God's children have to eat," he said.

The Blood Guardsman snarled and made a run at Fell, but Lucy fired her Glock before the man could get close enough to strike. The bullet struck the man between the eyes, and he went down.

"Bullseye," Lucy said, but her voice was shaky and her hand trembled.

"You goddamned monsters!" Walker said, more anger than fear in his voice.

Fell took his gun from Walker's head. His long, loose hair then started moving with a life of its own. Thousands of strands whipped toward Walker's face, elongating and extending. They speared his skin and drilled into his flesh like thin parasitic worms. Walker screamed and tried to pull away, but Fell grabbed hold of the man's shoulder with his free hand and held him in place as he began to feed. The strands of his hair took on a translucent quality and swelled as they filled with blood. They quickly became a dark crimson, and Fell sighed with pleasure. It was like watching a surreal, nightmarish version of a transfusion, Cybill thought. But even though it disgusted her on one level, on another, deeper level, it excited her, and she felt her hunger grow stronger, its voice rising from a murmur to a shout. *Feed! You must Feed!*

Cybill ignored the voice. She grabbed hold of Fell's arm and tried to pull him off Walker, but the man was too strong for her to budge. He was so powerful because he fed regularly, she realized. And not from animals—from the *real stuff*. Of course he did, she thought. A leader had to keep up his strength for his people, right?

A few moments later Fell released his grip on Walker. His hair pulled away from the Home Guard leader's face, and the man—now decidedly paler than he had been only a moment before—fell lifelessly to the stage.

The Home Guard began shooting then, and Lucy fired back. The Home Guard members standing in front of the stage vaulted up to join in the fighting, while the rest of the crowd erupted in panic, fleeing in all directions, shouting and screaming, shoving and being shoved, falling to the ground and getting trampled on. Other members of Unity rushed the stage, leaped onto it, and began attacking the Home Guard. Some fought with guns, some with tooth and claw, some with both.

Fell spun toward Cybill, his hair rising upward like a nest of snakes. He hissed at her—actually *hissed*—like a vampire out of some old movie. He dropped his 9mm to the stage and grabbed hold of her shoulders with hands grown hard and strong as iron. His skin color was almost normal, and the hollows surrounding his eyes had vanished.

"Thanks for the help, Cybill, but I'm afraid your services are no longer required."

She wanted to tell him that he didn't have to do this, that he could resist his hunger if he only tried. But before she could say anything, his hair darted toward her face and plunged into her flesh. It hurt less than she would've expected, like being penetrated by hundreds of tiny hypodermic needles. Except these needles weren't going to put something into her body, but rather take it out. But when they began extracting her blood, the pain began in earnest. It felt as if Fell was pulling her apart on a cellular level, bit by bit, breaking her down into her most primal essence and then drawing it into himself. The pain was excruciating, as bad in its own way as feeling her flesh burn in sunlight.

Well, you wanted to die, didn't you? she thought. *Here's your chance. All you have to do is stand here and let him finish you.*

But she realized she didn't want to die. Not here, not now, and certainly not like this: drained to death by vampire hair.

Her fingers transformed into claws, and she jammed their sharp tips into Fell's side. The man grimaced in pain, but he didn't pause in his feeding. Cybill was already beginning to feel weaker, and she knew she didn't have much time left.

Most Bloods could feed only on humans or animals, but some—like Fell, evidently—could also feed on their own kind when necessary. Cybill had no idea if she could too, but she was about to find out.

She extended her mind toward Fell, reaching out for his life essence. She sensed it blazing strong and bright inside him, and it was growing stronger by the second as he stole her life energy to add to his. She willed the light to come toward her, to move into her hands and suffuse her body. At first nothing happened, and she fought to ignore the pain and weariness that was coming over her. She focused her concentration.

Mine, she thought. *Your life is mine.*

Fell's light began to move into her, but as it did, her body convulsed. Instead of filling her with strength, Fell's life force was poisoning her. Nausea gripped her, pain lanced through her head, and her vision grew blurry and began to gray around the edges. It would've been so easy to let go, to let him finish the job she'd failed to do yesterday morning. But she continued fighting, continued drawing in Fell's energy, even though it felt as if it was killing her.

If I go, I'm taking you with me, you bastard.

She heard a pistol fire close by, and an instant later the hair needles withdrew from her flesh. Her vision cleared, and she saw Fell's hair coiling tight to his head, like the legs of a dying spider drawing close to its body. His face held a look of confused surprise, which was only natural since a good-sized chunk of his head was missing.

He slumped to the stage, his body pulling free of Cybill's claws, and she turned to see Lucy standing there, Glock in hand, staring down at the body of the man who had been her leader.

"I couldn't let him hurt you," she said.

Gunfire continued coming from all directions as Home Guard, Unity, police, and armed citizens fired their weapons at seemingly random targets. Or perhaps they fired at no targets at all, but simply out of fear.

Cybill knew that she and Lucy needed to get the hell out of there if they didn't want to get shot. She swept Lucy into her arms—the other woman letting out a "Hey!"—then she crouched down, leg muscles coiling, and with a great leap she bounded off the stage and soared into the air over the heads of the people remaining in the park.

"Told you I could jump!" Cybill said.

A short while later, Cybill and Lucy were walking down a sidewalk a mile or so from the park. Cybill looked human once more. The tiny pinprick wounds all over her face and neck were in the process of healing, and although she still felt sick to her stomach from trying to absorb Fell's essence, she thought she was going to survive.

Cybill handed the phone back to Lucy.

"Thanks."

Lucy tucked her phone into her back pocket.

"What did your mom say?"

"Not much. Just that she and Dad made it home safe. She sounded… scared. Of me."

They walked in silence for several moments before Lucy spoke again.

"Sorry we used you like that," she said. "Morgan convinced me that it would be a great way to make our point, and that when it was all over, you'd see that. You'd even *thank* us." She shook her head. "He convinced me of a lot of things."

Cybill reached out, took her friend's hand, and gave it a squeeze. Lucy turned to her, gave her a grateful smile, and squeezed back.

Cybill remembered something then.

"You said you can shapeshift."

"Yeah."

"What can you change into?"

"A giant bird. Want to see?"

"A bird? That's weird, even for a vampire. You bet I want to see, but not right now. After what happened tonight, the faster we get out of town—and away from the police—the better. My car's at my parents' house. We can take it."

"And go where?"

"First we head to the farmhouse and release the people in the barn. After that?" Cybill shrugged. "Nowhere. Everywhere. Someplace the police won't find us. Someplace where we can start our own Unity franchise, maybe. One that stays focused on the group's original purpose: peace—*true* peace—for everyone."

Lucy smiled. "Our corner of the sky, huh?"

"Yep."

They continued walking toward home—wherever that might be.

"A DAY IN THE LIFE" PT. 7

Sam Orion Nova West-Mensch

The song on the radio was by Lil Drip. Rapper, outspoken celebrity, top recording artist.

Vampire.

Hate me or love me
Hate me or love me
   you can't budge me
   can't change me
Can't faze me
   can't judge me
Don't like me?
Bite me
Fuck these
   critics and criticism
I can't hear it
   try to crucify me cuz I'm a little different
So Vampiric
   the explicit witticisms
   in this champ's lyrics
They can't hear it
Fans cheer it
Fear what you don't understand that's in man's spirit
Their plan is so transparent
Paint me as the enemy, create a reason for war
   but behind me there's ten of me
   behind that? a million more

292

so what's the point of the blood spilled and the gore?
Vampires and humans, we're both the same at the core
I don't screech like a bat, I'm like a lion I roar
They crossed the line in the sand outlined with a sword
I stand up in defiance, like I'm crying for more
No one would be dying if they didn't profit from war
But they do, so the bloodshed ensues
They cast us as Satan's sons, like we're the dangerous ones
I've only ever been a danger to myself and instrumentals
I get on a track and raise hell 'til you realize my potential
They hunt us down with big guns, ammo, and whistles
So we stay on the lam, but refuse to be sacrificial
See I am what I am, and that's so damn official
Vampires are alive, no more superstitions
I stepped out of the shadows and into the prism
Fuck the government and the New Red coalition
It's me against the world now with no supervision

"THE HIPPO II" PT. 1

Scott Sigler

That bitch is crazy.

The girl had to have a screw loose.

She wasn't a girl, though. A woman. Hard to tell what she looked like from this distance—the Barrett's night-vision scope wasn't the best for determining one's ranking on the *hot or not* scale. Not that Harry gave a squirt of piss about such things. He had more important things to do than ogle butts and boobs.

Instead, he ogled her gear. Couldn't really see from this far out, but she carried what looked like a squat submachine gun. Big KA-BAR sheathed on her left thigh, sidearm holster on her right, all of it clear of the black body armor worn over SPECAM urban camp fatigues.

Academi. Definitely, the woman was one of those contractor douchebags that were milking San Francisco taxpayers dry. Harry had seen a few of the mercs lurking around this side of the bridge, but they usually worked in teams. He'd never seen one alone, and the results were predictable—three Bloods gave chase, steadily closing in on her through this chewed-up area of Oakland.

Armed with AK-47s, they moved like a trained unit. That meant they were Charlemagne's people, and that meant Harry was interested. He could give two wet shits about the woman. If she worked for those merc fuckbirds, she knew what happened in Oak Town after dark.

If you can't do the time, don't do the crime.

"Harry Balls, what's that crazy bitch up to?"

"I don't know, Big Baby," Harry said without taking his eyes from the Barrett's scope. "She's all by herself."

"Crazy is as crazy does. Never seen one flying solo."

"That's what I'm saying," Harry said.

Why was she alone? Why was she sprinting down 20th at 2:15 a.m. in the most dangerous place in the Bay Area, a place where cops didn't even bother anymore and the only residents remaining were armed to the gills and battened down the hatches long before the sun went down.

The three vamps stalking her... they were trained, but not very well. Harry gauged that by movement alone. Lately, Charlemagne had been trying to keep her vamp goons quiet, keep them from roaming the streets at night. Except for the ones that were supposed to kill Harry, of course. Those fuckers seemed to have free reign.

Harry hadn't been able to figure out what Charlemagne was up to. Hell, he still hadn't found her most recent base of operations. Goddamn cell phones, email, and physical runners let her keep her forces spread out. The ones Harry found, Harry killed, but he hadn't found that many.

He knew that she'd been bringing something in from the North Bay, something that required cargo vans coming across the 580 to Richmond, then down to Oakland. Harry had learned this from his most recent capture. The vamp said she didn't know any details. Harry believed her. Harry believed pretty much everyone after they'd spent an hour in his truck.

So Charlemagne was moving something. Something important. Harry didn't know what, exactly, but it didn't take a Jet Age genius to figure it out: guns, guns, and more guns.

He suspected that she had some kind of shipping arrangement hooked up. Cargo ships launching light craft to land along the long coast of the Point Reyes National Seashore. Off-load, have her vamps carry whatever it was inland to the Shoreline Highway, then south to the 101, north to the 580.

Charlemagne wanted her vamps to rule the Bay Area. She wanted anarchy. She also wanted Harry dead. Which was fine by Harry, because he wanted her dead right back.

He just didn't know what she was doing, and that bothered him to no end. Only one of him, while she managed fifty vamps? Maybe a hundred? Maybe even more, and he couldn't figure out where they were. The numbers game made Harry face a difficult truth: Charlemagne was just plain smarter than he was.

For now, anyway.

But maybe those three chasing the idiot from Academi knew something. Maybe they'd been sent to kill Harry and had stumbled upon the woman, maybe decided to stop for a late dinner. There was only one way to find out.

"Big Baby, how would you feel about seeing where this plot leads?"

"Fuck yeah, fatso. Think I want to sit here all night doing the knuckle shuffle?"

"You have such a way with words, Big Baby."

"Blow it out your ass, fuzz nuts."

Harry slung the Barrett.

"Hands-free," Big Baby said. *"Does that mean the warrior can come out and play-yay?"*

Harry thought about it. Big Baby had a tendency to react on emotion only. He wasn't logical, not like Harry was. Still, Big Baby got the job done.

"Sure," Harry said. "Let's go."

———•———

Bad choices.

Two-thirty in the morning. Alone. In Oakland. The bad part, where the vamps ran free and no one came to stop them. As best as she could tell, three vamps were closing in on her.

In a lifetime of poor decisions, Karin Mulroney had to put this one in the top five.

She'd seen two of the vamps were carrying AK-47s. Vamps were bad. Armed vamps were worse. Armed, *trained* vamps were on another level. From the way they moved, they were clearly trained. Karin prayed they were inexperienced enough to make a mistake.

Up ahead, at the corner of 20th and Irving, was a small boarded-up house. Maybe it was pink, or salmon colored, but the streetlights in this abandoned area had given up the fight long ago; there was no way to tell. Karin was running, both hands on her KRISS Super V submachine gun, and didn't have time to be all that picky about the right place to make a stand. The plywood on the windows looked solid and the roof had no holes. The front door was gone, ripped off, broken in half and scattered on the front lawn as if it had been a bill torn apart and cast aside by an angry homeowner.

One clear way in, no other visible entrances that could be accessed without making a helluva lot of noise. She would have to take her chances that the back of the house was as reinforced as the windows.

An open front door meant no one lived there. The few people left in this part of Oakland were still alive because they knew how to shelter down for the night. With how bad the vamp situation had become, an open front door might as well be an "Eat At Joe's" sign.

She ran up the six concrete steps that led into the battered old house.

A broken couch, a leaning chair, a dog-shit stained, frayed rug over a chewed-up hardwood floor. Water marks on the walls, the general grime of a house lived in, loved, then become part of a slum, then abandoned altogether.

Once in, she looked for the best place to make her stand. The kitchen, straight ahead. No door, just an open frame. The walls in this place looked like old-style plaster and lathe: thick and solid enough to take some damage. She hoped, anyway, and she would probably find out soon enough.

Karin tugged an M86 free from her webbing. She set the one-pound metal and plastic mine—which was roughly the shape of a piece of pie and always made her want yellow cake with white icing—a few feet inside and to the left of the front door. She pulled the pin, then took half cover behind the kitchen wall, hugged the KRISS stock to her shoulder, aimed at the front door, and started counting.

The M86 took twenty-five seconds to arm. When you're being chased by vamps armed with AK-47s, twenty-five seconds is a long time to wait, and a lot of time to think.

Everyone made mistakes. She knew that, although most people hadn't collected as many as she had. Most people didn't leave behind a wake of horrible decisions that spread out from either side along the timeline of their lives, washing against the people they loved, eroding them like the tide rolling in on a sandcastle.

Joining the Army? A mistake.

Marrying Bob? A *huge* mistake.

Continuing to delude herself that she liked men at all, because that was what her family expected of her, what her culture demanded of her? A gigantic error.

Figuring things out, finally, then shacking up with Gretchen? That one made even the Bob choice look good.

Leaving her sister alone?

That had been the worst decision of all.

And now *this*. Five nights of stalking through Oakland, practically begging the Bloods to find her and tear her to pieces. Just so she could keep her job.

Karin had made mistakes before, yes, but none this bad, none that brought death.

Or maybe even worse.

"Just get out of this," she whispered. "You don't even have to go to work tomorrow, just get in the car and *go*, call and quit from the road. Colin won't find you. You'll survive. This isn't worth it."

But it *was* worth it. Because, where would she go? Where was safe? Her sister had tried to lead a quiet life, and her sister was dead. In a world of endless violence, where the darkness had come to life and walked in the light, the safest place was the place with the best defenses and the most guns.

Academi had the most guns.

San Francisco had the best defenses.

And to stay in San Francisco, to stay in Academi, to stay *alive*, she found herself in Oakland.

Oakland, which had no defenses at all.

It wasn't even a matter of getting back across the bridge to safety, not now. She wouldn't make it. She'd either have to scare her pursuers away, kill them, or die.

Or, find *him*. Maybe he would help her. Maybe he would slaughter her the way he'd slaughtered so many others. Karin just didn't know.

Twenty five seconds expired.

The M86 activated, blossoming out seven six-meter tripwires. She could see them when they launched in the lightless house, barely, but when they landed—one parallel to the threshold, two into the entry way, one reaching almost to the kitchen—Karin couldn't see them at all.

She'd seen all the intel Academi had on vamp behavior, especially on vamps that followed Charlemagne, the secretive local leader who operated like a guerrilla general. Her vamps moved fast, and they moved in groups. If the three pursuers entered, they would probably enter together, SWAT style, rushing in to cover all angles. Karin prayed they wouldn't come at all, but also prayed that if they did, they'd follow that training—the first vamp might blitz in so quickly he or she would escape the worst of the M86, but the ones following would be right in the sweet spot.

Karin breathed in slow, a four-second pull, breathed out slower, an eight second exhale. In through the nose, out through the mouth. This might very well be her last few minutes on Earth: she savored the coolness of the air, tried to feel the way it filled up her lungs, the way her skin stretched against her fatigues. Half-covered by the thick kitchen wall, her focus and her aim remained locked on the front door.

With almost no sound at all, they rushed in.

Three males, AK-47s at their shoulders, barrels instantly pointing in three different directions in perfect room-clearing form, but the first one caught a tripwire.

Karin ducked behind the wall.

The mine's internal propellant fired the kill mechanism upward, a lethal pop-goes-the-weasel shooting out of the cake slice so fast it smacked into the ceiling before detonating. The *snap* of the explosion sent fragments tearing through the ceiling, the floor, the walls... and Karin's pursuers.

She leaned out, keeping most of her body covered by the door wall. The first vamp had almost reached the kitchen, probably would have reached it were it not for mine fragments shredding his shoulders and driving him to the floor. His head was only a few feet away; Karin pointed her KRISS at it and squeezed off a short burst. Forty-five caliber rounds sprayed out. She saw at least one smash through his skull, splashing blood against the floor with a baseball-bat *crunch* when the bullet exited his face and punched into the hardwood.

She brought the muzzle up to locate the next two targets, but jerked her body back behind cover when she saw two AK-47 barrels swinging her way. She squatted down, froze in fear as the wall above her erupted in plaster-puffing holes. The shots were wild, as best as she could tell, hitting both sides of the door, going high and low—a bullet was going to punch through the wall behind her, hit her, tear her insides apart, she was going to die, they were going to take her…

A *boom!* so loud she flinched, far louder than even the mine's explosion or the AK-47 rounds. A fraction of a second later, a shout of surprise, of fear, a shout ended by a second *boom!*

"*I'm your Huckleberry*," someone said in a high-pitched falsetto.

All fell quiet.

Karin's heart hammered so hard she felt it in the base of her throat, wondered if it would make her throw up.

"You can come out now," said a deep male voice. "But I'm covering you, and unlike these idiots, I don't miss, so how about you leave your gun on the floor and let me see your hands?"

Karin couldn't even draw a full breath. Her body didn't want to obey. Her muscles seemed locked, glued onto her bones and shellacked in cold metal.

"Come on," the man said. "The worst is over."

Karin felt herself nodding. She had to come out. It was him—*the Hippo*—the reason she'd come here in the first place.

She set her weapon on the floor and stood, metal muscles fighting her all the way. A half-halting breath pulled itself into her lungs, and then she was gulping air. She raised her hands to shoulder level, turned and stood in the open kitchen door.

He seemed to take up most of the room. She had seen drone footage of him, but no one had ever landed a clear shot. So fat, he looked as wide as he was tall, flat-black trench coat hanging down to his knees. A Barrett .50-cal was slung over his shoulder, thick barrel angled up toward the pock-marked ceiling. And in his hand was the biggest pistol she had ever seen, barrel pointed at her face, the muzzle so wide you could drop a dime in it.

His black skin blended in with his black coat, black pants, black boots, and black gloves. A slight gleam of sweat on his skin was the only thing that made him look human. Bright blue eyes looked her up and down—those eyes hadn't been in the surveillance footage either, and they were almost as disturbing as the hand cannon aimed at her face.

"Academi," he said.

She drew in another half breath, unable to get a full one to go, then glanced at her black uniform and body armor as if she'd forgotten she was wearing it.

"Yeah," she said. "Academi."

"You're lucky," he said. "The mine was a neat trick, but it didn't stop the two I killed. You slowed them down, but the way you froze up in there, you—"

"I didn't *freeze up*," she snapped. She pointed to the dead one face-down on the floor in front of her. She made the mistake of actually looking—head half blown apart, chunks of red brain and splintered bone radiating out around him like a flat, fucked-up halo—then forced herself to ignore what she'd done, forced herself to again meet the blue eyes.

The big black man smiled. "One out of three will put you in the hall of fame, but you weren't playing baseball, honey." He lowered the giant handgun, used it to gesture at her other two pursuers.

Enough light came in through the missing front door for Karin to see the carnage. Moonlight glinted off curling strands of wet blood.

The one on the left was missing a head. No, not missing, just a few feet to the right. Whatever bullet that handgun shot, it was big. The man must have walked in and pointed the barrel right at the back of the vamp's neck before pulling the trigger. A line from *Dirty Harry* flashed through her head on rapid repeat: *the most powerful handgun in the world and would blow your head clean off...*

She didn't know if that was true of a Magnum, but the severed head and the ragged shred of a neck lying on this rat trap's floor showed it was true for the Hippo's artillery piece of a handgun.

The other vamp lay in a heap, a relaxed fetal curl. Karin could have put her fist inside the hole in that vamp's back.

Dead as shit, but the Hippo still reached out a toe and slid the fallen AK-47 away from the corpse.

"Academi always comes in force," he said. "Where're your friends? They already dead?"

Karin shook her head. "I'm here alone."

The fat man laughed. "Well, then you are one lucky lady, lucky lady. If I hadn't come along these kallikantzaros would be tearing you to shreds."

"I wasn't lucky," she said. "I was looking for you, Harold Chamberlain."

The man's smile faded. He stared at her for a second, long enough for her to remember she had her hands up, free of any weapon.

The Hippo half raised the pistol. Karin's breath again locked up tight, but he lowered it to his side just as quickly, like he'd changed his mind.

"Well, you found me," he said. His words no longer sounded jovial. "And how did you know where to look?"

"Academi's been watching you. Using drones to track your patterns, marking kills, shell casings, anything we could find. We know where you're living, we know about your father, Allan Chamberlain, know you're keeping him… "

Her voice trailed off as the gun came up again. Slower, smoother, and this time, it didn't go back down.

"You're watching me," he said. "*Tracking* me. Like an animal. And that's why you're in this part of town at this time of night? Because you knew I'd be here?"

Karin nodded. She couldn't look away from the gaping muzzle.

"Been looking almost a week," she said.

The man spoke again, but with a high-pitched voice, and he moved only the left side of his mouth.

"*Just shoot this bitch and be done with it. You know how bitches are, Harry.*"

The man glanced at his pistol. "Shut up, Big Baby."

"*But Harry, she—*"

"I said shut up!"

The Hippo slid his trench coat open and jammed the pistol into a hidden holster, then tugged the coat back into place.

Karin realized she could add another mistake to her list. She'd known this guy was crazy—you didn't saw open vamp skulls and take the brains as trophies if you were sane—but she hadn't thought him *this* crazy. He was talking to his gun, and to his mind, his gun was talking back.

She considered making one more mistake: turning and grabbing for her weapon. She could probably get to it before he could draw that obnoxious pistol, definitely before he could unsling the Barrett, and *maybe* before he could reach her. Then what? Shoot him? Try and coerce his help at gunpoint? No, she'd come here because she needed this man, needed this killing machine that had notched more Bloods than anyone Academi knew outside of Big Dog and his team of psychos in V-8.

The Hippo stepped closer. Just the *size* of him... so imposing, taking up so much space.

The fingers of her left hand flexed: she forced them to stop. That was where she wore her knife, on her left thigh. If he got his hands on her, she knew she was in trouble. She could do severe damage to damn near anyone, but she wasn't dumb enough to think she had much of a chance in a hand-to-hand fight with a man that outweighed her by two hundred pounds and killed vamps for fun.

The Hippo stared down at her with those odd blue eyes.

"Why is your company tracking me?"

"You're an unaffiliated operator in our sphere of influence," Karin said. "Proper intel gathering on any such individual is de facto procedure."

The big man smiled. "You guys always talk like that?"

"Huh?"

"I bet you asshats have tons of meetings," he said. "When you leave a meeting to take a shit, do you say something like, 'I will now extricate myself from this verbal engagement in order to open a new front in covert elimination'?"

Karin stared at him for a moment, confused, then laughed.

"No, we don't talk like that," she said, although, with the jargon that got tossed around in the corporate environment of the world's largest mercenary outfit, it wouldn't surprise her if someone did.

"We track you because you kill vamps," Karin said. "That's why I'm here."

The big man looked left, looked right, craned his head to look around Karin as if someone might be standing right behind her. Her finger flexed on the knife handle again, but she forced herself to be still.

"Huh," he said. "You say 'we,' but there's only *you* here. I've never seen Academi roll across the bridge with anything less than three APCs and a pair of Blackhawks. Since it's just little ol' you, something tells me you aren't 'operating within the confines of a properly demarcated theater of interaction and comma-delimited space.'"

"Comma-delimited?"

He shrugged. "I ran out of jargon. That's the first thing that came to mind. So you're using Academi intel to find me, and you came alone. Do we keep playing twenty fucking questions or are you going to tell me what the fuck you're doing here?"

"I want to help you with your dad," she said. "I can get you money and resources, maybe even space in San Francisco so he's not out here, chained up in a bus garage."

The big man leaned forward, ever so slightly. Karin heard the creak of leather gloves as hands curled into mallet-sized fists.

"You've been in my home?"

"Not *me*," Karin said instantly, shaking her head. "Academi operatives assigned to you."

As soon as she said it, she knew there would be no difference in this man's mind. He didn't know her. She could smell the anger brewing in him, and not just at Academi's surveillance. Harry Chamberlain had gone through hell. No, he hadn't gone *through*—he was still crotch-deep in it, every day, doing what he could to keep his vamp father, his only family, alive.

If Harry went ape-shit here, Karin would lose this opportunity she'd almost died to create. So she did the only thing she knew how to do: she went on the offensive.

"Don't you think calling it a home is a bit much, Harry? It's a garage. You've got your father in a shock collar that could kill a Rottweiler. You have him chained to the ceiling so he can't get away, because if he does get out, he'll kill anything he sees. You think a chain hooked to a winch is going to keep him in check forever? And don't forget that Charlemagne wants you dead. Eventually, she's going to find you *and* your father. When that happens, you—"

His left hand shot out, *teleported*, because she didn't see it before it was wrapped around her throat. It didn't knock her back, not even a bit:

the fingers tightened like they had been there all along, just waiting for the command to *squeeze.*

Karin's left hand reached for her knife, but found Harry's gloved fingers already gripping the hilt.

"Don't," Harry said. "And if you kick me in the nuts, I'll snap your neck so fast you'll hit the deck before I do."

The squeezing increased.

"Your... *father.*" Karin had to fight to get out the words. "I... can... *help.*"

The pressure eased off slightly, just enough for her to suck in a tiny bit of air.

The Hippo pulled the knife from her sheath. He held it reverse grip, blade up flat against his coat's black sleeve. The hand stayed low, but there was no mistaking the message: with that insane speed, Harry Chamberlain could slash at her legs, her belly, her throat, and do it so fast Karin might not know it had happened until she heard her own blood splattering on the floor.

"No one can help my dad," Harry said. He said it in a voice that sounded like it was woven from exhaustion and anguish, washed in bleach so many times that all color had faded away.

He let go of her.

She rubbed at her throat, coughed as if that would help the burning pain inside. It didn't.

"I can," Karin said. "I can get you resources and money... a place to hide him away in San Francisco, so you're away from Charlemagne."

"I don't want to be *away* from that bitch," Harry said. "I want to kill her for what she's done to my town."

Karin nodded, kept rubbing.

"Sure, but you could go after her when you want, not have to defend against her 24/7. Your dad, Harry... if he's in Fortress SF, he can be *safe.*"

She knew that was a ridiculous claim. Harry's dad was as far gone as gone got. When Academi's agents found a body with the skull-top sawed off and the brain removed, they knew that was the work of the Hippo. When they found bodies torn to pieces and gnawed upon—like they'd found in that old high school gym when Charlemagne's people had attacked Harry's previous hideout—they knew that was the work of Allan Chamberlain, former owner of Bup's Cups bakery and provider of confections to hundreds of Oakland residents.

Harry shook his head. "You came here alone, lady. If Academi wanted me, they would have brought the cavalry and a contract. That means your company doesn't want me, *you* do, and something tells me you ain't got the pull needed to set my dad up in San Francisco proper."

"If you help me, I'll have plenty of pull," Karin said. "My boss is crooked. If you help me, he'll be gone, and I'll take his place. *Then* I'll have the power to help."

The Hippo took up the entire doorway. Karin worked with bad-ass operators every day. Academi had the best of the best, veteran killers in top physical condition, but this guy? His intimidation level made her skin crawl.

"So you want me to help you get a promotion," he said.

"I want you to help me stay *alive*." Karin's words rushed free, a string of syllables that shot out like fishing line pulled by a monster fish. "Academi San Francisco has been infiltrated by Charlemagne. Senator Maria Giroux is speaking in San Francisco. Charlemagne's people are going to help the New Red Coalition kill her."

Harry again looked Karin up and down. "Funny, you don't strike me as the hero type. You're a merc. Why do you give a shit if some Bloods grease a politician?"

"Because my job is to be her escort," Karin said. "I'll be by her side the entire time she's in San Francisco. So if the NRC hits her, they also hit me."

And there it was. There were many layers of detail under that crust of reality, but she'd laid out the gist of it. The NRC was going to try and kill Giroux: Karin Mulroney didn't want to be caught in the crossfire.

Harry stared at her with those piercing blue eyes.

"The NRC is going to kill a senator, and Academi is going to let it happen?"

"Not everyone in the company," Karin said. "Colin Benthall runs Academi in San Francisco. He's been turned. They're paying him, or fucking him, I don't know. He's behind this. Maybe some of the others are in on it with him as well, I haven't figured it out yet. All I know for sure is that Giroux is the target."

"How many are coming for her?" Harry said. "Weapons? Tactics? Timelines?"

"RPGs," Karin said. "They're going to hit the motorcade that's taking Giroux to the Ferry Building for her speech. The timeline is tomorrow afternoon. Ten hours from now."

The Hippo nodded like Karin had just told him something he'd known for years.

"Of course," he said. "Tomorrow. Ten hours from now. Plenty of time to get ready." He handed her the knife, hilt first. "You know my name. What's yours?"

"Karin," she said. Had she gotten through to him? She returned the knife to its sheath. "Lieutenant Karin Mulroney."

Harry reached into his coat. Karin almost went for her knife again before she realized he was reaching into the right side, not the left where that crazy-ass gun was holstered.

His hand came out holding a small, square Tupperware container.

"Karin, do you like cupcakes?"

He popped the lid and held the container in front of her. Inside were four white-frosted mini-cupcakes.

"Uh... sure," she said.

A giant psycho who carried the biggest guns she'd ever seen anyone carry, who *talked to* the guns and had the guns *talk back,* and who carried cupcakes in his huge trench coat?

He gave the container a little shake. "I'm going to have one, just so you know I'm not poisoning you or anything. And also because I made these things and cupcakes are fucking delish. You pick one for me, and one for you, okay?"

Was this some kind of weird bonding ritual?

Karin pointed to the back right.

"For me, or you?" he said.

"You."

He nodded. "Good enough. And for you?"

She pointed front left.

"Tic-tac-toe," Harry said.

He pulled out the cupcakes, handed Karin the one she'd asked for. He peeled the paper from his.

"Red velvet," Harry said. "Made them myself. Did your little spies tell you about my kitchen?"

Karin shook her head. "They didn't go inside."

"I suppose they didn't," Harry said. "If they had, they'd be dead. But anyway, hooray for privacy, amiright? I love how you fuckers can get away with all this illegal shit. People give up rights for security at the drop of a hat these days."

Karin didn't really consider bloodthirsty vamps pushing civilization to the brink of collapse a mere 'drop of a hat.' And for that matter, Harry had been a cop once. She wondered if he'd been as high and mighty about civil rights back then.

He took a bite. A delicate bite, considering his size and the tiny cupcake.

"Eat up, girl. If we're going to do business together, the least you could do is try a brotha's baking."

She again thought about just quitting the job. She could wait out the night in this house, then in the morning just start walking. Someone, somewhere, would hire a woman with her skill set.

But that was the problem, wasn't it? Her skill set; the only people who would hire her were companies like Academi, or private forces, or some bodyguard firm, and at the end of the day she'd be more exposed and working for an outfit with fewer resources. She'd also find herself on Colin's radar. With Academi's endless resources, he'd find her.

But if she pulled this off, she could take over Colin's job. She'd never have to leave the city again. And the next time a VIP like Yuki Nitobe or Giroux came through town, someone else would work as their handler.

If a mini red velvet cupcake was what it took to make that happen, so be it.

She peeled the paper free and popped the whole thing into her mouth. The icing was sweet and creamy, the cake meltingly moist.

"It's perfect," she said as she chewed. "These are really good."

Harry smiled.

"I'm glad you like it. I need to finish up here, then we'll go to my truck. It's not far. Don't talk while we walk, don't talk while we drive."

"Where are we going?" She already knew the answer, but was hoping to hear something else.

"To the *bus garage*," Harry said. "I have to check on Dad. We'll talk there. Tomorrow is going to be a big day, and we have a lot to cover."

He reached into his coat again. This time, he came out with a small stack of square Tupperware containers, one insider the other, the lids layered on top. He put one on the body with the hole in the chest, the other next to the severed head.

Then, Harry again reached into the coat of many pockets. This time he produced a small bone saw. The circular blade gleamed in the dim light.

Karin's stomach flip-flopped. For a moment, she'd been having a normal conversation with him, sharing cupcakes for the love of Christ; she'd allowed herself to forget what this man was.

"You're not going to do that now," she said. "We've got a lot of shit to cover."

Harry smiled. "Your company watches me. You're familiar with my M.O. So, yes, we're going to do this now, before the brains go bad. Don't worry, I can talk and work."

Karin nodded. Don't worry. Of course. Why should she worry? She was recruiting a psycho who talked to guns and collected brains, a psycho with a *more* psycho father, and if this plan worked, Karin would have to find a way to provide for that more psycho father and hope that doing so didn't lead to more death somewhere down the road.

Maybe she could wait tables. Maybe she'd find a fake identity and work at Home Depot. Was staying in Fortress SF really worth being a part of this freakshow?

Harry pulled a thin vinyl gym bag from his coat and set it on the floor next to the corpse. Then, he pressed a button on the handheld bone saw. The blade whined to life.

"Wait a minute," Karin said.

Harry paused, looked at her.

"The brains," she said. "Why... uh... I know you take the brains, but what do you *do* with them?"

The big man smiled. "This and that."

He turned on the saw. When the blade touched bone, the whine turned to a scream.

"A DAY IN THE LIFE" PT.8

Jonathan Maberry

Chicago, Illinois

"**T**his is humiliating!"

It was the fourth time Brianna said it. Gus figured that he'd hear it, or some version of it, at least fifty more times today, and this was just day one of the braces. He couldn't wait until he drove his daughter to school next day. That was going to be so much fun. And afterward maybe, to keep the good times rolling, he'd drive at high speed into an El support.

This sort of thing was why, he was quite sure, so many parents drank.

"It's fine," he said.

"It's *not* fine," she wailed. Brianna was thirteen. Way too late to exchange her for a boy. Maria had made that quite clear way back during the first ultrasound. You get what you get. Parenthood is a lottery. For Gus, who did love his daughter and had actually wanted kids, a lottery win would have yielded a boy. Gus had grown up with four brothers and three male cousins. Boys, boys, boys. He understood boys. He coached a boys' soccer team. He loved being a guy. He understood "guy."

Girls? Not so much.

Maria had been his first and only girlfriend. She'd gotten pregnant on their fourteenth date. Brianna was their only child. A girl. In the thirteen years since he'd been married to a woman and father to a girl, he managed to understand none of it. They were both mysteries to him as surely as if they had come from some land of faerie. He could mollify with gifts and flowers, but in truth he was paying tribute to appease these strange beings that now ruled his world.

What made it even worse was that his two best friends, José and Terry, both had sons, so he couldn't even tap them for advice. He was a stranger in a strange land, and no matter where he placed his foot there was either a deadfall, or a landmine, or a bear trap.

"You look pretty," he told her.

Brianna kicked the dashboard. "I look *hideous!*"

"Of course you don't, pumpkin."

"Don't call me that. That's a kid's name."

"Sorry."

"I'm not a kid."

"Of course not."

"Don't patronize me," she barked. It was a line she'd picked up from her mother and used like a lash against her helpless father.

"I'm not."

She shot him an evil look, then turned and continued glaring hot ninja death out the side window. He cut quick, covert looks at her, and at the braces reflected in the window glass.

The orthodontist had gone—perhaps—a little crazy. The scaffolding he'd built around her teeth was impressive as a feat of engineering, but hardly the sort of thing a young girl wanted to be caught dead in.

"I had braces when I was your age."

"So what? You were a boy."

"A lot of girls get braces," he ventured, trying to land them both on the same field.

"So what?"

"Just saying. That girl in your class, Katie, she has braces. She's had them since last year. She looks fine."

Brianna turned toward him with the slow deliberation of a killer clown in a horror movie. The slow eruption of a smile, the shark-dead eyes, the burning promise of pain written in her body language.

"Katie looks fine?" she said in the coldest voice in North America.

"Well, sure…" he began, but didn't finish. The phrase *"Danger, Will Robinson"* was screaming in his head.

"You're just saying that because Katie Harraday has tits."

"Hey, language—"

"All the dads like her because she had big—"

"Language."

"—boobs."

"And that's not true."

"She *does.*"

"No, I mean that's not what I said. She has braces and—"

"Big boobs."

"Come on, pumpkin—"

"I *told* you not to call me that."

"Come on, Brianna. Don't make this weird. Why would I care about whether one of your friends has breasts?"

"Dad… we're all girls, we all have breasts."

"You know what I mean."

Brianna folded her arms. "Maybe I don't. Why'd you mention Katie?"

"Because of her braces."

"What about Alyssa and Naomi? They have braces, too. Why didn't you mention them?"

"I—"

"Because they both have smaller boobs than me."

"Will you stop with the boobs, for God's sake? This isn't about boobs."

"Then why'd you mention Katie?"

"Because she's the only one whose name I know."

"She's the only one whose name you remember because she has big boobs."

"Brianna, you're being disrespectful to your father."

Her answer was a cold little snort that was a perfect replica of the one Gus had heard from his wife thousands of times over the last fourteen years.

"Damn it," he snapped, "now you listen to me. This has nothing at *all* to do with how any of your friends are built and that is that. You're wrong and you're being rude and unfair. No, no, you listen to me for a minute. I'm your father. I love you. *You.* You're a beautiful young girl and you'll be a beautiful woman just like your mother. These braces are there to help you. You've been complaining about your teeth for two years now. You want them to grow in crooked? Of course not. Neither do I. Neither does your mother. Is wearing braces going to be a pain in the butt? Sure it is. I went through it. So did your mom. So do a lot of people. Will it be uncomfortable and annoying and embarrassing? Sure, maybe, for a while, until you're used to it. You say you have several friends who wear braces, then okay. You're still friends with them, right? You didn't drop them because they got braces, and nobody will stop being friends with you, either."

"Yes, they will."

"No, they won't. Kids get braces all the time and the world doesn't end."

"Oh, right, and like any boys are going to even look at me without throwing up."

What he wanted to say was, *Any boys so much as look at you, I'll run them through a wood-chipper.*

What he said was, "You're a very pretty girl, pumpk—I mean, Brianna. You're also thirteen, so maybe we don't need to worry about what boys are going to think for a couple of years."

"Why? Because I'm hideous, that's why." Her tone was almost triumphant, as if she'd won the key theme of her argument.

Not driving the car into oncoming traffic was becoming a real challenge. He took a breath to steady his voice and gripped the steering wheel hard enough to make the leather wrappings squeal.

"I. Didn't. Say. That," he replied, spacing the words out between gritted teeth.

"You don't know anything," she said, and disintegrated into tears.

Gus patted his pockets and found a plastic package of tissues, took it out and handed it to her. She snatched it out of his hand without looking at him. As she wiped her face, he studied her with more sly looks.

Brianna really was a pretty girl. Long brown hair that had red highlights, bright blue eyes, a splash of freckles across her nose. She looked so much like Maria had when Gus first met her in middle school. There was no doubt she'd truly be as pretty as her mother as she grew and matured.

Even the fangs were the same. Slender and not too long. Maria's had grown in straight, but Brianna had apparently only gotten one gene from her father and that was for crooked teeth.

Swell.

He couldn't wait for the moment when Brianna realized that and threw it in his face.

He wondered how the other parents handled it. Most of the kids in Brianna's school were vampires. Many of the parents were not. Maybe he should make more of an effort to bond with some of them. Find out. Get a clue.

"Are you even *listening* to me?" demanded Brianna, and he realized that he'd missed the last few sentences.

"Sorry, sweetheart, I was concentrating on traffic," he lied.

"I *said* that Katie got a tattoo for her thirteenth birthday. I want one too."

"No," he said automatically.

"But, *Dad*, it's not fair... "

And that started a whole different fight.

Gus didn't want a human child per se. He loved his daughter, fangs and all.

But a boy would have been so much easier.

"THE HiPPO II" PT. 2

Scott Sigler

Home sweet home.

Karin had seen pictures and knew what to expect.

This part of Oakland—most parts, really—looked like a functional war zone. Burnt-out buildings and abandoned cars sat side by side with bullet-pocked-but-functioning apartments and heavily gated storefronts. Graffiti covered everything, yet many of the streetlights still worked. Plate-steel window coverings with vertical slits cut into them promised bad juju for any vamps that had the poor judgment to rampage up and down the littered streets. As the city collapsed, it had also *shrunk*, pulling in on itself like a street-fighting hermit crab curling back into its shell, scratched claws still out front and raised in an aggressive warning.

The cops weren't a force any longer, but here that wasn't a factor, because the Oakland Militia certainly was.

Harry's garage wasn't much from the outside, just a typical cinderblock industrial building ideal for vehicle storage. Ideal for psychopath storage, too, Karin figured.

From the outside, the Hippo's food truck had looked battered and bruised, a punch-drunk has-been so graffiti covered she was surprised it had started at all. The inside, however, was immaculate—gleaming and sparkling like the product of an anal retentive housewife's infomercial for a revolutionary new cleaning agent. Stainless steel cabinets and counters, small fridge, an oven… even the surface of the grill shone with showroom spectacularness. Yet the scratches, dents, and dings showed this truck had been around a long time. It wasn't spotless because it was new, it was spotless because someone spent a *lot* of time meticulously polishing every single surface.

The Hippo wasn't just a serial killer; he was also a neat-freak.

He tapped a fast sequence on a number pad glued to the dashboard. A wide garage door rattled up.

The truck rolled in, headlights providing the only illumination. Karin saw a rusty Frito-Lay delivery truck, an RV that had to be thirty years old, and several boats. Harry backed into a space between the Frito truck and a canvas-covered speed boat.

Nothing much to the place, really, just a big open space and one room with long-gone windows that might have once been the office. The food truck's headlights pointed into that office, the metal window frames casting strange, angular shadows inside.

Karin saw a dirty, heavy-gauge chain leading out of the office door and into the darkness behind the RV.

Harry lowered the driver-side window.

"Dad? I'm home."

Karin heard a growl that made her skin crawl and her feet itch. The chain moved slightly, the metal ring hissing on the dirty concrete. The shadows crawled with barbed-wire threat.

Harry sighed. "Dammit, Dad, we've got company. Don't be moody."

Still nothing.

Harry reached into his coat and retrieved a small remote dotted with silver, handwritten words.

"Hold on a sec," he said to Karin, and clicked the button labeled RETRACT.

A whirring metal sound ended the silence. In the food truck's headlights, Karin saw the chain dragging across the floor, into the office. Yanked by the chain, a man stumbled out from behind the RV, tugged by the thick collar around his neck.

Wild eyes, the eyes of someone so far gone they couldn't even be described as human anymore. An old man with scraggly gray hair ringing from temple to temple, lips pulled back in a permanent snarl, white teeth blazing in the light. Not as overweight as Harry, not even close, but still chubby, black skin covered with dirt and grime.

"He's just hungry," Harry said. "Don't mind him."

The chain pulled the old man into the office. He snarled and grunted.

Harry stepped out of the truck onto the small warehouse's dirty concrete floor.

"It's safe," he told Karin.

"I seriously doubt that," she said, her voice thin and hard. She stayed where she was, in the passenger seat, shaking uncontrollably.

Harry shrugged. "Suit yourself."

He grabbed his black duffel bag from the van. He reached inside and pulled out the thing that had made all of this even worse than before, even worse that sawed-open skulls, and brains in Tupperware containers. Worse than those horrors, because Karin had suspected that this thing wasn't for Harry, but rather for his father.

From the bag, the Hippo pulled out a naked leg, severed just below the knee. Pale toes seemed ghostly in the reflected light.

One quick flip sent the severed leg spinning into the room. As it flew, Karin heard the chained-up old man squeal with delight before snatching it out of the air.

She didn't look, but that didn't help, because she could *hear* him eating.

"He doesn't like my cooking," Harry said.

Karin doubted if the thing that used to be a father and a business owner liked *any* cooking—that thing preferred its food raw.

Harry pointed to the RV.

"We can talk in there," he said. "That's where I live."

And what additional nightmares might be waiting inside? Karin didn't know and didn't want to know.

"Right here is fine," she said.

Harry shrugged. "Suit yourself."

He climbed back into the driver's seat. He waited for her to talk.

She said nothing, just sat there shaking her head, amazed at her ability to make bad decisions far, far worse.

———————◆———————

Harry didn't know what to say.

When you only talk to people you're going to kill, conversational skills can get a bit rusty. And when those "people" aren't even people at all, but monsters? Those skills might as well crumble into dust.

It had been a long time since he'd talked to a normal person. He'd spoken with vamps, sure, but those creatures weren't normal. Not by a long shot. And a pleasant conversation isn't exactly something that happens when you're torturing someone just before you kill them so you can bake their brains into cupcakes.

The thing with having a conversation is that it's shockingly easy to forget how to do it. Go long enough without human contact, and an effortless process becomes stilted, difficult. Even before the shit hit the fan, Harry had sucked at talking to people. The only people he'd ever experienced effortless conversation with were his wife, his daughter, and his dad. Two of them were gone. One didn't really talk that much anymore.

Sure, Harry talked to Big Baby, but Big Baby had a foul mouth and was more about saying something crass than carrying on intelligent discourse.

Karin still wasn't speaking. She looked freaked out. Harry would have thought the Academi goons were made of sterner stuff.

"Honestly, you're safe here," he said finally. "You can leave in the morning. It's not totally safe when the sun comes up, but it's saf*er*. You said the NRC is going to put a hit on this Giroux chick. You said your boss is involved. How did you find out about it?"

The only sound in the warehouse was the clink of the truck's cooling engine, and the wet smacking sounds coming from his dad and his dinner.

"She's a *senator*, not a 'chick,'" Karin said.

Harry rolled his eyes. "Oh for fuck's sake. Whatever. How did you find out about it?"

"I got a tip," Karin said.

Harry laughed. "You came out to Oakland at night all by your pretty little lonesome on a *tip*? I might be out of the loop, sugar pants, but I know it took more than just a tip to bring you out. Who did you get this tip from?"

"My name isn't '*sugar pants*,'" she said.

Harry sighed. She was one of those, was she?

Karin rubbed her eyes, rubbed them hard, then seemed to realize her eyes were closed—she opened them with a start, her hand sliding to the hilt of the submachine gun digging in her lap.

Harry sat still and just watched her.

"Sorry," she said.

He waited.

"The tip," Karin said. "Right. I got it from Yuki Nitobe."

She said that name the way a poker player lays down pocket aces, like the five syllables were so drenched in validity they'd hit the ground and splash the stuff all over the wall. Too bad they didn't mean shit to Harry, because he didn't know who…

… wait, he did know that name.

"Nitobe. She's the one who had that crazy story about me on TV."

Karin nodded. "When she came to town to do that story, I was assigned to her. I escorted her all over the place."

Harry knew this woman had rhino-sized balls to come to Oakland alone, looking for him. He admired her for that, but with the mention of Nitobe, he felt that admiration evaporate.

"She wrote crazy shit about me," Harry said. "Me and my dad. And you *helped* her?"

Karin's eyes widened. She opened her mouth to speak, said nothing. She looked dumbfounded.

"You *helped* her," Harry said. "Do you know what it's like to see some asshole on TV spreading lies about you?"

"I don't," Karin said quickly. "I… I don't know what that's like. But I didn't *help* her, you understand? I just escorted her around. That's part of my job. If a female VIP comes in, I get assigned to her. We knew you were leaving a trail of vamp bodies all over Oakland, we wanted to know who you were, so we called Nitobe and gave her a lead."

"What did Academi get out of it?"

"Your real name," Karin said. "Like I told you before, anyone killing vamps at your rate in the Bay Area is a wild card. Academi doesn't like wild cards."

Karin closed her eyes briefly, then looked down.

"Yuki used me. She played me. Of course, I was trying to play her, because that's what my boss wanted, that's what Colin told me to do, but… Yuki is better at the game than I am. A lot better."

Karin's body language reminded Harry of something. Maybe "heartbroken" wasn't the right word. Sad, though. Who did it remind him of? He shook his head; whoever it was, things in the grave of the past were best left buried.

"I don't get the connection," he said. "She used you to get bullshit for a story on me, and somehow that leads to you walking around Oakland like a buffet in combat boots?"

Karin's eyebrows raised and she opened her mouth a few times, tongue making a scraping sound. The two gestures together made it seem like she'd just woke up from an almost-nap.

"I think she was trying to make it up to me," she said.

"Make *what* up to you?"

Karin shrugged. "Doesn't matter. What matters is two days ago she told me she had info that the NRC wanted to take out Senator Giroux. Yuki didn't tell me where she got the info, but she had a time and a place. When I got it, I checked the intel against the planned route for Giroux's motorcade, and it's a match. She's supposed to speak at the Ferry Building in San Francisco. The NRC is going to hit her just before she gets there."

"The NRC already knows her route?"

Karin nodded.

"Is it public knowledge?"

"Of course not," Karin said. "Only Academi and the SFPD know it, but that's a lot of people. Someone in one of those two organizations obviously leaked it."

Harry shrugged. "So change the route."

"I tried," Karin said. "I started with Colin, my boss. I started slow. I told him I thought the route was too easy, that we should change it up and add a dummy motorcade just in case."

"You didn't tell him about your tip?"

She shook her head. "I was going to, but his initial reaction was… he got stressed, he got mad. He told me to shut the fuck up and do my job."

There wasn't much of Harry's past that filtered through. Weapons, tactics, all of that stayed wedged tightly in his memories, but his old job as a cop, not so much. Karin's words dredged up recollections of a woman, a captain. Harry had told her how tactics needed to change to handle the vamps. The woman hadn't listened. A few days later, a standard no-knock went south to fuckville and took the bullet train to get there: two cops dead, their throats torn out by a seven-year-old boy.

Sometimes, higher-ups didn't listen to the grunts.

Karin's situation was like that, but worse.

"You think he's in on it," Harry said. "Why?"

"The way he reacted," Karin said. "Changing the route is easy. Effortless, even. If there's any concept of a threat, a commander would at least give it some thought. But he didn't do that, he snapped at me. He asked me if I'd suggested the route change to anyone else. When he did that, all my alarm bells went off."

"So you didn't give him your intel," Harry said. "You have a time and place of the attack, and you didn't use that to convince him?"

"I'm telling you, he's in on it, Harry. If I'd told him what I know, I think I'd already be dead."

"So why didn't you go to the cops? Why didn't you go to Academi's big bosses?"

"Academi runs the police now," she said. "Let's just say that—" she made air quotes with her fingers "— 'financial contributions' to the local po-po are significant. I don't know what contacts Colin might have. If I go to the cops—or go over Colin's head—and he finds out, I think he might kill me."

Harry wanted to believe her situation, wanted to believe that she could actually help keep his dad safe, but it was hard to believe her when there were far easier solutions at her fingertips.

"So quit," he said. "No reason to put yourself at risk, right?"

She shook her head. "I'm trusting my instincts here. If I quit, if I don't show up for work, if I don't escort Giroux, he'll know I know something."

It was hard to rationalize what this woman was doing. She knew of a pending attack, or so she claimed, and instead of looking out for the people who could get hurt in such an attack, she was looking out for herself.

"So tell me how stopping this attack helps you," Harry said. "If you're right, you'll still have a boss that's corrupt, and he'll probably kill you anyway, just to be sure you don't know anything."

"I called Yuki and told her what I thought," Karin said. "She was shocked. She gave me the info about the attack because she thought it would help me at work, you know? She didn't think there was enough there to merit her time. When I told her Colin's reaction, she suddenly became much more interested. Corruption among the company responsible for making San Francisco the safe haven for the world's wealthy? That's a damn good story. Yuki used her power to get an interview with Academi's CEO to find out what the company is going to do about you."

"Me?"

Karin nodded. "You're a killer, Harry. You saw people's heads open."

He held up a finger. "Not *people*. I don't kill *people*."

Most of the time he didn't, anyway.

"Blood rights groups don't see it that way," Karin said. "It's no secret that the Oakland PD is overwhelmed and not investigating your victims. Academi has become the real authority in the Bay Area, so rights groups are putting pressure on the company to protect *all* people, not just their San Francisco fat cats."

Harry laughed. "Like that's ever going to happen. I don't know much about you guys, but I know you're motivated only by the almighty dollar."

"That's right," Karin said. "But part of any company is public relations. The CEO agreed to Yuki's interview request because having her grill you is better than *not* meeting with her and having her report whatever she wants."

"No shit," Harry said.

Karin winced. "Anyway, she scheduled her interview for the exact time of the predicted attack. She'll be with him when the attack goes down."

"If," Harry said.

Karin nodded. "If. Anyway, *if* the attack goes down, Yuki will pounce on the CEO, tell him that she provided Academi the exact time of the attack and the company did nothing. She'll say I tried to tell my boss about it and was threatened to keep quiet. So all you have to do, Harry, is keep me and the senator alive. The CEO will remove Colin, one way or another."

Or another. Harry was starting to suspect Academi was run more like the mafia than a Fortune 500 company.

People thought Harry was a killer? A reporter staging herself with a CEO *just in case* the attack happened, instead of making sure the attack didn't happen at all? And Karin, ready to gamble with her life—and Giroux's life—to take this Colin guy out of the picture?

People were crazy. That was the only explanation.

"What if you don't take Colin's place? Can you honor your deal to help my dad if you're not the boss of San Francisco?"

Karin thought about this before answering.

"I'll probably get the job," she said. "With Yuki's influence, saying I tried to stop it, saying I was brave enough to stay with the senator, Yuki says I'll become a bit of a media celebrity in my own right. On top of that, Academi can put a woman in charge of their flagship operation. It's a win for everyone."

"Probably," Harry said. "But not a lock."

"Not a lock. Also, because I'm a woman. Academi is definitely an old boys' network."

"Cry me a fucking feminist river," Harry said. "I don't give a shit about that. All I want to know is, if I keep you alive and you don't get the job—or there's no attack at all—what are you going to do for my dad?"

"Everything I can," Karin said instantly. "And I can do a lot. I'm on the inside, Harry. Academi runs San Francisco. It's just that simple. Your chances with me are better than without me."

"And if I help you, and then you fuck me and dad over? What guarantee do I have?"

Karin shrugged. "None. You have to take my word for it. Do you think I would have come to you alone if I had any other option? I'll help you, Harry. I promise."

Harry smiled. This Karin chick was eight flavors of crazy-cake—was any job this important to hold on to?—but she had conviction. If the attack did go down, this Colin fellow would be hung out to dry.

And if it didn't happen at all, at least Harry had a chance at improving things for his dad.

"Tell me how the NRC is going to strike."

"Yuki thinks they have an RPG-7," Karin said. "Already smuggled into the city."

Rocket-propelled grenade. Depending on which kind, how they were used, and where they hit, RPGs could take out a tank. Harry had seen the lightly armored Grizzly APCs Academi used. An RPG-7 would deliver a serious load of fuck-shit-up-itis to one of those. The VIPs, though, would be in Academi's souped-up limo/SUV/tank. A *Knight X* or something like that. Would that stand up to an RPG shot? Harry didn't know.

"You don't see RPGs around here very often," he said. "And by 'often' I mean 'fucking ever.' How did they get it?"

Karin shrugged. "Yuki thinks Charlemagne smuggled it in."

The trucks Harry had just missed the night before. His theory about cargo ships off the coast, sending small boats to Point Reyes. It added up. That was one way to get heavy weapons into the Bay Area. And it also matched up to why Charlemagne's people had kept such a low profile as of late—they didn't want to draw attention to themselves if they were about to smear a shitburger across the windshield of San Francisco.

"Got news for you," he said. "Your senator is fucked. If you ride in that convoy, you're fucked."

Karin shook her head. "Not if you can take them out. Yuki's info is that the RPG launcher was delivered along with a dozen HEAT rounds. Her info included the point of attack—an office that overlooks the route. If you can take the bad guys out at that place, capture the RPG, that busts everything wide open. The senator is safe, Colin is screwed, the RPG is off the streets so Charlemagne or the NRC can't just use it somewhere else. No one gets hurt."

"No one except the terrorists who have the RPG."

Karin shrugged. "You're concerned about them?"

"Fuck those guys," Big Baby said. *"They got it coming."*

"Shut up, Big Baby," Harry said.

Karin looked away again. She didn't seem to like it when Big Baby talked.

Harry thought it over. There wasn't much information. What they did have had been provided by a reporter who had lied about him, clearly manipulated Karin, and was choosing a big story over public safety. How could he trust that kind of information? Still, what the reporter provided seemed to jibe with his suspicions about Charlemagne shipping things in from the coast. Harry didn't know Yuki Nitobe from shit; if the connection between his knowledge and hers was just a coincidence, it was one *hell* of a coincidence.

But still… choosing to let things continue, instead of protecting the senator?

"It's not adding up for me," he said. "Why doesn't this reporter girlfriend of yours just blow the cover off of all this?"

He noticed that Karin winced a little when he used the word "girlfriend."

"Yuki thinks she doesn't have enough to go on," Karin said. "She doesn't have facts, just hearsay. She doesn't have anything on Colin, just my take on his reaction. If she reports this now, then nothing happens; Colin stays in play, the RPG is still out there, and it will get used someday."

Harry smelled something. He smelled *bullshit*.

"A credible threat on a senator is still a big story," he said. "You told her you had this handled, didn't you? You probably told her that you had a team on it or something, that you had people at Academi who would run this as a sting. Am I right? I believe the bit about her wanting to catch the people involved and get the heavy weapons off the street, but for anyone with a conscience to do this, you had to have told her there was *no way* the attack could actually happen."

Karin couldn't meet his eyes. It all clicked.

"You told her the route was changed after all," Harry said. "That's the only way she'd set up this meeting with the CEO, so she could be with him when your 'team' caught the terrorists waiting in vain for Giroux's motorcade."

Now Karin looked at him, stared at him in utter shock. She didn't say anything. She didn't have to. Once upon a time, Harry had been a cop; he knew guilty when he saw it.

"You lied to Nitobe," he said. "You're gambling with lives so that you can be the big boss."

Karin's face hardened. She pointed to Harry's dad.

"That's right," she said. "And if I'm the big boss, then *he* doesn't have to eat goddamn *legs*. You'll never get another offer like this, you understand me? This is it. You do what I want you to do, or you spend your last few days hiding in this shit heap and wind up torn to pieces."

Karin clearly didn't want to be there. She was terrified: of his dad, of Big Baby, of Oakland, of Harry. Terrified, but facing her fear, because in her twisted mind this plan was the solution to her problems. Harry wondered if she knew how close to the edge she really was. He could see it in her eyes. The one who is actually crazy is the last one to know—Karin Mulroney obviously hadn't got the memo.

But she was right.

Harry looked at his father. Such a great man, once. Now he had a bloody toenail stuck to his cheek and some thigh muscle caught between his teeth.

Charlemagne had almost gotten them both at the high school. She was adding tech, she was adding numbers, and now she was adding connections, as well as firepower. How long could Harry last out here?

The real answer: not much longer.

And with dad, there was no place else to go.

"I'm in," he said.

"*Fucking-a*," Big Baby said. "*Titties and beer and let's give a cheer.*"

Karin hid her face in her hands and slowly shook her head.

Colin Benthall had a face like a pig: pale pink, with an upturned nose that showed nostrils filled with hair. Karin wondered if the guy ever looked in a mirror.

"No Blackhawks once we get into the city proper," he said. "Those assets are otherwise assigned, and the mayor's been bitching about flyovers making people nervous."

Karin nodded. Of course there wouldn't be Blackhawks. She wondered if Colin would strip off any other assets while he was at it.

They were in the briefing room at Academi headquarters in San Francisco, well protected by thick concrete walls, armed guards, and machine gun emplacements. The safest place in the city, really. But they wouldn't be here for much longer.

Benthall stood at the front of the room before a wide monitor. He'd just finished showing the motorcade route that would deliver Giroux to the Ferry Building. As Karin had expected, there were no changes. Of course not; Colin wanted Giroux dead, and Karin along with her.

"Giroux's flight is on schedule," Benthall said. "So let's review one more time. SFPD cruiser and two motorcycle units up front. Grizzly 1 behind that. Five operators in back, plus one up front, plus the driver. Then the Knight XV with the package, followed by Grizzly 2, and a second SFPD cruiser bringing up the rear."

The man sitting next to Karin raised his hand.

Benthall glared at him. When Benthall glared, Karin imagined she heard a pig snort, although Colin didn't make any such noise.

"What is it, Meacham?"

"Sir, are you sure we can't clear all traffic?"

Gary Meacham was the Knight's driver. His face was always pinched, like he was holding back a fart. No one could handle that mobile monstrosity the way Meacham could. He and Karin would be in the car, along with Steven "Peck" Peckerton riding shotgun, and, of course, Senator Maria Giroux.

"Too late for that," Benthall said. "It's not like this is the president. It's a senator from Louisiana that half of you have never even heard of. You don't shut down a city for that. We go with the route as is. SFO to 101, 101 to 80, 80 to Fremont, Fremont to Market, Market to Steuart, then Mission to the Embarcadero and drop off the package on the south side of the Ferry Building, where I'll be waiting. Any questions?"

Meacham shook his head in disgust. A Knight XV made a Humvee look like a toy. He didn't like the thought of being stuck in Market Street traffic.

"This route is retarded," Peckerton said. "Could we possibly take nine vehicles through any more turns than that?"

Peckerton was a pretty boy, with perfect blond hair and a stubbly jaw made for lighting matches. He was a good enough operative that he could voice his opinion whenever he liked.

"'Retarded' is an offensive word," Benthall said. "And the route is fine."

The route was fine, all right, if you wanted to blow someone the hell up with an RPG. And thanks to Yuki, Karin knew exactly where that shot was supposed to come from: office number 304 of the Southern Pacific Building overlooking Market Street.

But the shot wouldn't come at all; the Hippo would make sure of that.

Karin tried hard not to glare at Colin Benthall. He was a murderer. He didn't have the balls to pull the trigger himself, but that didn't change what he was. After this, he'd be gone, and all of this would be worth it— the risk to find Harry Chamberlain, lying to Yuki, putting her life in jeopardy, putting Giroux's life in danger as well, not to mention Peck's and Meacham's and everyone else's in the motorcade.

This was going to work. It *had* to work.

"All right," Benthall said. "Get to it. Dismissed."

———————

Some people had the ability to blend in. Harry wasn't one of them.

He walked down the old office building's black-lined white marble hallway, moving as quick as he could without breaking into a run. A few people saw him coming, looked up from iPads or stapled reports in time for their eyes to go wide. They would stop, turn, put their backs against the smooth, lacquered wooden walls, and watch him shamble past.

Couldn't blame them, really. He knew he wasn't the friendliest-looking fellow in the world. Black trench coat, carrying a long, flat, black plastic case that might be mistaken as a guitar or bass case. Big ol' black man walking down these lily-white halls? He was surprised they didn't shit themselves when he passed by.

It didn't matter. He wouldn't be here long.

Room 304. That was where he was heading.

That room overlooked Market Street. Maybe sixteen meters up from street level. Couldn't be easier to hit the convoy coming down Market. With any training at all, it was damn near impossible to miss with an RPG from anywhere inside fifty meters.

The century-old building had once been the home of a railroad company, or something like that. Harry had come in through a back entrance, tried to avoid as many people as he could. Marble floors and dark wooden walls, it reeked of a time when the only black people allowed inside would have either been working the elevators or mopping the floors. Old-timey gold-lined black letters on smoked glass showed the room number and company name of each office.

He walked past 302, 303… ah, there it was, 304.

No guard. No lookout. Maybe there would be no one inside at all.

Harry gently gripped the knob and slowly, oh so slowly, gave it a soft, experimental turn: locked. He leaned close to the frame, careful to not let his bulk create a shadow on the smoked glass window.

He couldn't make out words, but he heard someone inside.

Then, he heard a sound he knew all too well: a burst of static and the squawk of a radio.

Unless there were cops inside, or kids playing with walkie-talkies, then the game was on.

Harry gently rested his Barrett case against the wall. He glanced up and down the hall. He had to wait for one woman to turn the corner, then he found himself alone.

He reached to his belt. Karin had given him a fancy radio of his own for this mission, one only she could hear. He pressed the "talk" button in place, unchecked it, repeated that twice more.

"A DAY IN THE LIFE" PT. 9

Jonathan Maberry

Burbank, California

J eremy Tripton sat like a king on a throne and watched the two vampires fight to the death.

Well, almost to the death.

The networks would never allow him to broadcast actual murder, though Tripton was sure the ratings would go through the roof. Ad rates would be amazing. And he was sure there would be plenty of people to subscribe to a show like that as long as it was vampire killing vampire and not Bloods on Beats. You couldn't even sell that mix in MMA. Couldn't have vampires whomping on humans ever since they decided that the V-Gene constituted "performance enhancement."

Whatever.

Tripton wasn't concerned about that kind of interspecies shit. It was problematic, and he'd never get it past standards and practices. But he was hoping the cultural temperature would change enough to allow pay-per-view death matches between Bloods. Put a *nalapsi* in the ring with an *alp* and that would be a license to print money. No way it wouldn't.

Ah well. A man can dream.

The match he was watching was pretty good, though. There would, as the saying went, be blood.

Lots of blood.

The match was being shot in studio ten, and he had a hundred people in the audience. Packed crowd, of course, and the set designer and lighting guys made it look like there were ten thousand screaming fans.

Smoke and mirrors. Literally, smoke and mirrors. The people at home would see what looked like the dingy basement of some illegal cage match. There were even posters and graffiti on the walls to suggest that this fight was in some blood den in Bangkok or Hong Kong.

Tripton bent forward to watch the performance.

The fighters were pretty evenly matched. The favorite was a Bohemian *ogoljen* from the Czech Republic. Tough son of a bitch, too. He was bald, with rotting skin and breath so foul that it could make a strong man swoon from ten feet away. His opponent was an underdog—an Irish kid right off the boat. A *sluagh*. He was a butt-ugly, pallid twenty-something with piercing dark eyes and a toothless mouth. But he had some kind of weird mojo; one of the seducer vampire subtypes. Ugly as fuck, but he got more ass than a casting couch. Crazy old world.

The fighters circled each other on the white mat. There were already spatters of blood on the deck, which is why they used white. The cameras were mounted on the struts of the cage and the director could choose from a dozen views to keep the viewer's eyes jumping.

The *ogoljen's* favorite trick was to flick his arm out and back like a whip, and the action always knocked off some bloody scabs that he could direct with great precision at the eyes of his opponent. Disgusting, but hey, nobody tuned in to *Blood Sports* for tasteful drama to watch while dining. You watched this shit with lots of beer and salty chips to calm your stomach.

When those scabs splatted home, the *ogoljen* would dart in, low and hard, and try to sweep his enemy's legs with a powerful arm-hook. After that it would be the usual MMA floor stuff that was borderline gay porn as far as Tripton was concerned. Two mostly naked grown men squirming around together on the floor. Sure, they punched the piss out of each other, but it wasn't as interesting as stand-up fighting. It also slowed the action down, which made the director have to change from camera to camera to camera so much that it was more nauseating than bloody scabs.

The Irish kid, though, didn't seem to want to go to the deck. He was a stand-up brawler from Belfast. After the first time he got suckered by the *ogoljen* he wised up and began ducking and weaving as if he was boxing a combination puncher. The scabs splatted on his head and shoulders, but not his eyes.

The *sluagh* had a favorite move, too. He roared like a fucking lion, reared up like a pissed-off tarantula, and then did this crazy flying Muay Thai knee kick that caught the *ogoljen* three of the five times the kid tried it. That was a damn good ratio for a novelty attack. Each time the Irish kid landed the knee it knocked scabs and blood from the Bohemian. People in the front rows—those who were smart enough and knew how this worked—cowered behind clear plastic sheeting, screaming and laughing and yelling like they were Romans at the arena.

Fun stuff.

Tripton sat on a raised platform between the judges and timekeeper, digging it all.

This was one of seven shows he had points in right now. All vampire-themed, all different, all hot as fucking lava in the ratings.

The one with the biggest consistent ratings was the absolute bitchfest that was *Real Vampires of the Hamptons*. Good lord, that was a gift from God. Three divas with more money than brains, no trace of class, plastic tits, faces like angels, fangs, and no trace of humanity before or after they transformed. They did nothing but complain about trivial shit ranging from whether to get their fangs sheathed in gold to the cost of rare animal blood. The biggest diva of them all had decided that chinchilla blood was the only blood worth drinking, and it impacted the rest of the world so hard there was a move to make chinchillas a protected species. Great stuff.

Just slightly less fantastic in the ratings was *Staking Amish*, which was a semi-scripted piece of fabricated bullshit about what it means to be Amish and a vampire. None of it was real, though the audience didn't know that. The disclaimer was in micro-font and flashed on and off the screen too fast for anyone to read. The show was in its second season and climbing in the Nielsons.

MYTV Crypts was good and steady, but not growing, getting spikes only when a new sports star or rapper outed himself as a Blood. There was an episode coming up featuring Lil Drip, though, that would probably get big play. He was the only Blood rapper who was "safe," at least as far as the mainstream crowd went. Like Will Smith, back when he rapped. White people could listen to Will Smith. Beats could listen to Lil Drip.

The other steady show was *Unholy Rollers*, which followed five evangelical tent preachers who had become vamps. Tripton didn't think it would have more than two more seasons before it jumped the shark.

Not like *Out of the Shadows*, which would probably only get bigger. It had started by having gay vamps out other gay vamps, but now half the shows were just about outing new Bloods of any persuasion. Last season had ended with them outing the blond on *Modern Family*, the one who played the mother. Not as gay, but definitely as a vampire. An *aufhocker*, one of the rarest of the German Bloods. That pulled serious ratings and upped the ante for advertising for the coming third season.

In the cage, the Irish was beating the living snot out of the *ogoljen*. Vegas odds only gave that seven to five, but upsets were conversation starters. People would be back for more of this kid. If the *sluagh* actually won, then that was PR gold and the network would have a new star. It would also set up the inevitable match for the Bohemian to try and grab his title back. And if the *ogoljen* pulled his own ass out of the fire on this, that would make headlines, too.

Either way, it was money in the bank.

Jeremy Tripton fucking loved vampires. They were money in the bank. Every blessed mother-biting one of them.

Money in the bank.

Down in the cage, blood splattered the audience, and the rubes cried out in the kind of horrified glee that made Tripton know he was in the right damn line of work.

He grinned and sat in his chair like a king on a throne, and all was right with his world.

"THE HiPPO II" PT. 3

Scott Sigler

Karin had to stop herself from laughing in relief; she'd thought those three clicks would never come.

She wore an Academi earpiece in her left ear, but in her right, she wore the one that paired with Harry's rig. Three quick bursts of static told her he'd arrived and found the bad guys.

Halfway home.

If Harry could take them out, the game was over. If he didn't, the NRC could still hit the Knight.

From the driver's seat, Meacham called out.

"Turning northeast onto Market."

"Northeast onto Market," Peck echoed from the front passenger seat.

Three blocks from the attack zone. With the current traffic, the motorcade would cover that distance in about two minutes.

"Excuse me, Karin, are you okay?"

Karin's head snapped right; Maria Giroux stared at her, a look of concern on her face. Blue pantsuit, long hair stylishly curled down past her shoulders, the kind of too-skinny face that only looked good on a woman of her height. Sitting in the Knight's tan bucket seats, legs crossed and relaxed, Giroux looked more like a fashion designer than a politician.

"I'm fine, Senator."

Giroux nodded, but didn't seem convinced. "If you say so," she said. "You looked like you just swallowed a bug or something."

Karin forced a smile. "Sorry, ma'am, just focused on my job."

A job that would soon be over.

Karin faced forward in her own bucket seat. She subtly reached to her belt and clicked the talk button three times.

Harry heard the three clicks in his earpiece.

He glanced up and down the hall one more time: *alone.* He needed to do this quietly. Slip in, take them out, make as little noise as possible so he wouldn't have any run-ins with the SFPD.

His father was chained up in a cinder-block building, probably gnawing on a tibia. Harry had to get this right.

The top half of the door was smoked glass; he couldn't shoulder his way in without shattering that. With his left hand, he quietly picked up the Barrett case by the handle. With his right, he reached into his coat and drew his Mark 3 knife. Good enough for the SEALs, good enough for him, he'd always thought.

Harry stepped back, raised his foot and delivered a fast push-kick just below the door handle.

The thin door *cracked* open, whipping fast on its hinges. Harry let his momentum carry him into the office: ten wide by twenty long, two desks crammed against the left wall, window with venetian blind down. A man and a woman, looking at him in stunned surprise.

Bloods.

The man had an RPG-7 on his shoulder, a four-foot-long green and tan tube with a loaded warhead that looked like two face-sized ice cream cones smashed together. Harry's second step into the room closed most of the distance—a straight thrust with the knife closed the rest. The blade drove through the man's eye, six inches of steel following the point all the way into the brain. Harry simultaneously let go of the knife and the case. He turned, black gloved hands reaching for the woman's throat.

Red hair. Pierced nose. Heavy eye makeup. Would have been pretty, save for the yellow skin; would have been pretty, if she'd been human.

She reacted faster than the man had, brought her arms up hard under his forearms to knock them clear. Quick move, definitive, would have worked great against some jackass off the street.

Harry Chamberlain wasn't some jackass off the street.

The defensive move bumped his hands up only a little. He grabbed her head, palms flat against her temples, and drove his thumbs deep into her eyes, felt them *pop* like small water balloons that splashed out a light spray of clear fluid. She twitched before she screamed. He ended that short scream with a sharp crank left, making her cheek parallel with her shoulder—it sounded like you would expect it to sound, a grinding *snap* muffled by meat.

He let the woman fall. The man was on the ground, trying to get up, knife handle sticking out of his face like a bloody cartoon telescope. Harry kicked the man flat on his back behind the far desk, then raised his foot high and stomped down on the Blood's throat—it sounded like he'd just stomped a carton of fresh eggs.

Harry moved quickly to the door and quietly pushed it shut. Not even five seconds from door kick to door close. If anyone had heard anything, if they peeked their head out of their office, they would see nothing but an empty hallway and closed doors.

"*Fucking Titanic dry-humping a horny iceberg, Harry,*" Big Baby said. "*Did you press the easy button on that shit, or what?*"

Harry shrugged. "That's what happens when you don't commit enough people to the project, I guess."

Big Baby was right… it had seemed easy. No guard, no lookout. The NRC didn't have that many people, maybe? Or maybe their travel budget wasn't all that big. Who knew?

Two RPG rounds lay on a towel in front of the window, ready to be loaded and fired. Hadn't Yuki's information said there were a dozen rounds?

Harry cleaned his glove thumbs on the man's shirt, then pulled the knife from his eye and did the same. He saw the walkie talkie strapped to the man's belt only a moment before it squawked.

"This is Watcher Three," said the tinny voice. "Bird is coming in."

Harry stared at the radio. Less than a second passed before it crackled, and a second voice called out.

"Watcher Two, here, I see them. Remember the plan, I go first."

"*Oh, shittyballs,*" Big Baby said.

Harry clicked the talk button on the radio Karin had given him, then threw his Barrett case to the floor and opened it.

"Come in," Harry said as he pulled out the rifle's upper receiver and slid the barrel into the firing position. "For fuck's sake, come in."

The tinny voice came back almost instantly.

"Go for Mulroney." Her voice was calm and confident.

"I'm at the target site," Harry said as he removed the weapon's upper receiver and flipped out the bipod legs. "You're about to get hit."

"*What?*" Not so confident now. "Didn't you take them out?"

His hands continued their automated work, putting the two weapon halves together.

"I did, but I got a feeling your girlfriend reporter got something wrong. I don't think it was 'RPG,' I think it was 'RPG*s*.' Plural. Get out of the fucking car and get to this building, I'll cover you."

"Harry, I'm not getting out of the—"

He had just popped the first retaining pin home when he heard the explosive *thump* of an RPG launch, and the hammering explosion of impact echo through the street below.

The short, intense detonation made Karin jump in her seat, made her stomach leap into her chest and flop down out of her body.

Giroux screamed.

Through the front windshield, Karin saw smoke billowing up out of the Grizzly's rear doors like steam venting from a high-pressure boiler, a spurting, intense burst that quickly faded to a steady stream.

The Grizzly rolled to a stop in the middle of Market Street.

"Fuck!" Meacham said. "RPGs! I'm getting us out of here."

He threw the Knight XV into reverse just as another detonation erupted from behind the vehicle. Giroux screamed again.

The Knight slammed to a stop. Meacham turned the wheel sharply left and gunned the vehicle forward—he didn't make it ten feet before he braked sharply to a halt to avoid hitting an oncoming car. The stop/start threw Karin and Giroux back and forth in their seats.

Karin knew two things: first, the Knight was blocked in front and behind, which made it an easy target. Second, the only person she could trust had told her to get out.

She reached across Giroux and yanked on the rear passenger door handle before pushing the door open, letting in the sounds of screaming, of chaos.

Peckerton turned in his seat, shocked.

"Karin, what the fuck are you doing? Stay in the vehicle!"

"We have to move," she called back to him even as she drew her Glock 21, roughly slid across Giroux, and stepped out onto the street. People were running in all directions, screaming like idiots. Smoke was already in the air. A fast glance to her right showed that the rear Grizzly was on fire. Ahead of her and to the left, the concrete pillars and curved arches of the Southern Pacific Building, topped by ten stories of old red brick and small office windows.

And peeking out a third story window, the green cone of an RPG.

Only it wasn't aimed *down*, it was aimed *across*.

Karin held the Glock in her right hand. Her left reached back and grabbed the senator's wrist.

"Come on!" Karin screamed, and yanked hard, pulling the senator out of the vehicle.

Karin heard gunfire, heard a different kind of screaming—the sound of men in agony, maybe shot, maybe *burning*—but she blocked it out, focusing only on the tall glass door that led into the Southern Pacific Building.

———◆———

Harry aimed the RPG at the fourth floor of the white office building on the other side of Market Street. There, two men were reloading an identical weapon.

Every window on that building had some kind of safety rail running across it, like a hundred white concrete ladders blocking the bottom half of a hundred gleaming windows. The men had shattered the glass of their window. The shooter leaned out, resting the RPG on the concrete ladder.

"*Fuck that guy,*" Big Baby said.

"I'm about to."

Harry pulled the trigger, felt the weapon lurch on his shoulder, and heard the sharp, roaring snap of launch.

Karin had almost reached the door when another explosion made her stoop and duck, shove the senator behind a wide pillar. Karin turned, unable to stop herself from looking. Across the street, chunks of concrete tumbled to the sidewalk, shattering and scattering like shrapnel amid a rain of tinkling glass. The first long, flickering flames shot out of the new hole.

"Jesus, Harry," she said.

Automatic weapons fire echoed through the street. Bullets ripped into the stone pillar not even six inches from her head. Who was firing? Terrorists, Academi, or the cops? She wasn't going to find out.

Karin pulled Giroux to her feet, yanked open the glass door and shoved the woman through.

"Harry, where are you?"

"*Third floor,*" he said instantly. "*Come to me, this is my spot.*"

She wasn't sure what that meant, but she didn't have time to ask any questions. Scared faces lurked at the edges of the high-ceilinged wood and marble lobby, people hiding behind tables, corners, the security desk, even potted plants. Karin looked for the stairs, saw them, yanked Giroux toward them.

"Come on, Senator, we're going to the third floor."

The senator yanked back, ripping out of Karin's grip.

"My legs work just fine, soldier," Giroux said. She pointed. "There's an elevator."

The senator ran for it before Karin could say a word. Karin followed.

The RPG roar carried through the street. The Knight XV lurched sideways onto its right tires, then dropped back to bounce heavily on its suspension.

Harry sighted in with the Barrett. Lucky for him the second RPG shooter was also on the other side of the street. Ground level, in a coffee shop. Everyone inside was probably dead. Everyone except the shooter and the shooter's buddy—something Harry was about to fix.

He waited until the shooter's partner came forward to help load another grenade. Idiots. They should have retreated inside, loaded, then come forward again slowly, but they weren't soldiers or cops or SWAT or mercs: they were thugs with weapons.

Harry fired. The .50-caliber bullet caught the helper above his left ass cheek, about where the kidney was. He lurched forward, knocking the shooter to the ground. The shooter man tried to get up, but he barely managed to sit forward before a bullet made a big red hole where his face used to be.

Harry swept the Barrett from left to right, a fast glance, taking it all in.

Market Street in San Francisco, *Fortress SF*, and it could have been mistaken for a Mideast war zone.

Far left: Cops taking cover behind a black and white cruiser, trading fire with someone firing an AK-47 from inside the white office building.

Mid-left: The rear Grizzly pumped smoke into the air from some unseen crack in the top. No one had come out of there. Five Academi soldiers, plus the driver and the man riding shotgun, probably dead, blown to bits inside by a heat round that punched through the armor before detonating.

Center: The huge, black Knight XV, smoke rising up from the side where it had just shrugged off an RPG round, trying to force its way past two cars in the other lane—had those cars been regular civilians, or were they driven by terrorists?

Mid-right: The lead Grizzly, back doors blown open, two men lying face down on the pavement, one smoldering. Wandering the street, a man in smoldering body armor and fatigues, missing an arm, screaming at the top of his lungs.

Far right: SFPD cops taking cover behind a cruiser and two motorcycles, the four of them looking around, trying to figure out what to do.

The attack had been fast. Maybe twenty seconds, tops, had gone by since that first RPG launch.

Harry saw two men rush out of the white office building, straight toward the struggling Knight. They carried AR-15s one-handed, shooting wildly at anyone they saw. Each of them also carried a heavy backpack by the straps in their other hand.

"*Bombs,*" Big Baby said.

"No shit," Harry said as he turned the Barrett, sighted, and fired.

The lead man's head snapped back in a cloud of red. His body flopped forward like a thrown toy, slapped against the pavement, and lay still.

Harry sighted in on the second man, but he was too late. The man whipped the backpack along the blacktop. It slid under the struggling Knight.

The man had time to turn and make it three steps before Harry's bullet caught him below the left shoulder blade. The AR-15 went sailing. The man managed two limp steps before he slumped to the ground.

A huge blast erupted beneath the Knight, bumping the vehicle into the air and shattering ground-level windows on both sides of the street. A fireball rose up, making the Knight vanish for a blinding moment, then continued on into the sky.

The Knight kept burning. It didn't move.

Turned out the NRC had plenty of people after all: two dead in the room with Harry, two on the pavement, two surely dead from that RPG hit across the street, and two more from the RPG team in the coffee shop.

Harry hoped they were all vamps. Hard to tell from a distance.

Over the crackling of flames and the staccato report of weapons fire, Harry heard distant sirens split the air. Cops would be coming. A lot of them. And SWAT. Harry knew all too well that dealing with those guys would be a far cry from the untrained bodies he'd just dropped on the street.

Maybe thirty seconds since that first RPG hit.

His experience as a cop told him he had about that much time before the first responders showed up.

Harry gave another fast sweep of the street below, then started breaking down the Barrett just as fast as he'd assembled it.

"Karin, you there?"

———•———

"Hold on," Karin said.

The elevator dinged to a stop at the third floor. Karin spread her feet slightly, pointed her Glock at the elevator door.

The doors slid open to an empty hallway.

She aimed right, stepped out of the elevator. Seeing nothing in the hall, she whipped around. Nothing to the left, either.

"We're here," she said. "We're coming to 304."

"No, I'm on my way," Harry said. "I'll meet you at the stairs, we have to get out of here."

"Affirmative," Karin said, then reached back to grab Giroux. The senator slapped Karin's hands away.

"I don't need you *yanking* at me all the goddamn time," Giroux said. "Just go, I'll follow."

The senator wasn't blowing any of this off, but she didn't look all that scared. She looked pissed. This woman wasn't some coddled politician. Karin wondered what Giroux had been through in her life to be this matter-of-fact while people were trying to kill her.

"All right, come on," Karin said. She looked for and saw an exit sign to the right. She headed that way. One turn revealed white marble steps leading down—and a man with a gun coming up.

Karin brought up the Glock on reflex, almost pulled the trigger before she recognized the face.

"Easy," Peckerton said, his left hand up palm-out in a defensive posture, his right hand holding his own Glock against his thigh. "I followed you in. Where's the—" his eyes flicked behind Karin, saw Giroux. "Okay, there she is. We have to get her out of here."

Could Karin trust him? "Why didn't you stay with the car, Peck?"

"Because you took the senator *out* of the heavily armored vehicle, you idiot," Peckerton said. "Or maybe that was brilliant, I don't know. Shit's crazy out there."

Karin paused a second, listening. The faint pops of gunfire, the sound of approaching sirens.

Peckerton reached a hand up. "Come on, Karin, we have to get the package—"

A gunshot—close range, ear-splitting in the stairwell—and Peckerton fell forward. On the landing behind him, pistol in hand, the pig face of Colin Benthall.

Colin's aim flicked left. For a fraction of time that stretched into an eternity, Karin stared straight down the barrel.

Impact on her right, flying left, the gun going off, something burning her cheek, smashing into the stair railing, falling on the stone steps, tumbling, another gunshot, and another.

Karin rolled again, landed on something far softer than marble, and came to a stop—she found herself on top of Colin Benthall, staring straight into his slowly blinking eyes. Beneath his left eye, a ragged, pinky-sized crater filling with blood.

Karin pushed herself up, away from him. Her Glock was still in her shaking hand. She aimed at Colin's face... but there was no need.

He was no longer a threat.

His body twitched, his eyes blinked weakly. On the marble landing behind his head, a pool of blood slowly expanded.

Karin looked up to the top of the stairs. There stood Senator Maria Giroux, Peckerton's Glock in her hand, the faintest trail of smoke rising from the barrel.

The senator suddenly turned to her left, aiming the gun like a professional.

"Wait!" Karin screamed, knowing what Giroux saw. "He's with me!"

She scrambled up the steps. Giroux's aim didn't deviate from the mountain of a man wearing a black leather trench coat, staring at them both with deep blue eyes.

"He's with you," Giroux said. "You're sure?"

Karin nodded, then remembered Giroux wasn't looking her way.

"Yes, he's the reason you're alive."

Giroux lowered the gun. She turned to Karin.

"No, *you're* the reason I'm alive," she said. "If he helped, I'm grateful, but I'd be dead if it wasn't for you. Thank you, Karin."

The senator then knelt next to Peckerton. His face wrinkled in pain. His hand clutched at his shoulder, trying in vain to stop the blood pouring from the bullet wound.

Karin didn't know what to say. She looked back down the stairs. Colin wasn't moving anymore. Giroux was one hell of a shot, it seemed.

Harry came closer, looked down the stairs.

"That your boss down there?"

Karin nodded.

"He looks like a pig," Harry said.

Karin nodded.

"Well, if you were gunning for a promotion, looks like there's a vacancy," Harry said.

"*Nice fucking pun, douchebag.*"

"Shut up, Big Baby," Harry said.

Karin nodded.

Giroux looked up. "We need to get this man help. But Mulroney, if this means there's a job that you want, I promise you that a phone call from a United States Senator carries a lot of weight. Now go get me an ambulance."

Karin nodded yet again. She walked down the stairs, easing past the senator and Peckerton, stepping over the body of Colin Benthall.

She was almost to the first floor when she realized the Hippo was right behind her.

"Time for me to leave," he said.

"Uh-huh," Karin said.

"Keep that radio on you," Harry said. "Do not make me have to come look for you, understand?"

That cut through her fog. She turned to look at him, at his black skin and blue eyes. He carried that rifle case like it was nothing more than a shopping bag. He was a psycho, a bona fide serial killer, and he'd also done exactly what Karin had asked him to do.

"I understand," she said.

Harry reached out a gloved hand, tentatively, like he wasn't sure what he was supposed to do with it. It hung in the air for a moment. He gave her shoulder a tentative squeeze, then ran back up the stairs.

Karin walked to the door. The glass had shattered inward, scattering across the marble floor. She looked through the concrete arch out onto the street. The gunfire had stopped. Police were running around, guns in hand and pointed at the ground. Wounded and dead lined the sidewalk and the pavement. Flames poured up from the Knight XV. Meacham was probably still in there, cooking to a crisp.

It should have been different. Harry should have captured the RPG, and that was supposed to be that. How many people were dead? Karin was going to get what she wanted, but was it worth it?

Or had this all been another installment in what she did best.

Just another bad decision.

"HEROES DON'T WEAR SPANDEX" PT.1

Jonathan Maberry

Los Angeles

The night was hers.
Hers.
She crouched on the edge of the rooftop and looked out at the sea of lights. Headlights and taillights. Streetlights, and the speckling of lighted windows on all the tall buildings.

Hers.

Her city.

Her people.

So many hearts beating just for her. For her.

For her.

Hydra.

That was the name she wore now. The name she owned. A perfect name for something that can't be killed.

She rose to her feet and ran along the edge of the building and then flung herself out into the air, twisting, turning, reaching, catching the heavy drainpipe on the far wall. The jolt tore something in her shoulder, but she didn't care. The pain was only a flash, and the damage would be healed by the time she slid to the ground.

The leather she wore, though, was still stiff and uncomfortable—still too new to move easily and silently. Not like the last set, which was as smooth as butter. But that was trash. Knives made a mess of it; blood had caked and cracked both jacket and pants. All she had left from that outfit were the gloves. They were still soft, they molded to her hands.

The new clothes would break-in over time.

She had time.

All the time in the world, according to the doctors at the clinic. She'd gotten the only golden ticket in the whole vampire genetics game: the self-regenerating cellular structure. Total freedom from senescence. All of her cells continually divide, continually renew. Complete morphallaxis—which meant that any cut, any bruise, even a nonfatal bullet wound closed and healed completely, leaving no scar. And it healed fast, especially if she'd just fed. Slower if she was hungry. The only marks on her body were the ones she'd had before the V-Gene fired.

Dr. Swann had interviewed her five times, and that was kind of hot, because *he* was kind of hot. A nerdy jock. She'd have slept with him if he'd asked. She'd have let him be her first. And if he wanted to keep on sleeping with her, he could keep being her first, because her hymen would keep growing back. An immortal virgin.

But Swann hadn't even looked at her that way. He was so straight, which was kind of nice, but also kind of frustrating.

He was the one who'd first called her "Hydra," though at the time he was suggesting that they use that word for a new species of vampire. A *hydra*. Lower case. Hydras were some ugly little water creature that regenerated and never died. One of only a couple animals that were actually immortal. Swann thought that this might be the root cause behind the legends that vampires were immortal. Only none of the other vampires were *actually* immortal. They'd done tests, and they all aged, even if some of them aged slower. And none of them were completely regenerative like her. Some were pretty good at healing, but none could heal from anything.

She could. Anything except incineration or a head shot, and the head shot thing wasn't for sure. There was just no way to test it. They could test the incineration by burning skin samples.

The scientists working with Dr. Swann went nuts. Everyone was looking for more like her. More hydras, but right now there was only one hydra and that was her, so she took the name and ran with it. Hydra. Definitely capital "h." Not a kind, but a person.

"I can heal from anything?" she asked.

"You need to be careful," he said. "We don't know how strong those abilities are, or if they'll last forever. And believe me, honey, you don't want to take any unnecessary risks. You're a new species of vampire, but you're not a superhero."

That's what he'd said.

Not a superhero.

Except that he was wrong. She *knew* he was wrong.

Hydra wished she was still in the study program, but Swann wasn't with the government anymore. He was hanging out with celebrities now. Clooney and Winslet and Swift. Cheadle and Elba. Those guys. The in-crowd that ran the OneWorld thing. A bunch of pretty people trying to keep the world from killing itself.

Nice, but not part of her world anymore. Hydra's world was the streets. That's where she was most alive.

Running with the night.

Hunting beneath the swollen breast of the moon.

In her mind, as she hunted, she cast her own movements into lurid prose, describing what she did as if she was the subject of a comic book or movie. Hydra, the immortal vampire, stalking her prey, ready to fight, always ready to kill.

Except that Hydra hadn't yet killed anyone. Or anything.

And so far she hadn't been in a fight.

It was inevitable, though. It had to happen. Fate would have it no other way.

That's what she told herself every night when she put on her leather and went out through her bedroom window into the alley and up onto the rooftops. She could have used the stairs and the back door, but that would have been lame. Batman didn't take cabs. Catwoman wasn't a latchkey kid. When you were a superhero—or even a super-villain—there were standards, even if no one was watching.

Hydra always played it as if she *was* being watched.

Watched by millions of people seated in the dark, crunching popcorn, sipping Sprite, eyes locked onto the sleek, lithe, incredibly dangerous and sexy vampire huntress on the screen.

Or, maybe it was a huntress vampire. She wasn't sure. Which one meant that she was both vampire and hunter rather than someone hunting a vampire? English wasn't Hydra's best subject in school.

She reached the corner of the roof and perched like a gargoyle on the edge. Above and around her, the night seemed to grow darker and bigger, colder and stranger.

Nice.

So nice.

Now all she needed was some prey.

She had no illusions about there being real super criminals out here, but a mugger or slimeball rapist would be great. Someone who absolutely deserved a beat down. Someone she could trash with the Hydra's wrath. And someone who was maybe good for a couple of pints of O positive.

This was her twenty-seventh night of hunting.

There *had* to be criminals out here somewhere. They were all over the news. So far, though, all she'd seen were hookers getting in and out of cars, and a couple of kids selling weed. That was all. Nothing that demanded Hydra display her awesome combat skills.

It was really pissing her off.

And she was losing heart.

What was the use of having superpowers if all they were good for was healing from cold sores or opening jars for her mom? She'd even tried wearing a ridiculously short shirt and push-up bra and hanging out near biker bars. Some of the guys whistled at her, but mostly the guys told her to go the hell home. They didn't even hit on her. Not after the one biker, Turk, came out and yelled at the guys who were talking trash to her. Turk had two daughters of his own, apparently, and said that if anyone tried anything he'd pull their assholes out through their mouths. Turk was six-eight and had to weigh four hundred. He also owned the bar that was home base to the Cyke-lones. After that the guys left her alone, and to make it worse, Turk yelled at her and told her to go home. He threatened to call the juvie people on her.

It was so humiliating.

After that she stopped trying to act as bait, and started wearing a mask.

Okay, so the costume was really a cosplay Catwoman costume, but Hydra had made some tweaks to put her own stamp on it. Her vibe. A stitched Hydra symbol. Borrowed from the *Agents of SHIELD* TV show, but covered in red glitter dust so it didn't really look like she stole it. Besides, all that stuff was superhero movies and shows. She was the real deal. An actual super hero.

A metahuman.

A vampire huntress seeking vengeance in the night.

Or trying to.

Damn it, why was it so hard to be a hero? There had to be bad guys *somewhere* out here.

Then…

Hydra heard the scream and for a moment all she could do was stare.

Like anyone would.

Like any kid would.

A scream in the night touched a reaction of protection, of avoidance. In a young girl living in the big, bad city it engendered a pull-back-not-me response. A cringe-and-turn-away response. That was hardwired into the lizard brain and reinforced by half a million years of human females being the targets for male aggression. A scream was not a call to arms; it was proof that the brutish takers, the ravening monsters, had never evolved out of the gene pool. They were there. Always there. And every girl and woman knew it.

That was Hydra's first reaction.

Female.

Girl.

Young.

Not me.

Please, I can't know, I can't get involved. They'll hurt me, too.

Then, as she crouched on the edge of a building with the dark and dirty sprawl of Los Angeles spread around her, as her fingers gripped the tiles, as her senses lifted into the breeze, she had a second reaction.

She needs me.

Me.

Hydra knew that her moment had come. This was her chance to step away from being a girl and into being a superhero.

She felt the wild grin blossom like night jasmine on her face. She felt her head suddenly begin to hammer. Her muscles tensed and then she was in the air, leaping from the edge of building, splaying herself in the wind as she sailed toward the roof forty-eight feet away.

The thud of landing jolted through her, but she took it, accepting the pain, knowing that any injuries would be healed before she took a dozen steps.

The scream rose and rose. Hydra did not yet know the flavor and assortment of screams. She could not tell the difference between a scream of horrified anticipation from one of pain. And she didn't care. The voice was female, and there was fear that anyone could read.

She ran, leaped, landed, jumped, slid down rain gutters, climbed fire escapes. Like Daredevil. Like Elektra or the Arrow. Moving through the city as if it was hers. *Knowing* that it was hers.

Another scream tore the air, but it was less strident, and that scared Hydra. The woman was getting weaker.

Or dying.

Or something.

Hydra poured on the speed. Two buildings to go and then…

She was midway through her leap before she realized the telephone wire was there.

Right there.

There was a split second of time to react. She wrenched her body, trying to simultaneously flip over it and twist away, and in both things she failed. With all the power of her leap still pushing her through the air, she slammed into the telephone line. It bowed, yielded, yielded…

And then snapped back.

Hydra felt herself flying upward and backward. Her own scream tore through the night as she hurtled toward the rooftop she'd just left.

The angle was all wrong.

She turned in midair to see the flat wall of bricks racing toward her.

The only thought she had time to think was that this never happened to Daredevil.

And then she hit.

"WEAPONIZED REVENGE" PT. 1

Weston Ochse

Fell stared through the window of the padded cell at their great leader, Calder Lang. The man's rage had been vast and had contained a universe of need. After the tragedy of Nemo, he'd surged across the plains towards Pine Ridge Indian Reservation. Pay-per-view had gone through the roof, as they shelled out credit and cash to watch Lang chase down first the remnants of Laughing Horse's men, then anything that got in his way. When he hit the reservation he'd almost died, getting shot twenty-six times as he roared through the roadblocks set up by the Native American separatists. Had he been human, he would have been dead. But he was vampire… he was *draugr*, or as one former sports broadcaster turned news announcer referred to them after Ekstrom Kriger's first broadcast, *the insane Viking linebackers of the vampire kingdom*. This was because a *draugr's* bones were stronger and denser. Their hearts were not in their chests, but rather in their pelvis where they were protected by the hardened pelvic plates. They had extra bone plates in the chest and back to protect organs, and their circulatory system had been rerouted to take advantage of this bone density. In summation, it is almost impossible to kill a *draugr* unless its head is removed.

The genesis of the berserker warrior in Norse mythology was believed to come from the *draugr*. In those battles of the old times, a *draugr* was like a tank, busting through the enemy lines, chewing, clawing, stabbing, hacking, kicking, pummeling, and pulping their adversaries. When the three extra adrenal glands began to pump, flooding the system with the adrenaline of four regular humans, the *draugr* was incapable of inaction, its body forced to move in herking-jerking spurts across the battlefield and into the gaping maw of violence.

And that's what Lang was, a berserker warrior, enraged because of the rape and murder of his wife, and the murders of his two daughters and only son. Weaponized revenge, he tore into his targets with jaws boasting razor-sharp teeth. His neck was swollen to five times its normal size, allowing excessive adrenaline to surge through his body, bloating his vascular system until blood and fluids roared through him.

He'd killed for Inger.

He'd ripped men apart for Brand.

He'd chewed through chests and stomachs for Amelie and Sigrid.

And it was all filmed by his GoCams, transferred through the video compiler secreted in his single-horned Viking helm, then transmitted to an Ostergard Industries satellite, and beamed into households worldwide for an obscene amount.

And then came Wounded Knee.

It was too much.

Even the most hardcore Ekstrom Kriger pay-per-view fanatics started turning away from their televisions.

The irony was that the federal government didn't care. They'd allowed Lang to do what they'd been unable to do, unwilling to do. Had Lang not killed a buffalo in his blind rage, they might never have stopped him.

Fell chuckled hollowly. The irony of it was astounding. The random killing of a protected species held more weight than the intentional murders of seventy-four Native American separatists. The men of Ekstrom Kriger were ordered to stop their own man. It took every one of them, but they did, and then placed Lang in this room for his safety, if not their own.

That had been two months ago.

Their boss, North Sea oil billionaire Brandt Ostergard, had allowed them to stand down for a much needed rest. The team had been on back-to-back-to-back missions for months, allowing Ostergard to rake in millions in pay-per-view revenue. The berserkers even had their own action figures and a Saturday morning cartoon dedicated to grooming children to become adult fans. The *draugr* of Ekstrom Kriger had never been more popular, despite Lang's meltdown.

But they had to get back to work.

Fell held his breath a moment, then opened the door to the cell.

Lang had been sitting on his cot with his head hung between his legs. He turned to Fell. Lang's blond hair had gone uncut during this time and was a shaggy mane. Gone was the anger in the man's face. It had been replaced by a resignation, an acceptance of the terrible.

"Are you ready?" Fell asked.

Lang took a moment, then pushed off the cot. "Yeah." He brought himself to his full height and shrugged the muscles of his shoulders. "We got a mission?"

Fell nodded. He was thrilled Lang was almost back to normal. Things would be forever changed, but working could be a terrific salve for the wounded soul. "One we can't pass up."

Calder Lang placed a meaty hand on Fell's shoulder and squeezed. "Then let's not keep them waiting."

"HEROES DON'T WEAR SPANDEX" PT.2

Jonathan Maberry

The Jacob Javits Center
New York City

"Luther!"

Swann turned at the sound of his name and looked across the sea of bodies. The living and the dead, lying in rows. Many under sheets or in body bags. Many more on makeshift FEMA cots or on tarps spread on the floor of the convention center. At first he couldn't see who'd called him, and then a figure pushed his way gently between aid workers, hailing him with a raised hand.

Swann raised a weary hand in reply and waited as Special Agent Jimmy Saint threaded his way through the pain and the blood. The FBI investigator was tall and gaunt, his Spanish black hair threaded with silver that had only begun showing up over the last year. His eyes were dark and haunted. Saint had been the lead investigator on several of the highest profile cases since the V-Wars began. He'd been with Swann in Pepper Grove and Dayton and Princeton, three of the bloodiest incidents in a war that was defined by its atrocities. The process had aged Saint, just as it aged Swann. They were young men with old eyes and broken hearts.

Saint offered his hand, and Swann took it.

"God, Luther, this is some shit."

"Yes."

"Are you okay? I heard you were in the middle of it," said Saint.

Swann shook his head. "I was only on the fringes, but… no, Jimmy, I'm not okay."

Saint searched his eyes for the meaning, found it too quickly, sighed, and nodded. "I was all the way the hell down in Asheville when the first bombs went off, working on the Rancid thing, but the deputy director pulled me off that and told me to get my ass up here." He looked around, clearly shaken by the scope of the disaster. The last of the bombs had gone off four hours ago, and although many fires continued to rage out of control, a strange hush had settled. Half hoped that it was over, half feared that there was more to come.

All told, more than forty explosive devices had been detonated in Manhattan. They ranged from car bombs detonated in underground parking garages or on crowded city streets to truck bombs that tore the heart out of skyscrapers. The press was all over the place with casualty totals. Conservative figures were putting the death toll at more than twelve thousand. The tally for injured was above six figures and climbing.

Swann took Saint's arm and pulled him into a quiet alcove. "Listen, Jimmy, I heard that thing on the news from the guy calling himself God's Soldier—"

"I know," said Saint, cutting him off, "that's why they brought me up here. The deputy director thinks this might be connected to Potter County."

"Jesus."

Last year, just before the Ninety-Nine Bombs went off across the country, Swann and Saint had been part of the investigative team called to the Barkey family farm in the small town of Ulysses in Potter County, Pennsylvania. The entire family had been brutally slaughtered and dismembered, and cryptic symbols had been left at the scene. One boy had been mutilated and his body twisted to form a swastika. And on the outside of the barn, someone had used fresh blood to draw a smiley face. Round, with dots for eyes and a wide, grinning mouth complete with fangs. A long vertical slash had been struck through the face. That alone was not too terrifying—it was a common hate icon found on t-shirts, buttons, tattoos, bumper stickers, even Pinterest.

No, above that symbol the killer had painted a cross and overlaid the crosspiece with another swastika. And beside these images were words:

GOD HATES YOU
GOD WILL NOT ABIDE YOU
WE ARE THE SOLDIERS OF GOD

That had been the start of a new phase of the problem because when the forensics techs lifted blood that was believed to have come from the killer, the DNA kicked out something no one had been expecting. The genes were a mingled corruption of two disparate types: human and *canis dirus*. The long-extinct dire wolf. There was no trace at all of the V-Gene, active or not, which meant that the killer was a werewolf, and not one of the lycanthrope species that were now known to be subspecies of vampires. This was something else. Possibly a third race of creatures in competition for the Earth. Humans, vampires, and true werewolves.

So far there was only one known example of the species, though forensic searches had linked this one killer to dozens of murders. Some of humans, many of vampires. Significantly, many *more* of vampires.

When the Crimson Queen had provided Swann with evidence linking the werewolf killer to a legendary serial murderer known only as "Rancid," a task force was formed and Jimmy Saint was given the task of finding the monster. The evidence Swann had received tied Rancid to the Ninety-Nine Bombs, calling into question whether that terrorist campaign was truly a vampire terrorist attack. General May and his hawk cronies believed that it was, and that sparked the second and more terrible V-War. Swann did not agree, and his disgust over the hardline ethnic hatred of all vampires had led to his resigning as the president's advisor on vampires and Swann's subsequent work with George Clooney and the other celebrities behind the pacifistic OneWorld Initiative.

"Rancid left his calling card on that barn," said Saint. "He said that he was one of the 'soldiers of God,' and now we have 'God's Soldier' taking credit for this."

"It's pretty clear this is an anti-vampire thing, Jimmy," said Swann. "Or is Washington still saying different?"

"After tonight? Christ, I don't know how they'll jump."

"Maybe it'll be a unifying thing," Swann said hopefully, but Saint gave him a sour shake of the head.

"And maybe blue pterodactyls will fly out of my colon, but I somehow doubt it."

Swann sighed. "Are you anywhere with identifying Rancid? I mean... who *is* he?"

"He's a fucking ghost is who he is, and before you say anything, no, I don't mean a supernatural ghost. He's a ghost in the system. The geek squad in Cybercrimes backtracked the video file from God's Soldier, and it jumped them through ten kinds of hoops and finally opened a trapdoor in the Federal database that activated a Trojan horse filled with viruses. Half the computers in D.C. are currently playing 'Bad Moon Rising' by Creedence Clearwater Revival in an endless loop while the screen flashes images of some hot blond chick tearing off her clothes and turning into a werewolf."

"Wait, you're saying Rancid is a woman?"

"No, the clip's from some stupid grade-Z horror flick from the '80s called *The Howling II: Your Sister's a Werewolf.*"

"Sybil Danning," supplied Swann. "I know it. Terrible movie."

"And besides, the DNA we got from Potter County and elsewhere pretty much establishes that Rancid is a guy. Mind you, I would like to change that by cutting his balls off and feeding them to him, but..."

He let the rest go.

"Are we anywhere at all with finding him?"

"We're closer to finding Jimmy Hoffa and D.B. Cooper."

"Damn."

The doors in the main hall opened, and teams of people began bringing in more victims on stretchers. They watched helplessly.

"Twenty-seven," murmured Saint when the doors finally closed.

The air was filled with a continuous din of screams and prayers, with shouts and sobs.

"If this is Rancid," said Swann, "he's one man. Werewolf or not, he's one man."

"Yes."

"How's he doing this? I mean, he can't be alone. Are we looking at a terrorist cell of werewolves, or is he working with a group of humans against the vampires?"

"I don't know," admitted Saint, but something in his tone made Swann give him a sharp look.

"What—"

Saint shook his head. "I shouldn't even be talking about this, Luther."

"Don't give me that, Jimmy. Not after everything we've been through. Besides, it's just you and me."

"And the Crimson Queen… " Saint said, half smiling.

"Don't go there, Jimmy."

"C'mon, Luther, I know you have her ear."

"That's not how it works. We share some views, but I'm not working for her. Or even with her. And she's not working against us. She's against the war and the terrorism on both sides."

"I'm not saying she isn't," Saint protested. "All I'm saying is that I have to be careful what I say, even around you, because I don't want anything getting whispered into the wrong ear."

Swann turned to face him. "Either you trust me or you don't, Jimmy. And by now you should know you can trust me."

The FBI agent was silent for a moment, his dark eyes unreadable. Then he nodded slowly, more to himself than to Swann. He took a small half-step closer and lowered his voice to a whisper. "You want to know why the case is going nowhere fast? One word: obstruction."

"By who?"

"That's the part that scares the piss out of me, Luther," said Saint, and he really did look scared. "I've been floating some theories about how the Ninety-Nine Bombs plan could have been put into motion. It was so big and so well coordinated that it had to have been well financed and put into play by a big team. And there are noticeable gaps in security at key moments. They've been officially labeled as either technical glitches— in security cameras, patrol schedules, like that—or they've been redacted from official reports for reasons of national security."

"Why?"

"I don't know why, and when I've pushed for answers I was given revised versions of those reports, and instead of having information redacted it was simply gone. Either replaced by new data that was definitely not there before, or simply removed and the documents reformatted. Now, get this, Luther, even my own files have been altered."

"What? How's that even possible?"

Saint looked even more scared. "It's not possible under any circumstance. There's only one way it could have happened, and that's someone inside the government doing it. Someone with truly frightening computer skills and a whole lot of juice."

"General May?" suggested Swann, but Saint shook his head.

"Aldous doesn't have that kind of power. No, Luther, this has to have come from further up the food chain. This has to be senior staff at very least." He paused. "This has to have come from the White House. I don't know who or why, but I think that someone in the White House is trying to keep me from discovering who Rancid is, and who he's really working for. And, Luther… I have never been more terrified in my entire life."

"WEAPONİZED REVENGE" PT. 2

Weston Ochse

Devil Ray checked the vid screens once more, then called for Child Susan. She stepped into a room that had once been an examination room and came to attention.

"Yes, Child Ray." She saluted.

He returned the salute. "Are the floors secure?"

"Child Frank and Child Manny have locked down the elevators. I have other Children posted at the stair doors. We control the second, third, and fourth floors."

He nodded. They weren't concerned about the first floor. With all the doors and windows, there was no way they could lock it down. It was administrative space anyway. He was more concerned about the victims. What bothered him, though, was their inability to take the fifth floor. It's where the facility director sat, along with his security forces. As close as they were, they were a constant threat and kept him on an unnecessary edge.

"What are we going to do about the fifth floor?" she asked, as if she could read his mind.

"Keep them bottled in." He gestured towards the barred windows. "Although they were meant to keep the patients in, they can keep security forces out just as well."

"Child Mindy says she's ready to broadcast."

"Just give me a moment."

She saluted, was about to leave the room, then paused. "Do you think the Smiling Man will see the broadcast?"

Devil Ray smiled. "How can he not?"

She dared to smile. "Do you think he'll be proud?"

He came to her and put his arms around her. "How can he not?" He kissed her on both cheeks. "Now go, prepare."

Her eyes searched his for several moments, then she lowered her head and nodded.

Once she left the room, Devil Ray checked his appearance in the mirror. He hadn't lost any of his physique since his unnecessary departure from the service. A pang of longing hit him as he thought about the men he used to serve with. But then they'd kicked him out because he'd changed. His honor and loyalty had meant nothing to his country. They threw him away like a piece of patriotic trash.

Then he'd found the Children of the Ninety-Nine. They'd come together under the leadership of Roger Croom. Father Croom, as he was known to the Children, was an exceptionally charismatic figure, reminding Devil Ray of the better officers he'd served under, even his own grandfather. After a few weeks, he'd joined them and had the fortune of being assigned to train a cohort of Children for a series of planned special missions. They'd previously acted in secrecy, but this was to be their big day—a coming out party, as Father Croom had called it.

He exited the room and strode down the hall. He passed several of the Children. He greeted each of them by name, just as Father Croom would have, had he been here. Here and there, a patient stared wide-eyed, still unsure whether they had good fortune, or if this was yet another trick by the facility director.

Devil Ray entered the operating theater where they'd set up the broadcast equipment. Child Mindy used to be a line producer for one of the major networks before she changed. She told him where to stand, made sure the sound levels were adjusted, then counted him down. Because of the satellite they'd hacked, he'd soon be in every living from Phoenix to Bagdad.

"In three, two, one… "

Cut into the network feed, then fade in.

The camera embraced a head-and-shoulder shot of him. Handsome, black hair, chiseled features of a fit twenty-something, with the complexion and cheekbones of his Native American ancestry.

"We are the Children of the Ninety-Nine. Where the original ninety-nine were bombs, we are the vampire versions." He spread his arms as the camera panned back to capture his entire upper body, including the explosives wired to his chest. "We are in every country. We are in every city. We refuse to take your abuse any longer." He made a gesture.

Child Pham and Child Ron brought in a sobbing, overweight, balding man in a cheap blue suit, tie loosened and off kilter. They made him kneel on a red-taped X.

"We are in Phoenix right now. Tell the world who you are."

The man sobbed until Child Pham slapped him on the back of the head.

"Doc—Doctor Na—Nathan Crosby."

"And where are we?"

"Cross—CrossCorp Research Facility."

"What is it you research?"

"Please—" he held up his hands. "Please don't hurt me."

"What is it you research, Mr. Crosby?"

"Vampires."

"Do you really? Tell us what you told me earlier. Tell the world what you really do here."

"I—We try and replicate the effects of the change through the manipulation of DNA and genome therapy on the offspring of the changed."

"You're conducting research on human children." It wasn't a question.

Now the producer would be switching video to the faces of the thirty-nine children they'd found in the facility. The world would see them one after the other, his voice the narration to the terrible story.

"Here's the whole story. CrossCorp has been contracted by the U.S. government to find a way to manipulate human DNA to replicate the change. Not only do they want to find a way to turn it on, but also to turn it off. To do this, they provided you with children of the changed who were in the country's foster care system, their parents either dead or incarcerated. They keep these children in a locked ward with bars on the windows. They have no access to education, or extended family, or social services. You're treating these human beings like lab rats."

That was the signal for the visual to switch back to him.

"We are the Children of the Ninety-Nine. We are all vampires. We are all bombs. We are vampire bombs and will not allow you to abuse us anymore. Nor will we allow you to abuse our children. You have been warned."

Child Mindy held out her hand and ticked her fingers as she spoke into his earpiece. "In three, two, one. We're out."

Everyone cheered except the poor man on the floor. When they were done, they took him to the cafeteria where they fed. Devil Ray fed first, enjoying the way the skin from his face tasted, along with both nipples and the soft, succulent jowls.

The men of Ekstrom Kriger sat in large leather chairs inside the Dornier 328 Executive Jet. A somewhat stunned hostess provided them non-alcoholic refreshments and snacks. The CEO had sent his personal jet because of the short notice, and the men grabbed the offered upscale snacks by the fistful. It was clear she wasn't used to seeing a dozen giant-sized men in the plane. It wasn't that she was intimidated, but she certainly looked awed.

Lang and Fell sat in the back. Lang watched the video once more before turning to Fell. "What do we have on this guy?"

"Former Navy SEAL. He was assigned to DevGru, their elite counterterrorism force. Full name is John Ray Tishomingo. He was named after a famous Chickasaw chief. Forcibly discharged from the U.S. Navy for violating Article 83 of the Uniform Code of Military Justice."

Lang raised an eyebrow.

"Article 83. It's what the U.S. government is using to separate the changed. It deals with fraudulent enlistment or appointment. Because he didn't disclose that he could be a vampire, he was forced to separate."

Dagner, who'd been looking on, snorted at this.

Lang game him a look, which eviscerated the other man's smile. "Continue."

"They called him Devil Ray in the unit because of his ability to sneak up on people. He had two silver stars and three bronze stars. He was a certified hero. Too bad the U.S.G. let him go."

"What kind of vamp is he?" Dagner asked.

"He's Chickasaw, so he's probably a *lofa*," Fell concluded.

Lang made a face. "Flesh eaters."

"Stinky too," Dagner added.

Lang nodded. "They can turn it off and on like a skunk." He pointed towards the screen. "What do we know about this group—the Children of the Ninety-Nine?"

Fell shook his head. "Nothing, boss. No intel at all. It's like they popped into existence."

"That suicide vest looked real," Dagner said. "How are we going to get past that?"

Fell shrugged. "Let them blow themselves up. What do we care?"

"I won't let the kids get hurt."

Fell and Dagner exchanged a look but said nothing.

Lang continued. "We need to figure out a way to get past them without blowing them up."

Fell seemed about to say something, but held back.

Lang noticed. "Spit it out."

"This really isn't our sort of mission. V-8 would normally go in on something like this, but they're busy down in Cuba doing something hush hush for the government."

Lang made a face. "Nestor's an ass clown and a homicidal maniac. Good thing he's not here."

Dagner snorted again.

Fell grinned. "Lang and Big Dog, the leader of V-8, have had an ongoing beef since long before the change."

"What happened?" Dagner asked

"I don't want to talk about it," Lang growled.

"You see, they were in Kosovo together and—" Fell caught the murderous look from Lang and snapped his mouth shut. "Back to the problem at hand. I'll have Oddvar contact Ostergard LLC home base and see if the eggheads have some ideas."

Lang nodded and stared at the still image. Fell was right. They shouldn't be doing this. But Brandt Ostergard was buddies with White House Chief of Staff William Gabriel. Lang had only met the man once, but came away with the impression that if this land wanted a king, he'd be the one to take it. Imperious, efficient, and ruthless; that's what Gabriel was.

"What if it's true?" Dagner asked Fell. "What if they are experimenting on children?"

Lang narrowed his eyes. He wasn't the same person he was before... before Nemo. There was a time when he didn't care about the fate of innocents, so focused was he on the mission.

Fell filled the silence. "We don't give a shit if it's true. We have a mission. We follow it. Isn't that right, boss?"

Lang continued staring at the screen, at the face of Devil Ray. Would he do it? Would he blow himself up? Who was the real leader of the Children of the Ninety-Nine?

"I said, *'Isn't that right, boss?'*" Lang repeated.

"I heard you." He ripped his eyes free of the screen and turned to Fell, giving his number two man a hard look. "We're not going to hurt the kids."

Fell's brow wrinkled. "But the mission—"

"We're not going to hurt the kids. Do you understand me?"

Fell blinked. "Yes, sir."

Lang glanced up and saw that pretty much every one of his men on the plane had turned in their seats to listen. "And that goes for the lot of you. We're not going to hurt the kids. Do you fucking understand that order?"

They gave a resounding "Yes, sir!" then turned in their seats. The men of Ekstrom Kriger were afraid of nothing... nothing except their leader, Calder Lang.

They landed an hour later and were taken to a helipad where a Bell 525 passenger helicopter awaited them. Although it had room for sixteen passengers, it didn't have room for Calder and his eleven men. He asked for another, but there was only one Bell 525 available. So he, Fell, Dagner, Colby, Ivar, and Gunnar took the first trip. The others would follow once the helicopter returned for them. Then it was a short ten minute flight to the research facility in Black Rock Canyon.

Reports had it that the group hadn't been able to take the top floor, so that left the roof safe for the time being and as good as any place to stage their possible attack. "Possible," because Lang wasn't yet sure about how they were going to get past the bombs. *Draugr* were almost indestructible, but even they couldn't withstand an explosion.

While they were in the air, Lang was contacted by Brandt Ostergard and reminded of the importance of the mission. He also received one last command. They were not to use their GoCams, proving even more that this was not the kind of mission they should be performing. Still, Lang agreed, then spread the word to both his men in the chopper and his men on the ground awaiting transport. They were met on the roof by the head of security, a human Type-A paramilitary wannabe with a hero complex—better known as a jack-booted asshole. His disdain for their presence and his sense of false superiority surrounded him like a *lofa* smell. He stood about five foot. He'd shaved his head but wore a died-black goatee and mustache. He wore black paramilitary fatigues like his men, as well as matching body armor; an LBE which held a flashlight, taser, handcuffs, and a baton; and a holster which held a Sig Saur. The only uniform difference between him and his three men, who waited with him, were the gold stars he wore on his collar.

Dagner saw him and made his own assessment right away. "Is he an admiral? If so, looks like his ship has sunk."

Lang ignored his man and stepped off the plane and onto the roof. He waited for all of his *draugr* to exit and for the helicopter to take off again, then headed toward the head of security and stopped in front of him. "What's the status?"

The man appraised him with lazy-lidded eyes. "To whom am I speaking?"

Remain calm and don't kill the asshole human. "Calder Lang. Head of Ekstrom Kriger."

The man gave them a practiced smile. "Ahh, the pay-per-view actors."

Dagner started forward, but Fell held him back.

Calder Lang decided to play the game. "And who are you?" He stepped forward so his seventeen-inch height difference seemed even larger.

The man stepped back. "Bill Picket, Chief of Security for CrossCorp."

"What happened here? Looks like you lost control of most of the building."

The man's smile fell a few millimeters. He licked his lips. "A temporary tactical decision. Our plan is in motion." He hooked his thumbs in his LBE. "Frankly, Mr. Lang, we don't need you."

Calder nodded. "You don't say?" Then he shrugged. "Clearly you haven't spoken to the White House Chief of Staff. We're here under his authority. Now, if you'll excuse me." Calder went to step past Picket, then the man made the incredible mistake of grabbing Calder by the arm. Calder stared at the offending hand for a hard moment, then slammed his gaze into Picket. The chief of security held the gaze for two seconds, then let go and stepped back, nervous eyes searching for his men.

Calder and his *draugr* exited the roof onto the floor below. They followed a long corridor with offices branching off at regular intervals. He stopped when he came to a conference room. On the wall was a schematic of the building. Several security men stared at it along with a tall, gaunt Persian, the ancestry revealed by the slight slant of the dark brown eyes and his complexion. They had virtually no information regarding the facility or who ran it, but this thing looked and felt like it was a vampire and was probably the leader.

"Calder Lang," he said as introduction.

The vampire was taller than Lang by six inches, making him at least seven feet. A long haggard face wore a mess of untamed wrinkles. "Caspar Bukhari. I run this facility," he said, barely opening his mouth.

"Doesn't look like you run much at all right now." Fell moved to the schematics, which showed the layout of the buildings five floors.

Caspar stared daggers. "Temporary. Setback."

Fell turned and gave him a mock smile. "We'll have it back to normal in a jiff!"

Dagner stifled a grin.

This mission was totally wrong for them, but Fell was making the best of it.

"How many men do you have? What other assets do I have at my disposal?"

Caspar turned back to him, seemingly a Herculean effort. "My men are my men. You are to do what you have to do with your own men."

Lang blinked. "Is that so?"

"It is."

"Have you been in contact with the man known as Devil Ray?"

Caspar gazed over Lang's shoulder.

"We've tried to establish contact several times." Picket came into the room and took his place at the right of Caspar. "He's refused any and all contact."

"How'd he take the building so easily?" Dagner asked.

Picket frowned, probably at the use of the phrase "so easily," but he answered. "They took the building during shift change. We only had two people on the main door."

Fell glanced at Dagner and Lang. "They either scouted, or it was an inside job."

Picket's eyes hardened. "None of my men would be a part of this."

Fell feigned shock. "Oh, so everyone feels that it's perfectly alright to kidnap human children so you can experiment on them. Not a one of your men has any decency or a working moral compass?"

Picket's face fell. "We're not part of that; we just secure property."

"Sounds like the guard force at Auschwitz," Dagner grunted.

Picket held up a hand. "Hold on now—"

Lang cut in. "This isn't getting us anywhere. What were your plans before we came?"

Picket glanced at Caspar.

After a few moments of silence, Fell said, "They were going to gas them."

Both Picket and Caspar looked momentarily shocked that Fell knew.

"It's on the schematics, plus I recognize the dispersal units. What kind were you going to use?" he asked, turning to Picket. "BZ or DHMP?"

The longer Picket remained silent, the more concerned Fell became. "It's not incapacitating gas you were going to use, is it? Dear God, you were going to kill them all?"

Now it was Caspar's turn to speak. "We needed a failsafe system that would be fast and effective. BZ and DHMP were too slow to take effect."

"What do you use then?" Fell asked.

"Zyclon B," Caspar said, as easy as saying Coca-Cola.

"The same shit they used at Auschwitz."

Lang shook his head. Fucking rookies, all of them. To Dagner, he said, "Find the control and disable it. Permanently. I don't want any of us to fall victim to someone's impatience."

"Hey, you can't just—"

Caspar laid a hand on Picket's shoulder. "Let them do what they have to do. Have your men stand down." The strange vampire gave Lang a look he might give an insect. "Let's get past this, shall we? I want to get back to the business of—how do you call it?—experimentation."

Lang stared for a morose second, then went to the schematics. "Show me."

"HEROES DON'T WEAR SPANDEX" PT. 3

Jonathan Maberry

The Jacob Javits Center
New York City

Thehe dawn light had to push its way through the pall of smoke that hung over the city. Columns of dusty yellow slanted downward like tent poles for a collapsed shelter. Swann stood on the steps of the Javits Center, filthy and exhausted, cried out, and drained in every way that mattered. The cup of coffee in his hand was bitter and cold. He leaned against the wall and slid down to the concrete, set the cup down, bent his head, and closed his eyes.

Defeat had begun to take on so many layers of new meaning.

When the V-Wars began there had been a sense of excitement, of anticipation because—despite the fear and wonder—he believed that his knowledge and ideals might make a real difference. The military had taken him on as an advisor, but over the months, he'd come to realize that all he'd become to them was a talking head, someone they could trot out to help sell the public on the fiction that they were not prosecuting an agenda of ethnic genocide. Later, when he'd joined Clooney's camp to make speeches around the world about tolerance and species acceptance, he thought he'd begun gaining some ground.

Now… ?

As he sat there, he tried to weigh what he'd managed to accomplish against the devastation here in New York. And against the battles, small and large, being fought around the world. Against the growing and lethal intolerance within families, schools, churches, communities. He felt like a surgeon who had successfully re-attached a severed finger only to have the patient die anyway.

"Luther... ?"

He looked up and saw her standing there. Yuki Nitobe. Like him, her clothes were stained with soot and splashed with blood, and her thick black hair hung in rat tails. In all the time he'd known her, Swann had never seen Yuki in any condition but perfect. Now she looked like a refugee from a lost war. Beyond her, down on the street, Lonnie Barlow stood beside the GSN news van, arms folded, head down on his chest as if he was asleep standing up. And next to him was Martyn, Yuki's lover and an agent of the Crimson Queen. He saw Swann and gave a single, grave nod.

"Is that seat taken?" asked Yuki, and without waiting for an answer sat down next to Swann. She kissed him on the cheek. "You look like crap."

"Lot of that going around."

She touched her hair. "I know. We were hosed down by accident."

"Not the worst thing that could have happened," he said.

"No," she agreed.

"No."

They stared at the smoke and the broken pillars of sunlight. After a while, Yuki cleared her throat and said, "We're reporting this as a terrorist attack by Beats."

"Of course."

"No," she said quickly, "not of course. Have you seen the news at all? Have you heard what the official response from Washington is?"

He shook his head.

"Person or persons unknown," she said. "With a warning not to make judgments based on a potentially unreliable source."

"Ah."

"And some of the networks are falling in line with that. Trotting out so-called experts to suggest that this was actually staged by vampires with blame unfairly shifted to the religious right."

"Christ... "

"I know."

He looked at her. "But that's not what you're reporting?"

"No. God's Soldier was pretty clear, and I think he was telling the truth, ugly as it was."

Swann nodded. "Good for you."

They watched helicopters fly over. Swann had never seen so many of them. At least two hundred. Ever since the RPGs had been fired at the National Guard, the president had sent in Marine, Army, and Navy choppers. Martial law had been imposed over the city and extended out to the other boroughs.

"Are you going to get in trouble?" he asked. "From your producers, I mean?"

"Probably," she said. "But that will change if a couple of the other networks pick up our story. It's already trending on Twitter and Facebook. Our version, I mean, so we have social media on our side."

"Will it be enough?"

She shrugged. "It's what we can do."

"Yeah."

They sat for a few minutes, then Swann said, "How brave are you, Yuki?"

"What?"

"How brave? How much courage do you have as a reporter?"

"I think you already know that, Luther," she said. "Why do you ask?"

He took his time before answering. "I have something to tell you. It's big, Yuki. Really big, but I can't prove it. I'm willing to go on record as the voice of it, but I can't and won't reveal the name of my source."

"Shit, Luther. You're putting me on the spot."

"I know."

She chewed her lip. "How big are we talking?"

He gave her a rueful smile. "Shaking the pillars of heaven."

Yuki rubbed the grit from her eyes and looked at the black stains on her fingers. Smoke. And since 9-11 everyone knew what was probably mixed in with the ash of building materials.

"Tell me," she said softly.

"WEAPONIZED REVENGE" PT.3

Weston Ochse

Devil Ray was sitting in one of the rooms, playing checkers with a young African-American girl named Chloe when they came for him. "We have movement on the south stairwell."

They'd planned this around V-8's departure. The last thing they needed was for them to come barging in. Devil Ray had run ops with several of those guys before the change and had found them all to be hotheads, if not competent hotheads. "Do we have a visual?"

"We do, but we don't recognize him."

Ray narrowed his eyes. "Him? It's only one person?"

"One big person, actually."

Intrigued. "Is he armed?"

"Not from what we can see."

It only took a second. "Bring him to me."

The man hesitated but a moment, then hastened to carry out the order.

"Who's coming?" the girl asked. She sat cross-legged on the floor across from him. She wore green scrubs. Her hair was done in braids. Blue eyes and freckles against her dark skin gave her an exotic look.

"A man who wants to stop me," Ray said. His red tile took one of her black ones, giving her the opportunity to make a king.

She saw it right away and glowed with her achievement. "Is it because you're helping us?"

"I'm not here to help you." He had set her up so that if she chose to get kinged, she'd lose all three of her other pieces. She took the bait, so he took her three pieces, leaving her with one lone piece on the board to his four.

She frowned. "Hey." Then she knitted her brows. "You're not here to help us? I thought that's why you came."

"Nuh-uh. I came to help the vampires of the world."

"But I'm almost a vampire. My mom was, before she ate my dad. She's an *ilimu*. Know what she can do?"

"No, what?"

"She can talk to animals and make them do things."

"That's cool, I suppose, except for your dad." They'd been playing the entire time they were talking. All she could do was move her lone king back and forth. He sacrificed one of his pieces so that when she took it, he took her piece.

"Hey! That's not fair."

"Welcome to the jungle, baby." He grinned and stood. He heard footsteps coming down the hall. He reached out and helped Chloe to her feet. "Sometimes when you have the opportunity to get something good, it's better to pass it up for something better later."

She gave him a curious look.

Even if he'd wanted to explain it to her, which he didn't, she was too young to understand. His man rounded the corner with a hulking monster who looked like he had stepped off the set of a modern-day Viking movie, if Vikings wore black camouflage and combat boots. As tall as Devil Ray was and with a flattop of shock blonde hair, but with twice the muscles, the man's presence and the possibility of his violence immediately filled the room even though his hands were flexi-cuffed in front of him. Ray noticed the GoCam in the center of his chest last.

He pointed at it. "Is that thing on?"

"Local feed only. My men insisted."

"They upstairs?"

The man nodded. He looked maddeningly familiar. The size, the gear, the muscles. Then he had it. Ray snapped his fingers. "You're Lieutenant Colonel Lang. I worked an op with you in the Sudan before the change."

Lang shook his head. "I don't remember you."

"You wouldn't have. I was just an ensign back then, working shore patrol."

"And now look at you. Navy SEAL turned militant."

Ray smiled. "I see you did your homework."

Lang remained silent, surveying the room and the young girl. When he saw the checkerboard, he asked the girl, "Who won?"

She gave a pouty smile and thumbed towards him. "He did."

Lang turned to Ray and smiled.

"Why so happy?"

"It means you're a realist."

"And that means what to you?"

"You could have let her win, but then that would have been sentimental. I hate sentimental. I have a hard time with sentimental people. But realists on the other hand, realists I can deal with rather easily."

"And how is that?"

"By providing the facts."

"And what are those?"

"Fact. You are outnumbered. Fact. There's a hidden gas dispersal system. Fact. Your mission is already accomplished because the world is on notice. Fact. There's a hue and cry in the media about the government's involvement in this terrible enterprise."

Ray nodded, then countered, staring not at Lang, but at the camera instead. "Fact. We don't care if we're outnumbered. We have one man on a deadman switch so if we're gassed, he will go off, killing seven children. Fact. The mission of the Children of the Ninety-Nine is not yet complete and it won't be until all vampires and their children are free. Fact. We'll only be in the media as long as we are doing something." Then he shifted his gaze at Lang's face. "Question? Since when does the United States government send in serial-killing entertainers to protect the men and women assigned to experiment on and eventually kill children."

Lang had no response, and his face betrayed no emotion.

Ray stood still, wishing, hoping this was being televised. Lang had said the feed was going to his men, but Ray had seen the *Ultimate Warrior* series enough times to know that you could never be sure when the cameras would be on or not.

When Lang finally spoke, it was as if Ray hadn't even asked the question. "Is there any way we can expect you to leave CrossCorp during the next twelve hours if I can guarantee your safe passage?"

"None."

Lang shrugged slightly as he glanced at the child. "Then we're done here."

To his escort Ray said, "Please take LTC Lang back the way he came."

Both the escort and Lang turned to go, but before they got ten steps, Ray called after them. "Hey, Lang."

The leader of the Ultimate Warriors turned to face him.

"You're on the wrong side of this, you know?"

"We don't take sides."

"Don't you think you should?" Lang seemed to consider, but before he could say anything, Ray asked, "Why twelve? Why not ten or fifteen or twenty-four?"

"Because that's how long it's going to take us to figure out how to come back and take you out." Then Lang turned back around and strode down the hallway. He didn't even look back.

Ray pondered the timeline. Twelve hours. It would give him time for a new broadcast.

⸻ ◆ ⸻

Back upstairs, Lang went straight to Fell. The time frame had come from Fell, who'd conveyed it through his earpiece. He'd said it and used it, but he didn't know to what it referred.

"What have we got?"

Fell grinned, something most people never wanted to see. "Ostergard came through."

Lang stared, waiting.

"You're gonna love this." Fell, drawing it out.

Lang stared, waiting.

"Fine. What do you know about EMPs?"

"Electromagnetic pulses. Generated as a result of a nuclear explosion. If you think we're going to set off a nuclear bomb, then you're insane."

Fell shook his head. "Not insane. Listen to this. Ostergard is sending over an EMP generator. According to the tech I spoke to, it can take out any unshielded electronics within ninety feet."

"Tell me why I care."

"Because we can render the Children of the Ninety-Nine bombless. Once the generator goes off, it will fry the circuits of their vests."

A smile slowly took over Lang's face. "I like that."

"Only one hitch."

"Isn't there always? What is it?"

Fell moved to the schematics and pointed to a spot in the center of the third floor. "Based on the building schematics, in order to have maximum coverage we need the generator here."

Lang thought for a moment. Using the EMP generator would allow them to open their tactical toolbox to the fullest. It was a terrific opportunity. "How long will it take to get here?"

"Six hours. Then two hours to assemble."

"Hope it comes with instructions," Dagner harrumphed.

"They're sending a tech."

Lang nodded. "Good, then you have that much time to figure out how you'll get the generator in place."

Fell crossed his arms and stared at the schematics. "Dagner, get the men. We need to brainstorm this."

Lang was happy to see his man taking charge. He might be the next leader of Ekstrom Kriger, especially if Lang decided that he'd had enough.

———— ◆ ————

"Good evening, America, and the world. How you doing, Mr. President?" Ray stared into the camera. "We are the Children of the Ninety-Nine. We are at CrossCorp research facility in Phoenix, Arizona, where a government-funded program was underway to experiment on human children. This is your government, America. This is your president."

At this moment the producer was using his voiceover with images of the president shaking hands, smiling at adoring crowds, even kissing babies.

"This is the president you elected. The president who took an oath of office to serve, to protect, and to honor the constitution."

Switched to images of the children, many taken from the files, providing graphic details about the experimentation.

"These could be your children, America. These could be your sons and daughters the president has ordered this company to experiment on. What are you going to do about it, America? Do you even care about your children?"

He turned to face another camera.

"And what about you, world? CrossCorp has facilities in over thirty countries."

Split screen with his face on one side and a list of the countries along with city locations on the other.

"Do you know where your children are? Have any gone missing in your area? Will your children be next?"

He smiled beatifically at the camera. "The president sent in his most trusted man a few minutes ago to negotiate with me, only you won't believe who it is."

Insert the image of Calder Lang walking down the hall, then entering the room. The entire previous conversation had been filmed using the security camera system installed in the building. The segment ended with Ray's last question.

"Question? Since when does the United States government send in serial-killing entertainers to protect the men and women assigned to experiment on and eventually kill children?"

Lang had no response, and his face betrayed no emotion.

Cut to Ray.

———•———

Colby came running into the room. "Boss, you got to see this."

Lang hurried after, running into the day room as everyone stood around the camera.

Fell pointed at the screen. "They just replayed your conversation. Looks like they used the security cameras to record your conversation."

The broadcast had switched to a montage of Ekstrom Kriger's first-person video footage of some of their most violent attacks, scored by Richard Wagner's "Ride of the Valkries." Stomachs were ripped open. Throats jerked free. Heads twisted off bodies. Blood, blood, and more blood filled the screen as a creative producer turned up the magenta until everything was red hued. The segment went on for a good two minutes.

Lang's men cheered, recognizing when it was them, reveling in the reenactment of their blood sport. Lang joined them. He didn't really care. They were beserkers. They were *draugr*. They were weaponized destruction.

The final scene was of Lang ripping into the buffalo and coming out the other side.

His men whooped and hollered.

Even Lang grinned.

Fell yelled, *"Meatloaf!"* and everyone cracked up.

Fade to black.

Silence.

Cut to Devil Ray.

"These are your president's men. These are the guardians of your democracy. Do you not see it, people? You have a president who is trying to cover up his experimentation on human children by sending in his professional squad of serial killers to stop the Children of the Ninety-Nine, the only ones trying to save these kids."

"This guy's good," Fell said.

Lang's phone began to ring. He looked at the screen. Damn. Ostergard himself. He glanced back at Ray on the television, then pointed towards the security camera in the corner of the room. "I bet he's been watching us this entire time."

All eyes went to the camera, then his men began to look at each other, clearly incredulous that they hadn't thought to check the cameras. Colby punched Canute in the shoulder. Gunnar facepalmed.

Back on the television. "We are the Children of the Ninety-Nine. We are all vampires. We are all bombs. We are vampire bombs and will not allow you to abuse us anymore. Nor will we allow you to abuse our children. You have been warned."

Lang strode into the other room and took the call. He didn't say much. It wasn't worth arguing. When it was over, he stared out the window at the Arizona landscape, thinking of the children on the three floors below them.

Fell came to the door, paused, then entered. "What's going on, boss?"

Without turning. "There will be no EMP generator."

"What? Why?"

"We've been told to stand down."

"Who's going to handle this then?"

Lang sighed heavily. "V-8."

"I thought they were on mission."

"They were pulled off. Seems as if the president doesn't approve of us and our ability to conduct this mission."

Fell balled his fists. "The president can go fuck himself." Then he lowered his voice. "They'll get everyone killed. Kids included. You know that, right?"

"I know."

"What are we going to do then?"

Lang turned away from the window. "We're not going to wait for V-8."

"But the bombs. We can't just—"

"Trust me."

"But—"

"Trust me. I have a plan."

Fell's face held a firm frown. "Fine. You have a plan. You going to share it with me?"

"Get the others. We don't have much time."

"HEROES DON'T WEAR SPANDEX" PT. 4

Jonathan Maberry

Los Angeles

She lay in a dumpster.

It's where she'd landed after hitting the wall. Cliché and ugly. A dingy place to die.

Except…

Hydra knew that her back was broken. She'd heard it snap when she hit the rim of the steel dumpster. Her arms were shattered, and there was only a shapeless cloud of pain where her face used to be.

A fly buzzed around her and landed on her face. She tried to brush it away, but her arms were sacks of dead meat and disconnected bone.

When she woke up she had no idea how long she'd been unconscious. It was still dark, though, so it couldn't have been more than a few hours. Dawn couldn't be that far away.

So what, she thought. Does dying in the morning feel better than dying at night? Would sunlight make anything better?

Hitting that telephone cable had been so stupid that it now seemed inevitable. Of course she'd hit it. And if not that, then something. Maybe a power line. Or she'd have misjudged a jump and simply fallen ten stories to the ground. Pulped herself there.

Or something.

Because that's what happens when you're stupid.

Because that's what happens when you think you're something special.

Because that's what happens when you believe.

So much for the immortal Hydra. Hadn't Dr. Swann said that there might be limits to how much she could heal?

You're not a superhero.

Dr. Swann's words echoed in her head. Instead of being the challenge she'd originally taken them for, they now rang like mockery.

You're not a superhero. You're a stupid little girl and you're going to die in this dumpster, and this stupid fly is going to lay its eggs and the maggots will eat you up.

That's what she heard him saying, as clearly as if he leaned over the rim of the dumpster and yelled at her.

The buzzing fly walked over her cheek and down toward her lips.

Would a superhero let a stupid fly lay its eggs in her mouth? Asked the phantom of Luther Swann. *Would a real superhero be that gross?*

She wished she could at least shoo the fly away. If she had to die, please don't let the fly lay its eggs in her mouth.

It crawled over the curve of her top lip.

"No!" She wanted to shout as she swept the fly away. Such a shame she was dying.

The fly buzzed, and then there was a second one. A third.

They were all coming to the feast. To lay their eggs. To make sure the maggots ate every last bit of her up.

No.

No.

"NO!"

The flies were gone in an instant. Swept off her face, smashed flat against the inside of the dumpster. Smashed to goo, eggs and all.

It took her a long time to understand why.

And how.

That's when she saw the thing that hovered above her face.

Five slender fingers. Covered with black leather.

An arm.

Her arm.

A forearm, an elbow, a wrist, and a hand.

The leather was torn and splashed with blood and garbage. The wrist was bent the wrong way. But the fingers twitched.

Twitched.

Curled.

Flopped forward toward the palm, and with a crackle of cartilage the hand fell forward.

Into place.

Hydra flexed her hand, curling the fingers into a fist. She could feel something weird inside her forearm. Bones shifting. Muscles moving to accommodate, then knitting. It hurt, but not like it should. It felt almost...

Good. Right.

It was nearly an hour, though, before her spinal cord reattached itself.

As dawn's light crept up the side of the dumpster and splashed across her face, Hydra rose on legs that were no longer broken. Getting out of the dumpster took work, effort, time. But she managed it, then had to lean against the side of the dumpster for another twenty minutes before her ankles finished reforming.

All the while she wept. And smiled.

Hydra.

The immortal vampire.

Hydra, the immortal superhero.

Last night was a mistake. Last night was a lesson. Last night had taught her so much.

Tonight, she knew, would be so much different.

Thinking heroic thoughts, Hydra headed home to shower, to repair her uniform, and to prepare for the night.

"WEAPONIZED REVENGE" PT. 4

Weston Ochse

An hour later, Fell, Brandt, Canute, Colby, Dagner, Gunnar, Ivar, Leif, Sten, Oddvar, and Tait stood in two lines before him. They wore the Ekstrom Kriger uniform—Viking helmets, black uniforms, black boots, and Kevlar gloves. The uniforms had Kevlar threads mixed in a 1:30 ration, making the cloth not necessarily bulletproof, but mostly fang proof. The Viking helmets, which could have come straight out of the Middle Ages, had they not been created using composites and containing electronics, were of all shapes and styles—some curved, some straight, some twisted, some rotated down, etc. Each horn contained a video compiler and a transmitter, which allowed the combined footage to be uploaded via SatCom. The helmets were strapped on to keep them from being ripped off. The only thing these Ultimate Warriors didn't carry were weapons, and that's because they *were* the weapons.

"Check your systems. I want a thirty-second buffer before transmission."

As his men adjusted their cameras, he thought once more of the plan. It was as if it had always been there, and he just had to realize it. This was the most logical conclusion to their participation in this farce. Plus, it felt right, and he hadn't felt right in quite some time.

"Fell, take your men to the first floor."

Fell headed to the elevator shaft. Brandt, Canute, Colby, Dagner, and Oddvar followed after. They'd climb down the maintenance access.

"Gunnar, Ivar, Leif, Sten, and Tait, you're with me. Let's flame on."

Each of them had three extra adrenal glands, which followed their desire to fight by pumping furious amounts of adrenaline into their systems. Their necks swelled in response. The skin of their faces tightened, pulling back their lips to reveal razor-sharp teeth. Their hands flexed and unflexed. Each of them began to growl, the sounds like the rumbles of idling NASCAR racecars just waiting for the starter's flag to fly.

Lang could hardly speak, but he managed, "Ready. Steady. Kill."

His men peeled off and began running through the fifth-floor halls.

Lang followed behind, his growing rage barely harnessed.

A security guard stuck his head out of one of the doorways to see what was going on. Sten grabbed the head and smashed it against the doorjamb nine straight times.

A female secretary screamed from where Leif had turned.

A janitor came out of a closet carrying a mop, only to find Gunnar standing in front of him. Gunnar took the mop and shoved it down the janitor's throat, roaring as he did so.

They were all guilty. They all knew what was going on and let it happen. Whether one is human or vampire, each of them had a moral responsibility to either stop or refuse. That they chose the easy path of moral relativism was their downfall.

Lang paused as his men killed and fed. His teeth chattered with the effort.

Three guards came stiff-legged scared out of an office, semi-automatic pistols held out in front of them with shaking hands. They were between Lang and his men, facing away from him. It was an easy thing for Lang to roar as he lowered his head and bulled into them.

He impaled the one in the center with his horn.

Another managed to get a round off, hitting him in the chest, before Lang shattered the man's arm.

Lang elbowed the third man in the head, sending him flying. Lang then concentrated on the man who shot him. The bullet had done no harm thanks to the strength of his uniform and the muscle and bone in his chest. But it had pissed him off. He leaned down and ripped away flesh surrounding shoulder using his jaws.

The man shrieked.

Lang chewed again and again, revealing the ball joint where the arm was attached to the shoulder. Lang heaved mightily and ripped the arm free.

The guard's eyes shot wide as his mouth opened, but the pain was too much for him to utter a sound.

Lang ignored him and used the arm as a bludgeon. Holding the arm by the wrist, he hammered it over and over into the guard he'd elbowed until his face was unrecognizable.

Then he returned to the one-armed guard and did the same.

Gunnar stood at the intersection of hallways, facing him, to ensure the violence made the screen. He was about to turn, when a giant figure barreled into him and took him down.

Lang, now lost in his berserker fugue, waved the dismembered arm above him as he roared with a warrior's joy. No more padded rooms. No more meetings. No more counseling sessions with a PHD who knew nothing about the glories of battle. This was what he needed all along. This was catharsis made real.

Lang took two steps and heard seven shots as he felt their impacts in his back. He fell to one knee as real pain sent a niggling finger into his rage.

He turned his head and beheld the chief of security wearing a full kit—body armor; Kevlar helmet; Kevlar gloves; elbow and knee pads; a pistol, knife, and baton at his waist; and a smoking Mossberg 590 shotgun in his hands. The killer's smile looked uncomfortable above his dyed black goatee and narrow nose.

Picket cocked a shell into the shotgun and fired.

But Lang had rolled to his right, out of the way. At the end of his roll, he slammed into the wall and used it to stand.

Picket went to cock another shell into the shotgun.

Lang threw the arm into his face.

Picket's head rocked back, and he struggled to avoid it. He somehow found his balance and fired, catching Lang in the chest.

Lang felt the impact but no pain.

Picket stepped back again and cocked another round into the shotgun. He fired, but Lang jumped aside.

Nine rounds gone.

Picket went to cock, but there were no more rounds. He brought up the shotgun to use as a club, but the effort was too slow.

Lang grabbed him by the neck and crotch and lifted. But instead of throwing him, his jaws went to work on the unprotected abdomen. The man screamed and screamed as Lang chewed, his face a charnel mess of

387

the man who'd been the head of security for CrossCorp. When the screaming abruptly stopped, Lang ripped his face free to take a breath and felt a presence behind him.

He spun and threw Picket at it.

The immense vampire before him shifted impossibly fast, and Picket flew by, landing a dozen feet down the hall. It was an *akvan*. Persian in origin, it drew sustenance from the misery and pain it caused; the perfect place for the administrator of a facility researching and experimenting on human children. Caspar Bukhari's mouth wrapped from ear to ear in an almost comic revision of the human mouth. Needle-like teeth glinted in the bloody maw of a mouth. Where before his face had wrinkles, now it was stretched tight—the metamorphosis turned man into monster.

Then Lang saw that Buhkari had Gunnar, his hand shoved inside the *draugr*'s pelvis. His *draugr*, his warrior, his man, stared back at him, still alive, face wan and agonized.

"That's the problem with the heart," said Caspar Bukhari. "It's altogether too soft… even in vampires." He glanced at his hand. "Oh yes. I researched you *draugr*. Very sneaky to hide your heart here."

Lang lurched forward.

Gunnar arched his back as Bukhari squeezed his hand.

"It feels so wonderful, this feeling of abject pain. Is this what you feel when you—what do you call it—berserk?"

Lang tried to form words, but he was too far into the fugue. All he could do was growl.

"So it's like that. You become a monster. Like Frankenstein."

"Frankenstein was the doctor, not the monster," said Devil Ray, coming up behind Bukhari.

The *akvan* turned.

Lang registered a smell coming off Aldo Ray, but other than that he seemed the same. Only now he was free of his bomb vest and wore commando gear instead—body armor with two lengthy double-edged knives, which he now held in each hand, tips pointed down.

To Lang he said, "I see you saw the light."

Lang growled, sizing up Bukhari for just the right moment to attack.

Bukhari squeezed Gunnar's heart one last time, then jerked it from the man's pelvis. He tossed it at Devil Ray, who batted it aside.

"I thought you *lofa* like to eat flesh?"

"Heart's not flesh." He flicked his knife out and sliced Bukhari's arm. "That is."

Bukhari made a face, then whirled on Lang. Punching him first in the eyes, then the throat, both blows like anvils.

Lang's vision disappeared as he brought his hands to his throat. He couldn't see. He couldn't breathe. What had Buhkari done? He fell to a knee. He fought for a breath, blinking furiously. Then he felt it. His throat had been crushed. So easily. His vision started to return, the world faceted before him.

He heard shots. One. Five. Eight shots.

Then he felt a sharp point of pain on his throat, then the luxury of air. He opened his eyes to find Devil Ray stepping back with his knife. Oxygen. He could breathe. Reaching up to his throat, he felt the hole the former Navy SEAL had given him. An emergency tracheotomy.

Lang also knew that the fugue had left him. With his body dying, his adrenal glands had shut down. Dagner stood behind Devil Ray, a pistol in his hand.

Lang tried to talk but nothing happened. He placed a hand over the hole Devil Ray had made. "Where is—" voice like crushed glass. He turned.

Buhkari stood down the hall, leaning against a wall. His chest was a mess of blood from the bullet holes Dagner had put there. Somehow the vampire was still alive.

Aldo Ray started towards him, but Lang reached out and grabbed his leg.

"Wait. Let me." He fought to his feet. When he got there he had to wait a moment for balance. But then he was ready. He stumbled down the hallway on stiff legs.

Buhkari stuck out a hand, but Lang dodged it. Now it was his turn to punch. With the last vestiges of his *draugr* power, he slammed his fists into the vampire's mouth, its teeth snapping like toothpicks.

Buhkari fell to the ground.

Lang climbed on top of him and punched him in the mouth once more. This time he didn't remove his hand, instead pushing it farther and farther until it was lodged deep in his throat.

Buhkari's eyes widened as his oxygen was cut off.

"How does it feel?" said Lang, his other hand over his trachea.

The vampire began to kick.

As much as it hurt to speak, Lang let his low rattle of a voice be heard. "You know, I think you're right. Giving pain does feel good." He shoved his fist farther down the neck. "This is for Gunnar… and for the children."

The vampire flailed at him, beating him on the back with his fists, but they'd lost all of their earlier power. He was more human now. He died with tears in his eyes.

Lang wasn't sure how long he sat atop him, but it was Fell who put a hand on his shoulder.

Lang removed his fist and wiped the blood and bile on his pants. "Status," he croaked.

"Lost Gunnar and Oddvar."

Lang frowned.

"Kids?"

"Still alive."

"Good." Lang depressed a button on the back of his GoCam which turned off everyone's feed. Only he had this master switch.

Lang turned to Devil Ray. It took him two tries to say it, but he managed, "You can go."

The *lofa* nodded. "What about you? We know you were told to stand down." When he saw the looks on their faces he added, "We intercepted your call." He shrugged apologetically.

Lang tried to speak, but the effort was too much. He gave Fell a pleading look.

Fell stepped forward. "We're fine. We'll explain that this wasn't a government-funded location, that the president didn't know about it, and that our mission here was because we were actually ordered to stop it. He'll come out looking like a hero and so will we."

"But you won't have us."

Fell shrugged. "We'll say you left during the fight. Mission complete."

Devil Ray stared hard at Lang and Fell as if he was waiting for them to recant.

Lang nodded, showing that he was in accordance with what Fell said.

Finally, Ray grinned. "Then we're off to the next place." He took a few steps and turned. "Hope to never see you again."

Fell laughed. "The feeling is mutual."

Once the *lofa* was gone, Fell turned to him. "Now come on, old fella. We need to get you looked at."

Lang narrowed his eyes. *Old fella?* His cell phone rang. He glanced at his pocket, but decided to ignore it. Ostergard could wait. After all, they'd just delivered to them the best possible solution, and the only solution that could guarantee the safety of the children.

… which reminded him of his own dead children, Brand, Amelie, and Sigrid. And his wife, Inger. All dead. A vision of them standing on the hill behind his South Dakota home came to him. The sun streamed behind them so he couldn't make out their faces, but he knew it was them. They waved at him as if to say goodbye… or was it hello?

Inside his mind he waved back.

"HEROES DON'T WEAR SPANDEX" PT. 5

Jonathan Maberry

The Jacob Javits Center
New York City

Yuki Nitobe looked deeply afraid. Swann could see the fear burn in her eyes. And yet, at the same time there was something else, a frequency of energy that he could sense, as if his words had flipped some kind of switch inside of her. She nearly hummed with it.

"God in heaven," she whispered.

"I know."

"You're *sure*?"

"Sure? No, of course not. This is hearsay, and as I said, I won't reveal my source."

"You don't have a choice, Luther. You're not protected by the First Amendment. I am."

"Neither of us is," he said. "Not on something like this. We're talking about accusing the government of the United States of treason, of conspiracy to commit terrorism, of mass murder. I don't recall seeing any amendment that would protect us from dropping that kind of bomb."

Yuki looked away, chewing nervously on her lower lip.

"What we need to do," continued Swann, "is find some way to prove it."

"How?"

"I… don't know. We need a source who would go on record and who would be believed."

She cut him a look. "What about *your* source?"

"No. He's going on assumptions. He's putting it together, but if he has anything concrete, then he hasn't shared it with me."

"Would he?" asked Yuki.

"Yes, I think so. But only if he had something irrefutable. Right now, no."

"Then we're nowhere."

Swann glanced down at the figures standing by the news van. Yuki followed the line of his gaze.

"What—?" she began, then stopped. "Wait, are you serious?"

"Maybe."

She pointed at Martyn. "You want me to take this to the Crimson Queen?"

"What other choice do we have? We know she has people inside the government."

"Right, and they haven't had a whiff of something like this."

"Maybe that's because they don't know where to look. The Queen's been looking at General May, or maybe a rogue congressman, but I don't think even she's looking higher on the food chain. Maybe all she needs is a nudge."

"To what end? Look, Luther, I know you admire her, and so do I. More than you know. But don't ever be fooled into thinking she's a benign player in all this. And don't assume that she'll make the choices you'd want her to make."

"Meaning what, exactly?"

"She told you once that you shouldn't force her to take sides because you might not like how that turned out."

"How do you know that? You weren't there… "

"It doesn't matter how I know, Luther. I know. What matters is that you're thinking this is a war between Beats and Bloods, with a handful of idealists trapped in the middle. Maybe that explains you and Clooney and others like that, but it's not a very good assessment of the Crimson Queen and her empire. How do you know she wouldn't try a coup? She might be positioned to overthrow the whole government. Would you want that?"

"Of course not."

"Then you can't bring her in… "

"And what other choice do we have?" he demanded. "I love my country, Yuki, but I love my planet more. I don't want to see global ethnic genocide. I don't know how many times or in how many ways I have to say that before someone listens. But that's where we're heading. The V-Wars aren't stopping, they're not slowing down. After last night, I think it's proof that it's only going to get worse until one side decides to completely exterminate the other. That's where we're heading, Yuki. Armageddon for half the world."

"Luther—"

"No, Yuki," he said, touching her cheek, "if we don't change the game, then every player at the table will lose. Neither side is going to allow themselves to be wiped out, not without doing appalling damage in return. But if we could prove that the so-called terrorist acts—the Ninety-Nine Bombs *and* what happened last night—were the actions of one group that has been trying to create a total war, then we'll be complicit merely by inaction."

She stood up. "And if we prove it, Luther, what then? How do you carve out a cancer like this unless you know where all the tumors are? How do we do that test? How do we diagnose this with any hope of accuracy? And how do we operate without killing the patient?"

Swann said nothing.

Yuki shook her head. "That's why my heart's breaking, Luther. Neither of us can answer that yet. And that's why this war is going to go on."

He stood up as well.

"I can't accept that," he said.

"We have no choice."

Swann looked past her at the smoke and then he turned and looked through the glass doors at all the dead and dying.

"Then we need to find that proof," he said coldly. "We need to launch our own war. Not just you reporting it, or me ranting about it. We need to find our own scalpels and begin cutting."

She gave him a puzzled, wondering look. "Are you… are you talking about creating a resistance movement?"

"Maybe I am."

"In partnership with the Crimson Queen?"

Swann walked to the top of the stairs and looked down at Martyn, who was talking on his cell. Probably to the queen or someone else in her court.

"Luther... ?"

Swann did not immediately answer her question. An ambulance pulled up, and the EMTs began off-loading another gurney. Another blood-splashed and soot-stained citizen. From this distance it was impossible to tell if the victim was a Blood or a Beat.

And it did not matter one bit.

"Luther?" Yuki asked again.

"I won't be a witness anymore," said Swann. "I won't stand by and do nothing. Not anymore. I won't let this war kill what I believe in." He shook his head. "Not anymore."

Then he turned and walked over to the glass door and held it for the EMTs. As they passed inside, he lingered in the doorway and looked at her.

"There has to be a way," he said. "There has to be. I am goddamn well going to find it. If I have to tear everything down to do it, that's what I'll do. It's up to you to decide if you want to help me."

With that he went back inside, letting the door swing shut behind him.

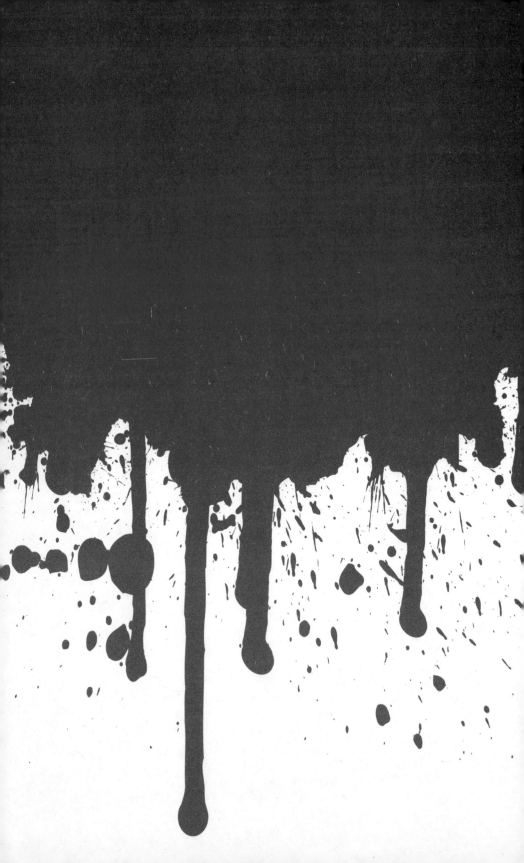

LARRY CORREIA's *Monster Hunter International*, despite being self-published, reached the *Entertainment Weekly* bestseller list in April 2008, after which he received a publishing contract with Baen Books. *Monster Hunter International* was re-released in 2009 and was on the Locus bestseller list in November 2009. The sequel, *Monster Hunter Vendetta*, was a *New York Times* bestseller. The third book in the series, *Monster Hunter Alpha*, was released in July 2011 and was also a *New York Times* bestseller. Correia was a finalist for the John W. Campbell award for best new science fiction/fantasy writer of 2011. *Warbound*, the third book in Correia's The Grimnoir Chronicles series, received a nomination for the Hugo Award for Best Novel in 2014. The Dead Six series started as an online action fiction collaboration with Mike Kupari (*Nightcrawler*) at the online gun forum "The High Road" as the "Welcome Back, Mr. Nightcrawler" series of posts. These works predated the publishing of *Monster Hunter.*

JAMES A. MOORE is an award-winning author of over thirty novels, including the critically acclaimed Serenity Falls trilogy and the Seven Forges fantasy series. His recurring anti-hero, Jonathan Crowley, has appeared in half a dozen novels with more to come. You can find him at *http://jamesamoorebooks.com/* and he's normally lurking around Facebook and Twitter when he should be writing.

JEREMY ROBINSON is the international bestselling author of more than fifty novels and novellas, including the robot-zombie thriller *Uprising* as well as *Island 731, Secondworld*, and the Jack Sigler thriller series. Robinson is also known as the #1 Amazon.com horror writer, Jeremy Bishop, author of *The Sentinel, The Raven*, and the controversial novel *Torment.* His novels have been translated into twelve languages. He lives in New Hampshire with his wife and three children. Visit him at *www.jeremyrobinsononline.com.*

JOHN EVERSON is a staunch advocate for the culinary joys of the jalapeno and an unabashed fan of 1970s European horror cinema. He is also the Bram Stoker Award-winning author of *Covenant*, as well as seven other novels, including the erotic horror tour de force of *NightWhere* and his latest, the seductive backwoods tale of *The Family Tree.* Other novels include *Sacrifice, The Pumpkin Man, Siren, The 13th,* and the spider-driven *Violet Eyes.* His tales have been translated into Polish, French, and German and optioned for potential film development. Over the past twenty years, his short stories have appeared in more than seventy-five magazines and anthologies. His short story collections include *Cage of Bones & Other Deadly Obsessions, Needles & Sins, Deadly Nightlusts,* and *Vigilantes of Love.* Learn more about John on his site, *www.johneverson.com,* or connect on Facebook at *www.facebook.com/johneverson.*

This is **KEITH R.A. DeCANDIDO**'s second foray into "V-Wars," having written "The Ballad of Big Charlie" (also featuring Mia Fitzsimmons) for the first anthology. In general, he's written about fifty novels, seventy short stories, and a mess of comics, articles, reviews, essays, blog entries, and more. Some other work due out soon: the novelization of *Big Hero 6,* the Stargate SG-1 novel *Kali's Wrath,* the novel *Mermaid Precinct* (the fifth novel in his series of fantasy police procedurals), the script for the graphic novel *Icarus* (based on the novel by Gregory A. Wilson, with art by Matt Slay), the short story collection *Without a License: The Fantastic Worlds of Keith R.A. DeCandido,* short stories in *The X-Files: The Truth is Out There* (also edited by Jonathan Maberry) and *Buzzy Mag,* and tons more. In 2009, he received a Lifetime Achievement Award from the International Association of Media Tie-in Writers, which means he never needs to achieve anything ever again. He contributes regularly to Tor.com, he's a freelance editor, a second-degree black belt in karate, a veteran podcaster, a member of the Liars Club, an avid baseball fan, and probably some other stuff that he can't remember due to the lack of sleep. Find out less at his cheerfully retro web site at *www.DeCandido.net.*

HANK SCHWAEBLE is a writer and attorney in Houston, Texas. A former Air Force officer and special agent, he is a two-time Bram Stoker Award winner, including for his first novel, *Damnable* (Jove, 2009). His short fiction has appeared in anthologies such as *Alone on the Darkside, Five Strokes to Midnight, Horror Library Vol. IV, ZVR: No Man's Land,* and *Death's Realm.* He is also a former World Fantasy Award nominee. His second novel, *Diabolical,* was released in July of 2011. His next novel, *The Angel of the Abyss,* is set for release some time in 2015. You can find him on the web at *www.hankschwaeble.com.*

SCOTT NICHOLSON is the international bestselling author of more than thirty books, including the After post-apocalyptic series, *The Harvest, Speed Dating with the Dead*, and many more. *The Red Church* was a Bram Stoker Award finalist, and *The Home* is in development as a feature film. You can find him at *www.AuthorScottNicholson.com*.

MARCUS PELEGRIMAS is the author of the Skinners series of novels chronicling the rise of the werewolf apocalypse and the humans who are crazy enough to fight the shapeshifting hordes. His recent works also include the Gillis Ledger series, which is a tasty blend of hard-boiled private eyes, depression era gangsters, and technology borrowed from alternate dimensions. Marcus's other interests include ghost hunting, the sweet nuances of junk food, and black t-shirts with skulls on them.

Shirley Jackson Award finalist TIM WAGGONER has published over thirty novels and three short-story collections of dark fiction. His most recent novels are *The Way of All Flesh* and *Dream Stalkers*. He teaches creative writing at Sinclair Community College and in Seton Hill University's MFA in Writing Popular Fiction program. You can find him on the web at *www.timwaggoner.com*.

SCOTT SIGLER is the *New York Times* bestselling author of fifteen novels, six novellas, and dozens of short stories. His hardcover horror-thrillers are available from Crown Publishing and Del Rey. He also co-founded Empty Set Entertainment, which publishes his YA Galactic Football League series.

WESTON OCHSE is the author of more than twenty books, including *Grunt Life* and its sequel, *Grunt Traitor* from Solaris. Both are military sci fi books exploring PTSD in a positive manner. His SEAL Team 666 series has been optioned by MGM for a major motion picture. Winner of the Bram Stoker Award and nominated for the Pushcart Prize, his work has appeared in comic books, and magazines such as *Cemetery Dance* and *Soldier of Fortune*. He lives in the Arizona desert within rock-throwing distance of Mexico. He is a military veteran with thirty years of military service and recently returned from a deployment to Afghanistan. Visit Weston at *www.westonochse.com*.

JONATHAN MABERRY is a *New York Times* bestselling author, multiple Bram Stoker Award winner, and freelancer for Marvel Comics. His novels include *Predator One*, *The Nightsiders: The Orphan Army*, *Code Zero*, *Rot & Ruin*, *Ghost Road Blues*, *Patient Zero*, *The Wolfman*, and many others. Nonfiction books include *Ultimate Jujutsu*, *The Cryptopedia*, *Zombie CSU*, and others. Several of Jonathan's novels are in development for movies or TV including *V-Wars*, *Extinction Machine*, *Rot & Ruin*, and *Dead of Night*. He's the editor/co-author of *V-Wars*, a vampire-themed anthology, and editor of the *X-Files*, anthologies *Out of Tune* and the forthcoming *Scary Out There*. He was a featured expert on several History Channel specials, including *Zombies: A Living History*. Since 1978 he's sold more than 1,200 magazine feature articles, 3,000 columns, two plays, greeting cards, song lyrics, and poetry. His comics include *Captain America: Hail Hydra*, *Bad Blood*, *Marvel Zombies Return*, and *Marvel Universe VS The Avengers*. He lives in Del Mar, California, with his wife, Sara Jo, and their dog, Rosie. *www.jonathan-maberry.com*.

SAM ORION NOVA WEST-MENSCH is a Penn State graduate, rapper and spoken word performer, travel enthusiast, and educator. He lives in San Diego, California. Get in touch with him on Facebook *https://www.facebook.com/sam.westmensch* or OrionNova on Instagram.

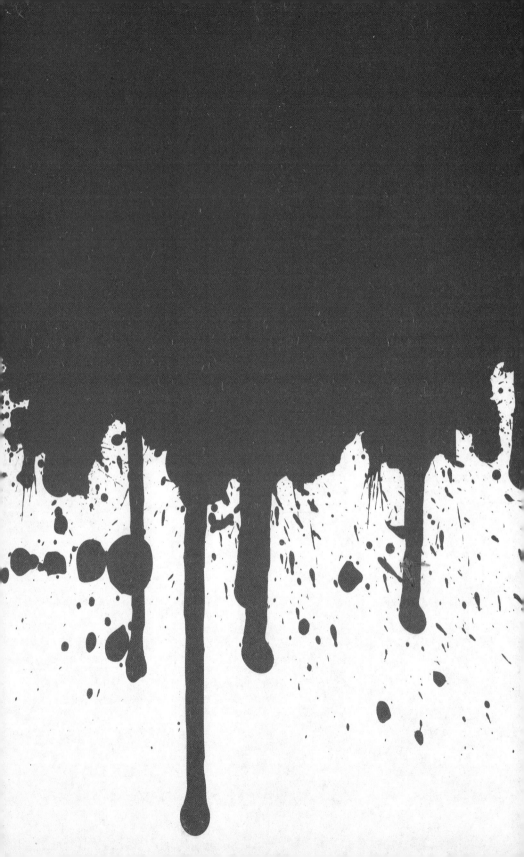